THE PRISON SHIP

Recent Titles in the Mariners Series from Peter Tonkin

THE FIRE SHIP
THE COFFIN SHIP
POWERDOWN
THUNDER BAY *
TITAN 10 *
WOLF ROCK *
RESOLUTION BURNING *
CAPE FAREWELL *
THE SHIP BREAKERS *
HIGH WIND IN JAVA *
BENIN LIGHT *
RIVER OF GHOSTS *
VOLCANO ROADS *
THE PRISON SHIP *

* *available from Severn House*

THE PRISON SHIP

Peter Tonkin

This first world edition published 2010
in Great Britain and in the USA by
SEVERN HOUSE PUBLISHERS LTD of
9–15 High Street, Sutton, Surrey, England, SM1 1DF.
Trade paperback edition published
in Great Britain and the USA 2010 by
SEVERN HOUSE PUBLISHERS LTD

British Library Cataloguing in Publication Data

Tonkin, Peter.
  The Prison Ship
  1. Mariner, Richard (Fictitious character) – Fiction.
  2. Terrorism – England – Chatham (Kent) – Fiction.
  3. Suspense fiction.
  I. Title
  823.9'14-dc22

ISBN-13: 978-0-7278-6880-0   (cased)
ISBN-13: 978-1-84751-234-5   (trade paper)

All Severn House titles are printed on acid-free paper.

Severn House Publishers support The Forest Stewardship Council [FSC],
the leading international forest certification organisation. All our titles that
are printed on Greenpeace-approved FSC-certified paper carry the FSC logo.

Mixed Sources
Product group from well-managed
forests and other controlled sources
www.fsc.org Cert no. SA-COC-1565
© 1996 Forest Stewardship Council

Typeset by Palimpsest Book Production Ltd.,
Grangemouth, Stirlingshire, Scotland.
Printed and bound in Great Britain by
MPG Books Ltd., Bodmin, Cornwall.

To Cham, Guy and Mark as always.
And to my Mother and Aunt Frances as promised.

CHATHAM

ONE
Thunderbolt

As Richard Mariner guided his beloved battleship-grey Bentley Continental GTC four-door sports saloon into the main parking area of the Historic Dockyard at Chatham, the first fork of lightning pounced down over the Medway immediately beyond the covered slipway buildings dead ahead.

'Are you sure you want to do this?' he bellowed as the immediate explosion of thunder added immeasurable depth to the relentless pounding of the downpour drumming on the roof and bonnet like doom. As he spoke he glanced sideways at his vibrant passenger.

'Of course!' Mary's youthful voice was bell clear, carrying as easily as his in the surprisingly capacious confines of the four-seater car. Even had she not possessed a tone of natural command and a cut-glass clarity of accent, the simple excitement she forced into the words would have carried far further than her doting father's ear.

Richard nodded, smiling a little grimly, and looked ahead once more, for he had known what the answer would be. He and his daughter seemed almost psychic on occasion. He guided the Continental across the car park along the tunnel of brightness cast by its headlights through the stormy gloom. He drew up as close to the entrance as possible, prevented from parking immediately outside it by a long, black official-looking saloon.

Richard had researched the trip with even more than his usual care and forethought, for this was the last of this summer's excursions with his darling daughter. He knew that the car park had been constructed over the site of the South Mast Pond. In earlier times, a great square man-made lake had stood here, where whole tree trunks had been seasoned into masts for the great wooden-walled ships of the British war fleets of the 1700s and 1800s. Under the weight of the torrential downpour it seemed to have reverted to its old self, for there was nothing to see in the whole place but water.

He had an instant of disorientating fantasy that the bumps beneath the Bentley's wheels as she slowed to a stop were naked fir trees rolling easily on the water as their flawless lengths were readied to become masts and spars, jibs and booms. And that the elegant sports car had been transported back in time somehow, like Doctor Who's telephone box or Captain James T. Kirk's starship *Enterprise*.

But Richard was here to look at far more traditional vessels than Federation starships. It was the last week of the long vac. Within the next few days and weeks every school, college and university in the land would be starting the new term and the new academic year. And he would be losing Mary to her studies. They had been planning this trip as a final treat for both of them. For she, like he, was fascinated by the historical roots of the maritime world that he and his company Heritage Mariner bestrode like a giant.

As the Bentley eased to a halt like a vessel coming to anchor, the rain eased and a beam of westering sun shone through the ghost of the lightning bolt.

'Let's go for it then,' he decided, killing the lights and the motor – and the pair of them leapt out of the black leather, kid-glove security of the car's interior. As they splashed side by side through the almost ankle-deep water, Richard turned. The wind blew his raincoat collar up around his cheeks, the right point just reaching the white line of the scar along his cheekbone. The wild blue dazzle of his eyes narrowed between long, dark lashes beneath the wind-ruffled jumble of his blue-black hair. The Bentley's lights flashed, confirming that the deadlocks were on. She sat, sleek, squat and strong beneath the downpour. It had almost been worth the brief cooling it had brought to his usually blissful marriage, he thought. When his wife Robin had discovered that he had gone for the James Bond classic sports car option rather than the more sedate Arnage she had wanted him to buy.

'Come *on!*' called Mary, a disorientating mix of the pair of them, running recklessly on without him.

And he turned to follow her as the rain returned with renewed fury. Blissfully unaware that this was the last time he would ever see his beloved motor car; how close he would come to never seeing his beloved wife again either. How close, in fact, he and Mary were to a thunderously explosive death at this very instant.

Out on the River Medway, hidden behind the long covered slipway buildings, the tide was coming to the flood. The weather had frightened away all but the most intrepid pleasure-boaters and there were precious few commercial vessels out and about these days. The rain-pocked surface of the grey-brown stream was all but empty, therefore. The banks stood deserted too, for not even the most dedicated fisherman would want to brave yet another deluge. Rochester, Chatham and Gillingham cowered on their hilltops above the dockyard as though nervous to be so near the restless sky. The Isle of Grain on the far shore looked more like the Isle of Mud.

The big pleasure boat *Jupiter* powering upriver from the south, pounding northwards with the tide beneath her counter, would have turned more than a few heads if there had been anyone much to watch her progress. She was the better part of sixty feet long, a sleek white Greek-built gin palace with a racily raked bridge-house three decks high to the bridge itself. She would certainly have turned the heads of the Kent and Essex police forces, and indeed of the river police as well, if there had been any out and about. For she had been stolen from her anchorage in the fashionable marina at Burnham on Crouch in Essex a week earlier.

During the interim she had been hidden in a covered dock at the head of one of the tiny waterways flowing into the Thames, just as they did in Dickens's day, up in the Pool of London upriver of the Isle of Dogs. Here her cavernous interior, the size of a couple of London double-decker buses, had been packed to the gunwales with high explosives, fuses and timers.

There were two young men aboard her now, guiding her rapidly and purposefully northwards on top of the tide towards her final destination. Like Mary, they both wore fashionable T-shirts, jeans and trainers under their rainwear. But they also wore *keffiyeh* scarves and *taqiyah* skullcaps. If everything went to plan, one of the men would die with the beautiful vessel – and with the victims she would claim – though he alone of all of them would be transported directly into *Jannah*, the

Paradise, as the mullah in the madrasa had promised. While the other would survive, if such was the will of Allah, and follow a longer and more devious, but oh so carefully calculated path to *shahada*, martyrdom and ultimate glory.

Richard saw that there was an unexpected level of security as soon as he reached the visitors' entrance. Years of experience told him at a glance that the young man with the open raincoat lounging apparently innocently beside the entrance barrier was an armed security officer. Counter-Terrorism Command or MI5 on special assignment by the look of things. In the old days he would have suspected Special Branch but the Branch had been subsumed into the new counter-terrorist order now, at every level from the Met to the Home Office. On the other side of the barrier stood two police officers, one male and one female. Both in uniform and stab vests; both armed.

That explained the black saloon that was sitting in the best parking spot, Richard thought, his eyes suddenly narrow and his mind racing as he turned his collar down and swept his wet hair back. Clearly Mary and he had chosen a day when some middle- or upper-ranking government official was visiting too. But at least the place seemed to be open as usual, he observed, joining Mary as she bought their tickets.

'Busy?' he asked the girl behind the counter as she handed Mary the tickets. He gave her a dazzling grin as she glanced up. Her eyes widened, then crinkled in response.

'Surprisingly busy,' she confirmed, glancing significantly out at the weather.

'And with special guests, too,' added Richard, glancing across at the security man, who met his gaze, ears pricked at his words.

'Well, we don't get government ministers every day,' she allowed cheerfully enough. 'Even junior ones.'

'Someone from Defence?' he hazarded, his tone lightly ironic. 'Checking up on a late-running contract for half a dozen four-masted ships of the line?'

'Culture, Media and Sport,' she answered with a twinkle. 'Checking up on preparations for the Big Event next year.'

'Father!' interrupted Mary impatiently. 'Will you stop flirting and let us get *on*!'

'Coming, darling,' he answered cheerfully. He gave the ticket girl the ghost of a wink and pushed through the gate, out from under the security officer's cool gaze and into the police officers' orbit.

'You know there are government people going all over the place,' Mary persisted as he hesitated at her side, looking across the rainswept expanse that stood between them and the covered slipways where the Lifeboat exhibition was. 'It was on the news. You said something about the government micromanaging everything down to the last detail getting ready for the Olympics next summer.'

'What they *need* to manage,' said Richard feelingly, 'is the weather. If it's like this in twelve months' time, they'll be up the creek. Or down the Swanee . . .'

The female police officer at his shoulder gave an automatic chuckle of agreement.

'Still,' allowed Richard, cheerfully ironic, 'I suppose it'd do wonders for the water sports . . .'

'Oh come *on*!' repeated his daughter, ruthlessly immune to his wry wit.

'. . . not to mention memorial 2012 umbrella sales . . .'

And off he went in Mary's wake across the flooded yard beneath the deluge that was not quite noisy enough to drown the sound of a laughing policeman.

Mary's weather-rioted curls bobbed well above his raincoated shoulder as they jogged side by side through the apocalyptic afternoon. They had started out as golden as her mother's in early childhood. Now they were almost as dark as his own thick mop. She had inherited her mother's willowy figure as well as her curls, but there was something of her father about the dazzle of her eyes, the breadth of her shoulders and the depth of her chest. She was taller than Robin already and looked to have some way still to grow.

Her character too was a strange amalgam of her parents', combining fearsome intellect with utter clarity of vision and ruthless ambition. She cut no one any slack, took no prisoners, suffered no fools – gladly or otherwise. By the grace of God she was also blessed with a ready, easy, self-deprecating wit; and more charm than an army of aspiring actors flirting with a flock of fetching debutantes. And she had a heart the size of Jupiter.

Richard and Mary arrived at Number 3 covered slipway side by side. At once they joined the outer fringes of a crowd consisting of a junior government minister with security entourage surrounded by the men and women of the Third Estate in the middle of a press call photo-opportunity.

'You know who she is?' asked Mary in a stage whisper that turned heads among others on the fringes of the crowd.

'Must be someone working for the Culture Secretary,' answered Richard, rummaging through his capacious memory, chasing an irritatingly elusive snippet of knowledge. 'There's too much security for the Department of Culture, Media and Sport – unless it's the Minister, which it's not. But the Culture Secretary works out of the Cabinet Office and the Culture Secretary has overall responsibility for the Olympics. And it's the Culture Secretary who's been making all the noise about ensuring every other tourist destination near the Olympic Village is up to the required standard. If this is someone from the Cabinet Office – even if she's fairly junior – then that would explain a good deal.'

Richard hesitated, looking around. Then, mercifully as it turned out, he added, 'Look. Do you want to get caught up with this, darling, or shall we get ahead of the scrum for the time being and come back later?'

'Yes! Let's do that,' Mary answered at once. 'I want to get a good look round the historic lifeboats and there's no way that'll happen for a while. So what next?'

'Lead on, my love! This is your treat. Let's start with somewhere properly designed to handle this amount of water, though, shall we?'

Mary gave a gurgle of excited merriment, which told Richard she had thought of the perfect place, and dashed out of the door into the deluge.

Aboard *Jupiter* the two men exchanged brief and silent farewells. The man destined to survive ran down the companionways from the bridge to the after deck, and on without an instant's hesitation to vault easily over the aft rail as though hurdling a garden gate. The instant the dead man saw his companion's head bobbing free of the filthy wake, he turned. He pushed the throttles wide and set the tiller dead ahead. Only then did he face east towards the long red-brick buildings

and the hills of Chatham and Rochester behind that hid distant
Mecca from his eyes. And he began to pray.

The last of the covered slipways stood at a slight angle, inde-
pendent of the rest. Its internal construction and massive grey
roof were completely different, as the gape of its open doorway
showed the fleeting figures of Richard and Mary sprinting
past. Then father and daughter were at the first of the docks,
where HMS *Gannet*, pride of the Victorian navy, sat. Her
yards were bare, her sails safely stowed. And that was just as
well, for the rain varnished her masts, spars, deck and sides
as though she had recently risen from the seabed. The wind
boomed in the top of her tall bronze-coloured funnel, and
howled in her rigging like the voice of every banshee in the
Emerald Isle.

They ran under the reach of her bowsprit and rounded the
corner to where the destroyer *Cavalier* sat quietly afloat, grey
as a ghost and silent as the grave. And also running with water
as though she had just returned from escorting the Arctic
convoys round Norway's North Cape on the murderous
Murmansk run.

In between, in dry dock – the dock being the only dry thing
about her – sat their immediate destination. Her Majesty's
Submarine *Ocelot*. Mary had taken her father at his word with
typically wicked literalness. If there was anywhere in Chatham
designed to handle the cataclysmic downpour on that thunderous
afternoon, it was the 'O' class diesel electric submarine – which
must have supposed, thought Richard wryly, that she was in the
midst of yet another crash-dive.

They paused under the cover of the little building designed
to house the queue to go aboard – mercifully empty at the
moment. They shook off the water from their coats, surrounded
by the posters and photographs of the submarine's exhibition.
They caught their breath, hilariously – almost hysterically –
amused by their situation. Then Mary plunged on with Richard
hot on her heels. Their way led forward between metal railings
in an 'S' shape familiar from countless rides in numberless
amusement parks. Then out into the downpour again, across
a plain concrete dockside and on to a level gangplank walled
with railings stout enough to prevent anyone from falling down
into the dry dock below. Twenty or so strides took them to

the narrow foredeck, where Mary ran lightly down the steps into the cramped hull below without a second thought, her feet light and sure in her fashionable trainers.

Richard hesitated, however, and looked about him, given pause by some subconscious part-prophetic thrill. The submarine's metal sail towered behind him, black against the steel-grey sky. The aft of the hull lay behind it like the black back of a recently surfaced whale, then the sturdy wall of the dry dock that held back the swirl of the muddy river water. Beyond that, the broad grey-brown reach of the Medway itself, and, reaching out into it, the skeletal 'L' of the Thunderbolt Pier.

And there, just to the south of the pier, surging through the little boats tethered opposite the long red-brick building that housed the Royal Dockyard Museum itself and bobbing restlessly at the top of the flooding tide, a pleasure craft was heading into dock. She was a tall white gin palace with a racy rake to her three-level bridge house. And she looked to be in the hands of some kind of amateur, thought Richard as he turned to look down after his vanished daughter. Because unless he reversed his engines pretty quickly, or put his helm hard over at once, he was going to give the pier a God-almighty whack!

Richard dismissed the vessel from his mind and clattered in his heavy leather-soled brogues down into the submarine's forward compartment, his mind suddenly filled with worried speculation as to how well his six-foot-four-inch frame could be adapted to the severely restrictive headroom requirements of the Silent Service.

TWO

Ocelot

There was no triumphal affirmation of the greatness of God at the moment *Jupiter* hit the Thunderbolt Pier. No '*Allah u akhbar!*' at the instant of the explosion. Instead the young man beside the locked controls, facing east, with his eyes closed and his thoughts of Mecca and Paradise, passed out of the living world mid-prayer. One second he knew no more of the nature of the afterlife and the existence of God than any other mortal – though he believed with an absolute faith. The next he knew for certain all there was to know. And in the instantaneous passage from one state to the other there was no pain, no sound, even; just the grating of impact, a force that rolled him sideways and a microsecond of panic that the fuses had not tripped the detonators after all.

The dead man's brother in God, bobbing breathlessly in the icy water, also hard at prayer, saw and heard the moment of impact. The crash of collision. The nanosecond of grating and groaning as the sleek hull tore into the skeletal structure. The overwhelming blast of the explosion. The wall of force that whipped his skullcap away, nearly scalped him and set his soaking hair steaming and smoking. That smote him on the forehead like a crusader's bludgeon. That flexed his eardrums with agonizing intensity so that he was screaming when the wall of muddy liquid hit him in the face and the force of the detonation in the river simply stamped him under. Filling his shrieking lungs with filthy, icy Medway water, washing away his patterned *keffiyeh* and his stylish rainwear alike.

The sphere of power unleashed by the detonation expanded in a circle; a wall of irresistible force moving across the Historic Dockyard at something like the speed of light. The pier and the vessels at its end simply vanished, literally blown to smithereens. The long buildings housing the World War II exhibition, the public toilets and the Police Museum were torn apart even as the little helicopter on the open area beside them was flung against the front of the Commissioner's House. Which in turn was hurled back into the Commissioner's Historic Garden as a jumble of blazing brick and timber. The Admiral's Offices behind the Police Museum were shattered and hurled into the main administration buildings, which were in turn torn from their foundations and thrown against the Officers' Terrace like a tidal wave of masonry. The Joiner's Shop was blasted north-eastwards into the Timber-Seasoning Sheds as the Ropery flew almost bodily south-eastwards towards the Lead and Paint Mill. Which survived almost as effectively as the air-raid shelters in between the buildings because Edward Holl, the architect, had made the mill blast-proof and fireproof at the direction of their Lordships in the

Admiralty when he constructed it in 1819. The main gate, with its arms of George III, the Guard House and the Royal Dockyard Church were not so strongly constructed or so fortunate.

HMS *Cavalier* was hurled on to her side as though by the greatest wave the Arctic Ocean could have thrown at her. Her square hull buckled, plates tearing asunder and rivets flying. Her masts, funnels, bridge and upper works were torn to shrapnel and hurled like grapeshot at the South Dock Pumping Station. The bank which separated her rolling poop from the writhing Medway was torn away and a wall of water washed over her crushed and blistered hull. HMS *Gannet* seemed to take wing. Her three naked masts were whipped away like tall trees yielding to a typhoon. Her funnel reared and rolled end over end into the side of the wide-doored slipway. The slipway's grey roof rose like a parliament of crows taking to the upper skies all at once as *Gannet*'s upturned hull, torn apart like *Cavalier*'s, was washed underwater by the same muddy tidal wave. The slipway's southern wall was stamped down and splinters of *Gannet*'s masts whipped through like machine-gun fire.

The slipways over the Lifeboat exhibition burst apart, roofs rolling back like the tops of sardine cans. Historic beams and timbers shattered as the roofs yielded, flew and rained in blazing shards. The lifeboats themselves were smashed as though caught in the greatest of killer seas. Only the oldest of them survived, its long, strong hull the furthest along the slipway, nearest to the river, protected by the other, more modern and substantial vessels which soaked up much of the blast as they flew apart. It shuddered as though a ghostly crew were piling aboard and unstowing the long sweep oars below its seats. Then it slid down the slip towards where the back wall had been, and launched itself into the swirling water of the Medway.

The visitors' entrance and gift shop, the Wooden Walls exhibition above it, the Wheelwright's Shop beside it and the restaurant behind it soared in ragged sections across the waterlogged remains of the South Mast Pond and the car park that had been built above it.

And, abetted by bludgeons of masonry and the still-smouldering breath of the overwhelming blast, the murderous

wall of force still had sufficient strength to tear Richard's
Bentley bodily into the air. The windows shattered. The roof
burst open. The doors jumped wide as though the flying car
had sprouted double wings like a huge grey dragonfly. The
bonnet crumpled as though it had run at full speed into a
wall – instead of the other way round. The fuel tank yielded
and the spray of petrol ignited into a fireball powerful enough
to take the red-hot wreckage a few hundred metres further
before it finally fell to earth. Later – much later – what was
left of the precious vehicle was recovered from the bottom of
the North Mast Pond, beside the cold charred wreckage which
was all that was left of the Lower Boathouse.

The lethal blast hit *Ocelot* less than a nanosecond after it tore
the upper works off *Cavalier* and a micron of time before it
destroyed *Gannet* and the covered slipways beyond her.

The submarine survived for several reasons. Because she
was seated deep within a dry dock almost as strongly
constructed as the air-raid shelter and the Lead and Paint Mill
beyond it. Also, apart from the slim fin, no part of her hull
was above ground level. Not even the bulbous housing that
contained the sonar and spoilt the sleek lines of her bow
section. So the instant after the blast swept over *Cavalier*,
scything lethally towards *Gannet*, *Ocelot*'s tall black fin was
stamped down as the hull writhed briefly below it. By the
time the blast was tearing the roofs off the covered slipways
and smashing the lifeboats to kindling, *Ocelot* was at rest
again, her upper works bent at a crazy angle, drooping sideways like the dorsal fin of a killer whale. Moreover, that hull
which had writhed so briefly as the fin bent, was designed to
withstand pressures in excess even of those that the explosion
delivered. The sorts of pressures to be found hundreds of
metres down in the deep ocean. Finally, the curved cigar shape
of the submarine itself was better placed than the angular hulls
of its surface-sailing cousins to shrug off the skirts of the
blast-wall passing over it at lightning speed.

Ocelot did not escape utterly unscathed, however. The movement resulting from the damage to the tall fin destroyed the
walkway that strode from the dockside to the foredeck
hatchway entrance. It also shattered the balks of timber that
secured the hull firmly upright and held it safely in the dock

itself. And that was particularly important because the blast
which tore the gates off *Cavalier*'s and *Gannet*'s docks did
the same for the wall keeping *Ocelot*'s dry dock dry. A wall
of water, six feet higher than the usual surface of the Medway
at its flood, swept into a dock that reached down a further
twenty feet below water level to its rain-puddled bottom. In
an instant, the wildly foaming ten-metre tsunami of river water
had swept into the dry dock. Flooded it. Exploded in a wall
of spray that rained on the smouldering ruins of the South
Dock Pumping Station and sucked the reeling submarine back
out into the river's muddy tidal flow.

Richard's experience of all this seemed to him to consist of
wildly accelerated mayhem punctuated by momentary flashes
of utterly unexpected stillness. Life, as he encountered it then,
became like watching reality presented by a faulty DVD.

Richard discovered Mary at the foot of the companionway
already deep in conversation with a wiry, steel-haired
pensioner. As Richard seemingly folded himself in half trying
to avoid bashing his skull on the deck-head, he caught the
end of their first few words.

'Seventy-one,' she was saying. 'You wouldn't think there
was room for a crew half that size.'

'They double-bunked,' he explained. 'Half on duty, half in
their bunks. Then they swapped. Thirty-five bunks and a bit
of privacy for the captain. I'll show you as we go back down
the length of her. But we need to start with the torpedoes
under the deck here. Welcome aboard, sir. Mind your head
there, sir.'

'Captain,' corrected Mary automatically. 'He's a captain.'

'Is he?' answered their chirpy sparrow of a guide. 'Not a
submarine captain, though . . .'

'Tankers,' said Richard, straightening as far as he dared.
'Container ships.'

'Wavy navy,' nodded the submariner. 'Big ships. Hardly a
surprise.' He stuck his hand out. 'Bob Roberts, Chief Petty
Officer, retired after twenty years as a submariner. Never
served aboard this vessel but I know all there is to know about
her. Been working here for five years now, ever since Mrs
Roberts went west, God rest her. Welcome aboard *Ocelot*,
Captain.'

'Thank you, Chief.' The handshake was firm. 'Sorry to hear your wife died.'

'She didn't. She discovered she couldn't stand living with me the instant I retired from full-time service. Went to live with our daughter in Canada. Good job too. Can't nag me from Toronto. Doesn't stop her trying, though. Call me Bob, Captain.'

'Lead on then, Bob. I see you've met my Mary.'

'I have, Captain. I was just about to tell her about old *Ocelot*'s firepower. Now, if you look to for'ard, young Mary, you'll see where the torpedoes that you're standing on were put – if they were going to be used in anger, so to speak. Those are the tubes. There are six of them and the old girl here went out with thirty Mark Eight or Mark Twenty torpedoes ready to fire out of them . . .'

They were the only visitors aboard, probably because everyone else in the dockyard was somewhere near the Lifeboat exhibition looking at the media circus surrounding the junior minister, thought Richard. So they had the garrulous pensioner all to themselves. Hardly pausing for breath in his patter, as polished as a snake-oil salesman, Chief Petty Officer Bob Roberts led them down the slim, packed, three-dimensional jigsaw that was the interior of the ninth of the fourteen *Oberon* Class vessels. The last of which, the second *Onyx*, had seen service in the Falklands some thirty years ago.

Ocelot had actually come home to Chatham, Bob explained, for she had been launched from the Number 4 covered slipway less than a hundred yards distant in 1962 when the pop music charts had been dominated by Elvis Presley, Chubby Checker and Sam Cooke. Everyone was still doing the Twist, though if they were humming 'Twist and Shout' it was more likely to be the version by the Isley Brothers rather than the Beatles. *West Side Story* was still in the local cinemas and *Lawrence of Arabia* was just about to go for the Oscars in Hollywood.

As Bob talked, he led them aft, swinging easily past a heavy bulkhead door through a circular vertical hatchway that Mary also wriggled through, feet first, holding on to a pair of handles above her head. Richard found it less easy for he was taller, broader and encumbered alike by his bulky raincoat and a pair of knees that had been damaged in a terrorist attack some years ago. But he refused to be left behind. Rather breathlessly, he caught up with Bob and Mary to find that they were waiting for him. They lingered at the mid-section of the submarine's long hull, looking aft past the radar and snorkel masts through a second hatchway into the engine compartment.

Bob was explaining to the more eager half of his audience about the vessel's control systems and Mary at once demanded that she should be allowed to sit at the helm. Bob hesitated a moment, then shrugged accommodatingly. She slid into the narrow space like an eel and put her hands on the helm itself, her eyes alight as she imagined herself in control of the wonderful machine. There was a more accessible seat nearby and Richard thankfully wedged himself into this. He raised his head and eased his shoulders. All this stooping and swinging was beginning to take its toll. Bob leaned forward beside him and began to explain the complexities of controlling movement that went forwards, backwards, left and right, then up and down into the bargain. He had just begun to describe the system of planes (fixed and dive) that she would see if she went to the wall at the end of the dry dock, put her back to the river and looked in at the stern from outside, when the whole hull leapt sideways and began to roll over.

Bob was hurled bodily on to his back – and was only saved from serious injury by the fact that there was so little space between his shoulders and the wall-mounted equipment behind him. Richard felt as though he was in some kind of ejector seat or fairground ride – but the unthinking care he had taken to wedge himself in as he sat down saved him also from any serious damage. And Mary fared the best, for there was simply nowhere for her strong young body to go, tight-packed in the helmsman's seat as she was.

But the rolling, accompanied suddenly by a cataclysmic banging, wrenching and tearing, had only just begun, it seemed, when the long, strong hull was pitching into the bargain and Richard realized with utter incredulity that the submarine was somehow suddenly afloat.

He felt the rolling, pitching, heaving, bellowing vessel begin to slide out of the flooded dock and into the deep water of the river.

And then the lights went out.

THREE

After

'**M**ary!' called Richard. 'Are you all right?'

'Shaken but not stirred!' As Mary answered she was shaken again – but this time by the movement of the hull rolling through the vertical, coming upright in the deeper water.

'Sit tight then, Miss Bond, while we work things out,' said Richard with the ghost of a chuckle. 'Chief. You OK?'

'I'll survive, Captain. What in God's name is going on?'

'Heaven knows. We seem to be afloat, though. Is the hull likely to be watertight?'

'As long as the old girl stays upright, I guess, Captain. The only holes I know about are in the fin and the forward main deck hatchway.'

'Good. So she should stay afloat for long enough to allow us a chance of escaping. But we don't want to be groping around in the dark while we try to get out. Is there a backup to the lights?'

'Yes, Captain. It should come on automatically if the batteries and circuits haven't been buggered by whatever the hell that was!'

Even as Bob spoke, the lights came back on, flickered, died and then settled into a dull gold brilliance. They seemed to be at about ten per cent of their original brightness, but it was possible to look around.

'Thank God for Health and Safety,' said Chief Petty Officer Roberts, feelingly.

Richard nodded in agreement, but his mind was elsewhere. He was immediately deeply grateful that they had stopped at the helm. The masts and periscope immediately aft of their position had all been twisted out of shape and now formed a tangle of metal between them and the engine room hatch that would have been all but impossible to get through if they had been trapped on the far side.

Richard automatically glanced upwards, understanding that the damage to the roots of the equipment down here must mean that there was severe damage to the fin up there. And that was worrying, because *Ocelot* clearly had no intention of remaining perfectly upright. Even as the lights flickered into renewed life, her hull began to roll back at an increasing angle to port, as though the damaged fin above them was the weight on a metronome. A metronome likely to swing wider and wider until the whole lot went right over and turned turtle.

'Right,' said Richard decisively. 'Let's get back to the forward deck hatchway and see what's going on. You lead us out, Chief. I want to keep an eye on Mary.'

'You want Mary beside you, Daddy dearest,' said the woman in question grimly, as she folded herself out of the helmsman's seat, 'in case you need help getting back through that nasty little hatch into the torpedo room.'

In the event, Richard got back through with no trouble at all. The immediacy of the crisis – whatever it was – overrode the hesitation that had slowed him the first time. Not even the increasingly crazy angle of the deck and the handles above it slowed him, for it only served to emphasize that his original concerns were well-founded – *Ocelot* was by no means content to settle vertically and float like a lady. But on the other hand, the compartment beyond the constricted little iron circle was flooded with clear grey daylight. They just had to pray that they could get out on deck, thought Richard. Before it was flooded with something darker, heavier and wetter.

One behind the other they staggered to the skeletal stairway that led up to the forward main deck hatchway. Bob went up first, his wiry frame as misshapen as Quasimodo's by the angle of the hull. By the time Mary was following in his footsteps, *Ocelot* was coming upright once again – but the upside-down pendulum swing of her movement was becoming disturbingly wilder. At least this allowed Richard to time his upward rush for the moments when she was nearest to being upright, and soon he was standing beside the other two on the narrow walkway that comprised the full extent of the submarine's foredeck.

Richard had only a moment to make his initial assessment of the damage and the position they were in among it. It seemed to him that the whole of the Historic Dockyard had been flattened. That all life had been extinguished as absolutely as the architecture housing it had been shattered. The silence alone – except for the thumping of the wind and the teeming of the rain – had a terrifying finality. He could see almost nothing that resembled any kind of building – any kind of order – any kind of movement.

'Christ almighty,' said Bob, his voice little more than a whisper. 'It's like Hiroshima!'

Ocelot had come round with her head pointing north, guided by the last of the tide. She was floating parallel to the eastern shore, just off the silently smouldering wreckage of the covered slipways. And there, its rudder wedged just securely enough in the lip of Number 3 slipway to hold her steady, was, of all things, an ancient lifeboat.

No sooner had Richard registered the lifeboat's existence than he realized that they were going to need it. And soon. *Ocelot* was rolling once again, and this time Richard felt she was not going to stop. The bent and broken wreckage of the fin was swinging relentlessly shorewards. The tilt of the narrow, slippery deck was steepening. Whether this was her death roll or not, it seemed likely that *Ocelot* would throw them overboard this time.

Chief Petty Officer Roberts jumped. 'Hang on a sec,' he yelled as he leapt outwards.

Whether Bob was talking to Richard and Mary or to *Ocelot* herself, Richard never knew. But all three of them obeyed. Father and daughter clung on to each other, feeling that four feet thus linked would stand steadier than two. And the submarine's roll hesitated too, possibly because Bob's weight – or the absence of it – had some impact on the weird physics of the situation. Perhaps because a gust of wind, given freedom by the sudden lack of any buildings along the shore, caught the fin and blew counter to the roll. Perhaps because the vessel obeyed the Chief after all.

Bob hit the water close to the lifeboat's broad, high-pointed prow. It was a clean jump, but there was still enough of a splash to shake the boat loose. She bobbed out towards him, the clever practicality of her design immediately obvious. For although her prow sat high and strong – ready to beat down and ride up over the wildest storm surf – her gunwales sat lower and her beam was wide and steady. It required little enough strength or energy for Bob to scramble aboard.

A moment or two later he had guided the lifeboat out against the submarine's side and was holding her there as Richard lowered Mary into its relative security, then scrambled down and stepped aboard himself – lucky not to get a ducking in the process. He and Bob took an oar each and rowed out from under *Ocelot* as she completed her death roll at last and plunged the twisted ruin of her fin into the heaving wash of muddy Medway water.

The waves created as the submarine turned turtle heaved the lifeboat further upriver. Past the northern end of the wreckage that had once been Number 1 covered slip. There was a little gut, leading to a boat-sized slipway, and Richard was just about to guide the lifeboat into this when Mary called out, 'Look! Dad, there's someone out there in the water!'

And sure enough, out among the wreckage of the smaller craft from around the Thunderbolt Pier that had been swept up-water by the blast and the last of the tide, there was the unmistakable shape of a torso. It seemed to be floating face-down, arms spread and lifeless – but even as Mary called out and Richard's keen eyes fastened on it, so it gave a faint heave of movement.

'Let's go, Chief,' grated Richard at once.

'Shouldn't we go ashore? See what's happened to the people there?' asked Bob – and Richard could see his point. A good number of them would be Bob's colleagues, probably his friends. But by the look of things, they were likely to be beyond anything the three of them could do. And here was someone they knew they could help.

'Let's get this one aboard as quickly as we can, then go ashore like you say,' said Richard.

'Fair enough, Captain,' said the Chief.

Mary knelt in the prow and guided them as the two men powered the lifeboat out into the littered flow. The strengthened sides bashed through the blackened debris a good deal more easily than they would have handled storm wrack, and the feebly twitching body was soon at the starboard gunwale. Mary joined Richard, who held the long sweep oar on that side, and they pulled it aboard. Richard got a brief impression of singed black hair and dark, blistered, blast-damaged forehead. Then Mary was leaning down, preparing to give mouth-to-mouth resuscitation. Richard went cold at once, thinking of the protective kits he and Mary's mother Robin had been trained to use to prevent rescuers catching infections or diseases or conditions such as AIDS. But when push came to shove, you were either serious about saving someone's life or you were not. Even so, he called, 'Wait!' He pulled a clean handkerchief from his pocket and tore a hole in the centre of it. 'Use that,' he directed. Mary obeyed, but her father's mind was hardly put at rest by the effectiveness of the makeshift barrier he had given her. He glanced at his Rolex at last, realizing he would have to be as precise as possible about what time this had all happened. Resuscitation at a quarter past the hour, he thought. So the explosion must have happened at, what, ten past? He settled the time in his mind and looked back at Mary at last. All in all, he was very glad when the young man gave a heaving shudder and turned aside to vomit into the scuppers. 'Job done,' he said to Mary.

'Mother's going to kill me when she hears about this,' said Mary cheerfully, chucking the handkerchief overboard and wiping her mouth with the back of her hand.

She took the puking man by his shoulder, her fingers trembling slightly as she touched the soiled white cotton of his T-shirt. 'Are you all right?' she asked.

He glanced up at her, wiping his mouth in turn. He had a fine profile, thought Richard. Lean, hawklike. All nose and cheekbones and huge, heavy-lidded, dark-lashed eyes the colour of ripe dates. He looked to be in his early twenties. And, considering that she had just saved his life, he was frowning at Mary in an extremely ungrateful manner.

He nodded at her, seemingly utterly disorientated. His face began to clear, his expression relaxing. Shock, thought Richard distantly. 'Yes,' he said at last, 'I'll live, *in'sh A* . . . Ah. I'll live.' He dragged a shaking hand over his forehead and hair, lowered it, stared in wonder at the black-smeared palm. His accent was midlands, Richard thought. But probably not too far north.

'What's your name?' asked Mary, apparently unmoved by his lack of gratitude.

'Sayed,' he mumbled, dragging his eyes away from her, sitting up, beginning to look around himself. The youthful face twisted into an expression of shock and horror once again. As it did so, the gusty wind carried a dreadful smell out across the Medway. And the sounds of the first murmurs of shock, groans of pain, calls for help and screams of terror. His eyes went wild, seemingly sliding out of shock into panic as he began fully to register the enormity of the destruction all around.

'Where are you from, Sayed?' Mary was covering her own gathering shock with pointless social chit-chat, Richard thought. As good a plan as any. 'What are you doing here . . .' she persisted.

'Mary. Pay attention!' Richard interrupted. 'We're coming ashore.'

The lifeboat's bow slid up the slick concrete slope with sufficient force to wedge it in place. Mary scrambled out and tried to pull the long wooden hull further ashore. She wasn't strong enough to do it alone. Sayed made no effort to help her. So Richard shipped his oar, rose and walked forward, stepping over the young man's sprawling legs.

It was only when he was standing on the slipway that the full weight of reality seemed to hit him. Suddenly breathless with the enormity of what he had become involved in, he strode forward and stopped. He looked at his watch. Seventeen past though he hardly registered the hour. Seven minutes in. Where in God's name were the authorities? The car park was immediately in front of him. It seemed to be completely empty. Where his Bentley had been parked – with the long black official limousine beside it – there was nothing. Well, not nothing precisely – there was the wreckage of the visitors' entrance buildings. There seemed to be no movement there. The shouts and screams seemed to be coming from what was left of the long slipway buildings on his right.

He closed his eyes, fighting to distance himself from the mental pictures he could suddenly see of the cheerful girl behind the ticket counter, of the suspicious security officer, the giggling policewoman, the laughing policeman.

He looked down at the face of his battered old Rolex. Eighteen minutes past. The afternoon was still dull enough to be making the luminous dial glow. Eight minutes and counting. Had anyone had time to raise the alarm? *Was* there anyone nearby who was able to raise the alarm? He reached into his raincoat pocket and pulled out his mobile phone, opening it automatically. He stood looking down at its illuminated face. The clock function said it was coming up to nineteen minutes past. Someone needed to do something pretty quickly. *He* needed to do something before he got sidetracked into trying to find whoever was screaming and give them what help he could.

Automatically he speed-dialled the first number that came to mind. His wife Robin's. Robin was in the office at Heritage Mariner, he thought. She would have one of the twenty-four-hour news channels on. If she heard of this before she knew that they were safe, she'd have a fit . . . He put the mobile to his ear. The connection purred three times.

'Hello, darling, what's up?' The cheery normality of her greeting almost destroyed him.

'Robin . . .' he started, but his voice failed him. 'Darling. There's been an incident. Mary and I are all right. But you have to get on to the authorities. Now. Police. Ambulance. Fire service. Tell them there's been a serious incident at Chatham . . .'

There was a noise behind him and the chimes of an iPhone being switched on. He turned. It was Mary. Sayed and Bob Roberts were coming up from the boat just behind her. 'What are you doing, darling?' he asked her.

'Calling nine-nine-nine, Dad,' she said forthrightly, using the tone that showed she thought him both stupid and senile.

He looked down at his own mobile and frowned, suddenly suspecting he was not so completely in command of the situation as he had fondly supposed himself to be.

'Who were you calling?' demanded Mary, her fingers busy on the touch-screen.

'Your mum. She's calling nine-nine-nine on the landline from the office.'

'Are you out of your mind? She's going to go *insane*! You do realize this is the last little jaunt she'll ever let you take me on?'

'Oh come on, sweetheart! She'll be cool. Especially when she finds out we're really both OK. If you knew some of the things she's been through herself . . .'

But Mary paid no attention to the bulk of this, for she was talking to someone at 999 central dispatch.

Richard's phone rang at once. Robin's picture lit up the

screen. The clock above her said twenty past. 'Hello darling,' he said as he put it to his ear.

'Richard! What in hell's name have you and Mary got yourselves mixed up in now?'

He opened his mouth to answer, but several things prevented him. Someone in the wreck of Number 3 slipway started screaming more loudly than ever. He felt an overpowering urge to act. To do anything he could to help. Robin's voice came distantly out of the speaker of his phone. The *wah-wah* of a siren suddenly bellowed surprisingly close at hand as someone – probably a policeman – came in under a blue-light run. And the young man they had pulled from the river abruptly took to his heels and went sprinting across the bombsite that was all that was left of the dockyard.

'Hey!' yelled Richard, breaking connection automatically. 'Hey, come back!'

The running figure hesitated amid the ruin of the visitors' entrance building. Half turned. Seemed to reel; to stoop. Then he was off again, running wildly into the middle of the bombsite.

FOUR
Math

As Richard sprinted towards the source of the loudest screams, he went over in his mind what he knew about the police response system for major incidents. He did this for several reasons. First, it stopped him speculating about the carnage he was likely to encounter. An old hand at accident and emergency work had given him the tip. *Don't frighten yourself before you get there. Arrive with an open mind and then deal with what you find. Scared first-aiders have lost the initiative before they even start.*

Second, he was trying to remain remote from the fact that Mary was at his heels. She was first-aid trained as well. It would be criminal to stop her helping – especially as it might well be less risky than the mouth-to-mouth she had already

given the fleeing boy. And after his last brief conversation
with Robin he certainly did not want to speculate on what his
wife would say when she found out about *that*.

Third, he was angry with himself for not dialling 999 direct
from his own mobile. He prided himself on his calmness and
decisiveness in a crisis. And yet he had automatically called
Robin when the going got tough while his daughter had been
thinking more clearly and effectively. Now he was trying to
rack up a score to balance things. Like a team that had gone
down by a goal, a try or a wicket in the opening seconds of
a match. Or had lost an easy starter on *University Challenge*.

It was called the Gold, Silver, Bronze system, he remembered. Or sometimes Strategic, Tactical and Operational. Gold
level was central command, in the Strategic Command Centre,
contacting relevant ministers of state, departments and services. And the COBRA committee if necessary. Assessing and
activating specialists when needed. Gold would be at Chief
Constable or Commissioner level – depending on the structure of the force involved.

Then there would be Silver, in overall command of the
tactical area. Someone at Commander or Chief Superintendent
level. And Bronze would be the man or woman on the ground.
Someone at Chief Inspector or Superintendent level. Someone
who didn't mind getting their hands dirty. Who would roll up
their sleeves and get on with the job – no matter how bloody
it might become.

The Bronze commander would take control of the scene,
coordinate the police, fire, ambulance and paramedic officers.
Richard wondered fleetingly what the target timescale was for
that. Fifteen minutes? Twenty?

These thoughts were enough to take Richard and Mary to
the biggest pile of wreckage, closest to the screaming. Richard
glanced back to see Chief Petty Officer Bob Roberts running
out across the parking area towards the police patrol car.

Richard gave a curt nod of satisfaction then he turned to
work. 'Remember the first rule,' he called to Mary. 'Safety
first. And that means *our* safety. We can't help anyone if we
need help ourselves. So look for traps and dangers. Holes.
Things that might be burning, scalding or corrosive. Electrical
cables that might still have power to shock . . .'

Side by side they began to pick through the jumble of

wreckage until they had located the precise source of the screams. Then, side by side, they lifted a section of partially collapsed roofing, almost thirty square feet of which was still being held up like a wigwam by something beneath it; like half of a pitched roof.

And there was a shock of another kind. Several shocks for Richard, as a matter of fact – though none of them electrical – as they pushed the wood back on to the top of the lifeboat section that had been supporting it. The first was that, while there was one person screaming here, there were others who were not. He glanced across at Mary, suddenly worried about the psychological damage this might be doing to her. But she was an intrepid young woman. And, by the grace of God, the other people beneath the planks of wood seemed merely to be asleep. But when he turned his attention back to his rescue effort, he received the next shock.

He knew the woman beneath the collapsed roof section. He knew her well enough to recognize her even though she was blast-blackened, her cheeks and forehead bruised, mottled and swollen, her hair burned and her whole face twisted by her screams. And he realized at once that he not only knew her but knew who she was.

He had been introduced to her at a charity fundraiser a couple of months ago. Then she had been a youthful, pretty, well turned out, executive-looking woman. Every inch the rising political star. Her name was Gloria Strickland and she was Member of Parliament for one of the seats in Sussex quite close to where he lived. And, he suddenly realized, she was ministerial assistant to the Culture Secretary. It was Ms Strickland, indeed, who had informed him that she and the Culture Secretary worked out of the Cabinet Office rather than the Department for Culture, Media and Sport.

'Hell's teeth!' he swore, glancing across at Mary once again.

For the final element that shocked him so much in the current situation was that some vagary of blast had blown off every shred of Gloria Strickland's clothing and left the poor woman stark naked. Not something a father wishes to deal with in front of his daughter.

'It's all right, Ms Strickland,' he said, leaning forward and focusing all of his attention on her face. Speaking almost in a whisper. Keeping the deep growl of his voice soft, calm and soothing. 'Gloria, we're here to help and there's more help coming. Can you tell me where it hurts?'

The screaming stopped. The blast-shocked woman's eyes flickered open. Fastened on Richard's face with a frown of partial recognition. He saw the irises contract as they reacted to what light there was. 'Gloria,' he repeated gently. 'It's Richard Mariner. We met a couple of weeks ago at a fundraiser in Dymchurch. There's been an accident. Can you tell me where it hurts?'

The eyes closed again. The frown deepened. 'I'm extremely cold,' she said in the accents of Cheltenham Ladies' College. Then she lapsed into silence.

'Dare we move her?' asked Mary.

'Not yet,' said Richard. 'We need to do a series of checks . . .'

'I know. Visual. Then, if need be, physical. My law studies suggest that we have to be very careful here, however, dearest father. We've got involved. That means we're responsible. If we get it wrong there could be a suit against us. A civil suit or a criminal charge. We've assumed a duty of care. We don't want to get caught for omission. Or negligence. We don't want you back in the Old Bailey. Or me for that matter.'

'Visual seems fine,' said Richard bracingly. 'Even if there's rather too much of her to see. No blood visible on her skin, at her orifices or on the ground beneath her. Do you feel competent to do the physical examination while I get my coat off and get ready to cover her up – or to wrap her up, depending on what you find? Feeling cold will be the least of her troubles if any of the cameramen who were surrounding her just now – or any of their cameras – have survived.'

'They wouldn't!' said Mary, genuinely horrified at the thought, looking up with her hands clasped gently round the MP's upper thigh as she checked the state of hip joint and femoral pulse.

'Don't you believe it, miss,' said a new voice, close enough to make them both jump. Richard looked up to see a tall man in the uniform of a sergeant in the Kent and Medway police force standing over them looking down with water cascading from the black peak of his cap. He was wearing a stab vest that made his square, powerful body look like some kind of a robot. 'That's the price of being a VIP. Just look in any of the tabloids or the gossip magazines. Still and all, this one's lucky to have survived.' He looked around at the devastation. 'God knows how many others will be that lucky.'

'I can't find anything wrong with her, Dad. I think we can risk covering her up at least.'

'Paramedics'll be here any minute now,' added the sergeant. 'Then Uncle Tom Cobleigh and all. There's a critical response unit up at Chatham, luckily enough. They'll be down mob-handed. That blast must have broken most of their windows so they won't have needed much more warning that there's a major incident in their own back yard. This is just about as major as incidents get, short of a train crash in the Channel Tunnel or one of those big new Super-Jumbos coming down in the middle of Ashford or Maidstone. You'll be Captain Mariner and daughter Mary, according to Chief Petty Officer Roberts. My name's Jimmy Lloyd. Sergeant up at Rochester nick on Purser Way and first officer on site, for my sins.'

Mary looked up. 'There was a boy,' she said. 'Sayed. We pulled him out of the river. He almost drowned. He panicked and ran when he saw all this. You'll need to find him. I think he needs help.'

Sergeant Lloyd nodded. 'We'll find him, miss,' he said. 'But first things first. There's teams coming ready to go out there after the walking wounded – I've counted half a dozen so far, with God knows how many calling for help apart from your poor lady there. The air ambulance is on its way. This lady . . .'

'Gloria Strickland MP, parliamentary assistant to the Culture Secretary. Works out of the Cabinet Office . . .' said Richard, looking up at the sergeant to make sure the message went home that the wounded woman was a person of considerable importance.

Sergeant Lloyd's eyes closed briefly. 'Jesus! That really ratchets things up,' he said. 'Thanks for the heads-up, Captain.' He glanced at his watch and Richard automatically looked at his. Twenty minutes dead, he thought. Sergeant Lloyd turned away, reaching for the two-way handset clipped to his flak jacket. Then he was off, jogging across the littered ground towards the car park, deep in conversation with his right shoulder. There, behind his shoulder, a helicopter settled on to the blast-swept car park. And then, as though this was all some kind of a signal, a colourful two-storey wall of head-lights and emergency flashers swept across the open area behind it as the first major response teams from the police service, the ambulance service and the fire service came screaming on to the site.

Richard and Mary accompanied Gloria Strickland on her stretcher across to the air ambulance, surrounded by para-medics who divided their time between making the MP comfortable and checking on the Mariners' state of health. But it was only as the MP was lifted gently into the ambu-lance chopper itself that Richard got his raincoat back. He was just – rather redundantly – shrugging it on over his sopping jacket when Sergeant Lloyd reappeared. 'Chief Inspector Clark would like a word with both of you now,' he said.

'Is the Chief Inspector setting up Bronze command?' asked Richard as they crossed towards a big square van the size of an old-fashioned ambulance.

Lloyd nodded. 'Bronze Incident Command Post,' he said, pointing with his chin. 'How do you know all this stuff, Captain? You on a police authority panel? Neighbourhood Watch? I guess you're not a part-time Police Community Support Officer.'

'I keep my ears to the ground,' Richard answered cryptically.

'He has a complete section of Heritage Mariner,' expanded Mary brusquely, 'who keep their ears to the ground for him. They're called London Centre. Half of them used to be Special Branch. Most of the rest of them are ex-spooks of one kind or another . . .'

'You'll be meeting some of their colleagues, then, I shouldn't wonder,' said Sergeant Lloyd. 'When the Cabinet Office gets to hear about poor Ms Strickland. They'll probably set up COBRA for this lot.'

They reached the Incident Command vehicle and Lloyd climbed three broad metal steps to pull the rear door open. 'Captain Mariner and his daughter, sir,' he said. 'Captain, this is Chief Inspector Clark from the Chatham Critical Incident Team.'

A tall young officer rose, hand held out. 'Tom Clark, Captain Mariner. I'm the operational commander at this scene . . .' He was in uniform shirtsleeves with epaulettes gleaming and tie neatly secured. He did not wear a stab vest.

'He understands the Gold, Silver, Bronze system, sir—' interjected Lloyd.

'Right. Thank you, Sergeant. That'll speed things up. Run along and bring Chief Petty Officer Roberts here, would you? Right, Captain. I'm setting up Bronze forward command here and I assume you know what that means.' He waved his hand around the inside of the vehicle, which seemed as well-packed with equipment as the submarine. Two women police constables were seated beside him, one at a fold-down table with a map of the dockyard and the surrounding area – a paper version copied and expanded on the computer screen above. The other was clearly in charge of communications.

'I have men and women out controlling traffic and access,' the Chief Inspector continued, 'and I'm setting up casualty and body holding. Liaison with the local hospitals is ongoing and they're all Major Incident briefed. Communication with Silver and Gold will begin when tactical and strategic levels are in place. But my major – immediate – preoccupation has to be the casualties. I need to find them, get them treated and start to clear them away to more suitable accommodation. I have my response teams almost here and the K9 sections will be ready when they are. I understand you have already done sterling work. But I wonder, until I get everyone organized and on the ground, whether I could ask you for more help. Both of you.'

'Of course,' said Richard. 'What help can we be?'

'I understand via Sergeant Lloyd from CPO Roberts that you are the only ones still standing who have any idea where people actually were immediately prior to the incident. I wonder could you guide my first response, paramedic and K9 teams? They'll be so much more effective with just a little more information. Such as you can supply. I mean, you can see the first teams are going through the area randomly and bringing back anyone who can walk, but we need to be more focused and methodical than that. As I say, the next teams will be here in just a moment, then I'd like to start a properly organized initial sweep.'

'Of course,' said Richard. 'If that's OK with you, Mary.'

Mary nodded, her dark curls gleaming, her face set determinedly.

He leaned forward and dripped on a map of the dockyard area spread on the fold-down table near the Chief Inspector. 'The obvious place to start is the ticket office. There were four people there – and I should guess there'll be visitor number records that will help. If we can dig them out of the rubble.'

'Two of the people there were police officers,' emphasized Mary. 'Armed police officers. And Dad said there was someone from security there too.'

'A security guard?' asked Tom Clark, surprised. 'Group Four? Someone like that?'

'More like Counter-Terrorism Command or MI5,' said Richard. 'Security for Gloria Strickland. Armed security.'

'Right,' said Tom Clark, grimly. He turned to the constable at the communications console. 'Sally, get on to Thames House. Make sure the duty officer is up to speed. They may want to alert the director general. This may well be a job for COBRA too if they can get the committee all in in time. Alert whoever arrives in Silver command as well . . .' He turned back to Richard. 'We'd better get a wiggle on,' he said. 'That's three guns lying around in that building alone. And Ms Strickland's personal security team will have had more.'

'Excuse me, sir,' interrupted Sally the communications officer, turning round. 'Thames House say they were on alert anyway. Their teams missed a scheduled check-in at a quarter past. They hit the panic button at once. There's a new team on the way and they're trying to track down Professor Stark from Imperial College.'

'Diana Stark? The mathematician?' demanded Mary. 'You won't get her. She's in Australia at the World Maths Forum . . .'

'What a team!' said Tom wryly. 'Is there anything you two don't know about?'

'I don't know why MI5 would be bringing a leading mathematician,' said Mary. 'Her field is post René Thom math, catastrophe theory, predictive patterns. Chaos theory. That sort of thing . . .' She saw the way her father was looking at her. 'No,' she said. 'It's not part of my studies. I'm just interested in outstanding women. I expect it's just a phase I'm going through . . .'

'Security has this theory that there is a mathematical model

somewhere that can predict terrorist incidents,' explained Tom
Clark. 'I think Intelligence and Counter-Terrorism – CTC as
we call them – have bought into it as well. I know both the
FBI and CIA are tickled by it . . .'

'Terrorist incidents . . .' said Mary. 'Using mathematical
models to predict . . . *Terrorist* incidents. Is that what this
was?"

'What else?' asked her father a little wearily. 'What else
could it have been, darling?'

'And in any case,' said Tom Clark quietly, 'you gave us the
crucial information. The vital clue.'

'*Me?*' demanded Mary, outraged. 'How did I tell you
anything about terrorists?'

'Sayed,' said Tom briefly. 'You said the man who ran away
after you had pulled him out of the river and given him the
kiss of life was called Sayed.And it so happens that we've
been looking for someone called Sayed.'

He gestured at the woman with the map in front of her and
the computer screen above it. She pressed a button. The young
man's face came on screen. There could be no doubt. The
cheekbones, the nose, the heavy-lidded, dark-fringed date-
brown eyes.

'That's what he told me his name was!' answered Mary,
her voice wavering uncertainly. 'But . . . *but* . . .'

'MI5, MI6, CTC, Thames Valley Police and the
Buckinghamshire Constabulary have all been searching for
Sayed Mohammed since he came back in through Gatwick
out of the blue – and vanished. Nightmare. How someone that
dangerous was able to come and go just beggars belief. He
slipped in through border security just over six months ago.
He was last seen in Milton Keynes, early in the New Year
apparently . . .' The face vanished off the screen to be replaced
by CCTV footage of a young man crossing a shopping mall.

'And that was all we knew until you fished him out of the
Medway this afternoon. Just after he had blown the dockyard
to kingdom come, by the look of things.'

FIVE

K9

By the time Richard and Mary stepped back out of the makeshift forward command centre, things had progressed considerably – even though it was still little more than twenty-five minutes since the explosion. As they descended the steps into the windy, rainswept car park they could hear Tom Clark's communications officer reporting that Chief Superintendent Jan Booth had set up Silver command in Tom Clark's office in the nearby Chatham nick. And Chief Constable Nelson Peake was on his way to the regional police headquarters in Maidstone where he was planning to establish Gold.

Things had progressed on the ground as well. The car park was becoming more crowded with ambulances, police vehicles and fire engines. A range of paramedics were out amid the rubble, helping walking wounded who looked to Richard disturbingly like the zombies in one of his son William's old shoot-'em-up video games. Fire officers and rapid response teams were being briefed by their team leaders. They were using the post-7/7 template. Hesitating briefly between the immediate requirement for urgent action – as emphasized by the increasing number of calls for help they could all hear – and the basic security steps required in case there were booby traps in the rubble. Or hidden among the bodies of the men and women trapped and calling – and those buried but unable to call.

The K9 units were designed to deal with both imperatives. Richard and Mary attached themselves to the first unit in place, Constable Patryk Zalewski and his springer spaniel, whose name was Brandy. 'Brandy is trained to sniff out explosives as well as bodies,' the constable explained in an accent that suggested the dog would have been better named Vodka. 'Also drugs, alcohol and contraband of many sorts. We follow where she leads and call for backup according to what she finds. Medics or bomb squad.' He grinned cheerfully and moved forward as the dog tugged eagerly at her leash.

Sergeant Lloyd reappeared, with CPO Roberts still at his side. He glanced up at the Bronze control vehicle and spoke into his two-way. Two teams of paramedics ran forward and grouped round the little team led by the eager dog. As soon as they all began to move forward, a small armed rapid response team appeared out of the gathering gloom to follow them. The three armed officers were wearing helmets, goggles and full body armour. Their leader's name, Sgt DUFF, was stencilled on his stab vest, back and front, just above POLICE. PC ABIVA was stencilled on the vest of the female officer behind him, as was PC BERGUNDO on that of her male companion. Richard looked narrow-eyed at the Glock 17 self-loading pistols and Heckler and Koch MP5 carbines the three of them were carrying. 'I don't think we'll need the guns, Sergeant,' he said quietly, eyeing an even more deadly-looking piece of weaponry attached to PC Abiva's belt.

'I agree, sir,' said Sergeant Duff. 'But let's wait until we're sure, shall we? Better safe than sorry.'

With PC Zalewski at his shoulder and Brandy bouncing at his side, Richard led the suddenly considerable group across to the pile of rubble that had been the visitors' entrance – the shop, restaurant and the Wooden Walls exhibition above. Brandy started snuffling through the wreckage at once, a long, excited, grumbling growl issuing from her throat. Richard, mentally reconstructing the plan of the ground floor in his head, walked across to the ticket office, placing his feet with extreme care. Glancing up, he noticed that everyone was doing the same, clearing and checking before they stepped forward for fear of walking on a buried victim – or some part of one. But, at the end of his straight-cleared trail, he found exactly what he was looking for, precisely where he had expected her to be. As Mary and he cleared the pile of debris that had been the little booth's wooden frame, so they found a lick of golden hair so bright that it seemed to have been painted on the rubble. The cheerful young woman was there, buried in the wreckage of her ticket office, so easy to find that he didn't need to call for Brandy's assistance. Mercifully, in Richard's opinion at least, the blast had knocked her cold without doing any damage to her clothing.

As the paramedics completed their initial checks and began to move her, so a computer printout fluttered into the light. Richard glanced at it automatically. It was a balance sheet of the day's takings so far. 'Mary,' he called quietly. 'Take this to Chief Inspector Clark, would you? It should give Bronze command some idea of how many visitors we're looking for.'

No sooner had Mary strode off back along the careful pathway they had cleared – like a soldier following a safe track through a minefield – than Brandy gave an excited bark and started digging. The rest of them joined in and soon they found their next survivor. Lying incongruously beneath a pile of stuffed toy animals, most of them singed and partly gutted, was the young man Richard had assumed to be an officer from MI5 or CTC. Like the ticket girl he seemed to be either deeply unconscious or dead, but as the paramedics began to ease him out of the wreckage and on to a tough moulded plastic stretcher, so he stirred. His eyes flickered. His hand went under the tattered remains of his raincoat. Richard supposed he was going to produce some kind of warrant card or ID. But no. The hand came out empty. 'I lost it,' he whispered, his public-school and Oxbridge tones just loud enough to hear.

'Lost what?' asked Richard.

'My gun. It's gone.'

Richard looked across at Sergeant Duff. The response officer leaned forward. 'What sort of gun? Describe it. Was it standard issue?'

'Not standard. Got it in Washington when I was seconded . . . Fast-draw, light and slick.' He laughed – not a particularly amusing or indeed pleasant sound. 'Better than a Walther or a Biretta.'

'What sort?' persisted Duff, more urgently. 'What are we looking for?'

'A K9. A Kahr double action K9.'

'Load?'

'Nine mm. Standard issue. One in the breach, six in the mag.' The young spook collapsed back into the paramedics' arms, gasping as though he had just run a marathon. By the time he was strapped on the stretcher he was deeply unconscious again.

'There'll be more guns out there somewhere, too,' said

Richard. 'The two police officers on the other side of the barrier were almost as well-armed as you, Sergeant.' There was a little pause, then he added, 'Perhaps you were right to come all tooled up.'

Richard was very glad indeed that Mary was still at the Bronze command vehicle when they found the next guns. Because the state of the officers who had been holding them would have given the most intrepid young woman nightmares. Just the roast-pork smell of them was going to linger in Richard's nostrils for a month. Richard took one sickened glance and left the messy stuff to the response unit and the paramedics. Instead he straightened and looked across the littered wilderness which was all that remained of the heart of the dockyard. He was suddenly overwhelmed by a feeling of bitterness and frustration, compounded by an uncharacteristic sensation of helplessness and depression. He recognized it at once as a dangerous cocktail of shock and survivor guilt, but that didn't help much. Suddenly, all he wanted was to get away from here. To take Mary, complete whatever formalities were required, answer any questions that still needed answering and get away as quickly as possible. There was nothing here but wounded, dead and dying. He and Mary shouldn't be trying to help, they should be getting out from under everyone's feet and going home. Except that, of course, his beautiful Bentley had vanished – blown to pieces like the rest of the place, as likely as not. So he would have to start begging lifts from the police in any case, like a teenager stranded at a party.

The phone in his pocket rang. Robin's face lit up the screen as he pulled it out. 'Hello?' he said guardedly.

'Hi darling. You sound tired. Poor old thing. Just the quickest call to tell you I'm at the cordon here waiting with William. He's texted Mary but no reply – her iPhone's switched off, I expect. It's all over the news. The worst incident in years. Trust you to be in the middle of it! The police won't let us any further so I've parked the Discovery as close by as possible. Tell Mary we'll be here waiting with sandwiches and flasks of soup when they let the pair of you out. Then we'll take you both home.'

Richard closed the connection without replying. He wouldn't have been able to talk in any case. But all the weight of weariness and helpless frustration seemed to have been lifted almost magically by her words.

PC Zalewski bustled past then, with Brandy straining at the leash. 'There is another team searching the covered slipways,' he said. 'We are supposed to go along the east side. Do you have any idea about who was in any of the buildings there?' He gestured up the slight slope towards the ruins farthest from the river.

'There was a tea room opposite *Cavalier* and another one down in the buildings there somewhere,' said Richard vaguely. 'Most of the buildings along the eastern perimeter were closed to visitors but I guess Chief Inspector Clark will have a list of any dockyard personnel who were working in them.'

Zalewski turned to Duff. 'I should maybe let Brandy off her leash. She will check fast for us. There is still enough light to follow her. It is the last chance to do this before dark.'

'Good thinking,' answered the sergeant. The constable released the dog at once and she went questing off among the rubble immediately, head down and tail high. Zalewski followed her at a run and Duff's little command jogged easily behind. The paramedic team assigned to them followed more slowly, hampered by their equipment.

Richard turned, his head still full of the welcome thought of Robin, soup and sandwiches. And home. He had had enough for one day. They'd sort out their bit of this whole colossal mess in the morning. But even as he moved, Mary arrived with Sergeant Lloyd in tow.

'The sergeant's got something to tell you,' she said grimly. 'I'll go and help the paramedics.' And she jogged off even before he could tell her that her mother and brother were waiting at the gate.

'Excuse me, Captain,' began the sergeant with sinister sententiousness, 'as soon as you've finished helping the rapid response team and the K9 section, there are some questions that we need you to answer. We've set up an interview room now and Bronze and Silver both agree – under Gold's direction I have to say – that we need to get as clear a picture of the last few moments before the atrocity as possible. Especially if this man Sayed Mohammed was involved in any way at all. It's clearly crucial that we find and detain him as soon as we can. And what he was doing just before might help us assess what he'll be up to this soon after.' The sergeant looked at his watch, glanced meaningfully at Richard. 'It's still only three-quarters of an hour . . .'

Suddenly the leaden weight of depression was on his shoulders once again. He opened his mouth to answer, but before he could get the first word out, the wild, excited barking started.

Then the gunshots. The shouting. And the high, unearthly agonized screaming.

'Mary!' shouted Richard, swinging round without a second thought to go pounding towards the sounds. He was only vaguely aware of Lloyd at his shoulder, and dark response teams closing in behind him. Eyes straining to make out the detail of what was happening he pounded forward. The pale shapes of the paramedics were scattering backwards, clearly looking for safety – perhaps shelter. He couldn't see Mary among them, so he bellowed her name again and heard her clear, familiar voice answer, 'Over here!'

She was crouching beside the low wall that surrounded the opening to the old air-raid shelter. A tree had stood over it before the explosion but that lay torn down now, its roots ripped from the earth as the explosion had stamped its topmost branches to the ground. The steps down into the shadowy pit that was the entrance to the underground bunker seemed to lean at a crazy angle and the outer wall at whose upper lip Mary was crouching bulged dangerously halfway down where the roots had damaged it as they were torn upwards.

Just at the point where the steps were craziest and the wall bulging most dangerously lay Brandy, wounded and screaming, sounding disturbingly like the shocked Gloria Strickland MP.

Mary was beside Pat Zalewski and she seemed to be holding the dog handler back by an incredible effort of strength and will. 'You're only wearing a stab vest,' she was saying. 'A bullet will go straight through it. You wouldn't stand a chance.'

'But she's so badly hurt! Listen to her . . .'

'Let us handle it, Pat,' grated Duff. 'We have the kit and the training. We know how to do this.'

Richard had mental pictures of the Stockwell fiasco that had led to the terrible, tragic death of Jean Charles de Menezes. 'Careful, Duff,' he said without thinking. 'Everyone from here to Helmand is going to want this guy alive.'

'Chief Inspector Clark has just made the same point pretty forcefully,' answered Duff, tapping the two-way on his helmet. 'We'll try to oblige. Bergundo. The gas canister. Can you get it round the corner into the bunker from there?'

'I think so, Sergeant.'

'Abiva. Ready?'

'Yes.'

'OK. I'll cover. Everyone else stand clear. That means you, Pat. For the time being. You can get Brandy back in a minute. One way or another. Go on three, team. One . . . Two . . .'

On *three*, Constable Bergundo leaned up over the lip of the wall and threw what looked like a grenade down past the screaming dog. No sooner had it vanished round the corner and bounced into the underground bunker than there was a dull thump. Acrid smoke billowed out into the stairwell and poor Brandy's howls became tearing chokes as the wounded animal fought for breath. The sound was horrendous.

Pat Zalewski tore himself out of Mary's grip and darted down the stair to rescue his dog. Without thinking, Mary followed him. Richard leaped upward only to collide with the unflinching solidity of Sergeant Duff's shoulder. Sergeant Lloyd grabbed him and pulled him back. Constable Abiva swung into position at the top of the steps, solid, square-on, straddle-legged – the strange, brutal-looking sidearm in standard two-handed firing position.

And that was the position they were all in when Sayed Mohammed came stumbling out of the bunker, choking, eyes streaming, waving the deadly little American Kahr K9 9mm pistol he had picked up after the MI5 man dropped it. Pat Zalewski was nearest to him, crouching with his arms round the choking, screaming dog. And it was at the pair of them that the half-blind man aimed his pistol first. He was squeezing the trigger when Mary, crouching two steps up from Pat, called out, 'Sayed! Don't!'

At once the gun jerked up to point at her. But for that one fatal instant the trigger finger hesitated.

Where Abiva's trigger finger did not. The bulky taser gave its flat airgun report and two sharp terminals flew unerringly twelve feet down into Sayed Mohammed's chest on either side of his heart. The wires that connected the terminals to the gun carried the shock of four thousand volts at the speed of light. He dropped where he stood and only Abiva's quick reactions saved Mary, Pat and Brandy from a shock as the wires fell across them.

There was an instant of silence, then Duff said into his two-way, 'Subject secured, sir. No major injuries.'

'No major injuries!' huffed Pat as he and Mary staggered up the steps with Brandy writhing and yelping in agony between them. 'He shot my dog! He shot my fucking dog!'

And the angry muttering of shocked reaction from the considerable crowd that seemed to have gathered around the little group made Richard suddenly certain of one crucial thing. That, no matter what other terrible crimes he might have planned or committed, Sayed Mohammed was truly for the high jump when the rest of the British public, and the press that served them so faithfully, found out that he had cold-bloodedly shot PC Pat Zalewski's dog.

DISCOVERY

SIX
Autumn

Press coverage of the arrest and detention of Sayed Abu Minyar Mohammed for the terrorist outrage at Chatham was treated exactly as Richard had suspected it would be. Mohammed's face was all over the news for a couple of weeks, accompanied at first by the faces of the twenty-four people killed. Then the press's interest seemed to fade a little.

And as the last days of the summer holidays passed, and then the autumn itself faltered with the gathering of winter, it seemed that only Richard and Mary – back with her law group amid her more general studies – were interested in the fate of Sayed Mohammed. Mary returned to her studies a little late because her parents were worried about the impact her experiences might have had on her. Robin was particularly concerned – perhaps because it was she, facing the enormity that she might have so easily lost half of her family, had the worst nightmares. William, too, seemed to suffer a kind of survivor guilt. Richard and Mary themselves, having faced the situation for real and come through it unscathed, were very much more blasé. And so, increasingly it seemed, were the press.

Even before Mary finally went back to her studies there was merely a glance in the popular press towards the implications of having a government minister involved as a victim in such an incident. An interest given legs and raised to prurience in some of the tabloids by the fact that the young and attractive MP had been discovered naked after the blast. A certain amount of more serious speculation in the London-centred media followed as to the implications for the capital and the Olympic festival it was due to host in the near and fast-approaching future. Then there was the three-day wonder of the funerals of the victims who had died, and the national day of mourning ordered by the government.

So, Sayed Mohammed was on every front page and news

station at first as he was detained without charge in Belmarsh high security prison, treated from the outset as a Category A prisoner, under a whole raft of anti-terrorist legislation, while the police built their *prima facie* case against him. All too well aware of the difficulties faced by previous prosecuting authorities who had taken years to obtain guilty verdicts even with cases supported by taped evidence, photographs, video footage and, in the final analysis, email conversations prised out of Internet providers through the American courts. Striving, in the first instance, to establish beyond a reasonable doubt that he had been on the bomb-laden boat before he appeared in the Medway. That he had been an active participant in the outrage. And then, satisfied that a jury might see his presence there as more than mere coincidence, they began to attempt to discover who had helped him in his murderous enterprise and sweep them into the net of criminal conspiracy before they could flee the country.

All this went on while the House of Commons was called back into emergency session to enjoy a lively debate as to whether now was the time to reintroduce the ninety-day limit, which they had already discussed at such length in days gone by.

And in the meantime, every soldier – in or out of uniform – on the British side in the war against terrorism was trying to get the vital details of Sayed Mohammed's precise involvement in the atrocity. Up to the moment before Richard and Mary had pulled his drowning body out of the Medway and into the lifeboat. Using to the maximum the added elements of secrecy and uncertainty granted by the fact that Sayed Mohammed had not been formally charged, had seemingly vanished into the legal machinery of the British state and, eventually, had vanished even from the news-hungry media themselves.

At first it seemed that Richard's involvement would progress no further than the evidence he had already given, and his awareness that, when Sayed Mohammed finally did come to trial, he and Mary would be called to repeat that evidence in court. And to expand or defend it as necessary under cross-examination should the need arise; at least that was what his legally orientated daughter warned him to expect. A busy man

with a global empire to run, he went back to work and effectively thought no more of the matter, beyond his discussions
with Mary and his steadfast refusal to employ any of his own
'tame spooks' – as she called them – in looking any further
into the matter. London Centre, he informed her, had better
things to do. And he really believed that they had better things
to do. While Sayed Mohammed was held without charge under
close guard in the country's most secure prison, at any rate.

But a couple of days before Pat Zalewski was due to take
Brandy up to receive her Dickin medal – the canine VC – a
call came through to Richard's office in Heritage House asking
if he was available to take a meeting with a member of the
Home Secretary's team. That was when everything started to
go down another track entirely.

Richard's first reaction to the summons was to do exactly
what Mary had been asking him to do for weeks. He took
himself out into Leadenhall and strolled thoughtfully past the
opening to St Mary Axe before turning left into Creechurch
Street. The afternoon shadows of an overcast but humid day
filled the little alleyway almost like one of the London fogs
so famous in earlier centuries. And they served, aptly enough,
to cloak the secretive door into London Centre. Richard went
through the outer security routine and then subjected himself
more cheerfully to the equally searching but slightly more
traditional scrutiny of Colour Sergeant Stone, Parachute
Regiment (Retd.).

The sergeant's scrutiny might be traditional, but everything
else in the foyer of the building was as high-tech, modern and
security conscious as it could be. In many ways this building
was the brains of Heritage Mariner, stuffed full as it was of
men and women who had knowledge of, contacts in and highly
educated speculation about absolutely everything that was
happening or was likely to happen in the world that Richard
and his company occupied. Or in any of the worlds which
impacted upon it, political, commercial, secret, military,
terrorist . . .

'I'm here to see Commander Bourne,' said Richard, as
though unaware that, as their employer, he could see anyone
in the building any time he liked.

'He's expecting you, Captain.'

'He'd be out of a job if he wasn't.'

The little byplay was one they enjoyed on all but the most serious or formal of Richard's visits. He stepped into the glass elevator and was whisked up to the top floor. Jim Bourne was waiting to greet him at the lift doors, his square, broad-chinned face split in a grin of welcome that seemed almost to stretch his pencil-thin black moustache from one jug-handle ear to the other.

'You look like the cat who got the cream,' said Richard, shaking his hand. 'What is it?'

'We got the proof you wanted about the Russian government's plans to build floating nuclear power stations and anchor them in the Arctic Ocean. Plans, anchorage points, prognostications, shopping lists . . .'

'That must have taken some doing.'

'Don't ask.' Bourne shuddered. 'Modern commercial relations with Russia – it's the new Cold War. Lucky you employ almost as many spooks of one sort or another as MI6 used to . . .'

'Do we want in? To the new Cold War or the floating power stations?'

'We're still making our initial assessment. On the power stations at any rate. Be with you soon, though the fact that they're going to be *floating* does move the whole concept firmly into Heritage Mariner's bailiwick. Not to mention the fact that all your Russian adventures and ex-Soviet contacts put you somewhere between George Smiley and James Bond in the new commercial Cold War anyway. Now. What did you want?'

On the question, Jim showed Richard into his office. The windows looked out across St Mary Axe towards Bishopsgate. The view westward was frankly ruined by the tall rear elevation of Heritage House rearing skywards on Leadenhall. But Richard crossed to the window as he always did, looking down with something akin to a shiver at the little raised graveyard that stood against the back of the building. Its elderly monuments leaned askew, its crosses crumbling and falling, like something out of Dickens's London preserved by a whim of fate. Like something out of a Hammer horror movie. Like the last haunt of Jack the Ripper.

'The Home Secretary's assistant assistant's assistant called. Could I pop across for tea and a chat?'

'What, with Alan Pitt himself?'

'No. With one of his minions.'

'Know which one?'

'Of course. I'm not going to the House completely blind-folded! Harry Blake.'

'So it'll be criminal justice and offender management. Could be to do with your involvement in the Chatham incident.'

'Can't see it. Not at ministerial level. It'll be policy, surely . . .'

'Some kind of new initiative they're sounding you out on. Yes, I'll buy that.'

'So, what's on the agenda?' Richard turned away from the spooky little graveyard and looked into Jim's speculative eyes.

'Terrorism,' said the head of London Centre at once. 'Terrorism is always on everyone's agenda these days. Then there's prison overcrowding. Civil unrest. Typical long hot summer stuff. Except that it's been long and *wet*. There's always the Olympics – that's got implications far and wide. Security – terrorism again, among the other aspects of health, crowd control, what-have-you. Transport. Accommodation. Maybe they want a long-range weather forecast from a horny-handed old sailor man. *Mackerel skies and mares' tails make tall ships wear short sails*. That sort of stuff.'

'Very funny!'

'No! I kid you not. They're looking in all sorts of areas. You know they've even got Diana Stark from Imperial working up mathematical models to predict the next terrorist outrage? Though, spookily enough, a lot of her work has been on weather prediction too. She's been swanning all over the world for the last couple of months by all accounts, rubbing shoulders with everybody who is anybody in the realm of predictive mathematics and how it can be applied to terrorism.'

'Yes. I did know Professor Stark was working for the govern-ment on this, as a matter of fact. Mary told me, I think.'

'She's got her finger on the pulse, that girl. You should get her a job here in the Centre.'

'Don't think I haven't considered it. She'd love it. But back to business. What is there on the Home Secretary's latest justice and offender agenda that's likely to be relevant to Heritage Mariner?'

'Well, now, let's see . . .'

SEVEN
Predictions

Four o'clock two days later found Richard taking tea on the balcony of the House of Commons, looking out across the broad reach of the Thames at Westminster towards St Thomas' Hospital on the South Bank basking in the torrid heat of a brief Indian summer. Aptly enough, he thought, in the sky-blue above the white bulk of the hospital there were the familiar patterns of a mackerel sky with one or two mares' tails hanging just below.

'I wouldn't bet on any barbecues this weekend, Harry,' Richard said. 'I'd predict a change in the weather during the next forty-eight hours or so.'

Seated opposite him were Gloria Strickland and Harry Blake, Under Secretary for Criminal Justice and Offender Management. It was Gloria who had greeted him at the security entrance. She was fully recovered now and dazzlingly grateful for the way Mary and he had looked after her at Chatham. He was charmingly modest and self-deprecating, looking her straight in the wide brown eyes and manfully quelling the image that kept springing unbidden to his mind. Of her body beneath the clothes revealed in his memory as effectively as the bodies of travellers passing through the new airport X-ray security machines. But it was Harry who had invited him here for tea and a chat.

Of all the members of Alan Pitt's team – and he had met a good few one way and another – Harry Blake was the one who appealed to Richard most. For a start it amused him that such a sylph-like Tinkerbell of a woman should call herself after England's most famous kings – even if Harry was actually short for Harriet. Even in a severely cut, if undeniably fashionable two-piece business suit she looked elfin, unlike the more robust, fuller-figured Gloria. Only the most discerning eye would have seen something more than girlish excitement in her wide blue gaze, more than the almost vacuous blondeness in her habit of gazing at her conversants with shiny lips slightly parted as though she was literally panting to know more about what they were telling her. Of the two women seated opposite, it was Harry who seemed like the secretarial assistant, hanging on her boss's every word.

But the Right Honourable Harry Blake MP was easy to underestimate – fatally, as some people had discovered. In fact she was next in line after Alan Pitt to run the Home Office. Harry had been a real person with a real job before she surrendered to the siren call of Westminster. She had started out like Mary, with ambitions in the law. Unlike Mary she had not set out to study the subject to first degree level, preferring to take Modern Greats at Girton. But she had gone through the CPE conversion course and the Bar Vocational Course then managed to find a pupillage like anyone else. In due course she had been called to the Bar and taken silk.

She had been fast-tracked to her current situation. But she had subjected herself to selection, nomination and election first; and was now, despite her background, the darling of one of the toughest parliamentary constituencies in the North East. All this and she hardly seemed more than a slip of a girl, thought Richard with an inward grin. Until she opened her mouth.

'Look at this bloody insanity,' Harry Blake said trenchantly, gesturing at the front page of *The Times*, barbecuing clearly not in her weekend plans in any case. 'Brandy everywhere. It's as though the whole of Fleet Street as was were fixated by that old movie: "*Throw more brandy!*" Nothing against the dog. Or the constable handler. Especially as he says it should have been your Mary up for some kind of an award for saving his life into the bargain. But I *mean*! God! We have the man who shot the poor beast sitting still without charge in the highest security we have. Ordinary prisoners of all sorts are being held in custody cells in police stations and courthouses up and down the land because we haven't got room in any sort of prison, from high security establishments to open prisons. The Muslim prison population is simmering on the verge of violent protest over the Sayed Mohammed situation – and all the rest are about to explode because of the overcrowding.'

At this point Gloria's pager sounded and she interrupted

Harry's diatribe long enough to repeat her thanks and make her excuses.

'There actually has been some civil unrest in the North over the head of the Sayed Mohammed business,' Harry continued trenchantly. 'And where does *The Times* put stories like these? Page five! Good God, I could smuggle out the news that the PM had gone into Happy Acres with a complete breakdown today – and all they'd want to know is whether he took his sodding dog with him!' She hit the offending paper hard enough to make the teacups rattle. Richard observed, not for the first time, that the table had been set for three – but Gloria had touched nothing before she left. This was all in the nature of a preliminary, therefore. Harry wanted him to meet someone else. But she hadn't said who or why. And he hadn't asked. He enjoyed fencing with her too much to cut to the chase.

'Is that why you wanted to see me, Harry?' he asked now, innocently, enjoying the little game. 'To tell me the PM's gone into Happy Acres?'

In actual fact, Richard had a list of probable subjects in the inside pocket of his suit jacket. The list that he and Jim Bourne had drawn up forty-eight hours earlier. And Harry's impassioned little speech had just ticked most of the boxes at the top of it. The likelihood of sending the Prime Minister to the funny farm was an exception, however. Not even Jim had come up with that one. Though the possibility of a meeting with someone else ranked high.

'No!' snapped Harry. 'As a matter of fact the PM's just behind you. And you know it because you saw Gloria stop and talk to him as she went off just now. But I *mean*! And *The Times*! What is it all coming to?'

Richard sipped his tea and wondered what Harry Blake was coming to. Where she was coming *from*, come to that. Her righteous indignation rather cleverly masked the fact that it was very much to the advantage of herself and her masters to have Sayed Mohammed so far out of the news. The debate about extending the period of detention without charge was raging in the chamber behind and below them, or it would be when the House sat for business later in the day. The terrorist's action was the central matter. The terrorist's current whereabouts and fate would be little more than a distraction. It suddenly occurred to him that the young man he and Mary had pulled out of the Medway might even have been spirited away to some friendly state unfettered by Britain's trenchant stand on torture. He might well have been subjected to what the Americans called 'extraordinary rendition' and be sitting somewhere with a fair section of the local power grid attached to various tender parts of his anatomy while someone from Security or Intelligence suggested questions to the man holding the electrical contact. And prepared to deny all complicity, of course. That had been done before. He himself had found the results of it on a derelict tanker in Archangel, of all places.

But no, thought Richard after a moment more. They simply wouldn't dare. They were up to something else. If Harry Blake was involved, it would be something less brutal but much more devious. The bottom line would take some teasing out of her. But he suspected it wouldn't be long before he found out the opening gambit of her real game.

It wasn't. 'What do you know about the *Discovery*?' she demanded, apparently apropos of nothing.

Richard shifted in his chair and sipped his tea again as he thought. 'Ex-cruise liner. Russian from memory, the old *Kalinin*. By no means one of your upmarket, all-singing all-dancing variety. Solid, basic accommodation and very little more. Bought by the British government, what, eighteen months ago? For a sum and a purpose yet to be disclosed. Dropped off the radar since. Rumoured to be somewhere in Barrow-in-Furness I believe. But if the question follows on from our previous discussions, I would guess that the spectre of the good old prison ship is about to raise its ugly head once again.'

'Not quite as Alan's predecessor John Reid envisaged them back in 2007.' Harry gave a shudder. 'I can still see the front page of that newspaper with that dreadful rusting barge affair! Made Auschwitz look like the Savoy in comparison.'

'Though it was apparently very clean inside,' teased Richard, who also remembered the picture on the front page of a leading red-top. And the article printed underneath it; 2007 was hardly that long ago, after all. 'Steel floors you could eat off if I recall. That would have kept the overheads down. Food on the floor. Eat it. Swamp the rest . . . But swamping out is no longer allowed, is it? Still and all, the outside just needed a lick of paint, I think, to bring the whole thing almost up to the standards of a Victorian prison hulk. But back to the *Discovery* . . .'

'She's almost ready.' The blue eyes parted, the gaze as fathomless as an ocean deep. The tip of her tongue flickered. Her lips gleamed as she spoke, and when she paused they remained a little way apart, allowing distracting glimpses of perfect, pearly teeth. For some reason, Richard was reminded more of Mac the Knife than of Marilyn Monroe. 'Two hundred guards and ancillary employees – kitchen staff and so forth – can look after just over one thousand prisoners. Facilities may not quite be up to modern cruise liner standard but they're better than any current prison by a long chalk. Absolutely secure but in a carefully controlled environment. The Inspectorate of Prisons has been satisfied by what we've done. And, put in the right place, it's almost escape-proof, of course.'

'The old Alcatraz principle. The only way out is to drown. Unless you're anchoring her where there are lots of sharks of course . . .'

'Not at all! *However* . . .'

'It really does depend on where you anchor her. Quite. I see that. And where is she now?'

'In the Thames, just upriver from Shoeburyness.'

'Of course! It's all clear now! You're working on the assumption that not even the most desperate criminal would want to escape to the lethal depths of the hell-hole that is Southend . . .'

'*Richard!*' Harry half rose, well aware that Alan Pitt, the Home Secretary, her boss, was MP for Southend. And that the Prime Minister, seated at the next table, was neither above eavesdropping on her conversation nor above passing Richard's comments on. 'Richard! Don't! Don't you *dare* . . .'

'Harry, you sound just like my wife . . .' said Richard, with a little inward frown. Harry had failed that little test, he thought. The PM's presence was not coincidental. Her assumption was that he was there on purpose. To listen to their conversation and learn from it without being actually associated with what they were talking about.

'I haven't met your wife but already I feel so sorry for the poor woman,' said a new voice, interrupting Richard's cynically guarded thoughts. It was a well-modulated feminine voice, but deep and a little mannish. Richard glanced up at the speaker, still smiling, then rose, setting his features into a more serious expression.

The woman striding purposefully and proprietorially towards the third tea setting was of an age with Harry – she had been famously at Somerville while Harry was at Girton – but could hardly have been more different. Her dark hair was swept a little severely over her forehead. The features were even, set and serious. Where Harry's skin was all peaches and cream, hers was tanned brown and not a little wind-burned. Brown eyes frowned out with a faint hint of myopia from under level brows. She was dressed in a high-necked shirt buttoned to the throat, corduroy trousers and a baggy waistcoat under a tweed jacket. What looked like riding boots almost reached her knees. The outfit might have suited Harry's mother – perhaps her grandmother – if she had been going for a hack around the country estate. And it covered her as effectively as a Muslim *burka*. She shook Richard's hand firmly, once. 'You're Mariner, I know,' she said. 'I'm—'

'Diana Stark. Professor of Predictive Maths at Imperial. I know. You're one of my daughter's greatest heroines. Welcome back from your round-the-world trip. It's a very great pleasure to meet you.'

He turned, not meaning to be rude. Dismissed the professor and focused all his attention on the Parliamentary Under Secretary of State for Criminal Justice and Offender Management. Dismissed, indeed, the sight of the Prime Minister's shoulders as he sat at the next table – all too obviously, now, in a suspiciously convenient position to overhear without seeming to be involved.

'Harry,' said Richard, his face folded into an earnest frown. 'Does this mean you're going to fill the *Discovery* with all the Muslim detainees and Al Qa'ida or Taliban terrorist suspects you currently have locked up in your more conventional prisons and whatnot?'

EIGHT
Prison

'The work I'm doing may have originally been based on the work by Lorenz and Glick. The famous chaos theories, the so-called "butterfly effect" of weather prediction and so forth. But it also expands on the modern ground-breaking studies by Saperstein and Woo, both of whom I've talked with on what you no doubt jocularly referred to as my round-the-world trip, at our first meeting yesterday.'

The professor needed to raise her voice above the thrumming clatter of helicopter rotors as the three of them were whisked down the Thames following a low, twisting flight path between City Airport and Shoeburyness. From up here, Richard was unaccountably struck by just how many little waterways, anchorages and marinas seemed to wander into the city off the main flow of the river itself. Some of them he could name – St Katherine's Yacht Haven, South Dock, Limehouse Basin and Gallion's Point. Others he could hardly recognize. But then they swept low over the Thames Barrier and he watched the river reaches run away below, dotted with shipping. Woolwich on the south bank gave way to Dagenham and Rainham on the north, Erith to Dartford and Greenhithe, while Purfleet and Grays were succeeded by Tilbury with Gravesend opposite. In the southern distance, the River Medway gleamed with all the disturbing associations of the Chatham atrocity, which made him look north again towards Shoeburyness and Southend.

And all the way through the journey, the professor bellowed her theories at Richard and Harry. 'The primary conclusions I have reached are deceptively simple. The first conclusion of my mathematical model is this. Closing borders cuts down terrorist activity exponentially. But it is hardly possible to close all borders – especially in a country geographically, economically and politically constructed like Britain. Which is why my theories have directed the authorities to *move* some

British borders, effectively repositioning crucial boundaries overseas. You may note that the border for immediate access to Britain from the Continent is now effectively in France. That access from the Indian subcontinent is effectively in Pakistan or in India itself. It is in those places that border checks are now carried out – not at Heathrow or Gatwick airports, Tilbury or Southampton docks. An added benefit, of course, is that there is no need to go to the expense of detaining or repatriating people who fail final entry tests. You see how it works, I am sure.

'The next conclusion is this. The use of large-scale counter-terrorist organizations adds to the effect of strengthening border controls in the ways I have just discussed, raising it by a level of magnitude or so. Large-scale counter-terrorist organizations keep terrorist cells small and relatively inactive. Recruitment becomes much more difficult for terrorists to achieve. Supplies are very much harder to get hold of. Spectacular events become all but impossible to arrange. Therefore recruitment is made even more difficult . . . And so on, in a positive spiral for the anti-terrorist forces and a negative one for the terrorist cells themselves, which will eventually wither and die. A strand of this theory has been the basis of the Americans' strategy against Al-Qa'ida, of course. And very effective it seems to have been. That and their UAV unmanned drones – their Predators and Reapers.

'But most important is the *isolation* of known terrorists from their communities. Communities out in society, in regional concentrations – in world communities – even in restricted communities, in prisons or detention centres, for instance. Isolation from these communities is the most effective counter-terrorist stratagem of all. This is particularly the case in a situation where there may be a considerable element of potential terrorist recruitment already resident, of course. As we may see in various areas in Britain itself where people of particular ethnic demographics are all clustered closely together.

'Ghettoization has always been a problem in this regard. Ghettoized communities are introspective, isolated. Young men turn to local leaders who all too often increase their isolation from wider society and foster a sense of division, paranoia and, ultimately, jihad. It works for university colleges, football supporter organizations and religions equally effectively.' She paused, lost in thought.

The professor had talked almost non-stop throughout the flight, shouting over the clatter of the motor. Neither Richard nor Harry had been able to get much of a word in. Though, to be fair, neither of them particularly wanted to interrupt the professor's flow. She was a very interesting woman and some of her theories were simply riveting. And there was always the slow unrolling of the river below to attract their eyes without really distracting their attention.

'Where my work offers a solid step forward is in the mathematical assessment of how the communities in question will react to any of the policies in the predictive pattern. The quantifiable prediction of which policies might best control the situation in the general populace – or to be more accurate in the subcultures most closely associated with any potential problem. The more precisely we define the groups in question, the smaller we make them mathematically, the more accurate the predictions will become.'

'So,' said Richard in a moment of unaccustomed hesitation by the professor, 'you take one thousand Muslim detainees out of the prisons currently holding them and put them all on the good ship *Discovery*. That gives you your small test group. It isolates them from the larger prison communities they might *infect*, so to speak. And it isolates them from the home communities where they may exercise the influence of martyrs or heroes.'

'More than that,' emphasized Harry. 'It's a very effective economic exercise into the bargain – as well as a mathematical one, of course. We centralize all the dietary requirements – one set of halal kitchens. We send in all the best-trained staff out of our top cadre of Muslim prison guards. We send in the most effective prison mullahs – all of whom are scattered from Belmarsh to Barlinnie at the moment. No more pointless duplication. One central repository . . .'

'The IKEA prison,' said Richard, dryly. 'I thought finance would be near the top of the priority list.'

The helicopter swooped under the clouds that Richard had predicted – without reference to any mathematical theory at all – yesterday afternoon on seeing the mackerel skies and mares' tails over St Thomas' Hospital. At this point in the conversation, the last reach of the River Thames before it became an estuary proper swung under them, running almost perfectly north/south. It was called the Lower Hope, Richard knew. And he hoped that the real driver behind *Discovery* was not the cash-strapped government's unending quest for lower overheads. No matter how persuasive Diana Stark's maths might be, or how well supported by her worldwide contacts, Harry's enthusiastic aside made him wonder more than somewhat. Wonder and worry.

But Richard too faltered into silence at that point, looking down, his mind suddenly and irrelevantly filled with something he had read by Joseph Conrad. Something about this stretch of the river. About the Lower Hope.

'The waters of the sea rush on past Gravesend, tumbling the big mooring buoys laid along the face of the town; but the sea-freedom stops there, surrendering the salt tide to the needs, the artifices, the contrivances of toiling men.'

A surf was breaking against the river-wall along Gravesend's northern shore now. A big sea must be heaving in through the sea reach of the estuary. The whole north/south reach of the Lower Hope seemed restless and ill-contained by its low, flat banks between Gravesend in Kent and Stanford Le Hope a couple of miles due north – as the river flowed – in Essex. Immediately opposite the ivory-coloured breakers in Gravesend, he could see the distinctive star shape of Charles II's great defence work, Tilbury Fort, with the power station just beside it. Then the Essex marshland stretching to Coalhouse Fort with Cliffe Fort standing opposite, isolated by the Kentish marshland he remembered so vividly from Dickens's *Great Expectations*.

But the professor was talking forcefully once again, as though outraged that the Thames should have distracted Richard from the explanation of her theories. 'The current prison population is eighty thousand, and set to rise to ninety-five thousand, with the current policies and rules on sentencing,' the professor continued. 'Twenty thousand of those eighty thousand are on remand. Of the sixty thousand in longer-term detention, about six thousand claim to follow the Muslim religion. These are by no means all men – and it is almost exclusively men, who come from Middle Eastern backgrounds and who are the main focus of the government's current anti-terrorist emphasis, and therefore of my work. There is a significant percentage of inmates in Brixton Prison in south London claiming Muslim beliefs, for instance. But statistics suggest that the vast majority of these men are of Afro-Caribbean background. The crimes of which they have been found guilty are almost by definition – given that particular demographic – *not* the sort of crimes that we are concerned with.'

'So, all in all,' interrupted Richard, earning and disregarding a stony stare as he cut to the chase. 'You have in the current prison population about a thousand Muslims who come from the correct demographic, who have committed the correct sort of crime, who have associated with the correct people, come from the correct mosques, taught by the correct mullahs, attended the correct madrasas, whatever, to fit in with your mathematical model. And the plan is to put them all on *Discovery* and see what happens. No! To see if you can *predict* what will happen.'

'The predictions are already made!' Professor Stark said, mellowed by his clear understanding of the point she was driving at. 'I don't have the figures in my head and I haven't brought my laptop, of course. So I can't be as exact as I would like to be – but the figures we have generated prove that there will be an exponential fall in terrorist activity in all the areas our suspects usually target or recruit from. There will be a parallel fall in inner-city unrest, especially in the predominantly Muslim areas. There will be a significant fall in the numbers of illegals attempting to cross our borders – no matter where those borders may be. There will be a concomitant fall in attempts to smuggle arms or materiel. And – this may well be a *marked* benefit – there will be a considerable drop in the drug trafficking associated with certain areas of terrorist finances! And of course we are still calculating the effect in home communities of the news that these men will not be held in standard and substandard accommodation – but on a cruise ship customized especially for them.'

The professor sat back and beamed at the Under Secretary. The peculiar odour of government finances was in the air. Richard suspected the dead hand of the Treasury. Almost everything Diana Stark had promised was going to save Harry

Blake and her department an absolute bloody fortune. The helicopter swung round on its final approach, its fuselage moving like a pendulum beneath the rotor. The grim shape of the *Discovery* swung into view, a dull blade slicing the brown heart of the Thames. The cruise ship upper-works – which should have been glass and metal Alps of snowy whiteness – had been painted government surplus grey. The decks, which should have been green or teak, were a drab slate. The whole thing was as depressingly leaden as the stormy sky slowly gathering close above them.

The helicopter started to settle towards it. 'And the *Discovery*,' Richard asked, his frown puncturing the happy glow that seemed to be brightening between the two self-satisfied women. 'What does your mathematical model predict will happen aboard the *Discovery*?'

'Ah. Well, I haven't been asked to do any predictive work on that,' admitted the professor.

'That's because nothing at all out of the ordinary will happen aboard the *Discovery*!' said Harry Blake decisively. Clearly echoing a dictum dictated by her boss Alan Pitt. Or, more likely, by his boss the PM. 'We will staff her with the most successful guards, hand picked from those applicants with the best possible background. There will be a slightly higher staff to detainee ratio than in other institutions, but that will be money well invested.' Another echo of the Chancellor of the Exchequer and his Treasury department, thought Richard cynically.

Harry saw his raised eyebrow and bridled. Came as close as a professional politician could be expected to come to an outright blush. 'Ancillary staff will be equally carefully selected,' she maintained, almost angrily. 'Suppliers of everything will be vetted at every level from security on down. Like staff working airside at airports and so forth, they will be required to carry ID cards. Like teachers and suchlike they'll be asked to go through a full CRB check. Security will be absolute.'

'I see,' said Richard. 'I was wrong to compare *Discovery* with an IKEA prison then. It's more like Colditz . . .'

'We've taken on board what the Americans learned at Guantánamo, certainly. And what we ourselves learned at Abu Ghraib . . .'

'Not the most impressive of authorities, if I remember the photographs on the Internet and in the press.'

'That's another of *Discovery*'s benefits,' riposted Harry as the chopper settled on the open grey square of decking that must once have been the aft deck swimming pool. 'We have absolute – *absolute* – control over communications. That's why the professor need not bother with her laptop or cellphone. There's a total signal block everywhere aboard – except for those areas where we need to communicate with such things as our helicopter here. No cellphones. No wi-fi Internet access. No Blackberries or iPhones. No Sky TV. Not even any radio signals. Nothing that we don't permit and monitor.'

As Richard was assessing the implications of this, the three of them climbed out on to the deck. A tall guard in the uniform of a senior prison warder saluted as smartly as a guardsman. 'The governor will see you immediately, ladies and gentleman,' he said. 'Please follow me.'

He led them off the increasingly gusty deck in through a drab door. The corridor they entered looked and smelt like all empty schools, hospitals, police stations, courthouse holding cells, prisons. But beneath it lay the slight rumble that told him he was aboard a ship whose alternators were running.

The power was on so their guide would be able to take them up to the governor's office – the captain's day room in all probability, thought Richard – in a lift. But just as the car came to a halt and the doors hissed open, something occurred which disturbed Richard. And disturbed him more and more as the rest of the adventure unfolded.

The doors hissed open on to a corridor seemingly identical to the first. But this one was occupied. A young man in a bright orange overall was standing between two officers, having clearly just come out of the governor's office.

Because Richard had seen the Medway in the distance so recently, a sight which had reawakened poignantly the feelings of the Chatham incident, the young man's familiar face utterly stunned him. It was Sayed Mohammed. So this is where he disappeared to, thought Richard, reeling with shock, when he vanished off the news pages all those weeks ago. And the young man seemed as thunderstruck as Richard. His face went pale with shock. His brown eyes opened wide. His lips pursed as though he was about to say something.

But the truly disturbing thing was that Professor Stark was, if anything, even more shocked than Richard or Sayed Mohammed. '*Sam?*' she asked, uncertainly.

'Please do not talk to the prisoners, Professor,' commanded the frowning warder.

'I'm sorry,' shrugged the professor dismissively. 'He just reminded me of one of my students for a moment.'

That seemed to satisfy Harry and the warder. But something in the exchange stuck in Richard's memory.

NINE

Ship

'That's all very interesting, Professor, and I am pleased you made that little mistake. Because it gives me the opportunity to show you and the Secretary of State that I know everything there is to know about everyone aboard. And everyone destined to come aboard. It is my job as governor, after all! I'll show you the young man's file. It's still up on my computer screen. And I can show you quite conclusively that he isn't the man you say you mistook him for. My trusty files have never heard of this Sam Newton. His name is Sayed Mohammed, as Mr Mariner has been kind enough to confirm. We know him here by his number, 4172. Though I have to tell you that we're not really interested in 4172 Mohammed's academic education. Where and how he learned to *add* things up is not quite as important in our view as where and how he learned to *blow* things up! Our focus is not so much *addition* as *demolition*!' Governor James Weeks looked around his guests with a knowing smirk of appreciation at his own wit.

Governor Weeks turned out to be a slight man of seemingly boundless energy and self-confidence. His dark hair was cut short and brushed to gleaming perfection. His eyebrows and nose hair – both copious – also seemed well-trimmed. He affected a thin beard that squared his jaw and strengthened his chin while the moustache above it emphasized a

wide, sensuous, ever-smiling mouth. The whole effect was
vaguely Middle Eastern, but slightly false – as though he were
an amateur made up to act a minor part in the pantomime
Aladdin.

It seemed to Richard that the smile didn't quite reach his
olive-brown eyes, though it showed off a range of well-
maintained teeth. And he assessed acutely that it was there
solely for the benefit of the professor and the Under Secretary.
4172 Mohammed had probably not seen the benefit of it, he
thought. But Richard's dark suspicions might have arisen
because Weeks focused almost all of his virile attention on the
women and only glanced rather coldly at the solid tower of his
masculine guest. Though to be fair, it might not have been
merely a gender issue and a sexist host. Both the women the
governor was schmoozing could do him a huge amount of
professional good – if they so chose.

Like many men of slight and wiry build, Weeks was a natty
dresser and the perfection of his well-cut and beautifully
pressed slate-grey pinstripe suit was matched only by the
mirror-bright parade-ground gloss of his shoes. A counterpart
for the oily gleam of his coiffure. He was a man who was
never at rest. He sprang out of his seat to greet them on their
arrival. Pumped their hands enthusiastically, cradling the
women's in both of his own as he did so. Led them to their
seats at a small side-table laden with tea and coffee things,
then bounced and buzzed around them, fussing with gleaming
utensils.

However, his every movement and gesture seemed to emphasize that this was his bailiwick; that he was in command here
and also a very important individual, for all that he announced
himself to be 'Mother' and served his guests with their coffee,
tea and biscuits personally. A rare privilege, his manner said;
and one not to be underestimated. Offered because of their
overwhelming importance to him.

It was a striking comment on the governor's view of his
own importance that his office was not – as Richard had
assumed it would be – the captain's day room. It was the
whole of the command bridge. As Weeks exercised his charm
and wit to the utmost on the women, Richard looked around,
surprised at the prodigal use of the vitally important space.
The command bridge crossed the whole front of the uppermost

deck. Through a doorway at each end of the long, thin room, you could step out on to either the port or starboard bridge wing. Both of these little navigating points were still in place, just visible through the thick glass panels in the tops of the doors, though the pilot's and captain's chairs traditionally placed just inside them had been removed. At about the same time as the whole place had been carpeted with thick, intricately patterned grey Axminster, Richard guessed.

The whole of one wall was dominated by the clearview window, reaching down – angling inwards as it fell – from the deck-head above to a wall of instruments standing waist high. Most of the instruments would be utterly redundant, thought Richard. The radar, the navigation systems; the propulsion systems; the helm and the suite of motion controls that clustered round it. He glanced over his shoulder. The equally redundant chart-room had been transformed into a secretary's office. However, he noted from the label on the door of the matching room on the far side of the bridge, which read COMMUNICATIONS CENTRE, that it retained its previous function. It was here that the man who had guided their chopper on to the aft deck lurked. But he had clearly been ordered not to cramp his boss's style. And in any case, Richard half heard, he was already in contact with another aircraft or vessel of some sort.

As Weeks redoubled his efforts and excluded his third guest entirely, Richard rose to wander apparently aimlessly around. In fact his interest had been piqued by the strange amalgam of Civil Service and Senior Service that the room now represented. Could one call it a deck if it was covered in a couple of inches of Axminster, he wondered. Or was it really now a floor? If there was a huge copy of the Queen's portrait hanging opposite the clearview windows, it must be hanging on a wall. Could one even call it a command bridge with a great big mahogany partners' desk in the middle of it? A desk with a laptop open on it – but no sign of any of the instruments needed for command or navigation. And a tea-table instead of a pilot's chair surrounded by four admittedly comfortable overstuffed armchairs? This wasn't a bridge at all, he decided. It was an office with some nautical features. And this wasn't a deck, therefore it was a floor. It wasn't even a ship – it was simply a floating building. And yet . . .

And yet . . .

And yet he was drawn to that bank of instruments like a moth to a flame. Or more precisely – he thought wryly – like Dr Frankenstein to a recent corpse. Looking for flickers of life.

For the ship was alive in a way that a building never could be. As he had felt from the moment he set foot aboard, there were alternators and generators throbbing somewhere far below, supplying electrical power and light; and heat no doubt. And pressure to the water systems. His huge hands rested, apparently by chance, on the familiar controls as his narrow eyes gazed thoughtfully through the rain-beaded clearview almost due west up the river. The view at least was nautical. Riverine.

On his right, the Essex bank gathered into the grey, rain-washed conurbation of Southend. The famous pier reached out into the salt-water estuary well aft of the ship on that side. Under the low, drizzling overcast, a helicopter was swooping out towards them, appearing and disappearing though the rain-laden skirts of cloud in an unsettlingly random manner, like something out of a dream or a fantasy.

Dead ahead, Canvey Island all but obscured the twist of the estuary southwards to the left, down into the first section of the river – the Lower Hope. It was the Lower Hope that had claimed his attention during the flight in, he remembered. Something about the way the twisting brown snake of water had narrowed suddenly out of the broad stretch of the estuary – like the first section of a king cobra immediately behind the spread hood.

Away due south on his left hand there were five or so miles of the broad estuary itself, reaching across towards Kent. In the southern distance, the south bank gathered out of the tidal mud flats into the low mounds of the Isle of Sheppey and the Isle of Grain. Beyond them, right in the farthest distance that made his keen eyes ache for binoculars, he could just see some kind of mast or aerial. That must be standing above Cliffe Fort, he thought: certainly there was nothing much between the high bridge and the ancient fort except the low brown marshes. But he had supposed the fort to be deserted. At least as far as he knew, Palmerston's mid-1800s companions to Charles II's seventeenth-century Tilbury Fort had been deserted for years.

But between the twin humps of Grain and Sheppey, due south, opened the mouth of the Medway. There was talk of putting a barrier across the Medway, he remembered, to stop a repetition of the Chatham bombing. Perhaps that explained the distant bustle down there. Well, he thought – they'd better be bloody careful. That was where the wreck of the Second World War Liberty ship *Richard Montgomery* still lay aground. With 1,700 tons of high-explosive bombs aboard. If that lot were to detonate it would send a wall of water upriver that would do untold damage. He remembered a conversation with an old friend in the fire service about the famous wreck. If the *Richard Montgomery* went up, the fire officer had told him, it would be raining nuts and bolts in Tunbridge Wells. And, if his experiences at Chatham were anything to go by, the forts along the Lower Hope would be the only buildings for miles around that would be left standing.

He looked down at his hands lying apparently idly on the ship's defunct controls. And his mind turned to more immediate speculation. Just how many of the still and silent wheels and levers, knobs and screens were really dead? How much of the massive, powerful and very expensive equipment to which they were supposed to be attached was now permanently off-line? How much might still be brought back to life like Dr Frankenstein's monster in Mary Shelley's story?

Richard was suddenly aware of movement behind him. A moment later Harry joined Richard himself at the controls. 'What do you think?' she asked.

'I'd need to have a look over the whole vessel,' he said guardedly. 'I can't make up my mind if it's a ship or a building. It's certainly all prison. But like I say, I'll need to look her over more fully.'

'That will be our next order of business,' promised Harry. 'But what's your first impression?'

'Mixed, frankly,' he answered, dragging his eyes back from the enormous view ahead. 'Wasn't there a famous historic prison hulk named *Discovery*?'

'And *Warrior* and *Justitian*. There were lots of them up and down the Thames. Haven't you read *Great Expectations*?'

'And not only in the Thames,' he answered as he nodded 'yes' in answer to her question. 'New York harbour as well, if memory serves. At least you didn't call her *Jersey*. That would

have really ticked off the Americans. How many died on
Jersey? Fifteen hundred American freedom fighters in the War
of Independence? Prison hulks really do not have a happy
history.'

Harry forbore to make any comment on Richard's seemingly encyclopaedic knowledge of arcane shipping history.
She contented herself with, 'I'm sorry you're so negative. We
were wondering . . .'

'Whether Heritage Mariner could find and fit out a few
more,' said Richard as she hesitated fractionally. All too well
aware that his habit of finishing other people's sentences
showed that his stress levels were higher than he would have
liked. 'Jim Bourne and I have already put it on the list.' He
tapped his jacket over the inside pocket where the London
Centre list still sat, carefully folded.

'Interested?' she asked, as though she knew exactly what
he was talking about.

'May be a little less toxic than getting mixed up with what
the Russians are planning . . .'

Governor Weeks interrupted. 'Under Secretary . . . Ma'am
. . . Are we ready to proceed?'

'Ready when you are, Governor. Lead on.'

'*Lead on, MacDuff*, eh? As the Bard has it . . .'

There were seven accommodation decks, containing altogether
five hundred and twenty-five cells – seventy-five per deck.
Per deck or per floor or per level. Richard kept losing sight
of the fact that this was a vessel. Something that had never
happened to him on shipboard before – no matter how old,
ugly, battered or disgusting the ship in question had been.

But once you had seen one you had seen them all, he thought
sourly. True of the cabins – Richard could not bring himself
to think of them as cells – and true of the decks. A refit costing
ten million pounds seemed simply to have prepared the ship
for a drab cruise in a cold climate.

TEN
Drama

Weeks led his little tourist group along constricted corridors to the lifts. Richard glanced at the tweed and corduroy-clad professor as they reached the spot where they had bumped into Sayed Mohammed. Seemingly deep in thought, her face was closed, and remained so as Weeks pushed the button and the doors hissed open like thoughtful serpents. Then he took them down. They looked at one cell on each deck. Not only were the cells depressingly similar, so was the governor's gratingly cheery banter. And his constant repetition of the intimacy with which he knew everyone aboard – prisoners, warders, everyone from one side or the other of the prison service associated with the project.

On the main deck – Richard mentally called it A deck – things changed for the better. As though they had arrived in Limbo on their way to some kind of Paradise below. Here the constriction of the passenger decks with their secure cells and narrow corridors opened a little into more common areas. There was a decent-sized dining room that looked as though it could accommodate a couple of hundred at a sitting. The galleys behind it were clean, spacious and well-fitted. The governor lingered here, seemingly working on the assumption that the female section of his audience would find the domestic arrangements of the galleys of particular interest. He opened the refrigerators and took them into the cold room. He showed them the stainless steel cooking equipment. 'The inmates use plastic trays, cutlery and beakers,' he explained. 'But the kitchen staff have to use steel. Knives, forks, pots, pans, tureens. They could all make very effective weapons so we have to be very careful with security. And even more so here,' he continued, crossing to the cooking ranges and gesturing at the big gas canisters that fuelled them. 'If the prisoners got access to all this there would be serious problems, I can tell you. But even in that disastrous extremity – one which is unthinkable under my tenure and regimen, I assure you – where would they go? What would they do – other than immolating themselves and drowning a few of their comrades?'

On this level also there were the communal recreational facilities. A library with a range of books. All of them seemed to be new. Written, Richard noted approvingly, in a range of languages and dialects, scripts and prints. There were no pictures that might offend any true believers among the proposed inmates. Though, he suspected, what pictures there were might well prove a source of friction after a while. There were solid, old-fashioned PCs all round the walls.

'No laptops,' observed Richard thoughtfully.

'No,' confirmed Weeks. 'Laptops are heavy enough to use as weapons. Keyboards are not – and they are the only sections of the PCs not firmly secured in place. And, as I believe you have been informed, no unrestricted Internet access. Everything comes aboard in cable form. There is an absolute block on wi-fi. Your mobile phones will find there is no signal for them here.'

Weeks led them to a well-fitted and spacious gymnasium. 'No free weights, of course,' he continued, warming further to his theme of security. 'No ropes or bars. We must be aware at all times of the twin danger of serious assault and suicide.' He crossed to a treadmill. 'This is my favourite,' he admitted with a little show of modest shyness. 'Running is my great passion. I prefer to do a few laps of the promenade deck, though. That's my morning routine, even on a wet day like today. And when we have established a privilege regime, that will also be something that a few trusties will be allowed access to as well. As well as the staff, of course.'

'None of this is particularly unusual, except for its placing aboard,' emphasized Harry, her voice beginning to betray the irritation of nascent boredom. 'But there are other, less workaday facilities.'

'Indeed,' enthused Weeks, apparently insensible to her tone. 'I was planning to show you one . . .' He looked at his watch, frowning. And just the instant that he did so, the figure of the warder who had welcomed them aboard appeared in the doorway.

'Governor Weeks, sir,' he said. 'They're ready for you now.'

'Excellent, Burke!' said Weeks, as though he personally had arranged every detail. 'Perfect timing! Good man.'

The four of them followed the warder across the central area towards a door a few steps beyond the library door. The warder opened it smartly and they all stepped in. Governor Weeks led the way, confident of what he would find. The other three followed a little hesitantly. Richard was particularly deep in thought as he entered, for he knew a fair amount about the layout and facilities of ships such as this one. And the space they were entering would have been the ship's cinema, had this still been the cruise liner *Kalinin* instead of the prison ship *Discovery*.

It was a court room.

The tiered seating and cinema screen had been torn out and replaced with a sizeable, almost theatrical space with enough chairs for a modest audience in the middle. And in place of screen, popcorn and ice-cream facilities, the main trappings of the legal process now occupied three walls around the edge. As might be expected of a cinema, there were no windows or portholes. Instead, the walls had been panelled in gold wood.

There was a raised bench, also panelled in pale gold wood, straight ahead with the royal coat of arms painted on the wall behind it in royal blue, red and gold. Between the bench and the coat of arms were three tall chairs.

Opposite the bench, in place of the first row of audience seating, was a lower bench clearly designed to accommodate legal representation of one sort or another. To one side of the bench, at right angles to it, was a raised witness box. To the other, facing the witness box, there was a box for the accused. All of these were panelled in gold wood. Richard was reminded yet again of IKEA.

The bench was occupied. Not by a judge, but by a panel of magistrates. There were three – two women and a man. One of Middle Eastern appearance, one of Indian or Pakistani and one of Afro-Caribbean. All in formal day-dress suited to their position as well as their ethnicity. At a smaller desk at floor level in front of them sat a red-haired young woman whose porcelain skin and faint freckles suggested to Richard a Celtic gene. She must be the clerk to the court, he guessed; she wore a severely cut pinstriped business suit.

There was a young man in an even more formal pinstripe sitting in the front row immediately opposite the clerk. He, like one of the magistrates, was of Middle Eastern, Indian or Pakistani background, judging from his skin colour; though he might equally have been Indonesian in origin.

In the witness box stood Chief Inspector Tom Clark, in full uniform. Richard had last seen Tom in the Bronze command vehicle in the car park above the South Mast Pond, at the storm-swept, bomb-ravaged desolation which had been Chatham Dockyard. And that had been exactly – Richard looked at the date function of his Rolex, making double sure – twenty-eight days ago. It was the law's magic number, of course. The accused had to be charged today. Charged or released, whether the police and the Crown Prosecution Service, the Ministry of Justice, Special Branch and MI5 were happy about it or not. There was no alternative.

And opposite him, therefore, with a warder solidly at each shoulder, stood Sayed Mohammed.

Weeks leaned conspiratorially towards Harry and the professor. 'This is so much cheaper and more effective than running the prisoners under escort up to Horseferry Road or Woolwich, you see,' he said in a stage whisper. 'The magistrates, recorders and circuit judges may need a lift in a chopper down from City Airport but they don't need a full police escort each. And when they arrive, they need a cup of tea not a holding cell. The cost isn't even faintly comparable and the savings will be enormous. We'll discuss the implications – and indeed the process – of setting up our own magistrates' and Crown courts here aboard later, but no matter what the Minister of Justice thinks, the Chancellor of the Exchequer is ecstatic!'

'Sayed Abu Minyar Mohammed,' said the clerk, rising formally to her feet. 'You are charged with murder, attempted murder and assault on a police officer, and with the offences as listed under the Terrorism Acts. How do you plead?'

Silence.

The chief magistrate leaned forward from her position in the centre of the bench. 'You have refused to confirm your identity or to address the court in any way,' she said in clear, ringing tones. 'Nevertheless I must now inform you that your silence will not protect you from due process of the law.

Quite the reverse, in fact, as you will find as you proceed through further hearings to the Crown Court itself.'

'That'll probably be the Central Criminal Court,' added the governor, earning a stern glance from the chief magistrate. 'He's bound for the Old Bailey, as I'm sure you know,' he finished in a whisper, 'just as Chief Magistrate Patel has observed. Even the so-smart new prefabs at Woolwich would send out the wrong message, if you see what I mean. To our American colleagues at the very least.' He winked knowingly at Harry, who frowned in return. Water off a duck's back. 'The wingers by the way are . . .'

'*I will ask you one last time, sir,*' repeated the chief magistrate, raising her voice over the governor's whisper and silencing him mid-sentence. 'How do you plead to the charges?'

The young counsel half rose from his seat on the front row opposite the clerk. His body genuflected as he spoke, beginning to sit down again even before he was properly up. 'I'm afraid my client persists in his refusal to answer. He refuses to recognize the jurisdiction of the court, Ma'am.'

But even as he sat down again, sharing a helpless shrug with the male winger on the bench, the charged man spoke after all.

'I do not recognize this court,' he said clearly. 'You desecrate Ramadan by holding these proceedings as and when you do.' He turned to face the group at the door, his gaze raking over the governor to rest somewhere between Richard and Professor Stark. 'Even were this not so, I do not recognize this court or anyone within it.'

HUNT

ELEVEN
Power

Governor Weeks reacted first to Sayed Mohammed's ringing pronouncement. He turned to Harry Blake with that familiar roll of his eyes, like a parent tacitly apologizing for a screaming child in a supermarket. 'You see what we have to deal with?' he asked quietly. 'I mean, he kills almost as many as Mohammed Sidique Khan and his co-conspirators on July seventh and he just shrugs it all off. And calls upon one of the holiest of feasts in the Muslim calendar as though it is some kind of an excuse. The act, its consequences and the process that arises as a direct result! Unbelievable! It's almost as though he *wants* to spend the rest of his natural life cooped up aboard here. Not that he has a heck of a lot of choice in the matter, of course.'

As the governor was speaking, the chief magistrate gestured to the warders and they took Mohammed down. The young man shot one long frowning look at the people by the door and allowed himself to be led silently away by the two phlegmatic guards. The legal representative stood up and followed the three of them out of the court – no doubt hoping to get some kind of sense out of his recalcitrant client. Some kind of commitment to more amenable behaviour at the next stages of his arraignment, which the chief magistrate had already detailed for him. The clerk rose and exchanged a quiet word with all three of the magistrates before they too rose, gathered their clothing about them and filed out, taking with them their folders of notes.

'I thought perhaps you'd want to discuss our little innovation here,' Weeks was saying to the women. 'And there will be tea and biscuits of course. Chocolate biscuits. For anyone not fasting during the daylight hours!' He leaned towards Professor Stark and stage-whispered, 'Ramadan!' Then he guided Harry in the magistrates' wake as Diana Stark spat, '*I know!*' and followed. 'The JPs are expecting to have a bit of a chat and the clerk's been briefed to discuss legal precedents for this kind of arrangement,' he continued, apparently unconscious of the professor's reaction, his mellifluous tones fading away across the courtroom as Richard stayed exactly where he was. 'I mean, Under Secretary, I'm sure you are completely *au fait* with the process for setting up a court – no matter where – but I thought you might be interested in the process we went through here. Particularly as we plan – with the Justice Secretary's acquiescence – to use this not merely as a magistrates' court but to add it to the list of Crown courts in due course. Again, the question of court security will be a major aspect of the plans. Security and economy.

'Of course if we had a proper captain aboard, we could probably dispense with the magistrates and even the judges – and let him do the flogging, wedding and hanging . . .'

Tom Clark caught Richard's eye as the proceedings closed. Now he picked his way forward across the court and shook hands with Richard, who was waiting for the policeman and watching the governor's busy little back thoughtfully as it bustled the women away across the room towards tea and chocolate digestives. Richard was a gingernut man himself. As Tom approached, he found himself ruefully thinking that, as a fully qualified and widely experienced ship's captain, he would dearly love to be able to do a little flogging and hanging. Starting with the irritating governor.

'It was a bit of a surprise to see you here,' said Tom quietly as he approached. 'I wasn't expecting to come across you again until we got this matter up to the Bailey at least!'

'It was a bit of a shock for me too, in all sorts of ways,' Richard answered. 'What do you think Mohammed's up to?'

'God knows. It's too deep for me. He's a clever bloke, though, from what I can tell. Which isn't a hell of a lot, to be fair. We've learned next to nothing from questioning him. Counter-Terrorist Command went in first like gangbusters, all threats and deadlines – you remember the CIA approach after 9/11? *We'll kill your kids and rape your mother. And have you met my friends Mr Black and Mr Decker?* It was something like that, I gather. And he clammed up. MI5 have sent in a quiet bloke to talk things over more gently with him when the Branch drew a blank and extraordinary rendition was ruled out of the question. The softly, softly approach seems to be making progress, especially as the interrogator was born and raised in Bahawalpur, Pakistan. But it's slow work. And I rather think Mohammed's calling the shots most of the time in any case. He's got some kind of an agenda, you can bet your life on that.'

'Bet my life? Been there. Done that. But for *Ocelot* I'd have bet my life and bought the T-shirt too. As well as a one-way ticket to Paradise. Or somewhere hotter.'

Tom gave a bark of wry laughter.

'How's the case coming overall, though? May I ask?' pressed Richard, emboldened by Tom's unexpected candour. He had begun to suspect that there was a hidden agenda here in any case.

'Slowly,' admitted the policeman. 'That's why we went to the full twenty-eight days. If the government had pulled its collective finger out we might have gone over ninety, but there's no use crying over spilt milk.'

Side by side they walked out into the open area and crossed it to what Richard would have called the A deck bulkhead door that opened out on to the weather deck. Side by side still, they stood on the narrow promenade deck where the governor liked to do his morning run. They looked across the rainy grey of the estuary to the twin lumps of the Isles of Grain and Sheppey, which stood behind the wide mudflats that marked the northern edge of Tom's patch as they stretched round into the Lower Hope and Cliffe Fort.

The overhang of the first passenger deck above kept most of the fine, penetrating rain off them as they talked.

'We wanted to try and get a net round the whole conspiracy,' Tom continued. 'And there must have been one hell of a conspiracy. Worldwide if previous experience is anything to go by. I mean he can't have even begun to get something like that organized on his own. He could have got the explosives here at home – or made them up using the *Terrorists' Cookbook*, even if he didn't get one-on-one instruction from Ubaida al-Masri, the Al-Qa'ida bomb-maker the Americans say they killed five years ago. But the quantities alone are astonishing. And the power. And there's more organization here than we reckon he's anywhere capable of working on his own. Then there's that visit to Pakistan. Why did he go? Who did he see? Who sent him? Who brought him back?

He seems to have arrived there, disappeared off the face of the earth for a month or so, then reappeared and come on home. But we're having a hell of a time defining any kind of a circle of friends or associates for him.

'And of course there was at least one other person involved in the actual Chatham attack, independently of any further help needed getting the boat loaded up like that. We're absolutely certain about that. Quite apart from anything else, forensics tell us there's the DNA of someone else on what little is left of the boat they blew up. There's not much of it, mind. But there's not a hell of a lot left of the boat either, come to that.'

'This is all a bit vague, surely, after twenty-eight days . . .'

'You don't understand the focus on a case like this. The overriding imperative. Almost, you might say, the policy. Still, there's no reason to suppose you would. Look. Have you ever read a book called *The Man-Eaters of Kumaon* by a bloke called Jim Corbett?'

'Not that I recall. Why?'

'It used to be a great favourite of my dad's and I remember reading it myself when I was a kid. Corbett was one of the most famous of the white hunters between the wars. Worked in Africa and India. Wrote a series of best-sellers about his life after he retired. There's a scene in *Man-Eaters of Kumaon* I remember – at least I think I do. You know how things are when you're a kid . . .'

'Yes. But I—'

'Corbett is hunting a man-eating tiger. He's been called in by some terrified villagers who have had some children and old folks eaten by the beast. Somewhere in India I think. Or maybe Pakistan. That would be bloody apt! Still, what he does is to tether a goat in a clearing near where the tiger has been hunting. Then he hides up a tree overlooking the clearing with his rifle and he waits for the tiger to come for the goat.'

'Yes. OK. I get the analogy. The hunter doesn't pay too much attention to the goat. Any old goat will do. All of his attention is going to be focused on the tiger. Where will it come from? What will it do? How much warning will it give him? Will he get a clear kill-shot?'

'You've got it in one. And the point is that Sayed Mohammed

is more of a goat than a tiger as far as most of the authorities are concerned.'

'A goat who blew up a fair number of people,' insisted Richard, less than impressed with this apparently casual attitude

'A goat who was involved in a plot to commit a terrorist atrocity. Who jumped ship, by the look of things, just before the suicide bomber actually blew himself – and his victims – to kingdom come,' Tom insisted. 'And what did he do after you pulled him out of the Medway? He ran away again. It does seem to fit, you see?' He paused for a moment, staring thoughtfully across the estuary at the distant bustle due south, a little less than five miles distant. 'But we don't seem to be able to get a handle on this end of it – while the pressure is all on checking out the other end. We still don't even know for sure who the actual suicide bomber was. The guy who drove the gin palace you saw into the Thunderbolt Pier. She was called *Jupiter*, by the way, and had been stolen from Burnham on Crouch in Essex a week or so earlier.

'And we're fairly certain that there's a tiger – maybe more than one – out there now, as we speak. The nightmare that the CIA are wrestling with is the rumour that maybe some of the Predator victims that the Americans thought they had killed with their unmanned drones between 2007 and 2009 aren't quite as dead as they hoped. That somewhere out there there's a Rashid Rauf, an Ubaida al-Masri, a Khalid Habib, a Saad bin Laden. And these are the guys who Sayed Mohammed went to see while he fell off the screen in Pakistan.'

He gestured vaguely upriver towards the darkening greyness that was London. 'The CIA think there's a real, deadly dangerous, honest to God man-eater. Maybe a gang of man-eaters, like I say. They're the guys with the real clout. The real *power*. And they put Sayed Mohammed and his dead friend up to this but then they've stayed in the bushes. Or, much more worryingly, in whatever little nook or cranny in East Ham, Isle of Dogs, Limehouse or Wapping – *Wapping*, mind you, right up beside the Tower and Tower Bridge – they might have packed her with all the explosives.

'And, of course, the fear is that they're setting up other impressionable kids with more spectaculars like Chatham. We don't know who they are or how they did it yet. So we don't know if we stand any chance at all of stopping them doing it again. Any old time and any old place they want. So we have Mohammed staked out. But he's the goat . . .'

'And everyone's too busy looking for these tigers – the whole senior command structure of Al Qa'ida by the sound of it – to study him as closely as maybe they should. I get you.' There was a tiny silence. Then Richard said, 'My daughter Mary came through the Chatham business with me. She actually gave Mohammed mouth-to-mouth resuscitation – though we don't know whether she actually saved his life.'

'Yes, I know. It's in your evidence. And hers.'

'Mary has become intrigued with Mohammed. She wants me to use my Heritage Mariner people, we call them London Centre, to look into his background. Rummage around. See what we can find.'

'Does she? Sort of Stockholm Syndrome I suppose. Almost as though he had kidnapped her and held her long enough for her to start identifying with him. Yes. I can see why she might want you to do that. Very understandable. And the people in this London Centre, who are they?'

'Ex-Special Branch; ex-spooks. People with contacts who know the ropes, so to speak. You may have heard of Jim Bourne, he's the director . . .'

Tom nodded. There was no surprise in his eyes. Unstated recognition. Satisfaction, perhaps. Maybe a hint of victory.

'So you wouldn't expect there to be any problems if London Centre rooted around a little? Just to keep my Mary happy? We wouldn't be treading on any toes? Even if we tried to find out where he went when he fell out of your frame in Pakistan? I mean, we'd pass a copy of anything we found directly to you.'

'And I'd pass it straight to my superiors; up to Silver, so to speak, and Gold – and to that young interrogator at MI5. Even the CIA if need be. Can't do any harm. Can't do any harm at all.'

Tom's casual words closed the conversation. And Richard, veteran of thousands of conversations like this one, frowned thoughtfully as he looked south towards the distant bustle at the mouth of the Medway, aware that a kind of semi-official, totally deniable, partially secret deal had just been done.

'Ah. There you are,' came a familiar voice – though Richard

had not heard the A deck bulkhead door swing wide. 'Chief
Inspector, the helicopter and the magistrates are waiting for
you. Mr Mariner, the ladies and I are keen to continue our
survey of my, ah, *command*.'

The warders' accommodation was brighter, warmer and much
more spacious than the decks above. It was homely rather
than luxurious, but the contrast was still striking. On the far
side of the strong metal door through which Governor Weeks
led the three of them a moment or two after interrupting
Richard and Tom's conversation was a corridor that seemed
almost airy – in spite of the fact that there were no windows.
Instead, on either hand, doors opened into well-proportioned
single cabins that looked to be comfortable and well-fitted.
There were well-lit common areas. A modest library with
current papers and periodicals. A TV lounge. A pleasant little
canteen. As Richard allowed himself to be guided through
these areas, his mind kept drifting out of the present and into
the immediate past, assessing and reassessing his conversation with Tom Clark.

Weeks led them along the corridor towards the aft lift shaft
– which, Richard observed, did not go up any further, empha-
sizing how secure it was down here. As he did so, he continued
his proprietorial little chat, apparently unaware that neither
the Under Secretary nor the professor shared Richard's genuine
interest in what they were seeing here.

'The original specifications of this vessel had accommodation for more than four hundred crew,' the governor
informed them. 'But we don't need so many, even to oversee
a thousand inmates. That has allowed us a little more elbow
room with accommodation down here. We don't need engineers of course. Nor, naturally, do we need any deck or
navigating officers or crew. Except for one temporary exception. We do need the equivalent of what I believe is called
a lading officer. His only real responsibility is to oversee
the fuel oil we need to keep aboard in order to drive the
generators that you can hear. He actually doubles as a
kind of chief engineer, because he's the one in charge of
the maintenance of our major electrical and generating
equipment. Funny chap. Always complaining that there's far
too much for him to do now – and when the place has its

full complement of detainees as well as warders and whatnot he'll be run right off his feet!'

Richard, who had snapped back to the present part way through the speech, opened his mouth to ask a question, but Weeks cut him off, perhaps unintentionally. 'And that's about it for the old-fashioned sailors such as Mr Mariner is used to dealing with. Everyone else is the kind of person doing the kind of job you would expect to find in a modern prison facility. As well as warders of various grades and seniority, we need catering staff and a basic cleaning and maintenance team together with a laundry. But, as with engineers, we *don't* need stewards, a purser or any of his staff, fitness instructors, masseurs, croupiers, entertainers, salespeople, guides, so forth, so on, all of whom used to be accommodated down here.'

'No engineers apart from the one you mentioned,' persisted Richard. 'Didn't you say something about sailing out beyond British jurisdiction – or was that simply a pleasantry? Or have you actually had the motors taken out? Certainly, I was wondering which of the controls up on the command console on the bridge was still connected to anything. Most of them seemed dead to me.'

'Oh no. That's not the case at all,' Weeks corrected him, rolling his eyes at the two women as though to say, *What is the man thinking?* 'The motors are still in place, but they have been most carefully disengaged. And everything up on the bridge can be brought on-line again should the need arise. I mean, why on earth would the government buy a Ferrari – so to speak – and then take the wheels off it? No. No. No. That's not the plan at all. We were due to look at the engineering sections next in any case. So let's go straight on down, shall we?'

The aft lift took the three of them straight down to the main engineering level. As they descended, the distinctive throbbing of the alternators grew more pronounced. The almost soporific sound started Richard thinking back again. Just what did Tom Clark want him to do, Richard found himself wondering. Use Heritage Mariner's London Centre intelligence arm to put Sayed Mohammed's life and times, friends and relatives, teachers and lecturers under the microscope? Examine them like the Martians were said to be examining

the earth at the beginning of H.G. Wells's *War of the Worlds*?
How did that famous opening go? *They were being scruti-
nized and studied, perhaps almost as narrowly as a man with
a microscope might scrutinize the transient creatures that
swarm and multiply in a drop of water.* Something like that.

Almost unconsciously, Richard found himself scrutinizing
Professor Stark, though he was suddenly hilariously aware
that he could hardly claim '*an intelligence greater than our
own*', or, indeed, '*an intellect, vast, cool and unsympathetic*'.
Certainly not when compared with Professor Stark's.

She caught his glance and gave a weary little smile – two
kindred spirits sharing a moment of understanding in the face
of enormous boredom. He smiled back, the fact that he was
mentally laughing at himself making the smile wider and
warmer than it might otherwise have been.

The lift bumped to a halt and the doors hissed open to
reveal a strange space. It was almost a quarter of the ship's
length – some fifty metres. It was as wide as the hull itself
at this point – twenty metres or so. And it was three decks
high. But the deck levels themselves ended in balconies that
overlooked the beast, crowding in towards it. The effect was
part way between a gloomy cave and a claustrophobic theatre.
An effect made more powerful by the fact that most of the
lights were out and the central space around the monster itself
a mysterious mass of gloomy, gently throbbing shadows.

Both women hesitated, apparently a little overcome, but
Richard stepped forward almost eagerly. The motor lay like
a sleeping giant and his mind, still in classic sci-fi mode,
switched effortlessly from Wells's *War of the Worlds* to
Lang's *Metropolis*. The gigantic mass of the sleeping diesel
would have dominated the closely overhanging space even
had it been lying naked there. But it was not. It was clad in
level upon level of scaffolding, which led from one dully
illuminated maintenance point to the next. And, like a
Himalayan peak surrounded by foothills, it was surrounded
by housings which, Richard knew, contained among other
things the gears that controlled the naked power of that
massive motor and applied it to the twin shafts that drove
the propellers. Gears that must, for the time being at least,
he thought, be unconnected. For the shafts and propellers
were surely not meant to turn while there were no officers

or crew aboard to control the engine's colossal power or the hull's majestic progress.

But even as Richard, entranced, strode out of the lift and into the engine space, a voice rang out. '*Oi!*' it bellowed, setting echoes resounding loudly enough to drown the grumble of the generators. 'Who the hell are you and what are you doing in my frigging engine room?' it concluded in a thick Glaswegian accent.

Richard stepped forward again as a square figure in overalls appeared out of the shadows to face him. The engineer was square-bodied – made to look squarer by his overall. He held a heavy spanner and an oily rag – though he himself was as pristine as a mannequin in a chandlery store. A black spade of a beard covered the upper half of his breast, but his head was as bald and shiny as a bowling ball. His long, dark, narrow eyes had widened now with unaccountable outrage. He had a long, slightly hooked nose whose nostrils were flared. The ragged moustache all but hid his puffing mouth and there was just enough light shining out of the lift to make one or two drops of spittle sparkle in its depths.

'It's all right, Archie,' called Weeks, putting his hand on the lift door to hold it open while he and the women stepped out. 'I'm just showing these guests the facilities. We don't want to disturb you and we won't be long. We all call him Archie,' he whispered to the professor as though a university lecturer would appreciate schoolboy wit, 'because it's short for Archi*bald*.'

The engineer grunted and turned away, apparently unconscious of the governor's whisper.

'Just a moment,' called Richard, taking another step after the man, his footfall ringing in the metallic space. 'My name is Mariner. Could you show me the gearings that connect the motor to the main shafts, please? The governor and I were discussing whether they were still connected. Whether the ship could still be brought under power.'

'I dinna need to show you,' said the engineer. 'I can tell you. The answer is yes. Everything is still connected up. I could sail her out of here in a couple of hours if I wanted to. Maybe even less. If I had some help around here. As it is, ye're looking at a motor that's too much for one man tae handle. In a system that's too much for one man tae handle.

In a whole facility that's just too much for one man tae handle. As the governor there will learn tae his cost when he gets all his prisoners aboard and the urinals all start overflowing and the shitters all seize up!'

He turned on his heel and stalked off. As he walked away back into the shadows he pulled a cap out of his pocket and slipped it on his head. Perhaps he had heard the governor's comment on his nickname after all. Richard recognized the style of headgear. It was a flat-topped, gold-embroidered *taqiyah* cap, the sort worn by men all over the Muslim world.

TWELVE
Board

The full board of Heritage Mariner traditionally met on the last Thursday of every quarter. Thursday so that reports to section and action on matters arising could be put in train on the Friday. They usually met either at ten or at midday – depending on which of their members from abroad were due to attend through video-conferencing facilities. Today they were meeting between twelve and three to accommodate New York time.

The full board met in the boardroom of Heritage House, surrounded by seeming centuries of tradition. Although the impressively spacious room was high in a modern building, it was filled with an atmosphere of almost Georgian solidity. As though it had stood there, filled with generations of seafaring businessmen assembled to oversee the good running of their empire through calm seas and prosperous voyages, since the War of American Independence instead of the Second World War.

The floor was made of long teak boards, carpeted with priceless Aubusson, brought back from long-past adventures in the Middle East. The walls above were panelled to waist height in mahogany. Brocade wallpaper reached from here to the ornate moulding around the long edges of the tall, intricately decorated ceiling with its thirty-six-candle brass chandelier – slightly larger than the one in the Cabinet Room at 10 Downing Street. The wallpaper's Regency stripe had long faded out of garishness into respectability. Aided by the earlier generations who had smoked cigars in here over their brandy, liqueurs, port and coffee at the end of long gourmet luncheons where enormous fortunes'-worth of business had been done over a Havana and a handshake.

The brocade in any case was almost hidden by one of the finest collections of maritime oils outside Greenwich and the National Gallery. The collection had been started by Robin's father, Sir William Heritage, before he retired to the South of France, and continued by Robin herself. Father and daughter shared a passion for oils of sailing ships, and preferred the Romantic era. There was nothing much older or more valuable than the Turner that hung behind the chairman's chair on the chimney breast above the mahogany mantle of the wide open fireplace – except for the Canaletto behind the deputy chair's seat beside it. Three sides of the great chamber were covered with rich and rare originals. Winslow Homer jostled with Walter Lansil and Kaspar David Friedrich. The huge Roger Desoutters, Thomas Gowers and Robert Taylors seemed positively arriviste by comparison. Or they might have done so had the massive flat-screen on the wall opposite the Turner – and beneath the long oil of Brooking's breathtaking *Flagship Before the Wind* – not brought the twenty-first century so forcefully into the place.

But the huge screen was by no means the only modern intrusion. In the centre of the boardroom sat the board itself – a huge mahogany table the better part of fifteen feet in length and a good solid six feet wide. Arranged around it, opposite the well-spaced chairs set out for the meeting, were old-fashioned blotter pads framed in green leather. But a laptop computer sat on each blotter instead of a notepad. These accessed all previous minutes of earlier meetings at the touch of a button. They displayed the minutes of the current meeting as they were typed in beneath the headings of the agenda. And they could Google any reference and answer any query raised within moments.

At the opposite end to the tall, wide door, above which blinked a battery of motion sensors, alarms and wireless Internet access contacts, long casement windows looked out over Leadenhall and Bishopsgate. On the deep mahogany sills beneath them sat glass cases filled with detailed models of the vessels which, individually or as the foundation of a series, had brought so much wealth and power into this room. The first *Prometheus* supertanker – now in its fifth incarnation. *Atropos*, the industrial waste transporter. The *Sulu Queen* container ship, whose route had been around the China Seas in the days when Heritage Mariner had enjoyed a brief reign as Noble House in Hong Kong and Shanghai. *Poseidon* – with her tiny remote DSRV *Neptune* – which still carried the HM flag in the Far Eastern seas while her sister *Poseidon II* was undergoing tests in the North Sea, where she was destined to support Heritage Mariner's increasing involvement in oil exploration. In the case beside her stood *Lionheart*, the jetcat whose offspring sailed at huge speeds across most of the major tourist waterways from the Channel to the Great Lakes.

Under Richard's Spartan chairmanship, all indulgences of food and drink – not to mention tobacco – were dispensed with in favour of fast, efficient business. Long lunches at the huge mahogany boardroom table were replaced by late lunches at favoured restaurants nearby. During the last couple of months, in spite of the gathering of a wet autumn, the most favoured eateries had been within what Richard considered easy walking distance – somewhere between one mile and two – which covered the City and the West End as far as Soho.

Robin accepted this collective penitence – centred as it was on the self-immolation of her husband as part of the process of mourning his beloved car, whose space in the company car park many storeys below still stood forlornly empty – and she teased him only occasionally. Occasionally and with increasing circumspection, for he was becoming genuinely irritated by the apparent slowness of their usually reliable insurers in completing the paperwork that would allow him to replace his sleek, grey, all too powerful darling.

After Richard and Robin, Jim Bourne was the next most senior officer present. He was of course Chief Executive (Commercial Intelligence), running London Centre, and so was just senior to Rupert Bligh, Chief Executive (Human Resources), who ran The Bounty.

Chief Financial Officer Anthony Ho had replaced Charles
Lee a couple of years previously. The chief executive in charge
of design was Doc Weary, the massive, leonine Australian
whose design of the *Katapult* series had stood the company
in such good stead over the years. Doc may have started with
sailboats, but he had graduated with little apparent effort to
become the head of a team capable of designing anything that
would float, no matter how large or powerful. Not to be
outdone by such titles as London Centre and The Bounty, they
called themselves The Outback.

Chief Executive Audrey Gunnel ran the HM subsidiary
Crewfinders, a vital subsection of Rupert Bligh's human
resources empire – and a company originally founded by
Richard himself during a brief period when he had fallen from
grace with the sea.

Finally, the company secretary was the solicitor Andrew
Atherton Balfour, husband to the breathtaking QC Maggie
DaSilva – close friend and ex-colleague of Harry Blake, Under
Secretary of State for Criminal Justice and Offender
Management. And it was Blake, as fate would have it, who
the board were just discussing, under Any Other Business, at
the end of their meeting as the clock ticked round to 3 p.m.
on that rainy Thursday afternoon.

'What are the financial implications of getting into prison
ships, as the Under Secretary seems to want?' asked Anthony
Ho, leaning forward intently. 'Will we be expected to meet
the initial outlay on purchasing these ships? Will we be
expected to refit them fully and then invoice the Home Office
– or will there be cash up front? Plans and estimates
presented to Procurement. I have been keeping a close eye
on government procurement systems, such as the one run
by the MoD—'

'Over contract, over budget, under-performing. Yes, I know
. . .' said Richard.

'By millions and millions at the last audit. But of course
that could be enormously to our benefit,' answered Anthony,
used to Richard's interruptions. 'I hesitate to suppose that any
companies commissioned by the MoD to supply their arms
and armaments – and doing so at twice the price quoted in
twice the time stipulated – have actually suffered financially.
Quite the reverse, I should imagine. Even with pretty hefty

penalties built into the more recent contracts. No. The British government is a pretty deep trough. We could well benefit from joining other businesses feeding at it. Under the right circumstances.'

'I didn't like the *Discovery* when I looked round her last month, though,' said Richard. 'I didn't like the vessel, what they had done to her, or how they were staffing her.'

'Then maybe we could do it better,' suggested Jim Bourne. 'Turn a profit and make a difference. Like we do with the toxic waste disposal vessels that we run between Europe and the States. Like we do with the tanker recycling facilities up in Archangel.'

The American C.J. Martyr interrupted then, his voice a little distorted by the connection from New York. 'Toxic waste seems to be a good parallel, Jim. The people up at State are a little uncertain about this – even though it does reflect our old policy at Guantánamo pretty accurately. Our old *discredited* policy. Putting all your bad eggs into one basket in the Thames Estuary is a high-risk strategy, even if you can up your anchor and sail them out to God knows where if there's any trouble brewing. And who are you going to have aboard there? Al Qa'ida sympathizers – even some active soldiers like as not. Taliban sympathizers. Guys with a grievance, especially after the invasion of Waziristan in 2009. Guys who may or may not have contact with all sorts of desperate elements . . .'

Annie Bledsoe chimed in, her bell-like tones seemingly unaffected by the distance or the electronic interfaces. 'Director Hayden's sent one of the CIA's leading experts on this kind of thing over to Grosvenor Square. They're still looking to track down the Haqqanis, Maulay Nazir Ahmad, Mullah Omar and some of the others who may or may not still be active. Not to mention Rashid Rauf, al-Masri, Bin Laden al Zahwahiri and the others who may or may not have been taken out by Predator and Reaper strikes over the last five years. And they think there may be leads in London. Paranoia rules, I tell you!'

'You're not telling me that any of these men could possibly be aboard *Discovery*!' said Richard. 'Most of them are certainly dead or detained by distantly foreign governments, and those who aren't are keeping profiles so low they're almost subterranean. Especially when there's Predators or Reapers overhead.'

'No,' grated Annie, her voice losing its usually golden tone. 'What I'm telling you is that there are guys over there – our guys working with your guys – who think there's a chance that some of the guys destined for *Discovery* have possibly – conceivably – been in contact with the last of the 9/11 leadership sometime – somewhere – in the recent past. And that if our guys and your guys are right, then there's something really dangerous being planned. And the good ship *Discovery* might . . . just might . . . be something to do with it.'

'*Might* and *just might*,' said Richard thoughtfully. 'We need something a little more solid to go on than that, Annie! We'll take it on board though. Sounds like one for you and London Centre, Jim. Still, on with business. Where were we?'

'Discussing *Discovery* and how we could improve on her,' said Doc Weary slowly, sounding only half convinced. 'And I guess we could do it at that. Better quality vessels, better fitted. We have the contacts, God knows.'

'Better staffed,' added Rupert Bligh. 'We don't have contacts in the prison service at the moment. But I bet I could get some.'

Audrey Gunnel laughed. 'God, Rupert, will you ever stop empire building? You won't be happy until we're all berthed somewhere on The Bounty, will you?'

'No seriously,' insisted Bligh, too used to her teasing to be wounded by the accusation – even though they all knew it was true. 'We moved into the new fields of supplying domestic service to help Robin look after Cold Fell and Summersend when the National Trust had trouble.' The two great houses had come to the couple from their parents when they collectively retired to France. Robin refused to let Bligh and The Bounty staff Ashenden, the home where Richard and she lived high on the Sussex cliffs of the south coast. Much to his chagrin. 'It's turned into quite a profitable little sideline,' he continued. 'I don't see why we couldn't do the same with prison staff.'

'OK,' said Richard, bringing discussion to a close with his usual ruthlessness as three o'clock approached. 'We'll examine the possibilities. I'll tell the Under Secretary – unless you and Maggie are having her over for dinner anytime soon, Andrew? No? Well, I'll get on the phone to her tomorrow. We don't

usually have so many projects on the back burner, but we'll
just leave it there with the Russian floating nuclear facility
project until we get clearer figures – or better intel. I suppose
I'd better phone Felix Makarov . . .'

'Max Asov would be better,' suggested Robin. 'Though you
can't get on to anyone until Monday, you workaholic man!
You promised me a long weekend at Ashenden, starting tonight.
Anyway, Max is working in that area too – and he's still pretty
grateful to you for rescuing his daughter from those kidnap-
pers in Africa . . .'

'Yes,' said Richard shortly. 'Or he was until Anastasia eloped
with that heavy metal rock group. What did they call themselves? Simian Artillery? But point taken. I'll get hold of him.
On Monday. That's it then, thank you, ladies and gentlemen.
Time for lunch, I think. Time for brunch for you two in New
York. Thanks to both of you.' The Americans nodded and the
screen went blank. 'Right,' continued Richard, turning to the
rest of them. 'We'll sit down bang on the turn of the first dog
watch by the look of things. Just the same as always. Robin,
where had you got in mind?'

'L'Atelier de Joel Robuchon,' she said firmly, knowing he
would probably have preferred the Bleeding Heart, as Bleeding
Heart Yard was nearly a mile closer than Covent Garden. 'I've
booked a table for the eight of us. And yes, at sixteen hundred
hours as always. And two taxis. We have to be prompt. In my
opinion we're very lucky indeed that they agreed to stay open
for us – they close after lunch at two thirty and we'll have
the place to ourselves. But we'll have to be out by five thirty
when they open for dinner,' she added, firmly.

'That's all fine, darling, thanks,' said Richard, his amenability
sounding a little suspicious – to her wifely ears at least. 'Jim,
a word with you, please. We'll catch up with the rest of you
in a moment . . .'

As the suspicious Robin led the other six out of the boardroom, Richard took Jim Bourne to one side. 'Look,' he said.
'Two things. Firstly, Mary's coming home soon and I'd like
to take you up on your offer of finding her some work experience at London Centre. Secondly – and this might or might
not overlap, I don't know – I want you to set up a little section,
reporting to me and to me alone, dedicated to finding out all
you can about this fellow Sayed Abu Minyar Mohammed.

From the sound of what Annie Bledsoe said we could do some good work by just ensuring he hasn't been in contact with Osama bin Laden or whoever. That he doesn't have another nasty little surprise up his sleeve.'

Jim Bourne's eyes narrowed. 'Won't we find ourselves treading on some very tender official toes if we do that? I mean I'm not saying we couldn't do it – we've got the contacts, heaven knows, and feet on the ground from Peckham to Pakistan. But I'd hate to find ourselves waltzing around with Counter-Terrorism Command, Security, Intelligence and now, of all things, the CI bloody A!'

'It's not going to be like that. At least I'm almost certain it won't be. And God knows, I've spent the last week or two tapping every source I have before I even considered bringing it all to you. Look . . .'

And all the way down to the taxi, and then right across to Covent Garden, Richard went through what Tom Clark and he had discussed on the promenade deck of *Discovery*. And the fears that had begun to form in Richard's own mind since then.

THIRTEEN
Surprise

Richard's conversations in the back of the taxi continued all the way along London Wall, Newgate Street and Holborn Viaduct, down towards Shaftesbury Avenue and the West End. His co-conspirators were Jim Bourne, Rupert Bligh and Anthony Ho. He had engineered their presence in his taxi easily enough. The others had gone ahead with Robin in the other cab. Robin herself had been so preoccupied that she hadn't even seemed to notice that she was being managed by her husband.

The four men were still deep in their discussions as they ran through the drizzle across West Street and into no. 13, beneath the modest sign announcing that this was the London version of the world-famous gourmet brand.

Robin was waiting just inside the door, deep in conversation with the sleek young manager and the chef. The secretive conversation faltered as she led them into the ground floor of the famous restaurant.

Although he was still deeply preoccupied by his discussions, Richard was given pause by the stunning effect of the pitch-black and flame-red décor. 'My God!' he said, struck. 'This is simply breathtaking!' He hesitated for an instant, staring around at the high stools and the efficient bustle of the chefs in the open kitchen that would be overlooked by a heaving clientele in ninety minutes or so. But then Robin, smiling secretly to herself for some clandestine reason of her own, hurried him on upstairs in the wake of the others to the more comfortably traditional environs of the first floor restaurant.

At 16.00 hours precisely, therefore – just at the moment when the afternoon watch on their ships at sea was dogged into two halves – the eight Heritage Mariner board members who had attended the meeting at Heritage House in person arrived upstairs in L'Atelier de Joel Robuchon's formal dining room. Apart from staff taking care of the party themselves and others laying up for the Michelin-starred restaurant's evening session at five thirty, they were alone.

Once again, Richard was momentarily distracted from his rapidly fragmenting conversation with Jim Bourne to wonder how Robin had managed to swing this little miracle. But then the conversation took over almost all his concentration once again.

'Richard!' called Robin, as they sat amid a gaggle of attentive staff, 'No *shop*!' It was a company tradition that no business could be discussed once the board was at table, and Richard reluctantly drew things to a close.

But he had achieved his prime objective even before the taxi had turned off Shaftesbury Avenue into West Street. As the conversation around him turned to social chit-chat at Robin's dictate – the last raking-over of summer holiday memories, plans for the festive season, old acquaintance and errant children, babies and birthdays – his mind was more than capable of settling matters for itself. Especially as the usually fraught business of selection from the gourmet menu had been settled for them as part of Robin's achievement of the modest miracle of keeping the place open for their benefit.

*   *   *

Well aware that Richard would have been happier at the Bleeding Heart enjoying their outstanding sirloin steak and *frites* or sea bream and pan-fried fennel, Robin had agreed courses that came closest to spoiling her man.

To tell the truth, Robin was beginning to feel that, after a long wet summer fraught with too much work, topped off by the horror of the Chatham atrocity, things had been a little strained in their usually blissful marriage. The credit crunch might have led to a shorter and shallower curve of depression than everyone once feared, but business had been hard for the last couple of years – even for Heritage Mariner. And hard business soaked up Richard's time particularly, pulling them both apart.

Sorting out the vital details of the twins' seemingly never-ending education, keeping a weather eye out for their increasingly elderly parents happily retired to Grimaud in Provence, running three large houses and meeting her own responsibilities within the company had soaked up much of her time too. Not to mention the charitable work she under-took in what she laughingly called her 'spare' time.

Then Richard's more recent seduction into government plans that seemed to be almost a knee-jerk reaction to the terrorist outrage had put yet more distance between them. Distance that the twins had easily bridged in the past, pulling their parents together as they tried to sort out some scrape or another. But the twins were on the verge of flying the nest now and had spent much of the summer spreading their wings away from home. The arrangement and oversight of their adven-tures had yet again fallen largely to their mother.

Robin was acutely aware that, on top of all this, it would soon be just the two of them again. The old team. She desperately wanted that to be a good thing; a positive thing – something to be anticipated with excitement and enjoyed with relish. It would soon be Richard's birthday in any case and she had decided to surprise him a little early. And so, like the Martians in Wells's *War of the Worlds*, she had slowly and secretly drawn her plans . . .

And the plans were coming to fruition in the carefully stage-managed surprise. Starting here.

Starting now.

*   *   *

Over an exquisite langoustine carpaccio, Richard chatted almost automatically, avoiding Robin's eye as he mentally reassessed the plans he had drawn up with Jim Bourne. There would be a discrete section of London Centre set up within the next couple of weeks. It would be given a designated office and all the backup it required. Richard himself would help and advise Jim on the selection of his little crew. Jim would be focused on organizing a team that was ready, willing and able to go over every moment of Sayed Abu Minyar Mohammed's life.

Jim, of course, would know the best suited, best motivated and best connected people at London Centre to fulfil these tasks. Richard really only wanted to vet the team to make sure Mary would fit in seamlessly when she took up her work experience placement in her next vacation.

But as the langoustines – or the clean plates which were all that was left of them – were succeeded by the next course, Richard's mind turned to the next leg of his discussions. Jim Bourne gave way to Rupert Bligh, much as the seafood was giving way now to Robuchon's world-renowned miniburgers of Aberdeen Angus beef (in preference to the Japanese milk-fed, at Robin's insistence) ground with foie gras and served with extra-crunchy chips, accompanied by a green salad.

While Richard mixed his own light dressing, surveying the food with the liveliest anticipation and continuing to avoid Robin's eye contact, at the back of his mind he was occupied with a rather more problematic matter.

Jim's team at London Centre had some kind of blessing from Tom Clark and an assurance that their work was unlikely to tread on too many tender toes. His discussions with Rupert had gone well beyond that secure little pale. Only Rupert would have agreed to the plan, Richard suspected. And only Richard would have asked it. Only Anthony Ho would have agreed to become complicit – for all of them liked living a little more dangerously than the rest. And, aware that he was sailing a little too close to the wind, Richard had asked that it be kept from Robin and the rest of the board.

Rupert was planning to use The Bounty's personnel resources to find a professional prison warder. One who would fit every detail of the criteria Governor Weeks and Harry Blake had described as their requirements for officers aboard

Discovery. Once the man – and it would have to be a man – was found, he would apply for a position on the prison ship and go aboard undercover. They would have to move quickly, for Richard was pretty sure the ship's complement was almost filled. But the process of placing teams of officers and moving the detainees aboard was still in its early stages, so there was a chance. Anthony Ho advised on those legal aspects of the plan that occurred to him – a brief monologue which might have flattered the careful solicitor Andrew Atherton Balfour, consisting mostly of warnings and suggestions that they might like to stop and think. But as the cab pulled up in West Street, at least he had cheerfully agreed to deny all knowledge and say no more, unless he could think of anything that might help. Or unless he – or the Dragon Head his father – came across anyone who might help.

Richard had never tasted anything like the miniburgers, a symphony of prime beef and foie gras; never experienced such crunchy-coated, fluffy-centred perfection of chips. Under the lightest of French dressings scented with just a trace of truffle oil amid the Spanish extra virgin, the green salad was flavoured with rocket and chard with the faintest hint of tarragon.

The others spoke of the South African Pinotage with awed tones after Robin had held intense discussion with the tall blond sommelier and raided the legendary cellar accordingly. Richard himself was more than content with sparkling Ashbourne water. And, in due course, coffee.

With an eye on the clock and timekeeping every bit as ruthless as Richard's own, Robin broke the party up at five fifteen on the dot, so that the eight of them were stepping out into the windswept street on the point of five thirty. Just as the considerable queue outside was allowed in, bubbling with an anticipatory excitement that standing in the chill rain had clearly been unable to dull.

Somehow, the excitement seemed to have infected Robin too, thought Richard as they settled back into the cab that had been waiting for them. Or maybe she had enjoyed just one glass of Pinotage more than usual. Richard leaned forward, about to order the cabbie to take them back to Heritage House – where there was a flat they often used as a pied-à-terre.

But she forestalled him, passing the man a card instead. 'Sit back, darling,' she said a little throatily. 'Enjoy the ride.'

There was just enough emphasis on the last word, Richard thought, to give it a promising double meaning. Distracted, he leaned over and took her in his arms. The taste of the rich wine on her lips was intoxicating. And as she returned the gathering passion of his embrace, the cab moved through Soho and into Regent Street.

It was only as Robin felt the vehicle swing sharp left that she broke his grip and sat back, patting her hair into place. 'Down, boy!' she purred. She watched him look around, wondering where they were and orientating himself by the half-familiar shop and showroom frontages, still bright because Thursday was late night shopping in the West End. Almost aglow with excitement, she watched the blue dazzle of his gaze narrow as his mind grappled with the half-familiar sights. Suddenly the brightness seemed to expand in a way she still found breathtaking as his eyes widened with overwhelming surprise. He glanced down at her, his chiselled face in the sharp-edged shadows and golden planes a mask of pleasurable anticipation. The scar along his cheekbone disappeared into the laugh lines that seemed to join the corners of his eyes to the fronts of his ears and his lean cheeks to his square jaw, as his expression became one huge grin of boyish excitement. Because he was just beginning to suspect what his surprise might be.

FOURTEEN

Darkness

The taxi drew up outside the Bentley showroom. 'I have a little surprise for you,' said Robin breathlessly, well aware that he already suspected the truth. Or part of it at least. Always that one step ahead. But even Richard would never guess how carefully she had worked to make this surprise one of the greatest he had ever enjoyed.

Andrew Assay, Bentley's chief London salesman, met them

at the door and took them past ranks of Arnage and Mulsanne
saloons and Continental sports cars directly into the fragrance
of his gleaming office. Around the walls hung prints and photographs of almost every model in the great marque. Richard
gazed at them, dazzled as always, his mind leaping back to
the childishly pleasurable research he had done in the selection of his own first Bentley. A suspiciously juvenile amount
of it, he now thought, in the pages of James Bond novels, as
he had followed his boyhood hero through the 3.4 litre blower
destroyed by Hugo Drax in *Moonraker*, past the aberration of
the Aston Martin borrowed from the MI6 garage during the
matter of *Goldfinger* to the specially adapted Continental that
Bond had called the Locomotive, whose Arnott supercharger
put so much strain on the motor and the chassis that Bentley
had regretfully cancelled their warranty. He felt his heart beginning to race as though he was driving in the Le Mans with
W.O. Bentley himself. Or facing Ernst Stavro Blofeld in his
Japanese garden of death at the heart of *You Only Live Twice*.

On Andrew's desk lay a neat pile of paperwork and two
sets of keys. 'Everything ready, Andrew?' asked Robin, her
voice slightly choked with anticipation – her identification
with her beloved Richard almost absolute. Her heart was
beating almost as fast as his, her breath coming as short. She
was literally tingling. She could hardly believe it.

'One hundred per cent,' said Bentley's London manager.
'I'll only need a couple of signatures, and then we can go
though.'

'Better be quick,' said Robin, glancing across at her man.
'I think Richard's going to explode if we don't hurry.'

Andrew smiled in the fullest understanding. He had supplied
Richard with the car destroyed at Chatham. It had been a long,
secret process involving trips from Ashenden not only to
London but to Crewe, where Richard's measurements had
been taken as though he was having a suit fitted rather than
a motor car customized. Test drives on the Bentley test track.
Tiny adjustments to guarantee perfection. And, as with his
shoe size at Lobb's and his leg, waist, chest, collar and arm
at Gieves', the measurements were all on file.

Feeling a little drunk – though he had not touched alcohol
in ten years and more – Richard followed Andrew Assay and
Robin through into the covered yard behind the showroom.

'And there you have her,' said Andrew smoothly, fitting his words into the awed silence. 'The brand new Bentley Continental Supersports. The very latest model – only been out for a year. You'll notice several differences from your old Continental GTC, Richard. The most obvious of which is that she's a two-seater.

'In truth almost everything about her has been redesigned in some way or other, from the fact that she can take ethanol for severely reduced emissions to the fact that she can now officially reach more than two hundred miles per hour.

'Reduction in weight and development of power have enhanced performance at every level. Your old car could do nought to sixty in, what, five point four seconds? This one can do it in three point seven. Nought to a hundred in just over eight . . .'

Andrew's voice seemed to Richard to drift away into the ether. The car sat there ferociously. It was a black panther of a machine. Crouching, ready to spring. Dark and dangerous-looking. Lower than his old Continental, wider at shoulder and hip, it seemed longer, somehow; sleeker. Its dark grey paintwork seemed to soak up the light. There were no gleams of reflection, even under the flat stage-brightness of the show-room lights. It was matt, he realized with a pleasurable frisson of surprise – the darkest of greys and almost velvety in texture. It looked to him in the rainy overcast of an early winter evening as though the whole beautiful machine had somehow been made of shadows and darkness.

The windows were tinted. The grille, the wheel trims, light bezels and window frames seemed smoky rather than chromed or steely. She was a thing of shadowy power and almost inter-stellar beauty.

He took a deep, shuddering breath, realizing with distant surprise that this was the first time he had breathed since he first set eyes on her.

Andrew leaned down and reached for the all but invisible door-handle, but Robin beat him to it. She opened the door herself, and the car's interior seemed to gulp down the light like a black hole even as the fragrance of new leather spread out on to the evening air. The two deep seats were black – Beluga, Richard would come to know. Hand-trimmed in piping and stitching of the brightest blood red – Hotspur.

For a disorientating moment it was as though he was back on the ground floor of L'Atelier de Joel Robuchon.

'Get in, darling,' whispered Robin. 'See if it fits.'

'It's been set to your personal specifications,' prompted Andrew.

Beginning to come out of his dream as he moved, Richard stepped forward, stooped and eased himself into the cabin. The seat groaned a little as the beluga-black, red-trimmed, diamond-patterned leather yielded to his weight. The key slid into place. The steering wheel seemed to press its soft leather rim against his right palm, the smoke-dulled winged B of the marque gleaming mysteriously at its centre, as his left settled sensuously against the unexpected warmth and softness of the kid-covered gearshift. His long legs plumbed the shadowy depths of the footwell. The pedals placed themselves unerringly beneath the soles of his shoes. The showroom aroma of the leather was as heady as any Chanel fragrance. It was as though he had known this car all his life. As though he had never driven another.

'Everything is in the same place as in your old Continental,' Andrew was saying as he leaned in through the open door. 'But most of it has been adapted slightly. It's a Quickshift six-speed gearbox. Very fast. Very smooth. You'll soon get used to it. The power's more full-on, though, you'll have to watch that right foot. You'll have to programme a code on to the starter when you get home, but I've left it open now. Start her up whenever you like.'

Richard checked that the shift was in neutral and pressed the starter at once. The engine fired instantaneously, with something between a roar and a snarl. The whole vehicle vibrated gently, and Richard luxuriated in the Bentley's desire to be off and out on to the open road. No sooner had he pressed a gently experimental foot on to the accelerator than the passenger door opened and Robin slid in beside him.

'Now you know why the insurance company seemed to be so slow,' she said breathily. 'In fact the paperwork came through almost immediately. It's been almost impossible to keep everything secret from you while I got things organized with the loss adjusters and then with Bentley. But it was worth it just to see the look on your face. Now, don't be shy about taking her out at once. The tank's full. All the bumf is in the boot – and it's a big boot too, given that there are no back seats.

'Andrew's been briefing me during the long dull afternoons while you've been playing politics and going boating with your adoring parliamentary bimbettes on your prison ship,' she added. 'It's lucky he's so happily married or we might have got up to some serious mischief . . .'

She leaned over, her grey eyes huge in the shadows of the dusky interior. 'Now, lover, why don't you take your new toy out and I'll give you a bit of a driving lesson all the way down to Ashenden.' She punched in the destination – their home, Ashenden's postcode – into the SatNav, watching the recommended route pop up but knowing that Richard would probably choose his own way. In this as in all things.

'And you can give me a nice ride home . . .' she whispered, still tingling with the excitement he was feeling. Andrew Assay closed the driver door as though it were made of glass instead of steel.

Richard added an afterthought to the SatNav – *via Gatwick* – and pulled gingerly away from the cheerily waving salesman. He found himself at one with the car almost at once as he guided her through Belgravia and down on to Vauxhall Bridge. Then he eased her past Vauxhall, through Stockwell and round The Oval, where England had managed to retain the Ashes at the end of a rain-sodden Test series. He and the Bentley's SatNav seemed in cheerful accord as he pushed on down the A23 up Brixton Hill and through Streatham. It was as though the car knew that his cunning plan was to get on to the M23, where – subject only to the SatNav's careful advice with regard to speed traps – he could open her up and see what she could really do.

At first, Robin fussed over him, passing on the nuggets of knowledge and advice that Andrew Assay had given her during the afternoons that had not after all been filled with serious mischief but with advanced driving tuition. But she soon saw that Richard was in complete control, so she settled back and let him learn through play. And, once they had crossed the M25, he learned a good deal. About the unfettered roar of the turbocharged V12 beneath the long grey-black bonnet. About the lively, responsive handling, no matter how fast – or slow – she was going. About the way the gearbox flashed him up and down from first to sixth as the accelerator threw the car forward with astonishing power and acceleration. And just what speed he needed to be doing for the elegant little spoiler to lift itself out of the rear bodywork and settle the back wheels even more firmly on the road.

It was at the moment that the headlight beams first cut through the gathering gloom ahead and the cabin lit up with the eerie display that Richard suddenly said, 'Two seats? Not four?'

'The twins will be living at home less and less,' she said easily. 'I'll be having their rooms redecorated for when they come down to see us. Clearing spaces in the garage for when they settle on their own cars. But it's soon going to be just you and me, rattling around in Ashenden and roaring around Sussex. I thought this would be a really good way to get ahead of the game. And I wanted to give you a nice surprise.'

She did not say how hard she had been hit by the sudden thought that, had it not been for the *Ocelot*, she might never have had the chance to surprise him or Mary ever again.

She didn't really need to.

He looked across at her in the ghostly shadow of the speeding cockpit. 'Nicest surprise in years . . .' he said. 'And I'll have one for you as soon as we get home.'

Three hours later, Robin rolled over and snuggled contentedly against Richard's shoulder. 'Now that,' she said contentedly, 'was what I *call* a ride . . . Though I have to say, it wasn't that much of a *surprise* . . .'

Richard laughed quietly and cradled the vital warmth of her naked length against him. Over her duvet-wrapped shoulder he could see out of the big broad window across the balcony outside the master bedroom at Ashenden. Through the tracery of Art Deco ironwork that was the balcony's safety rail, he watched the navigating lights of the vessels passing relentlessly up and down the Channel. Beyond them, the sky was beginning to brighten as the cloud cover thinned and began to break. By the time Robin was snoring quietly, a full fat moon was sailing through the cloudy skies just like the ships sailing the sea lanes below.

Ten minutes later, Robin sprang awake, suddenly cold. She felt the vacancy in the bed beside her and chuckled to herself.

She knew exactly where her errant husband would be – standing naked in the back bathroom, looking down through the window that commanded a view of the gravelled drive and parking area outside Ashenden's front door. Gazing with boyish wonder at the elegant, shadowy picture made by the breathtaking Bentley's beautiful – if almost invisible – dark grey satin paintwork in the pale winter moonlight. She had suspected acutely that it was more than overwhelming passion that had led him to leave the beautiful motor car out there while he swept her into his arms and carried her into the house like a new bride.

After another ten minutes, she felt him snuggling back down beside her. His long lean body felt cool but as she turned over, a sudden, sensuous heat sparked between them. She lifted one warm thigh over his lean hips and rubbed herself lazily against him. 'Now this *is* a nice surprise,' she whispered.

With a deep, voluptuous chuckle that raised goosebumps across her shoulders, he clasped her buttocks in his huge hot hands and began to guide her suddenly thrilling body with that same easy, irresistible command that he exercised aboard his ships. 'Have I thanked you properly for my present?' he growled, the timbre of his words seeming to reduce a good deal of her insides to tingling jelly.

He rolled on to his back, kicking the duvet free with one imperious stroke of his leg. She rose seated astride him, and yet somehow moving at his command alone, as though she was his puppet. She took one shuddering, ecstatic breath, filling her lungs as deeply as she could.

And the bedside phone began to ring.

FIFTEEN

Nightmare

Richard stroked one thoughtful finger along the thin white scar on his cheekbone, looking narrow-eyed out across the Thames Estuary towards the Medway.

There was a light-hearted rumour in Heritage House that Richard had come by the scar duelling with a pirate chieftain over Robin's honour somewhere in the mysterious East. Which told more than a little about the way the majority of their employees saw both of their employers – especially, perhaps, the swashbuckling Richard. And the thin white line on the crest of his cheekbone did indeed look like the honour scar prized by Prussian aristocrats a century since. But he had come by it in a more prosaic way, while trying to secure the deep-sea remote vehicle *Neptune* on the foredeck of her mother ship *Poseidon* during a typhoon in the Yellow Sea.

He was stroking it so thoughtfully now because he was standing on the deck of *Poseidon's* sister ship, watching as the new-generation *Neptune* was lowered into the water of the Thames Estuary at the point where the Medway flowed out into it, forming a considerable sub-estuary of its own. And a consequent complex of inflows and outflows, tides and currents out in the mighty river. *Poseidon II* looked like a state-of-the-art corvette. Her long lean hull was raked and angular, the bridge rising from the weather deck in solid steps. It was not until the high command bridge that there was any glass at all. Up there now, the captain and her senior officers stood awaiting Richard's orders. Orders that would only come when the bright yellow DSRV, the crablike *Neptune*, was in the water and ready to be deployed. For it would be Richard and Robin who would operate her. They had been trained on the original vessels out in the Yellow Sea, and had used them – to worldwide acclaim – in the River Yangtze last year, after the catastrophic earthquakes in Hunan Province had destroyed the Three Gorges Dam and sent a terrifying wall of water smashing down the reeling river valley to the sea.

Robin was standing on one side of him now, with Gloria Strickland in turn beside her. On the other side were ranged a series of more official officers, including Chief Inspector Tom Clark and Chief Superintendent Jan Booth – a hurried amalgam of the Silver and Bronze crisis teams that Richard recognized from the Chatham incident. Gold, apparently, was once again assembling at the Maidstone headquarters under the Chief Constable's control. And even Maidstone, it seemed, was dangerously close if anything at all went wrong. He glanced over at the hump of the Isle of Grain with the Hoo Peninsula behind it. The Cliffe Fort on this bank of the Lower Hope was hidden from where he stood. But it was likely to be the safest place nearby, he thought inconsequentially. Except for the Coalhouse Fort opposite, or the massive Tilbury Fort beside it on the Essex bank.

Richard was recalled from his instant of wool-gathering by Gloria Strickland's honeyed tones. 'I'm getting a serious attack of déjà vu,' the MP whispered. 'I just hope I can keep my clothes on this time if this lot goes up as well.' Everyone laughed politely, but without amusement. Ms Strickland had the grace to blush, for she had not meant her aside to become public property. Robin allowed her lip to curl for a moment as she noted wryly how often Ms Strickland's eyes lingered on her husband when she thought no one was looking.

Poseidon herself sat just north of the main channel into the River Medway, in a little less than fifteen metres of water, with the tide coming precisely to the flood beneath her. She was facing west, the flood peaking under her counter, looking upriver towards the shallower Yantlet Flats with the Isle of Grain and the Hoo Peninsula behind them as *Neptune* was lowered carefully into the deeper channel under her port side.

Richard swung his bright gaze firmly south, past Robin and Gloria, over the port-side rails beyond the swaying DSRV, towards Sheerness where his brand new Bentley was currently parked like a little thundercloud on the point overlooking both of the estuaries, just less than a mile distant. He had left it there as Robin and he were picked up and hurried aboard by helicopter late last night, though *Poseidon* had been out between the Gabbard lights off Harwich when they arrived, heading in at flank speed.

The Bentley was about the only car left in Sheerness now, except for the police vehicles that had overseen the town's evacuation. While that had been going on, the night had waned, the dawn had gathered and the tide at last had turned. Richard and Robin had prepared everything they could, while *Poseidon* came on to her appointed station with the rising flow beneath her and waited for the tide to come up to the flood.

At this precise moment, Richard, gazing southward and stroking the scar on his cheekbone, was oblivious of almost everything around him. The brightening overcast of the morning, the whispering gurgle of the peaking tide, the stench of the estuary on the blustering drizzle-filled wind, the screaming of the breakfasting gulls. The fact that Gloria

Strickland was gazing almost worshipfully at him and the fact that Robin, narrow-eyed, was watching her.

He was thinking of how he had lost his beloved old Bentley in one terrible explosion. And how he really, truly, did not want to lose his beautiful new one in another.

Except, of course, this time he wouldn't know anything about it.

If anything went wrong, none of them would know anything about it.

It had been Under Secretary of State for Culture, Media and Sport Gloria Strickland who had phoned him so inconveniently twelve hours earlier, directly from her office in the House of Commons.

He had answered, fearing that only someone with bad news about the twins would call as late as this.

But no. 'We have a bit of a nightmare, Richard,' announced the breathily familiar voice. 'It's come to me via several other authorities. Apparently the buck stops here because of the potential damage to the Olympic facilities. And Secretary for Culture Maggie Emin is in Geneva with the Olympic Committee in any case. Several people I talked to, including Harry Blake and even the Home Secretary, suggested that you'd be the best man I could possibly consult about it . . .'

'That's the price you pay for saving politicians' lives,' Robin observed tartly some little time later, as Richard finished explaining the situation to her. 'You're Gloria Strickland's knight in shining armour now. If she ever was a maiden, which I doubt, you'd be the answer to her prayers. *You'd* better pray she never becomes Prime Minister or you'll end up as Defence Secretary or something.'

She wrapped the duvet around herself and marched off to the bathroom, leaving him nonplussed, naked, chilly and more than a little deflated. 'First Sea Lord?' he called after her, a little plaintively.

'Still,' she called through a moment or two later, 'she's right.' Her tone had mellowed but it was still a little grudging. 'They're all right, for once. You can't argue with that. We'd better get on to Heritage House and see who has the first night watch on *Poseidon* . . .'

*   *   *

As he stroked his scar, still deep in thought, Richard's narrow eyes were at last dragged back to *Neptune*. The bright yellow crab of the DSRV settled into the thick, oily, green-brown water, her flat top with its lowering ring a couple of metres above the surface. The surface roiled and twisted lazily around the remote vehicle's carefully guarded main propulsion and movement control system, which stuck out like a stubby tail as it bobbed there, dragging gently at its lowering ropes. Richard's wise eyes observed that the whorls of water which were twisting out from under the hydraulic arms and claws at the opposite end all seemed to be coming northward towards *Poseidon* herself. *Neptune* seemed keen to snuggle up against the side of her mother ship, like a kitten seeking warmth and reassurance, the saucer-like eyes of her cameras watching wide and hopefully.

This confirmed to Richard that the tide in the Thames itself had reached the flood and faltered. There would be dead water now for a while as the inwash of the tide balanced the outflow of the great river. He expected a call of confirmation in a moment or two via the bridge from the coastguards downriver – and more a few minutes after that from the relevant authorities upriver. But he knew the truth of it himself just by looking. Now it was only the outwash of the more modest Medway that was working on either vessel. 'It's time to move,' he said decisively. 'Dead water won't last long here.'

'*Dead water*,' echoed Robin as the pair of them ran down into the DSRV's handling facility. 'A very nicely chosen phrase, lover. Let's hope it's not too accurate.'

'That will depend on whether we've lost our touch since the last time we had *Neptune* working in a river,' he answered bracingly. 'That wasn't so long ago.'

'That was in the Yangtze, Richard. With all due respect to the Thames, there's only limited areas of comparison, no matter how recently we were doing it.'

'Still, we're the only people this side of the world who have ever done anything like this – though I agree, the Yangtze in full flood with seventy-five cubic kilometres of water thundering down on you and half of Nanking city washing down in front of it doesn't really bear comparison. It's a hell of a lot scarier in my book.' He gave his most reassuring chuckle. And only wifely ears would have detected the faintest hint of uncertainty within it.

'This is going to be a lot more like when we used *Neptune* to free the Chinese navy submarine that had got trapped by the undersea cable,' he continued, as though he was trying to convince himself as much as Robin. 'And that was a piece of cake.'

'Lover of mine,' she persisted, clattering off the last companionway and walking briskly along the short corridor to the control-room door in the lowest and farthest forward section of *Poseidon*'s hull, 'the Chinese cable wasn't a deflated boom with chain and netting dragging under it. And the People's Liberation Army navy submarine wasn't loaded with seventeen hundred tons of ancient and extremely unstable high explosive, liable to go up like an A-bomb if we made any kind of mistake at all.'

'There you go, you see – looking on the dark side . . .' He stopped trying to reassure her, focusing on surviving the vital task ahead.

By the time they had finished talking they were in the cramped little control room and settling into the remote vehicle operators' chairs there. Robin was switching on the cameras that circled the whole of *Neptune*'s hull. 'Looks like the dark side is all there is,' she said. 'I've never seen such filthy dirty water. Not even Darth Vader could see through this lot. What do we have in the way of light sabres, young Skywalker?' As she spoke, Robin was slipping the communication headset over her ear. Through this she could talk on open channel to *Poseidon*'s captain on the bridge, the coastguard upstream of them and downstream on the river – and to any other authority likely to have anything important to tell her. She wore it rather than Richard because it was crucial that the DSRV's handler be capable of absolute and uninterrupted concentration. Though she knew this particular handler well enough to be certain that her almost non-stop commentary was something he could take on board or disregard as circumstances might dictate.

'Is she always like this?' asked Tom Clark, coming through the doorway behind them.

'Only when she's terrified out of her tiny wits, Chief

Inspector,' answered Robin cheerfully, fielding the question before Richard became involved at the risk of his vital concentration on the task in hand. 'I hope you brought Captain Han Solo with you, Tom. Because we'll need to talk things through here.'

'Captain Han*cock*,' said Tom's companion, a pompous little ball of a man in dirty overalls and grubby seaboots who clearly did not see the funny side of any of this *Star Wars* talk at all.

But then, as the man responsible in the first place, he probably had good reason to be a little less than buoyant, thought Robin. Especially as he would have the coastguard, the Medway Port Authority, the MoD and the commercial marine safety company they had appointed as overseers of the wreck, the Secretary of State for Culture, Media and Sport, the Home Secretary and the Mayor of London, all on his back. If he survived.

As Richard ran through the shortest possible systems check, letting the irrelevant conversation flow by him, he looked at the all but featureless view that *Neptune*'s cameras revealed, even though Robin had switched on all her lights as she was babbling about sabres. The water in front of the submerging cameras was a thick green-brown, not unlike pea soup. Without the lights it was impossible to see even the hydraulic arms that sprouted from *Neptune*'s forward sections. Even with all of them on full, it was almost impossible to see beyond the bright crab-claws and ancillary equipment that stood ready at their ends.

The green soup of the water heaved and swirled with the balletic tree trunks of the whorls and eddies that he had observed on the surface. 'Switch on sonar please, Robin,' he ordered more formally. 'Thermal imaging, Google Earth, anything you've got. Keep me up to date with anything the coastguard has to say about tidal movements and time-frames. I'll need a pretty precise countdown when we're expecting any major movement of the water here. And, Captain Hancock, if you could talk me through this once again, inch by inch if you please . . .'

SIXTEEN
Boom

'I was positioning the inflatable boom across the mouth of the Medway in accordance with my orders at seventeen hundred hours yesterday when the control cable parted,' explained Hancock in the voice of a man who has repeated his story so often that it's beginning to damage his brain. 'The cable parted at the stern of my vessel, tug *Atlas*. It was not immediately obvious, but it later became clear that the cable lashed back against the inflatable boom – the so-called *unburstable* boom – and punctured several sections. The slackening of tension was so sudden and presented such potential danger to my partner's tug, *Ajax*, that her captain let slip his end of the cable for fear of fouling his propeller . . .'

Hancock faltered here, distracted by the complex of graphics on Richard's monitors. Robin was obeying Richard's orders and had started adding in a range of computer-generated images.

'So the boom was washed out of the estuary of the Medway into the estuary of the Thames,' prompted Richard, calmly, as though this were an everyday experience for him.

On the screens in front of him, the almost impenetrable brown-green pea-soup fog, which was the Thames' water at this point, was suddenly pierced with schematics based on sonar images. Sound able to discern so much more than light was able to reveal in these strange, almost nightmare circumstances.

A weird under-river world was forming and pulsing in front of him as the submersible's sonar pings began to pierce the green gloom. But it was the multicoloured thermal imaging that made it possible to see the sunken boom, which was a degree or two warmer than its surroundings – as were the nets and chains, providentially.

'A boom consisting of several inflatable sections with slow punctures at the surface, with chains and nets hanging beneath it to prevent submarine attacks on what little is left of Chatham,' prompted Robin, less understandingly. She was working, narrow-eyed, to ensure that the slow progress of the fully submerged *Neptune* was into areas whose details they could see – in the confusing complexes of computer images if not in perfect pictures.

'The slowly sinking boom washed out into the Thames Estuary,' admitted Hancock unhappily. 'That was where the tide took hold of it and moved it out of the Medway's outwash. And the tide was still coming in across the estuary quite strongly at that point. The last flood tide, as a matter of fact. There's been one ebb since – and we were a bit disappointed there wasn't enough buoyancy left in the boom to pull the whole lot free. Though on the other hand, thank God on bended knee that the counter-current didn't set anything off!'

'Can I have exact references for the sequence of movement as the boom drifted west?' asked Richard. 'Then I can match them up to *Neptune*'s satellite locator beacon. Follow the precise course of the boom across to its current location.'

Robin started talking into her headset. Coastguard computers, linked to Richard's through limited wi-fi and Internet, began to add the information requested to what he was able to see on the screen in front of him.

Captain Hancock suddenly saw the relevance of the *Star Wars* talk. All this was beginning to look like science fiction to him. Especially when the details of his own initial report clicked on to the screen and a little section opened up in the top right-hand corner of Richard's screen that showed the DSRV's progress across a schematic of the area. Like the little orientation maps on his children's shoot-'em-up video games.

'Very, very slowly,' advised Robin. 'Extend the top arms a little more and open the claws. They'll act as buffers if nothing else. *Feel the force*, young Richard. Which arm has the syringe?'

'Middle right. It's the one I have firmest control over. Are those location references accurate now that they seem to be coming in? Good. Moving forward, then.'

'Very, very slowly,' advised Robin once again.

'Carry on, Captain,' said Richard, quietly. Hancock jumped. He had been sucked into the strange world on the screens – a world where vague shapes were beginning to glimmer in the near distance under the lights. Shapes overlain by pulsing outlines as the sonar defined them more precisely and the computers arranged them into three-dimensional graphics based on minute variations in the times it took the sonar pings to return. Pulsing graphics given sharper definition yet – like the screen on an HD TV – by the blues and reds of the thermal images. It was becoming possible for Hancock and Tom beside him to see what Richard and Robin had understood almost instantly.

'The boom was swept westward with the tide,' continued the tug skipper. 'We went after it at once, but I stopped and asked for advice when it drifted past the buoys and into the exclusion zone. The coastguard told us to wait while they sought advice from the chief salvage officer with overall responsibility. So we waited. And it was only then, when it was in the zone itself, that we saw it was sinking so quickly. And beginning to snag, of course.'

The screens showed the three-dimensional picture of the river bed quite clearly now. The bed sagged like a hammock. At the centre of the hammock shape it was just possible to see the outline of a sunken vessel. A looming thing, ghostly and imprecise under the lights, but given vital definition by the sonar. Tiny, restless combinations of numbers gave measurements that allowed some idea of scale. The vessel was broken in two at the waist. The bow section lay leaning five or so degrees to the left. Two hundred feet behind, the after section lay leaning a further ten or so degrees, also to the left. On both sections there were stubs of broken masts and a funnel, some of which were tall enough to break the surface at low tide.

'And when the authorities realized that the whole lot – boom, chains and netting – had become wrapped around the *Richard Montgomery*, all hell broke loose,' concluded Captain Hancock. 'I mean it was a nightmare. A total nightmare.'

'What do they reckon will happen if I get this wrong?' asked Richard. He eased *Neptune* forward infinitesimally and held her still again, his narrow eyes busy; his concentration absolute despite the conversation. The screen was beginning to discriminate between the vital elements of the old Liberty ship's hull, the partially deflated boom and the mess of netting and chain that had hung like a curtain beneath it.

'Tom?' prompted Richard. 'You should be briefed on this as Bronze commander . . .'

'Leaving aside the obvious danger to ourselves,' answered Tom, 'the best guess seems to be this. If all the munitions aboard were to go up at once, the resulting explosion would send a tidal wave upriver that would peak at between five and ten feet. If that happened now, at the top of a high tide, we should probably lose most of Sheerness and Southend on the Thames alone. More if the wave went down the Medway as well. The Tilbury docks would be at extreme risk. The Thames Barrier would be hard put to handle the wave – always assuming it had time to close, because the wave would be moving very rapidly indeed.

'The Americans did a lot of work during World War Two and subsequently – apparently – looking at the possibility of using large underwater explosions to trigger tsunamis. Would have helped a lot in the Battle of the Pacific, so my basic briefing tells me. They didn't achieve much success but they did establish that the most effective scenario is when the explosion happens at the mouth of a funnel, so the surf runs into a narrowing area . . .'

'Like an estuary or a river mouth,' prompted Robin.

'Yes,' answered Tom. 'And the outflow of a river can steepen the wave, make it taller and more destructive under certain circumstances. So, if the Thames Barrier can contain it, we will just lose all riverside properties this side of Woolwich. If the Thames Barrier is swamped, we could lose a certain amount of London. Especially all those bits – like the London Underground and what-have-you – that lie beneath the Thames's normal water level. And there are some further sections of London itself that lie pretty far below the Thames's natural level in any case, even at street level, because the river's built up its banks quite considerably over the years while London itself has been sinking into the clay it was built on. While the whole of the South East has been quietly slipping deeper into the North Sea into the bargain. Which, of course, has been getting deeper because of global warming. So in theory a good deal of the city could be at risk. If they don't get the Thames Barrier closed in time.'

'Not to mention,' added Robin trenchantly, 'the further theory that even if they did get the barrier closed, the wave might simply wash out of the Woolwich Reach through Silverton and the Albert Dock system into the Blackwall Reach. Then of course it's goodnight Olympic Island, and a great deal of wasted work by Sir Harry McAlpine and co., even if the West End and the City survive.'

'But,' persisted Tom, 'Jan and I are here with Bronze and Silver teams because of the potential damage that the blast would do independently of the wave. Particularly to Kent and the Medway towns. I mean, seventeen hundred tons of high explosive wrapped in shell casings contained in boxes – metal for the most part – in more than four hundred feet of American steel has to be just about the biggest hand-grenade in the world . . .'

'Yes, I know,' grated Richard. 'It'll be raining nuts and bolts in Tunbridge Wells . . .'

'True,' agreed Tom grimly. 'And there'll be a good deal more serious damage within that blast radius in Kent alone. Sheerness, Sittingbourne, Rochester, Chatham, Gillingham, Maidstone, the whole Thames Gateway development . . .'

'Sounds like you'd better not screw this up, lover,' whispered Robin. Only now her tone was absolutely serious.

'I agree,' said Richard.

Richard's steady hands began to move *Neptune* forward once again. The DSRV's progress moved the vivid blip across the Google Earth schematic in the top right corner. In the rest of the screen, *Richard Montgomery*'s hull seemed to stir into life and creep stealthily towards them out of the muddy fog. Framed as it was by the crab claws of *Neptune*'s multiple hydraulic arms, the picture looked disturbingly fantastic and deeply dangerous. More *Alien* than *Star Wars*.

The lines of the long-sunk Liberty ship's forecastle head, dulled by mud and weed, bloated by sixty-five years of submersion in the restless tidal estuary, were further veiled by the nets and chains of the partially deflated boom. The boom itself still bobbed a little clear of the whole lethal mare's nest, a line of silver, something like a sausage-shaped bubble trapped here by some other-worldly physics. It was towards this, rather than towards the ship itself, that Richard was guiding the little remote submersible.

With shocking suddenness the boom leapt forward. The reaching arms with their widespread crab claws touched it, then seemed to bounce back. All four of the people in the little control room gasped with shock. Richard let his breath out slowly and eased the vehicle forward once more. The crab claws kissed the smooth silvery surface of the part-inflated boom. Richard closed them so gently they would have carried eggs safely. Sets of figures scrolled, detailing the precise pressures that the claws were exerting. When the grip seemed tight enough to hold the material without damaging it, Richard reversed the motors and tried to pull the whole mess gently free. Although he reversed to the degree, minute and second the course the boom had followed as it drifted in, his initial effort failed. The mare's nest moved quite promisingly, but then progress slowed and stopped. Richard made the game little vehicle shake its head like a terrier with a rat – only much more gently. The tangle of nets and chains yielded a little more then caught once again.

'Plan B, I think,' said Richard.

'The guys at Greenwich estimate you have about ten minutes of slack water left,' said Robin, now that he had initiated conversation.

'Ten minutes. OK. We'll factor that in. Get me some kind of estimate as to water pressures when the Thames starts flowing right on out past us, please. Oh. And the precise direction of the major tide axis here.'

'Right. The tide axis should be easy enough – with any luck it'll be similar to the figures you have for drift. I don't see the wind having much effect on a sinking boom dragging all that underneath it. Pressure will probably be a guesstimate, though.'

'Any port in a storm. Ready for Plan B. If you have fingers, prepare to cross them now.'

Richard's deft hands moved on the controls in front of him. The claws retained their grip on the half-inflated material. A new arm suddenly jerked into life. This one ended not in a claw, but in a long needle that was joined to a thin strong hose. Like the lines joining the tanks to the regulator on a scuba set. Unerringly, Richard guided the point of the needle into the bulge of material between the claws. As soon as the tip broke the silver surface and penetrated a centimetre or so into the bag, Richard flicked a switch. Yet another set of figures rolled by on the screen as the control system recorded exactly how much CO_2 was being pumped into the boom.

'But it's burst and leaking,' said Hancock.

'It's a slow leak,' answered Richard shortly. 'I can pump gas in far faster than it's leaking out. With luck I can reinflate all the damaged sections. How long did it take to sink? Twenty minutes according to the figures you gave in your initial report. I can get them back up and holding in less than ten and then we'll see . . .'

As he spoke, the claws slipped off the first section because it had inflated past their capacity to hold on. Richard pulled the needle out and bubbles began to leak at once. But slowly, as he had said. The whole section was now tugging upwards, like a balloon on a gusty day. He moved *Neptune* on to the next section.

'How long now, Robin?' he asked.

'Seven minutes. Tide axis is identical to the drift figures you already have but reversed through one hundred and eighty degrees, of course. They're working on the water pressure but they say it'll start pretty gently and then build up. But you knew that.'

'I knew that. Captain Hancock. How many sections did the cable damage?'

'Three.'

'Two more to go then. And no time to waste.'

Richard guided *Neptune* across to the next sagging section and smoothly closed its claws on the wrinkled side. The needle went in. The silver skin plumped up, seeming to shed years in a manner that consumed Robin with sheer envy. She was already green, for that was the primary colour of the readouts on the screen in front of her.

The moment the claws lost their purchase, Richard was guiding *Neptune* on to the last section. But even as she moved, a range of new figures flashed on to the screen on the top left, opposite the orientation map. The boom seemed to reach out towards the DSRV even as the claws reached in. 'Looks like we're out of time,' said Richard. 'The tide – as they say – has turned.'

Nothing daunted, he took hold of the last flaccid section, stabbed the needle home and pumped in CO_2 as fast as he was able. The upward pressure of the reinflated sections was tugging at the chains and nets ever more strongly now, as though the balloons of the boom were caught in an increasingly powerful gale. They began to yield to the upward, outward pressure that was trying to push them back along the course they had followed when last night's tide had pulled them in here.

At last it was possible to see the individual chains that joined the sections to the nets themselves as the whole mess started to slide back off the wreck's forecastle head.

The claws slipped off. But Richard did not withdraw the needle yet. Instead, he kept *Neptune* hanging there, fighting to stay still despite the gathering current, pumping CO_2 into the straining section as powerfully as ever. With one eye on that most delicate and easily severed connection, he extended the arm nearest the chain that shackled it in place.

Only the most practised hand, moving at the dictates of the steadiest nerves, perhaps, could have completed the manoeuvre. But Richard managed it. As soon as the claw closed on the chain he flipped another lever. A little red message flashed up, warning MAX PRESSURE. The claw could not possibly grip any more tightly than it was doing at that moment.

'Robin,' ordered Richard. 'Positive buoyancy please. Feed it in slowly, but don't stop unless I shout.'

'Ayeayesir!' answered Robin, turning the phrase into one word. 'Until you shoutsir! Or until the *Richard Montgomery* blows us all to kingdom come.'

Like any submarine, the DSRV had to be able to make itself lighter as well as heavier in the water if it was going to be able to move up and down as well as forward, back and from side to side. She could exert seven hundred and fifty kilos of lift. And so she did. Just as the fully – if temporarily – inflated sections of the boom came under the full pressure of the river's outward rush to the sea. And, just as Richard had calculated, the combination of forces was simply – and safely – irresistible.

Helped by the game little submarine, the reinflated boom sections lifted and dragged the chains and nets safely away from the sunken wreck. Then, with the long falls dragging like the tentacles of some massive Portuguese man-of-war, she guided it back precisely along the route that had pulled it in. With Richard's narrow eyes on the SatNav track across the Google Earth display and his hands steady on the controls, the whole mess came out of the exclusion zone altogether.

Until, at last, amid a good deal of shouting and cheering, the whole lot was nestled safely at the surface along *Poseidon*'s long starboard side, with *Neptune* in the midst of it all like a kitten in a cat's cradle.

SEVENTEEN
Helm

R ichard and Robin were not expecting any great show of public gratitude for their work with the *Richard Montgomery* and the errant boom. But there was complete media silence about the incident. 'No news is no news, I suppose,' said Richard when Robin expressed mild surprise at the breakfast table a few days later. 'What is it Milton says – *Bad News gallops while Good News waits*. And No News just stands around sucking its thumb, I expect.'

'Fair enough,' allowed Robin.

'All the news on the radio this morning was about what they're expecting the Home Secretary to say in his speech today,' she continued. 'And how the Opposition are likely to react if he does say what they expect him to say.'

She took a crisp bite of toast and crunched thoughtfully as Richard sipped his English Breakfast tea and mentally went through his itinerary for the day.

'And – I kid you not,' she continued now. 'They've even started trying to guess how the relevant government department will defend the Home Secretary against any attack the Opposition might make if the speech goes as they think it might. *And*,' she concluded darkly, as though this was proof of some truly Machiavellian plot, 'the minister they trotted out was your old friend Harry Blake!'

'Now you're back into Professor Stark's field,' Richard acknowledged, taking a covert glance at his Rolex. 'Perhaps someone on the BBC's *Today* programme has a degree in predictive mathematics, chaos or catastrophe theory. Or, more likely, the government has given notice of the contents of Alan's speech so they can start to spin it before he even opens his mouth.'

'Professor Stark's not so far off the mark either,' Robin observed, reaching for the last slice of toast. 'The speech will be about the reaction in the Muslim community to this prison ship of yours.'

'*Discovery* is not my ship. Though some of the later ships in the series might well be ours, if we proceed along those lines.' Richard put his tea cup down and sat back, suddenly giving Robin his full attention. 'But what's the story about? I must have missed it. We must get a showerproof radio, then I'll never be out of touch.'

'The usual. About how some sections of the government are worried that putting terrorist detainees on an ex-cruise liner will send out the wrong kind of message. Even though it's their own policy, mark you! They've suddenly realized it might make trouble in the rest of the prison community – and some sections of the country as a whole – because these prisoners are going to have such an easy life. Cruise ship accommodation, dedicated chefs, special diet and so forth, specialist teams of warders, their own private mullahs. You can see how it might look in some quarters. Apparently someone in the British National Party was complaining and the government is addressing their concerns.'

'God knows what the BNP would have had to say if we'd allowed the *Richard Montgomery* to take out the East End of London, half of Kent and most of Essex!' said Richard lightly. But his attention had been caught by her version of the news story and he was a little frustrated that he had not heard the details of it himself. For the matter of prison ships was on his agenda at his meeting this morning.

Robin rose, unconscious of his change of mood, and started stacking the dishes in the sink – tea and toast for the two of them wouldn't make much work for the cleaner when she arrived. 'That's the point,' she said, glancing over her elegantly tailored shoulder. '*We did that*. That happened. It was real, not speculative. And there's not a word about it anywhere. Not a whisper! No one's taken any notice of what we did at all. What's the time?'

'Seven fifteen.' He glanced at his watch again, knowing the time exactly but caught out by her sudden change of tack.

'God! We're running late!' The dishes clattered dangerously as she turned and abandoned them. 'My first meeting is at

eight thirty. Personnel committee. And you know how Rupert
Bligh gets if anyone is late, even the chair!'

'*Especially* the chair!' As he rose and pushed his own chair
straight, he put on an accent that wavered dangerously between
Charles Laughton, Trevor Howard and Anthony Hopkins.
'"Flogging's too good for 'em, Mr Christian! Break out the
keelhaul . . ."' He grinned, suddenly. 'Looks like we'd better
take the Bentley then . . .'

Richard's first meeting was in London Centre. He parked the
Bentley almost invisibly in the shadows of the chairman's slot
beneath Heritage House and saw Robin into the lift with ten
minutes to spare before Bligh started to live up to his name-
sake's reputation. Then he strode purposefully up the slip to
street level, round the corner, and, disregarding the overcast
and the light drizzle, plumbed the shadowy depths of
Creechurch Street before going through the usual routines
with the automatic entry system and Colour Sergeant Stone.

Heritage Mariner's 'Way Ahead' or 'Steering' Committee
was familiarly known as The Helm and those who served on
it – men and women alike – were known within the company
as Helmsmen. The main orders of business for today's meeting,
under Richard's chairmanship, were the matters that he and
vice-chair Jim Bourne had been chewing over most recently.
A fleet of floating nuclear power stations anchored in the
Arctic Ocean off the north coast of Russia and the government's unofficially expressed desire that Heritage Mariner find
and fit some more prison ships. Research and discussion on
both topics meant that they were firm enough to bring to the
committee now, for a test run at least before they were referred
up to the next full board.

They dealt with the matter of Russian nuclear facilities
swiftly. Then they turned to the matter of prison ships.

'You have your ear to the ground, Jim. What *is* the government's current position on prison ships?' asked Richard. 'Robin
heard something on the radio this morning and I haven't had
a chance to check with Harry Blake, though she must be in
her office because she was on the radio before seven . . .'

'As far as I'm aware the Home Office are keen to proceed,'
answered Jim. 'Though you've heard about Alan Pitt? The
gossip is that he has prostate cancer and will be in hospital

for some time in the New Year. We'll know more soon, but in the meantime they're talking about appointing a caretaker as Home Secretary if it does come to anything – and that might mean new faces in some places. But every government briefing seems to be promising steady as she goes.

'Anyway, I heard that news report too but I think there's a longer, deeper game being played. I see the puppeteer's hand of Professor Stark and her mathematical models here.'

'How do you mean?' demanded Anthony Ho, leaning forward. 'I heard the report myself and it seemed that the Home Secretary may be having second thoughts . . .'

'Wait a minute,' said Richard, his voice thoughtful. 'I remember Professor Stark saying something about her predictions allowing some control of reactions in the demographic areas where the terrorists were most likely to recruit from. If the facts were spun in the right way. Is that what you're driving at, Jim? Is that what Alan Pitt's up to?'

'Probably. The one really big problem that the *Discovery* might bring with her is negative publicity. Like the bad publicity that arose out of internment in Ulster – out of the old "H" blocks and the Maze Prison. Like Guantánamo more recently and Abu Ghraib. And the way almost any prison with a harsh regime gets immediately compared with a Nazi concentration camp. That kind of emotive issue can stir up a huge amount of trouble.'

'It's something the professor mentioned when we were looking round *Discovery*,' admitted Richard. 'Harry Blake seemed very much in agreement that it was quite a worry for the Justice Department and the Home Office as well.'

'Then this is a good way to deal with it, isn't it?' suggested Jim knowingly. 'How do you stop rumours that these men are being sent to a modern Auschwitz? Tell everyone you're worried that they're actually going to something more like the Hilton. Start a bloody great debate about how cushy things really are aboard the Prison Service's latest five-star luxury liner!'

'Such a simple double bluff is too childish to work, surely!' snapped Anthony Ho, flinging himself back in his chair.

'Kite flying is a major part of this administration's policy procedure,' riposted Jim. 'And it's only a double bluff under certain circumstances. If the howls or outrage get too loud then there may indeed be a subtle change of policy and hey presto, the simple double bluff will suddenly be the careful forethought of a listening government sensitive to issues of particular public concern!'

Anthony gave a reluctant laugh. 'Now that,' he said approvingly, 'is more like it! As though Sun Tzu had written *The Art of Politics* instead of *The Art of War.*'

'But it leaves us in a bit of a bind, doesn't it?' argued Richard. 'I was hoping to take a firm proposal to the next full board. Now I'm not sure that I can.'

'And the new lot might well change the whole policy after the next election in any case,' continued Jim cynically. 'So we really need our legal sharks in a feeding frenzy before we sign on the final dotted line.' He sat back, glancing across at Richard. 'But I can't believe we're too worried about buying a couple of second-hand cruise liners for Whitehall – we've just been discussing getting into bed with Moscow over floating nuclear power stations anchored in the Arctic Ocean!'

The discussion wavered back and forth for the rest of the morning without getting anywhere and Richard closed the meeting at midday with a vague, frustrating sense of wasted time. 'Hang on, would you, Jim?' he said as the others left. 'I know you're busy but I've got more I want to discuss with you.'

As he spoke, he was flipping open his cellphone and calling Robin on the speed dial. Her face lit up the screen and she answered at once. 'Hi darling. All finished? We're just about through here.'

'Yes. Jim and I are on our way over to Heritage House. Hang on to Rupert, will you? I'll buy the four of us lunch.'

EIGHTEEN

Stones

As Richard and Jim walked down Leadenhall towards Heritage House, Richard said, apparently quite casually, 'I wanted to pick your brains about something else too, Jim.'

'Pick away. What's the problem?'

Richard explained Robin's surprise that the *Richard Montgomery* incident hadn't received more media attention. Jim gave one of his cynical laughs. 'It'll be one of the new DA Notices,' he said. 'The ultimate government spin.'

'DA Notices?' asked Richard.

'It'll be a fairly long discussion. I may need to fill you in on some background. Over lunch maybe.'

Richard nodded. The sun came out as though this had been some kind of a signal. He narrowed his eyes, looking upwards, and gave a contented little grin.

Richard had chosen a restaurant just off Leadenhall called Stones. The four of them rose in a lift to the level marked *ROOF*, then stepped out into what seemed to be a sizeable glasshouse. Built on the huge flat slab of concrete that had been put on the top of a venerable Victorian building whose pitched roof had been blown off in the Blitz, it commanded breathtaking views over the City. And, now that the sun was trying to come out, it was very pleasantly light and airy. Also, because the unseasonably springlike weather had only just replaced the formerly wintry conditions, it was not too full.

Fifteen minutes later, Richard leaned forward over his carefully selected chicken Caesar salad and prompted Jim. 'DA Notices, Jim,' he said. 'Tell us about them.'

Jim looked up from an excellent lasagne al forno. 'I don't know if you remember what they used to call the old D Notice,' he began thoughtfully. 'D stood for *desist*, I guess.' He looked across at Robin – barbecued tiger prawns on salsa verde – and Rupert – good old-fashioned steak and kidney pudding. 'It was a formal forbidding notice designed to stop the publication of anything that the powers that be didn't want in the public arena. But then the Blair/Brown lot brought in the Access to Information Acts in 2000 and 2005. So it seemed that the old D Notice was defunct. Deceased. Dead. *However*, it soon became clear to one and all that they would still have to hold some information back for reasons of security and what have you. And so the D Notice became the brand new DA Notice.

'It's where the government alerts every strand, arm, web or what-have-you of the media that they must not publish anything at all about a particular subject. Not a suggestion.

Not a request.' He took a sip of his Peroni, sat back a little. 'A DA Notice has immediate force of law. If any paper publishes, the editor goes straight to prison. Any TV channel breaks the silence, the local editor is banged up at once.' He glanced across at Robin, who was eyeing Rupert's steak and kidney pudding with some envy. 'Your beloved *Today* programme breaks the news, then it's not only "Goodnight Vienna" for John Humphrys, Ed Stourton, Eddie Mair or whoever, the director general gets a closer look at Brixton Prison than he was planning for. In the States they call it spiking a story.'

'OK. I can see several reasons why they might want to spike the *Richard Montgomery* incident, I must admit,' said Richard. 'For a start, the existence of the thing isn't something they'd want to advertise, especially as it's so terribly dangerous.'

'Certainly not during the build-up to the London Olympics,' added Robin thoughtfully. 'Talk about tempting fate!'

'Nowadays the DA Notices cover the five vital areas of military ops, weapons, codes and communications, sensitive matters like installations and home addresses, and security and intelligence,' Jim continued. 'But of course it's up to *them* to decide what each of the categories might actually cover when the going gets tough . . .'

'And I suppose they don't want anything to get in the way of what Alan Pitt is going to say in his Home Secretary's speech,' allowed Richard thoughtfully. 'So it looks like a DA Notice ticks all the boxes for them, no matter whether we're talking military, weapons, sensitive installations or security.'

'Is that what you wanted to talk to us about?' asked Jim. 'DA Notices?'

'No,' answered Richard shortly. 'What I really want from each of you is an update on how things are proceeding off the record. Jim. How is your investigation into the life and times of Sayed Mohammed coming? Was Professor Stark right when she thought she recognized him as a student of hers? Rupert, how's the search for an undercover warder to send aboard *Discovery* going?'

The two men looked at each other, neither, clearly, too keen to speak first. Rupert pushed his empty plate away and looked at Richard. 'Really and truly, Richard, I've hit a brick wall on this. The Bounty can select and supply almost any kind of person you might need on board an ordinary ship, as well as the kinds of people – not too different from stewards and so forth – who can maintain and run a home. Even a stately home. But prison warders are pretty much of a closed shop, you know? Particularly as the Justice Department seems to have been serious when they decided to make sure any officer aboard *Discovery* would be subject to full CRB, identification, ID cards, the lot. Like people working airside at airports.

'And Muslim prison warders who can tick all those boxes and then are still willing to act independently, undercover, within the service . . . I'm afraid it's a bit of a bridge too far, if you follow my drift. Particularly in the face of the rising need for the kind of people we normally deal with as the world comes out of recession. Suddenly we're needing to find and send officers and crew all over the world. Navigators and engineers. Big ship specialists and small. Men and women to crew supertankers, container ships, waste transport vessels, ferries, jetcats – you name it. The only HM vessels I haven't been asked to crew recently are *Katapult* and *Marilyn*. And that's because Doc Weary's in charge of them!'

'OK, Rupert. Clearly we need a bit of a rethink on that. Jim?'

Jim shifted guiltily on his chair. Clearly he too was the bearer of bad news. But before he could begin to deliver it, the waiters arrived to clear their plates and suggest desserts. The dessert menu was as varied and crowd-pleasing as the main menu. Soon Robin was tasting a low-sugar raspberry sorbet with an expression like Joan of Arc at the stake while eyeing Jim's rhubarb crumble and Rupert's spotted dick. Richard was digging into an ice-cream, and waiting none too patiently for the rest of the bad news from London Centre.

'It's the time factor that's the problem, Richard,' admitted Jim at last. 'Finding the man hours. London Centre isn't what you'd call huge. I put together a little team just as you asked, but they keep getting pulled off task by more immediate concerns. Obviously the Russian nuclear platforms are soaking up man hours like you wouldn't believe. Then there's the West African involvement. The ever-increasing links with Shanghai and China as a whole. If that keeps up we'll have to start looking to expand in Hong Kong as well, and you know how

much background research that's going to take. Then there's
North Sea security – an increasing worry. Global warming
alone is beginning to push up sea levels enough to put some
facilities at risk – and there are time implications to getting
realistic predictions there. Let alone the security consider-
ations. Things coming and going in the Great Lakes – anything
that can be smuggled is being smuggled . . .'

Jim sat back and pushed his empty plate to one side. 'The
problem really seems to be that no matter who I put in Al
Azhar, they have some other work or expertise that keeps
distracting them. The sort of expertise that they were originally hired for. Something of more immediate importance to
Heritage Mariner.'

'*Al Azhar*,' said Robin thoughtfully. 'That's what you call
your research unit, is it?'

'It seemed appropriate. After all, Al Azhar is . . .'

'Just about the oldest Muslim university in the world. Yes,
I know,' answered Robin. 'Richard, it sounds like we need
someone in there who has no ties to any other aspect of HM's
work. Someone we can trust to do the work and keep the
results to themselves.'

'Mary comes home next week,' said Richard. 'I had always
thought she would get some work experience in this section
in any case. Perhaps she can do more than just *work* in it.
Someone else would have to do the footwork – visit
Mohammed's home town, check out his friends and family,
school, sixth form college . . .'

'But at least she could go up to Imperial herself,' said Robin.
'Diana Stark is one of her greatest heroines . . .'

'You'd be happy with that?' asked Richard, surprised. He
had been uncertain how Robin was going to react to his plans
for Mary. But, if her emails, texts and – very occasional –
letters had been anything to go by, she was still fascinated
with the man she had pulled out of the Medway. Whose life
she had probably saved. Terrorist mass murderer or not.

'As long as she didn't get too fixated. You know Mary.
She's always been part terrier.'

'A considerable strength in a researcher,' suggested Jim.
'She would be a welcome addition, if you're still focused on
getting this information about Mohammed's background . . .'

'Really and truly,' said Richard, 'I think it's possibly of

vital importance. It isn't anything I can put into words, but I do feel that what we're discussing now is incredibly important. Finding out all we can about Sayed Mohammed' – he swung away from Jim and slewed round to look at Rupert – 'and getting someone on *our* team placed undercover somewhere on *Discovery* so that we can find out the truth about what's really going on aboard her too.'

'You may be asking the impossible, Richard,' said Rupert, shaking his head and laying down his spoon, defeated at last. 'As I said, prison warders are so far beyond our usual run of employees . . . What other sort of employees do they have aboard on a regular basis?'

'Well . . . No navigators, obviously,' said Richard, going through a mental list of The Bounty's usual contacts.

'I should hope not. *Discovery*'s not going anywhere, is she?' asked Robin, half jokingly.

Richard frowned, her words stirring something in his memory. But he had started on his list and so he continued with it almost automatically.

'No stewards . . .'

'One or two *bar-stewards*, if rumours about some sections of the prison service are true . . .' Robin was still hungry – but well aware that she needed to be ready for a big meal this evening – and getting a little bored.

'Because the prison service are supplying specially trained halal cooks and what-have-you,' persisted Richard, still focused on his list.

'All apparently CRB checked with full ID and so forth,' warned Rupert. 'Though to be fair, we do have a bit more access to stewards and so on with Muslim backgrounds . . .'

'Nothing like general purpose seamen, obviously.'

'Because she isn't really a ship, is she?' persisted Robin. 'She's just a prison that floats. The closest thing to a sailor she'll probably need is someone to change the light bulbs.'

And that innocent remark clicked something vital into place in Richard's mind, the germ of which had been placed there by Robin a few moments earlier.

'Archie,' he said.

The other three looked at him with the kind of sheer incomprehension usually reserved for someone speaking Klingon. Or a madman speaking gibberish.

'The good ship *Discovery* has an engineer,' he explained. 'A single, unassisted engineer who feels he is badly over-worked and under-supported. Hardly surprisingly, because he is in sole charge of the electrical supply to the whole vessel – as well as maintenance of everything from the plumbing to the oversight of the mothballed motors they still have aboard her. An engineer whose name the governor doesn't know, so he calls him Archie like the warders do.'

He looked around the others and sidetracked into a word or two of explanation. 'Archie. Short for Archibald. They call him that because he hasn't any hair. But the point I'm making is this. Archie is the chink in the armour. The governor doesn't know his name. And he made such a point of calling everyone else by their names. Not to show that he particularly cared about them or respected them, I think. More as a demonstra-tion to Harry Blake of his power over them; of his total command of the situation. To show her that he had read, learned and inwardly digested their security files, their CRB records and so on. Don't you see? I don't know if it's still the case, but I'll bet anything you like that it is! Certainly when I visited the ship, there was no security check on the engineer, or if there had been it was so low-grade that it hadn't even registered on the governor's radar. Or Governor Weeks would have known the man's name the same as everybody else's. And he would have carried on showing off to Harry!

'And, Rupert, I know you would be able to find me an engineer with just the background that we want – and the qualifications and expertise that Archie would need in a very welcome assistant. Then I just have to have a subtle word with the Under Secretary for Criminal Justice and Offender Management and our man will be in on the engineering deck.'

NINETEEN
Al Azhar

Richard and Mary hurried towards the warmth of London Centre through a freezing flurry of snow in the teeth of a truly Arctic wind. There were no flakes. Merely tiny grains of ice seemingly made capable of flaying cheeks and foreheads by the power of the sub-zero northerly gale blowing them through London as though it were Murmansk.

It was nearly a fortnight to Christmas and Mary was not due back at her studies until mid-January. In the meantime she was destined to join Al Azhar. Expanding the manpower of the little research department by 33.3 per cent, thought Richard; and expanding its enthusiasm almost infinitely.

'You won't be going from a standing start,' he told her as they turned into the relative calm of Creechurch Street. 'All sorts of stuff has turned up and as far as I know your co-workers have been sorting and cataloguing it for the last week or so. Though I haven't been as much on top of things as I would have wished, I must admit. There's all the news research done at the time of the Chatham incident. And Tom Clark has sent across some boxes of stuff the local police sent down to the Met and they passed on to him, as well as the edited highlights of the counter-terrorism file . . .'

'Edited highlights . . .?' she echoed questioningly.

'I don't think the whole file ever came down to him. And of the bits that did, a good deal has to remain restricted.'

'For reasons of national security . . .'

'Precisely.' He hesitated, the simple little exchange reawakening deep concerns in his mind about the appropriateness of this whole adventure. But Mary hit the entry button with her signature mixture of impatience and excitement and Colour Sergeant Stone came forward to welcome them into the foyer.

Jim Bourne met them in the foyer as Stone completed the security routine and then led them inwards and downwards to the little research facility. Al Azhar didn't look much like a top-flight research establishment, and the two men occupying it didn't seem all that enthusiastic or impressive either. It looked to Richard like a hastily adapted cleaning store, and the two researchers Jim had assigned to it seemed quietly discontented. But they stood up, shook hands and welcomed Mary into their midst.

There was Patrick Toomey, a big, bluff, square-faced Irishman in his late thirties, with blue eyes and crinkly red hair and a lilting Dublin voice. And there was Ahmed Haroun Tewfik, a tall, almost skeletal boy with a South London accent and the face of an angry Pathan brigand.

After Jim had performed the introductions, Richard assured himself that Mary knew what she was expected to do, how she would fit into the structure here, and that she knew how to get hold of both Robin and himself up the road at the Heritage Mariner building. Then he left her to it.

'You fuss over her too much,' said Jim as they walked back to his office. 'She'll have the Chuckle Brothers twisted round her little finger and eating out of her hand in no time.'

'The Chuckle Brothers?'

'Ask Mary tonight. If she can tell you, then she's made a good start.'

'Fair enough. And I don't fuss over her.'

'No more than any dad over any daughter, I guess. And yes, I know Robin is just as bad.'

'Worse! With both of them. She really and truly did not sleep for one whole solid month when William went to Guatemala. Even though he went with a group of friends all properly organized by Voluntary Services! And when Mary proposed to do the same she put her foot down so hard I'm surprised there wasn't an earthquake.'

Jim laughed. 'I suppose it's because the pair of you have been mixed up in so many scary scrapes that she's terrified the twins will get mixed up in more. Look at that situation in West Africa you were involved in. It was a miracle no one got hurt. I mean, Robin and that girl getting kidnapped and us going after them up a bloody great river into the heart of darkness to find ourselves in the middle of a civil war.'

Richard nodded in grudging agreement. 'I think she's started to believe that we've used up so much blind luck simply in surviving as we have that there'll be none left for William and Mary if they do anything hare-brained too.'

'Well,' promised Jim blithely as he ushered Richard into the lift back down to the foyer, 'I promise we won't let her get mixed up in anything even a little bit dangerous while she's here with us.'

'I hope that's not a case of famous last words,' riposted Richard as the doors hissed shut between them.

Despite his apparent lack of concern, he pulled his phone out of his pocket. And by the time he stepped into the foyer his secretary had cleared his schedule for the morning so that he would be doing paperwork in his office – in case Mary had to call on him for any reason at all.

Mary sat in a black swivel chair with a blank-screened laptop open on a cramped little work surface immediately in front of her. The work surface wasn't the only thing that was cramped. The whole of the room seemed hardly larger than a broom closet and it was bursting at the seams. It was too small to contain the equipment, notes, files and boxes of information packed into it. It was too small to contain three black faux-leather swivel chairs, each filled with a body of above average size. And it was certainly too small to contain the atmosphere of angry negativity and almost childishly sulky resentment that began to burn in here the instant that Jim and her father had walked away.

Mary considered just putting her head down, ignoring the atmosphere and getting on with what she had come here almost psychotically fixated on doing. But that would be like walking away from a fight. And Mary never, ever walked away from a fight.

'OK,' she said, swinging round to face the two backs hunched against her, facing the walls behind her. 'Forget I'm related to the boss's boss. Assume that whatever you tell me will stop here unless I can do anything to help. Tell me what's got you two so fed up with this assignment. Pat?' she prompted after an instant, assuming – correctly as it chanced – that a big red-headed Dubliner could be counted upon to speak his mind on most matters without a shadow of fear or favour.

'Well now,' the big Irishman swung round, resting his huge

freckled hands on a pair of rugby-playing prop forward's thighs. 'Since you're kind enough to enquire . . .'

During the next ten minutes Pat Toomey described the high-lights of both Ahmed's and his own experiences in the fields of counter-terrorist intelligence. Their reasons for leaving their respective services when and as they did. Their motivations for joining Heritage Mariner. The work they dreamed of doing. The work they had been promised they would be doing. The respect in which they had been held by their original – if secret – employers. The respect in which they had been held until so recently by Heritage Mariner, London Centre and their colleagues in both. But how this assignment had under-mined all that. How they had been moved from the upper echelons of a commercial intelligence unit of almost legendary reputation. Out of the company of men and women whose job it was to discover, discuss and assess the most crucial aspects of economic, commercial and political security around the globe. To looking into the life of some school-kid who had become mixed up in a terrorist outrage. Out of a war room buzzing with information and speculation on everything from global warming to Middle Eastern nuclear ambitions, from the implications of diminishing supplies of oil to the effects of continued political instability in West Africa, from the commercial outcomes of the rise and rise of tiger economies to the insurance implications of continued piracy in Somalia and all points east. Into a stinking broom cupboard with three laptops, enough paper to start a recycling plant and a student for company.

'And they laugh at us now!' added Ahmed, literally shaking with outrage. 'They call us the Chuckle Brothers!'

'What! Call you what?' All Mary could think of was a TV programme from her childhood. The Chuckle Brothers performed sporadically funny slapstick routines loosely woven into half-hour narratives. She herself had loved the Chuckle Brothers, with their simple gag-line, *to me . . . to you . . .*, that almost always heralded some hilarious disaster.

'*Too mey . . . Tew fik . . .*' said Pat, in a remarkably accu-rate impression.

Mary maintained a straight face – but only at some cost. 'That's so . . . silly!' she said at last, a little gustily, threatened by an overwhelming attack of the giggles.

'That's workplace bullying!' said Ahmed angrily. Like William on occasion, far too quick to take himself seriously and stand on his honour. His dark eyes were wide and wounded. He looked very young suddenly, in spite of his square-cut beard and the devilish sweep of his eyebrows, very deeply and genuinely aggrieved. All at once, Mary's heart went out to him and the desire to giggle withered. Pat was watching her speculatively, and Mary was abruptly aware that the guardedly cheery expression in the square Irish face was a habit; a mask. Pat was almost as wounded by this as Ahmed clearly was.

Her normally wide eyes narrowed – and for an instant she looked very much like her father did when he went into deep dark thoughts. 'The problem here is not with you,' she announced after a moment. 'It's with us. This is our fault and I think I know how to put it right.' She reached into her pocket and pulled out her iPhone. Flicked it into phone mode and touched her father's speed-dial contact.

'That was quick!' he said with no preliminaries. 'What can I do for you?'

'I have a couple of colleagues here,' she answered shortly, in the voice that Richard recognized as indicating that she was unlikely to take no for an answer, 'who need a proper and detailed briefing. They need it now and they need it from you. Can we come over?'

Fifteen minutes later the three were sitting in Richard's chairman's reception room with coffee, tea and gingernuts laid out on the Chippendale table in front of them. Mary was tucking in. Pat and Ahmed were sitting like statues, waiting for Richard to start talking to them.

Jim Bourne had arrived five minutes ago, his presence requested by Richard, who was far too good a manager to be doing anything behind a section leader's back. Jim was still frowning from Pat's pithy restatement of the concerns he shared with Ahmed. 'To continue the Le Carré London Centre concept,' he had concluded. 'It's like we have a building full of George Smileys – while Ahmed and I are just like Alec Leamas and some other poor sod, likely to be lied to, patronized, never allowed to see the whole picture, stabbed in the back and shot in the end . . .'

Richard glanced across to Jim, who gave a minuscule shrug. 'I see,' said Richard thoughtfully. 'If you'll allow me, Jim, I think I can answer some of Pat and Ahmed's concerns.' All of their attention focused on Richard, all of their intelligence assessing his every word. And he paid them the compliment of treating them with absolute candour.

'You haven't seen yet just how important the work you've been asked to do here actually is. And if you don't feel you've been shown the whole picture then that's probably my fault – though to be fair I haven't been shown the whole picture myself. As nearly as I can work it out, the situation seems to be this,' he explained, his voice gaining pace and timbre as he broadened his narrative, coming swiftly and effectively to his most charismatic, forceful and convincing. 'Sayed Mohammed is a much more sinister figure than he seems to be – or is involved in a much more dangerous conspiracy than he appears to be.

'He may be relatively young, but he has some much more experienced contacts. Only no one seems to know exactly who or where these contacts are. Or what they might be plotting. As to their identities, the best guess of the people I've talked to seems to be that they are the last survivors of the Al Qa'ida/Taliban alliance that cleared out of the tribal lands in South Waziristan a couple of years back when the Pakistani army went in mob-handed. Those few who may not have been wiped off the United States' hit list by air strikes from the remotely controlled Predators and Reaper drones after all.

'There seems to be no real intelligence on why Sayed Mohammed could have contacted these people – or how, or where. But a lot of important folks in the intelligence world here and elsewhere seem to think he did. The Chatham incident wasn't the end of whatever is being planned, but the beginning.

'So, when Sayed Mohammed so conveniently survived the destruction of the Historic Dockyard and got himself arrested, Counter-Terrorism Command seems to have taken over – at Home Office level. Tom Clark and Jan Booth were warned off. So Kent Constabulary – and even the Met – seem to have been sidelined. The Public Prosecutor's Office seem to have been dancing to the Intelligence tune as well – though what the Ministry of Justice and the Director of Public Prosecutions must have had to say about that one can only guess.

'CTC, perhaps manipulated – certainly advised – by the CIA, seem to have hoped that while Sayed was being held, tethered like a goat in a hunt, some tigers would have come out of the terrorist jungle, but nothing of the sort seems to have happened. So, by all accounts, CTC stood back. MI5 went in – but we have no knowledge or record of what they've discovered so far.

'CIA are still involved – one of their most influential and highly regarded experts in the field is still in Grosvenor Square. Chap called Harvey Swann. And the long and short of it seems to be that the normal authorities who would be working on this incident – Kent Constabulary and the Met – have both been simply warned off. Which they don't like.

'But it so happens that at least one relevant officer is a contact of mine – and he has a nasty feeling about the whole situation. I can't read his mind and he's keeping everything pretty close to his chest as you'd expect, but I have a shrewd suspicion that I know what he's thinking. What if the CIA – who are playing in another ballpark altogether, so to speak – has convinced Counter-Terrorism to take its eye off the ball here? What if they're so scared of another 9/11 that they've forgotten about the possibility of a bigger, more devastating 7/7? What if MI5 are going too slowly – and are already too late? What if there is a terrorist conspiracy already running and its target is here – no matter where its roots might be?

'Then, the only lead we've got, the only link we have, is Sayed Mohammed. And if they have been told to leave him alone for the moment while everyone searches for the men who programmed him – wherever in the world *they* are – then they're failing to follow up the only – the *only* – chance we might have of stopping whatever might be planned to happen here.

'So we've been asked – unofficially and with thorough deniability – to use London Centre to see what we can find out before the next stage in whatever plan Mohammed is involved in comes to fruition. And we've asked you to do the spade work for us. Everyone else thinks we're wasting our time on a little pawn who is more likely than not to be something between a red herring and a double bluff. But we think he just might be the linchpin in the whole conspiracy. The short fuse. The trigger.

'And we want you three to find out the truth before it all blows up in our face.'

TWENTY
Mohammed

'What we're doing here, d'ye see,' said Pat, rocking back in his black swivel chair, his prizefighter's fists on his prop forward's thighs, 'is walking the finest of fine lines between the Freedom of Information Act and the Data Protection Act. Between the Devil and the deep sea. Between the rock and the hard place.'

'Or getting someone else to walk it for us,' added Ahmed, swinging round as well. Stooping forward into an equally characteristic pose – as though he was about to leap out of the black seat and attack the listening Mary. Attack her or embrace her – it was always hard to tell with Ahmed. 'The whole western news industry has walked parts of it for us already. As have the BBC, ITV and various interested foreign news services. As have the Metropolitan Police – if briefly – and the Kent and Buckinghamshire constabularies. As has Counter-Terrorism Command – though anything we have from them is as heavily censored as an old MP's accounts sheet. But here's another one. The Sunday after Chatham.' He brandished a folded newspaper like a scimitar. 'The *Observer* has a good long, detailed investigation.

> '*Milton Keynes, once most famous as the first of the new towns, has earned a darker place in history this week as the community that bore and nurtured terrorist suspect Sayed Abu Minyar Mohammed. Like all too many terrorists in the recent past, Sayed Mohammed was born, raised and educated in the heart of England, only to become radicalized by clerics both here and in the Indian subcontinent. Trained by terrorist organizations abroad. Equipped by them and their sinister web of international contacts – who are apparently able to cross our borders at will. And set on the path of terrible* jihad *against the very country that raised him . . .*'

'OK, OK,' cried Mary, amused by the change in the Chuckle Brothers in the week since their meeting with her father. 'Hold your horses, the pair of you. The basic facts seem pretty clear so far. Let's sum them up again for the record.' She swung back to face the screen of her laptop and read from it, her fingers busily adding details as she talked and the others added input. The three of them were almost a machine now, losing their individual identities in the three-way effort as they worked. They made unthinking allowances for each other and supported each other with increasing ruthlessness. With Mary on board, the Chuckle Brothers were rapidly becoming the Three Musketeers.

Pat's habit of humming snatches of music from great classical masses no longer proved an irritant – or even a distraction. Unless his fine baritone suddenly rose unexpectedly on the wings of Mozart, Rossini, Fauré or Verdi. He visited the great Catholic cathedrals in his spare time, and loved a Latin mass. But he never seemed to have settled on one particular church, not even near his own home. He said a little defensively that his heart belonged to St Patrick's in Dublin, where he had worshipped while reading theology at Trinity College. In the days when he had believed in any of that sort of stuff.

Ahmed's little timer, which tinkled a warning like a musical muezzin just before the hours of prayer – and his absences in answer to it to perform the *wudu* rituals of cleanliness as required and the *salat* prayers themselves – simply fitted in the warp and woof of their working days. At least he seemed to have held on to his faith, thought Mary, in spite of what-ever experiences had darkened his life – when it was less lonely. And it must have been less lonely, like Pat's when he was younger, studying engineering at the University in Peshawar. Unless, of course, that was some sort of cover too – and had been accompanied by the kind of isolation that never quite seemed to follow the spies and agents whose fictional adventures had filled her tomboy youth.

But if Pat's masses and Ahmed's prayers did not disturb the harmony, then neither did the ringing of Mary's iPhone, kept on at the insistence of her parents, but accepting calls from a seemingly infinite circle of friends and fellow students. And if her constant stream of muttered conversations empha-sized to the Chuckle Brothers that their lives might be a good deal fuller than they were, then neither of them disturbed the new-found calm by saying so.

The transformation resulted from more than her father's pep talk. From more than Jim Bourne's new-found respect – or the Chuckle Brothers' new-found sense of purpose. Mary herself had proved to be the catalyst. Both of the men she was working with were solitary. Pat had a bachelor flat in Willesden and Ahmed roomed with a family in Lewisham. Both of them had extensive families – but at some distance from town. Some distance from the country in fact. Sufficient distance to ensure that neither man had any particular plans for Christmas next week. Not that the Muslim Ahmed would be observing that particular feast in any case, of course.

'Sayed Abu Minyar Mohammed,' announced Mary now, pulling them together and jerking herself out of her more maudlin thoughts. 'Born in the maternity unit of Milton Keynes General Hospital at or about midnight, December 24th/25th 1985. That's nice. It'll be his twenty-sixth birthday on Sunday. Though I must admit he doesn't look twenty-five years old to me.'

On that thoughtful aside, Ahmed took up the narrative that they had checked and double-checked during the few days in all the various overlapping sources that were available to them. Sources to be painstakingly discovered everywhere from the scraps of paper in the boxes on the floor beside them to the government department websites on the screens in front of them. 'Birth accomplished in hospital as opposed to at home in a more appropriately Muslim atmosphere because of antenatal complications. The baby was blue – wrapped in the umbilical cord and lucky to survive an emergency Caesarian section. Mother died during the procedure. Baby put in the natal unit and was lucky that it was state of the art, by the look of things.

'Baby Sayed strong enough to be taken home by his father and his mother's sister on the seventh day after birth, though a mullah had been called previously and performed the necessary birth rituals for the boy before attending to the mother's death rituals. No detailed record of the full rituals due to a newborn boy but the assumption is that his father, Yussif Mohammed, saw them all properly performed.'

Pat took up the story. 'Yussif Mohammed. Shop owner,

benefactor, pillar of the local mosque. Killed in a car crash in Ordsall, Greater Manchester, summer 1990. Not listed as a fatality of the riots but there was apparently much speculation locally – and in Milton Keynes. Manchester police report states that the deceased was seen driving in an erratic fashion away from a disturbance during which shops had been set alight and shots fired. The shops on fire were Muslim properties which Sayed's father may have been visiting. Though there is no suggestion that the shots were fired at *him*.

'Witnesses state that the car was driving very fast and weaving from side to side of the street. The car crashed into a parked vehicle at some speed and both vehicles burst into flames. Attending officers who saw the last few moments of the incident gave evidence at the inquest that the driver was in all probability drunk.'

'A devout Muslim?' asked Mary, her voice dripping with cynicism. 'A pillar of the Milton Keynes Mosque? *Drunk?* Maybe we should look into the father's death after we've looked into the son's life.'

'Sayed was taken into his aunt's family – his father's elder sister's family. The Tantawis,' continued Pat, brusquely. 'The shop technically went with him, run very successfully by his aunt's husband Hassan Tantawi and Sayed's elder cousins Aamil, Lais, Raashid and Saami, until such time as Sayed was old enough to take it over himself. In the meantime he was educated. And well educated, it seems. The uncle owned a chain of shops and wanted Sayed to be in a position to expand his own shop likewise when the time came. And it seems the uncle, while he appears to have been just as active in and around the mosque as Sayed's father, wanted to make sure the young man had a fairly broad education as well as a good one. Teddybears nursery from the age of five. Very highly spoken of.'

'There would have been Islamic education in the evenings, though,' added Ahmed. 'Religious instruction by the mullahs at the mosque. As well as practical lessons in business, maths and so forth – from the uncle and cousins if from no one else. Charitable work locally too. And support for international Muslim charities, not just financial but active and personal, when he and two of his cousins began to work with the Islamic Humanitarian Association, going first to Pakistan and then more generally abroad. That was before they took him on the Hajj to Mecca in the millennium year. And all that becomes crucial later, I believe.'

'His formal education continued at Wilberforce Primary School, in the meantime,' added Pat. 'The best in Milton Keynes. *Now*, according to OFSTED. And *then*, according to gossip as collected – but not collated – by the Buckinghamshire Constabulary. Outstanding student according to the testimony of teachers interviewed by the same local police officers. Worked very hard to fit in with the local white students as well as with his Muslim brothers – both before and after his visit to Mecca in March 2000.

'Popular and successful by all accounts. The fact that he was effectively an orphan doesn't seem to have had much appreciable effect on him. Unlike the fact that he was apparently near or above genius level in mathematics. Of which, again, more later. Transferred to Lord Brook's very highly rated secondary school and sixth form college in September 1996, aged eleven years and eight months, give or take.'

'The Buckinghamshire police have got some old reports from somewhere,' Ahmed added. 'They cover achievement in both schools. More solid than witness statements and local hearsay evidence.' Paper crackled as he consulted a photocopy. 'Sayed Abu Minyar Mohammed. Unique Pupil Number 2179444. Level Eight and above in all core subjects at Key Stage Three as taken in May 1999. Says here that his maths score was one hundred per cent. That sounds like genius level to me, Pat. Straight A student at GCSE, July 2001. In spite of the fact that he must have missed some of his secondary schooling on the *Hajj* in March the previous year. All ten subjects sat in summer 2002 either A or A starred. Top score for maths again.

'Taken straight into the sixth form September 2002. And they must have been pretty glad to keep him, I'd say, surrounded by grammar schools, private and public schools as they are. Still, maths, physics, chemistry and religious studies at A level. Predicted straight As in all subjects. The school has a reputation for pushing their students in all sorts of ways at every level. So Sayed was in on several national science, debating and maths competitions. Did really well. Especially in the maths, as you'd expect . . .'

'There's a news article here,' said Mary. 'It's from *Milton Keynes Today*. Dated June 2003. I found it this morning and was going to add it to the record. It seems even more relevant now, judging by the way this is going now. Where is it? Ah. here we are.'

LOCAL WHIZ-KIDS MATHS CLUB HONOURED

The Sixth Form Maths Club at Lord Brook's School has won the first National Mathematics Competition of the new millennium. During the last eighteen months they have proceeded through all the heats, quarter-finals, semis and, in a nail-biting final, swept to victory.

The whole winning team of six boys and six girls will be awarded the famous Newton Prize tomorrow. The ceremony will be seen by millions when it is broadcast by the BBC at ten p.m. tomorrow on BBC Two. Team captain Joanna Wu said,'It was Sam who won it for us really. He made absolutely no mistakes at all. Sometimes I think he has a computer instead of a brain. He's our Newton all right!'

The ceremony will take place at Imperial College, London, and this year the Newton Prize will be awarded by Diana Stark, Professor of Predictive Mathematics, authoress, journalist and popular television personality . . .

'Damn! I wish we could see that programme!' said Mary.

'We can, if we can find an old video cassette recorder,' Ahmed said. 'Whoever talked to Joanna Wu as part of the Buckinghamshire Constabulary's investigation got the cassette her mother made of the broadcast. It's here in the Buckingham box. All nicely labelled up for us – by the good Mrs Wu, by the look of things. In some kind of Chinese script and – praise be to Allah – in English.'

It took the better part of two hours to get to the programme. First they had to find a VCR – and unearthed one eventually in Colour Sergeant Stone's little hideaway. But only after they had peeked in every office and disturbed every meeting in the building. Fortunately, the sergeant – unlike some of the colleagues whose blue-sky, out-of-the-box thinking had been disturbed by the video search – was prepared to be indulgent. Especially as the wise ex-Para was very well aware that on the Friday before the Christmas weekend, it was more likely to be blue-wrapping-paper thinking. And any boxes on any minds were likely to contain Christmas presents. But the fact that the Three Musketeers seemed to have no idea that it was the last working afternoon before the festival only made him more helpful. Accommodating, in fact. He cleared the work table and set up the little VCR/TV combination just in front of them. Then, always keeping at least one eye on the security cameras which were his responsibility, he produced some 'proper military' tea for them that made builders' brew seem anaemic and insipid in comparison. And Garibaldi biscuits.

TWENTY-ONE
Newton

They watched the little programme four times.

The slightly old-fashioned BBC credits rolled over a series of shots of Imperial College taken from the outside. Then the picture settled on the interior of a large hall packed with people. An audience facing a stage, as though this were a theatre. The stage was set out with twenty or so chairs and an imposing lectern.

Professor Diana Stark appeared in close-up, head and shoulders. She looked surprisingly young, vibrant, excited. The seven and a half years since seemed to have aged her, thought Mary. The headscarf she had chosen to wear for the evening made her look a little like Benazir Bhutto – another of Mary's heroines and one for whom she still mourned. 'Mathematics and science are being severely undervalued in the new school curriculum,' Diana Stark was saying trenchantly. 'Unless we support the next generation of mathematicians we'll end up with a crop of second-raters. Not because they don't have the intellect, you understand. Not because they don't have the drive or the ambition – one must particularly observe how hard those students with back-grounds from both Chinese and Indian subcontinents work in this context. But because they won't have the top-flight teachers. Innate ability and outstanding effort are not enough. The best minds need the best preceptor in order to flourish.

'And the Newton Prize is designed to ensure that the best mathematical minds of this generation are discovered and nurtured so that they can become the instructors of the best mathematical minds of the next generation. That is a great mission of mine. As we live in such an international society – a society with such wide and international roots – I cannot call it a *crusade* for fear of offending our Islamic brothers and sisters. Nor dare I call it a *jihad* – for the word has such unfortunate associations after the atrocities of 9/11. But it is very much a part of my life's work . . .'

The interviewer steered Professor Stark into safer waters and a voiceover explained, 'Professor Stark talked to us earlier this evening. As we look down on to the stage now, we see that the students themselves are taking their seats.' The screen faded to show the stage with a line of youngsters filing on to it out of the wings. The students were all dressed in smart school uniform. They seemed very self-possessed and calm – but even so, something of their excitement seemed to reach through the screen to Mary's wide eyes.

Excitement that seemed as nothing compared to the excitement on the face of a teenage girl clearly of Asiatic parentage. 'Joanna Wu,' said the interviewer. 'Can you please tell the viewers a little about your school, your team and how you came to win the Newton Prize?'

'Well . . .' Joanna began. 'I don't know how well you know Milton Keynes, but we always thought it was named after the great poet John Milton and the great economist John Maynard Keynes. At the Lord Brook School, we always strive to follow in the footsteps of men such as these. And of women such as Professor Stark. So, when our maths teacher Dr Abu-Sharkh suggested we form an after-school maths club we leapt at the opportunity . . .'

The screen began to fade away from the excited young woman, though her voice continued as slightly grainier, black and white footage faded in. '*We started going on local competitions and one or two of the later ones got on local radio and even local TV.*'

The screen was split into an upper and a lower level now, as though for an episode of *University Challenge*. In the top half, above a simple label stating LORD BROOK'S SCHOOL, sat Joanna and three other nameless team-mates. But beside her on her right was the unmistakable figure of Sayed Mohammed. Hair slicked down, immaculately parted. Shirt white. Tie tight. Blazer apparently recently cleaned and pressed. Every inch the top-flight British student. Face pale. Eyes large. Focus absolute.

Mary found it hard to breathe the first time she saw this close up; though it was hard for her to say why.

In the lower half of the screen, anonymous and unregarded, sat a team from, as the label stated, WICKHAM COLLEGE. The sound of Joanna Wu's voiceover was replaced at last. By a voice on the tape that was just a little distorted – the soundtrack no better than the visuals – doing its best to sound like Bamber Gascoigne. '. . . and multiply that number by the square root of two hundred and fifty-six. What is the ans—'

Even before the quiz master could say *answer* Sayed's buzzer buzzed. A light lit up in front of him. 'Three point eight seven eight,' he said decisively. 'Three point eight seven nine corrected, of course. I can go to six decimal places if you would like . . .'

'Well,' said the quiz master, clearly nonplussed.

'That would be three point eight seven eight seven eight four.'

'Correct!' announced the quiz master. 'Though I must admit I only have the answer corrected to three decimal places. Three point eight seven nine is what it says here. And that means Lord Brook's School have won this section of the competition. Bad luck, Wickham College. You've clearly come up against a team that is really on tip-top form. Lord Brook, what can I say? . . .'

The local television footage faded as the lights in the hall went down. A spotlight shone on to the lectern and a tall man strode forward. 'Ladies and gentlemen, honoured guests, boys and girls, viewers at home. May I welcome you all to the awarding of the first Newton Prize of the new millennium. And, as we forge through the early years of that millennium, it is perhaps most apt that the prize be awarded tonight by Professor Diana Stark, whose work has taken mathematics and forged it into a very potent force for seeing ever more clearly into the future. Some would say, indeed, into a tool through which it might one day be possible to *control* the future.

'But let us for a moment return to the past. It seems particularly apt that the story of this running of the competition whose victors we are celebrating tonight should have begun with a mathematical debate. To wit, the one that raged some twenty-four months ago, as to whether the new millennium would begin at the moment 1999 became 2000 or whether it might more properly be celebrated as 2000 passed into 2001 and the new age attained its *first birthday*, so to speak. For it was as a result of this debate that the competition we are seeing finish tonight was started in the summer of the latter year – rather than of the former. Calls went out to local authorities, and through them to governors and schools, boys and girls all over the country, that they should organize themselves into teams. That parish heats become town heats, so to speak; that town heats become district heats; that district heats become constituency heats and county heats. And so on and so forth . . .'

'*And so on and so forth*,' Mary mimicked, reaching for the fast forward.

After the first time of listening, she fast-forwarded even Diana Stark, for the professor's speech was largely a rehash of the interview she had already given to the presenter earlier. It was not until the camera turned its focus upon the students themselves as they started coming up to accept the individual prizes and certificates that accompanied the Newton itself that she returned the tape to normal speed. And indeed, in the later reviews, to slower and slower motion. For there was a little flaw in the presentation which caught Mary's notice at first – and then pulled in the rapt attention of the others.

The indefatigable Joanna Wu came up first and exchanged a few words with Professor Stark. As the women talked, their lips moved silently and the presenter gave a potted version of what they were saying to each other, extrapolated by his own imagination, as likely as not. The only point at which the sound and picture came anywhere near synchronization was when Joanna Wu said her own name, introducing herself, as the presenter said who she was. Then, as the girls were called up in order, the lip-sync came and went as Joanna introduced each of them. 'Sharon Keeping,' said the commentator. *Sharon*

Keeping, said Joanna's lips. Sharon, Joanna and the professor had a little chat. Certificates and prizes were handed over. Hands were shaken. Sharon curtsied and went to stand at the far side of the stage. The same thing happened with Aisha al-Rahman, Bashair Zamani, Jenny Chu and the rest. Joanna's lips moved, the presenter spoke.

The same happened with Charles Christopher O'Leary, first of the boys. But then the little glitch occurred. 'Sayed Mohammed,' said the presenter's voice. But Joanna's lips said something else. Sayed bowed courteously, shaking the professor's hand. Joanna chimed in, face animated and lips moving enthusiastically. Sayed, Joanna and the professor spoke for far longer than any of the others. The presenter burbled on, drifting into repetitions about the way the competition had been organized. At last Sayed was released to take his place with the others. Jonas Pratt, who succeeded him, and the others following Jonas, got very short shrift indeed. Until at last Joanna accepted the Newton Prize itself and held it above her head, looking more like an FA Cup winner than a staid mathematical student. The credits started to roll. And, 'Let's just go back to Sayed again, shall we?' suggested Mary. 'Let's see if we can finally get some kind of a handle on what Joanna is actually saying.'

Colour Sergeant Stone stuck his head round the door just at that moment. 'I'm afraid I'll have to chuck you out soon,' he said. 'It's obviously later than you think . . .'

'I don't suppose they taught you any lip-reading in the Paras, did they, Colour Sergeant?' interrupted Mary.

'As a matter of fact, Miss, yes. Well, not in the Paras precisely. I did a Black Ops course. All very Bravo Two-Zero.' He stepped in, began lecturing them as though they were a brick of favoured squaddies. 'There are circumstances when signals don't quite cut it, d'you see. And others where it's good to know what people are saying even when you can't hear them. Know what I mean?' He put his hands to his eyes as though holding binoculars. 'I'm surprised neither of you gentlemen got in any of that. I'd have thought it would be basic spook-craft. I'll bet James Bond can read lips.' He chuckled.

Both Pat and Ahmed shrugged. Stone came right in and stood easy, his interest piqued. 'What's it all about then, miss?'

'This. Look.' Mary pressed play. Sayed Mohammed leapt

out of flickering stasis and set off across the stage towards Joanna Wu and Professor Stark.

'The Chinese girl,' said Mary. 'Tell us what she's saying. It'll be a name first, I'd guess, and then some other stuff.'

Sayed came up to the professor. His hand reached out. He smiled modestly and tensed himself for that little bow. Joanna's lips began to move.

Mary's iPhone started ringing. She snatched it out and slammed it to her ear. '*Not now, father!*' she spat and hung up on Richard for the first time in her life.

Stone's concentration hadn't been disturbed at all, however. His lips were moving. Independently of the voiceover. Forming the same shapes as Joanna's. But no sound was coming out of his mouth either.

'Well?' demanded Mary. 'What's she saying?'

'She's saying,' said Sergeant Stone slowly, as though replaying the conversation in his head and repeating the words he heard without any understanding or intonation, 'she's saying, *And this is the star of the team, Professor. We couldn't have won without him. I think he'll be applying to Imperial and he's hoping to study with you. His real name's Sayed Mohammed but we all call him Sam because he likes having an English name too.* Then the tall bird in the headdress says, *Well, maybe we'd better call him Sam Newton in future.* Yeah. I'm pretty sure about that . . . *maybe we'd better call him Sam Newton in the future. Because he's apparently the best natural mathematician anyone's seen for quite a while. He comes from a famous new town. And he's just won you the Newton Prize.* And the kid says, *Sam Newton. Yes. I like the sound of that . . .*'

TWENTY-TWO
Imperial

Christmas fell on Sunday that year and the phone call Richard attempted so inopportunely was to remind Mary he was picking her up early to beat the rush out of town. Heritage Mariner was closing its main London offices

early. And it came as quite a shock to the Three Musketeers
to discover that London Centre was doing so as well. No
sooner had Colour Sergeant Stone finished reading Sayed
Mohammed's lips than he booted the three of them out of the
otherwise empty building with all the brusque efficiency of
Scrooge before Marley's ghost came visiting.

But on her way out, Mary pleaded a moment or so's indul-
gence to powder her nose. The carefully chosen little-girl-lost
phrase had the desired effect. Sergeant Stone suffered a
moment of uncharacteristic weakness. Instead of going to
the ladies', however, Mary ran down to Al Azhar and grabbed
her laptop and the memory sticks on to which she had been
saving everything. This time she answered her father's call,
though she was too busy to bother with a call of nature.
And when she pressed a quick Yuletide kiss on to the sergeant's
weathered cheek, he had the grace not to notice the big black
carry-case she was removing from the site, against the dictates
of company policy.

Mary hesitated on the corner of Creechurch Street,
suddenly utterly alone. Great big feathery snowflakes were
tumbling out of the upper darkness into the city lights, turning
black, white and yellow for a moment before they became
part of the grey-brown slush on the pavement. She pulled
up her collar and looked around. For an instant she felt list-
less, let down, bitterly disappointed. There was no sign of
the Chuckle Brothers, both of whom seemed to have vanished
into the shadows like more of Scrooge's ghostly guests. In
the handbag hanging on the outside of the carry-case there
were cards and little gifts for her partners in crime, and now
she had lost the opportunity even to wish them the compli-
ments of the season.

But then the opening bars of the *In paradisum* from Gabriel
Fauré's lovely Requiem Mass came floating in a baritone hum
on the gusty wind and suddenly Pat and Ahmed were beside
her. '*There* y'are, me darlin',' boomed Pat, who seemed to
have kissed the Blarney stone in the minutes they had been
apart. 'And *here* y'are!' A little box was thrust into her hands.
'Merry Christmas!'

'It's from both of us,' said Ahmed quietly. 'Though of course
my half's not really a *Christmas* present.'

'Then neither is this, Ahmed,' she answered a little breathlessly, pulling the gifts from her bag. 'Though yours is, of course, Pat.'

And she found herself swept into a thoroughly Irish bear-hug. Over Pat's shoulder, she saw Ahmed turning away, glancing at his watch, and as he hurried down the street she thought she heard the tinkling of his call-to-prayer timer.

Suddenly the winter evening seemed to take a lean and dangerous-looking form on the busy roadway in front of her. Headlight beams led back like the blaze of two great cat's eyes to the crouching darkness that was her father's Continental. The snowflakes defined it briefly, as though a swansdown duvet had burst just above it. But then the wind blustered it all away and that familiar snarling, throbbing black-panther shade returned. The passenger door swung open and she wriggled free of Pat's overwhelming embrace like a fly-half escaping from a ruck and maul.

'So Professor Stark was right. She did know him as Sam,' said Richard thoughtfully a few minutes later as the Bentley snarled towards south London. 'Now what are the implications of that little nugget?' Although his narrowed eyes were focused absolutely on the treacherous road ahead, his mind and imagination had been sucked into the strange world of Mary's investigation even before they had purred out of the City.

'The first thing as far as I'm concerned is that I'll have to go and see her,' announced Mary cheerfully – in exactly the same tones as those her father used when he was forced – against his better nature of course – to drive the Bentley in to work. 'Can you swing that? I mean, you know her well . . .'

'I don't. But I know a woman who does. I'll see what I can do.'

In fact he knew more than just any woman. Alan Pitt's prostate cancer had worsened rapidly and unexpectedly. The poor man was now in hospital and *hors de combat* – perhaps permanently. Southend West was beginning the long search for a new parliamentary candidate. The Prime Minister had been forced to reshuffle his Cabinet. The redoubtable Harry Blake was now Home Secretary. And as part of her price for accepting the notoriously poisoned chalice of the Home Office, she had poached Gloria Strickland from Culture Secretary

Maggie Emin. And so the survivor of the Chatham bombing –
cheerleader for the Richard Mariner fan club – was now Under
Secretary of State for Criminal Justice and Offender Management,
replacing Harry herself as the minister in charge of the prison
ship *Discovery*. In constant contact with Professor Stark as the
ship was slowly filled with carefully selected, mathematically
suitable prisoners. And more occasionally with Richard as she
tried to wheedle him into joining the administration's plans for
more ships like *Discovery*. Much too regularly for Robin's taste,
however – and not a little to her disgust.

'You won't be able to see Diana Stark till the New Year,
though,' warned Richard.

'Imperial goes back a week before we do,' announced Mary
airily, as though this was mere general knowledge. 'I could pop
in and see her sometime during the second week in January.'

'I'm surprised you haven't booked yourself in already . . .'
growled Richard, frowning.

Mary stole a glance at her father's lowering profile. 'Well,
her *secretary* said . . .'

'Mary! I was joking! You haven't . . .' Richard even swerved
a little as the shock of what she had said sank in. Fortunately
the road ahead was all but empty and the snow had stopped
falling.

'Gotcha!' she giggled wickedly. 'Are we *supposed* to be
driving on the right side of the road these days?'

'Devil-child!' he chuckled, straightening up.

'Still,' she said more sensibly, 'if Diana Stark did recognize him and he did use the name Sam Newton, then he almost
certainly did go to Imperial. And he is certainly an outstanding
mathematician. So if he *was* working with her, then he's an
expert in the same kinds of maths as she is an expert in . . .'

'That seems logical,' allowed Richard, sucked straight back
into the strange half-world of her researches.

'And, from what you've told me . . .'

'Which is everything . . .'

'. . . then that's the kind of maths the government is trying
to use to control the men aboard *Discovery* and the people in
the communities they come from.'

'And the terrorist organizations who programme, train,
fund and equip men who perform atrocities like Chatham
Dockyard.'

'Men like Sayed Mohammed, alias Sam Newton,' concluded Mary thoughtfully. 'That's more than just circular. That's spooky. That's almost *incestuous* . . .'

'It's certainly unsettling,' allowed Robin later that evening, as she and Richard sat over the remnants of dinner, alone at last. 'Perhaps even sinister.' She leaned forward a little, allowing the steam from her coffee cup to bathe her face with its Blue Mountain aroma. 'I can see why Mary wants to push on with her research. And why she wants to use you as a sounding board.'

'And why I'm keen to help her out,' persisted Richard. 'As long as she's not going to come hammering on the bedroom door at midnight looking for some help like she did during the last of her exams.'

'Don't flatter yourself, dearest. She and William are both far ahead of anything that we could actually help with.'

'Academically, perhaps . . .'

'But midnight is about the only chance she'll have for either research or for sounding you out, if our Christmas calendar is anything to go by,' Robin declared firmly. 'You know we're expected out both at lunch and dinner tomorrow. We do drinks for half of the parish after church on Christmas morning . . .'

'But we've Christmas dinner to ourselves . . .'

'By the skin of our teeth. Unless people just "drop in" like they did last year. Then there's all the traditional Boxing Day engagements.'

'Cold ham and turkey for the half of the parish who didn't come round on Christmas morning . . .'

'*And* of course we're supposed to be at the Greatorexes for lunch on the twenty-seventh, and you know their lunches usually last until supper time. Then, on the twenty-eighth . . .'

'And William and Mary are supposed to be coming to all these with us?'

'You know very well that William will be helping us out at all times as usual. He'll also be going to the rugby club bash on top of everything else. And you couldn't keep him away from the Greatorex girls with a cattle prod. That's where he's gone now, in fact. Mary's promised to do her bit too and *she* has always gone to the hunt ball into the bargain because she's known all the girls from their pony club days.

And I expect William will make her drag him along this year because . . .'

'Yes. I know. The Greatorex girls will be there.'

'Still, we'll see. Anyway. Early bed tonight. Choir rehearsal tomorrow – the vicar wants a full choral carol service as usual – and you'll be church-wardening both at midnight service and at ten o'clock carols on Christmas morning.'

'Serving God as well as Mammon. Well, Hammon . . . turkey. But I see what you mean. If Mary wants to push her researches much further then she'll simply have to miss out on her beauty sleep. Like she's doing at the moment, in fact. You want a hand clearing up?'

'Of course . . .' Robin began, getting busily to her feet. Richard rose a tiny bit less enthusiastically.

'*Father*,' came a distant summons. 'Father, I need you . . .'

'Bloody man!' said Robin as though Mary's call for help was Richard's fault. 'Off you go! She might have found out where Osama bin Laden's been hiding all these years.'

'Look,' said Mary excitedly as Richard entered her bedroom. 'The Met's input came in electronic form. Just a folder on a memory stick, so I transferred it straight over to this one.' She waved the miniature device at him. 'The whole thing. This is the first time I've opened it. I had no idea there would be so much information!'

The screen was filled with icons for about twenty folders, Richard saw at a glance. And a glance was all he got. For Mary, all uncontrolled enthusiasm as always, was pushing on. 'And if I click on this one marked Imperial, look what comes up!'

The screen filled with Word file icons. Each one had a few identification letters or numbers beneath. She clicked on 'StuReg0405'. A list of names appeared. '*Look!*' She scrolled down at breakneck speed. There, among the M's, the name was highlighted: 'MOHAMMED AL HAJJ Sayed Abu Minyar'.

'I expect his A level results are in the Buckingham box somewhere,' she said. Richard agreed heartily but found the pronouncement a little obscure. 'They'll have been straight A's though,' she continued thoughtfully. 'Top score in maths.'

'Is this what you wanted to show me?'

'Not all of it, no. Look . . .' She closed the file and sent her cursor scurrying around the icons once again. At last she settled on 'MalHCrs'. Clicked.

'*MOHAMMED AL HAJJ Sayed Abu Minyar. Courses 2004/5*' appeared as a heading. Beneath was a list. Pure Mathematics: Analysis. Algebra. Foundations of Analysis. Geometry and Linear Algebra. Mathematical Method. Mechanics. Probability and Statistics. Predictive Mathematics.

'He must have had to choose,' said Richard. 'Surely there's too many here . . .'

'No. He'll have done three units and each of these is likely to be part of a unit. He'll have done all of them over the full year. But he will have been able to specialize. Especially later.'

She closed that, clicked on the next. '*MOHAMMED AL HAJJ Sayed Abu Minyar. 2005/6*' appeared. This time the list of courses was shorter. Mathematical Method. Probability and Statistics. Predictive Mathematics.

And again: '*MOHAMMED AL HAJJ Sayed Abu Minyar. 2006/7*'. Predictive Mathematics: Probability. Chaos. Catastrophe.

She closed Sayed's final year course description and, to prove her point, clicked on the icon labelled 'PredMath':

Predictive Mathematics, said the heading on the University Maths Department page that came up.

Professor of Predictive Mathematics
Professor Diana Stark Room 666
Internal 48590 d.j.stark@imperial.ac.uk

'That's nothing new,' said Richard. 'Once we knew Professor Stark really did recognize him on board *Discovery*, the rest was pretty much inevitable.'

'No,' said Mary. 'No, but wait. That's not all.'

She scrolled down the page and there, hidden on an unsuspected extension, the helpful Maths Department handbook added:

Associate Tutor in Predictive Mathematics:
Dr M.F. Abu-Sharkh Room 667
Internal 48591 m.f.a.sharkh@imperial.ac.uk

'So what?' demanded Richard, who had not seen Joanna Wu's videotape of the award ceremony for the Newton Prize, or read any of the news clippings in the Buckingham box.

'It's the same man, it must be,' said Mary. 'Dr Abu-Sharkh was Sayed Mohammed's maths tutor at Lord Brook's School!'

'No!'

'Yes! I remember the name because it's so unusual. I'll check it again as soon as I can get back into London Centre. But I'm sure. I'm *certain*!'

'Well,' allowed Richard, grudgingly convinced, 'after all, there can't be *that* many Sharkhs in the sea . . .'

TWENTY-THREE
Sharkh

Bang on midnight, just as Robin had predicted, there came a thunderous knocking on Richard and Robin's bedroom door. 'It's for you,' Robin told her sleepy husband and he rolled out of bed. 'And it had better not be Gloria bloody Strickland this time,' she called after him as he shrugged his dressing gown over his pyjamas.

It was, of course, Mary. Still fully dressed, looking as though she was no more likely to sleep than a vampire on Red Bull. 'Sharkh,' she said, waving a printout triumphantly. 'Gott'im. It's the same man all right, *look . . .*'

'Look *somewhere else*,' called Robin. 'I gave up on two-hour sleep patterns when I stopped commanding supertankers.'

Mary dragged her still groggy father out into the corridor. Over her shoulder he caught an edifying glimpse of his son William tiptoeing towards his room with his shoes in his hand and his mop of golden hair and his clothing alike in the most spectacular disarray.

'Oh, don't mind *William*, daddy dearest,' stage-whispered Mary, her honeyed voice dripping sisterly poison. 'He's just escaped from the *Greatorex girls*.'

William, hearing as clearly as he was meant to, gave his sister the finger and dropped his shoes in the process. Wisely he decided to leave them where they were as he went through to his room in slow-motion mime, like a not entirely sober Marcel Marceau.

'Looks like a pretty narrow escape to me,' said Richard paternally, refusing to rise to Mary's bait – recalling vividly the way the twins had squabbled endlessly as children. 'I'll maybe have a word with him in the morning. Now what's so important, Mary?'

'I went on to the Imperial website after you left,' she said, pulling him imperiously after her. 'All the staff details were locked away. Even the click-throughs give you very limited info. Security in the modern age! But, I thought to myself, all the proper schools, colleges and unis that I know of have their magazines for old girls and alumni and so forth. And then it was just a question of tracking down the relevant magazine for Imperial. *Then* it was a matter of hunting the relevant issue. And look . . .' She surrendered the printout at last.

By no means a large article, it was headed simply, 'MATHS DEPARTMENT WELCOMES NEW ASSOCIATE'.

Dr Muammar Faisal Abu-Sharkh will join the Mathematics Department from the beginning of next semester. Dr Abu-Sharkh will replace Dr John Swain who has been appointed to the chair of Predictive Mathematics at Adelaide University, thus returning to his own *alma mater.* Dr Abu-Sharkh's treatise *The Catastrophe of Global Warming: weather prediction after René Thom* has garnered much positive comment among his peers and appeared briefly on the *Sunday Times* Best Sellers list. Dr Abu-Sharkh has been working at the Lord Brook School in Milton Keynes and will be relinquishing the post of Head of Maths there to join our faculty. He will be associating most closely with Professor Diana Stark who met him in 2003, when she awarded the Newton Prize to a Mathematics class from which he had created a winning team. She was so impressed by his work – as a mathematician, a catastrophe theorist and a teacher – that she remained in contact with him. And it was she who advised him to apply for his current position when it became apparent that Dr Swain might be moving on. But his appointment was as the result of the University's usual advertising, interviewing and appointment procedures.

'OK,' he allowed. 'More spookiness. Unless there's a mathematical theory to explain it all of course. Newton's equivalent of Jung's theory of synchronicity. Or Diana Stark's chaos theory of Six Degrees of Separation. But where does all this get you?'

'I don't quite know,' she answered. 'But I'll be very surprised if there *is* actually any kind of mathematical theory. And I'm a firm believer in the James Bond theory: Once is happenstance, twice is coincidence . . .'

'And three times is enemy action,' he completed thoughtfully, handing the paper back to her.

But it was William rather than Mary – or, indeed, James Bond – who proved to be the wave of the immediate future. His effective socializing with General Greatorex's granddaughters – another pair of twins but some eighteen months younger than William and Mary – was simply a warm-up for the festivities and responsibilities that filled the Christmas period.

So no more research was done until a good deal later in the week, and even that was a short and sketchy search for Abu-Sharkhs of any sort which revealed precious little that was either new or interesting. There were a lot of Abu-Sharkhs in the sea, after all; or there were on the Internet. But only one Muammar Faisal Abu-Sharkh, Doctor of Philosophy in the area of Predictive Mathematics, made it on to Google. There were reviews of *The Catastrophe of Global Warming* and one or two articles about the secondary school mathematics teacher who had written it. A man born in the obscure township of Buurhakaba, who had travelled the world, it seemed, before he attained his doctorate at the Islamic University of Karachi. And even then seemed to have become an economic migrant when he found that neither his qualifications nor his work were particularly welcome either in the Indian subcontinent or in Africa – where his membership of the Islamic Humanitarian Association had made him try for employment first. Now, as confirmed by the article from the Imperial magazine, he was beginning to gain the recognition he deserved.

The only other reference to Dr M.F. Abu-Sharkh that Mary unearthed was a brief report on an incident which had occurred

long ago in Pakistan, where several men working for the
Islamic Humanitarian Association had been hurt and killed
during an attack by an American unmanned Predator drone.
The group were helping local families to organize a wedding,
explained Dr Abu-Sharkh from his hospital bed. The suggestion that this was some kind of terrorist meeting was
outrageous. And the author of the tiny article tended to agree.
A list of dead and wounded was attached, together with the
note that one of them, a lad named Aamil Tantawi, had domi-
ciled like Dr Abu-Sharkh in England.

By the time Mary had managed to get that far, of course,
the New Year 2012 celebrations were seriously under way
and, in the face of a wall of absolute silence that answered
any further enquiries – even on the Internet – she became
distracted once again. She didn't even discuss her new find-
ings, such as they were, with her father, for he too was
becoming swept into the seasonal maelstrom. Not waving, as
the poem has it, but drowning.

If the Mariners' family Christmas was traditionally a whirl
of activity, it was as nothing compared to the demands of New
Year. And, of course, on top of their parents' celebrations,
there were more sporting and hunting revels for both William
and Mary, as well as the burgeoning social whirl resulting
from old friendships reawakened – made more irresistibly
urgent by the sense that there was so much catching-up to do.
And so little time.

Thus it was a thoroughly guilt-ridden Mary who arrived at
London Centre at ten o'clock precisely on the morning of
Monday 9th January. 'I need hardly have sneaked this out
past you,' she confessed to Sergeant Stone after he had admitted
her and she had dutifully wished him a happy New Year. 'I
did no real work at all.'

'Parties, was it?' he asked easily. 'Up to your armpits in
keen young Ruperts, I should guess, you being the old man's
daughter . . .'

'Ruperts? Old man?' asked Mary, sidetracked into thinking
of adventurous bears from her childhood and a bearded figure
rising from the sea.

'Junior officers. Your dad, the CO. Still. Never mind. You're
young. It's only a hobby with you. And anyway . . .'

The sergeant meant his words well – but they could hardly have been worse chosen. It was like telling Joan of Arc that the voices in her head would soon be advising her to put up her sword, take off her armour, settle down and have babies. Mary turned away from him mid-sentence and positively thundered down to Al Azhar. But the little room was dark and empty. Even the Buckingham boxes were gone.

Mary looked at her watch. Not that she was at all interested in the time. It was the present that the Chuckle Brothers had given her – opened in private and well away from the general celebrations round the Christmas tree more than a fortnight ago. And wept over a little, for it was exquisitely beautiful and rather unusual – the result of lengthy negotiations, she thought, and an extremely painstaking search. It suddenly seemed an absolute age to her since she had opened that lovingly wrapped little gift and admired the Arabic numbers on the dial. The gentle golden chimes of Ahmed's half of the present warned her suddenly and musically that it was time to prepare for prayer. Or that it would be if she were Muslim. She swung round, tensed to run back up to Sergeant Stone, but he had followed her down and was standing in the doorway. 'They've been reassigned,' he said simply. 'I was trying to explain. Al Azhar was closed down while you were away.'

'Who by? Why? What's going on, Sergeant?'

'Best ask your dad. He's the commanding officer. If he didn't order it, then sure as eggs is eggs there'll be a pile of bumf on his desk right about now, explaining who did and why. And I'll be wanting that laptop back as soon as you'd like as well, please, miss.'

Mary opened her mouth, though she had no idea as yet what she was going to say. Her iPhone started ringing.

TWENTY-FOUR
STARK

'Things seem to have progressed rather swiftly while we were down at Ashenden, even though I kept in touch with HM business as usual,' Richard explained as Mary prowled up and down his office like a caged tigress. 'There's a message here from Chief Inspector Clark, who asked me to look into things in the first place, warning me that the Crown Prosecution Service is ready to take Sayed Mohammed to trial. The letters warning us that we will be required as witnesses will arrive as soon as a court date has been set. We have to stop associating with any aspect of the case forthwith, therefore, or our testimony will be hopelessly compromised and we'll be useless in court.'

'But Pat and Ahmed aren't going to be witnesses . . .'

Richard held up his hand. 'They felt that they were getting nowhere with their work in Al Azhar. Both of them asked for reassignment last week – they were in London Centre from the twenty-eighth to Friday the thirtieth of December and came back in again from the third of January too. Pat's a field man and he's apparently convinced Jim Bourne to send him out to do a little digging around on site, so to speak. Ahmed has defected to The Bounty, effectively. Or, if I know anything, he's simply been poached. Rupert Bligh was still scratching around for an engineer to send aboard *Discovery* – again at my request and . . .'

'And Ahmed was trained as an engineer. I remember. I didn't realize it was as a ship's engineer though . . .'

'It wasn't. But they've got a ship's engineer on board already. What they need is someone who knows his way around the civil stuff – electrical and plumbing. That sort of thing.'

'Christ, Dad, I thought Ahmed was a spook, not a plumber . . .'

'Bit of both. Think about it. Even in Waziristan, they need guys to fix the lights and the toilets – plumbers can get in anywhere.'

'Jesus! That's thinking outside the box!'

'You have no idea, my love. I read an article somewhere that the CIA stopped using cash to fish for information – they started using Viagra instead. Think about it! All those tribal leaders getting on in years needing to have harems of a certain size in order to protect their standing. Viagra was the wave of the future there for a while. Guaranteed that everyone stayed happy in every conceivable way. The answer to a lot of prayers. So a Muslim who knew about plumbing was the answer to Rupert Bligh's prayers, I understand.' Richard gestured to a pile of flimsy printed memos on the big mahogany desk in front of him.

'*Bumf,*' said Mary, remembering Sergeant Stone's word for it. 'One favour before I go back to my studies, then. One that you *promised* . . .'

'Already done,' he said with just a trace of weariness. 'Professor Stark will see you at eleven a.m., Friday morning. That's Friday the thirteenth,' he added warningly.

'Oh, you superstitious man!' she laughed, suddenly sounding a lot like her mother. 'But thanks anyway, Dad! Thanks a lot.'

Friday 13th January 2012 dawned bright and clear. It was unseasonably warm by nine o'clock and as Mary ran up the steps to the main entrance of the maths department, she seriously considered slipping her pullover off. She glanced at her watch instead. Although the Arabic numerals still struck her as strange, the hour hand pointed towards the '11' position and the minute hand lingered behind it over the '10'.

Her mind was teeming with questions and in her bag was the sheet of A4 lined paper on which, during the last few days while she tried to get to grips with her holiday homework assignment, she had scribbled a list of the most important. On one side were vague musings on the practical, legal and constitutional implications of the replacement in 2009 of the Law Lords – the Lords of Appeal in Ordinary, to give them their full official title – with a Supreme Court. On the other were questions such as, *What was Sam Newton's main area of study?How well did you know him?Why do you think he preferred an anglicized name to Sayed Mohammed?Did he ever do anything that made you suspect he had terrorist links?*

Mary signed in, too excited and apprehensive to take in much about her surroundings. The directions to Professor Stark's room went way over her head in a dreamlike haze, but she found the main corridor where the maths tutors' offices were and wandered down it, looking at the names and numbers stencilled on the doors. The last two were ajar and she ended up going halfway into the room as she tried to read the name.

'Yes?' demanded a sharp voice suddenly, just as she made out the name of Dr M.F. Abu-Sharkh on the label.

'Oh, excuse me, Dr Sharkh,' she said, looking towards the sound of the voice. 'I was looking for Professor Stark's room.'

'That's Dr *Abu*-Shark*h*.' A slight, hunched man was standing by the desk, watching her coldly and suspiciously with eyes so brown they seemed like black holes ringed with ivory set in the ebony mask of his face.

As she repeated the name, adding the *Abu* and aspirating the final *h*, she studied him. His skin was darker than she had expected. His hair was dense and curly, greying at the temples but still black and glossy over the crown of his head. He wore a short grey beard that matched his temples, but on the left cheek it was a little wispy because the flesh there was shiny with scar tissue. Tissue that stretched up towards his forehead far enough to make his eyebrow droop and pull a black cowl partly over his eye, giving him in Mary's imagination a vaguely piratical air. His left ear seemed to have melted. His left hand, little more than a claw, leaned on a stick that led her to suppose the leg was little better preserved than the cheek. She remembered the brief web article about the wedding party and the American drone in Pakistan. Dr Abu-Sharkh's statement from his hospital bed.

'Professor Stark's office is next door,' said Abu-Sharkh firmly. 'Please close the door behind you. I do not want any more uninvited guests today.'

Professor Stark's reception could hardly have been more different. 'Do sit down, my dear,' she ordered, fussing about her office as she spoke. 'I have some tea here – Twinings or Earl Grey from Waitrose – or rooibos from my African adventures. Though there's coffee if you'd prefer Java, actually bought the last time I was in Jakarta. And chocolate biscuits. *Belgian* chocolate, too. I was across in Europe last week and brought back as many as I could carry with me. What

---

can I do for you? You come *very* highly spoken for, you know. Gloria Strickland, Under Secretary for Law and Order or something, was on the phone on Tuesday and she said even Home Secretary Blake would recommend you if need be. As though I would ever refuse to see a student! The very idea . . .'

She leant forward, tea things and piled biscuits all on a round tray with a strange, vaguely Arabic pattern on it. As soon as she put it down, she sat opposite Mary and rested her hands on her cord trousers in a gesture oddly reminiscent of Pat Toomey. And she, like him, seemed to have kissed the Blarney stone. 'Though I have to say, your charming father's kind little message would have been enough – more than enough. He's a past Master of the Guild of Merchant Venturers of course, and the Merchant Venturers are the London City Guild who give far and away the greatest amount of money to the college. Have done for years, and I mean *years*. They funded the original College of St Gregory and St Martin in fourteen forty-something. Though I expect that was a *little* before your father's time, so he may not have real-ized how much naked power he can actually wield over us poor lesser mortals.' She swept back the fall of her hair, settled the brooch on the high Victorian collar of her blouse and picked up her plate.

Somewhat overwhelmed, Mary sat with a lovely Spode teacup steaming in one hand and a Belgian chocolate biscuit melting in the other.

'Was it something to do with my theories, dear?' asked Professor Stark more gently. 'Something to do with my travels and contacts? I've been everywhere in the last year alone. Melbourne, Sydney, Jakarta, Shanghai, Hong Kong, Singapore, Somalia, Egypt, Saudi, *Moscow*.' She rolled her eyes. 'Hamburg, Antwerp. Brussels, Liège, Bruges. That's where the biscuits came from – do take a another one, dear. What about my charity work? Or did your devious father send you to spy out what I'm up to with my government work in case he's finding it too hard to resist both Harry Blake and Gloria Strickland combined? Or did you just want a more general chat?' She settled herself back in her chair, and looked down at Mary a little like a cobra eyeing a dormouse. 'Let's start at the beginning, shall we dear? Are you a mathematician yourself?'

Under the goad of a direct enquiry, Mary at last found her voice. 'No, Professor. I'm studying law. Ethics . . .'

'Ha!' exploded the professor. 'Mutually exclusive, I'd have thought! Unless it's Islamic law, of course, coming straight out of the Qu'ran. And it's Diana! No one calls me Professor in that way. Except your father sometimes. And a dreadful little man called Weeks. But go on . . .'

'English. History . . .' Mary took refuge in a sip of tea, fearful that she had already said too much.

'Nothing to overlap with my disciplines then! But go on! You must have wanted to ask me something, child . . .'

'I was in the Chatham bombing,' Mary blurted, surprising herself.

'Oh, you poor thing!' Diana Stark leaned forward. Her hair fell over her face like a veil. 'Were you injured?'

'No. My father and I were very lucky. Not like Dr Sharkh next door . . .'

'That's *Abu*-Shark*h*, dear. He's very particular.'

'We weren't hurt and actually we managed to help one or two people.'

'Gloria Strickland, among others. She told me your father helped her. Didn't mention you.'

Mary plunged on, given increasing courage not only by the professor's kindness but also, oddly, by the way the veil of hair was hiding her face. 'The first person whom we helped was a young man we found in the water. I gave him the kiss of life . . .'

'That was very brave of you, dear. Though not very wise. Or *proper* . . .'

'His name turned out to be Sayed Mohammed and he has been charged with causing the explosion . . .'

'Then you were *doubly* lucky to have survived, were you not?'

'I don't know. But my father says that when you saw Sayed Mohammed on the prison ship *Discovery* you thought he was a student of yours called Sam . . . Sam Newton or something . . .'

'Did he? I don't remember. I see so many students that they all start to look the same in the end.' One hand swept back the veil of hair. The blazingly intelligent gaze settled on Mary and she felt her tongue begin to shrivel. Or that might just have been the effect of the scalding tea and the thick sweet chocolate.

'But you must remember this one. You awarded him the Newton Prize . . .'

'I awarded the Newton Prize to a girl called Joanna Wu. A student of Dr Abu-Sharkh's. He had trained the team from his school, but none of them was called Newton. It was one of the things that recommended him to me. We stayed in contact . . .'

'His real name is Sayed Mohammed. He called himself Sam Newton to fit in with the others at school or something, I suppose. And he did come here. He studied pure maths from September 2004 to July 2008. He specialized in predictive maths – chaos theory and catastrophe. When you thought you recognized him on the *Discovery* you were right. You did. He was one of your students!'

'I'm sorry to disappoint you, my dear. I may have thought I recognized him. It is encouraging to know that I got his name right – at my age, the precision of recall is beginning to go out of focus, as I said. But he wasn't one of my students. If he studied what you say he studied, then he must have been one of Dr Abu-Sharkh's young men.'

'What does that mean, Professor?'

'It means he studied a completely different branch of our mathematical disciplines. What, did you suppose he had picked my brains about my terrorist control theories? That I had given a terrorist suspect the keys to my particular kingdom so he could use everything I have worked with – against the government, the Home Secretary, the Under Secretary of State for Criminal Justice and Offender Management? Did you imagine some terrible terrorist plot centred aboard that ship your father and I went round? This is real life, my dear, not some kind of spy story. If this deluded boy studied here, and I must suppose that he actually did, do you know what he would have been working on with the good doctor? The butterfly effect! Lorenz. Feigenbaum and Libchaber. Mandelbrot. Gleick. Predictive mathematics and the forecasting of weather. Not terrorists or terrorism, dear. *Weather!*'

Mary put down her empty cup and the last bite of her biscuit numbly. She had no real idea what she had been expecting to learn from her heroine, but the revelation was so bizarrely unexpected that it made her mind go utterly blank. 'Not bombs

– barometric pressures,' insisted Professor Stark, warming to her theme. 'Not outrages *– rainfall.* Not jihad *– jet streams.'*

Mary found herself on her feet with her chocolate-smeared handbag clutched to her chest like a stab vest. 'Thank you, Professor,' she began uncertainly.

'*Diana*, my dear,' insisted the professor, rising as well. 'Now, if that's all . . .'

The chimes from Mary's present sounded, warning the faithful that it was time to start preparing for noon prayer. Diana Stark jumped as though stung. She looked around the room, frowning. Mary spread more melting chocolate as she switched the watch's function off. 'That's my alarm,' she said, breathlessly. 'It's time I was—'

But at once the mechanical chimes were taken up. And this time there was no doubt. They came from a cupboard in the professor's office.

'And that's my alarm, dear.' she said easily, her composure regained and her smile firmly fixed back in place. 'Off you go now. And give my regards to your father . . .'

A moment later Mary was outside in the corridor, hesitating outside Dr Abu-Sharkh's door. Behind both the professor's door and the doctor's there were quiet, restful sounds. Sounds very much at odds with the uneasy thunder of Mary's own heart. And, indeed, as she felt the icy threat that seemed to emanate from Dr Abu-Sharkh's closed office – in sharp contrast with the friendly warmth and chocolate odours of Diana Stark's – the tension across her shoulders seemed to be telling her emphatically that she had only narrowly escaped the most dreadful danger of her life so far.

TWENTY-FIVE
DHUHR

Ahmed Haroun Tewfik stopped working the instant that his tiny prayer timer tinkled. Fifteen minutes to *Dhuhr* noon prayer, he thought. He would certainly have to perform a very careful *wudu* ablution today, for his work on the plumbing had made his hands uncommonly dirty. But at least he had not become so soiled as to require a full shower or *ghusl*.

And yet even that inconvenience had been of benefit to his secret mission. For his handler – later his trainer – in Peshawar had been correct when he said that a screwdriver and a plunger open all doors. Ahmed had been to every part of the floating prison. He had replaced lightbulbs and fuses in every cell. He had seen to the wiring of the computers in the prisoners' library. He had cleared the plumbing in the communal ablutions and had unblocked pipes in personal washbasins. He had met Sayed Mohammed on several occasions now, and had found himself almost looking into a mirror. For the terrorist prisoner was a man of his own age, who filled his cell time reading the Holy Qu'ran, who discussed matters of faith with the mullah and occupied his free time on the computers, apparently working out complicated mathematical formulae. Ahmed found this disturbing, for, like everyone who successfully led a double life, he was well aware that other apparently simple people could be harbouring the darkest and most dangerous thoughts and plans.

Ahmed had set the gentle unbeliever Mary Mariner's gift to ten minutes before prayer times – but as soon as he had come aboard, he had been forced to set his own to the earlier time. For he was all too often called to deal with substances that the Holy Qu'ran defined as filthy. He allowed himself a good fifteen minutes to prepare for prayers, therefore. Some mosques where he had worshipped in his youth called the faithful a good half hour before prayers to allow a very full ritual cleansing. But such a requirement should hardly be needed in the almost antiseptic environment of a modern city – or even of a modern ship such as this one.

Ahmed was finding some aspects of life aboard *Discovery* unexpectedly pleasurable. His objectives were to simply follow the dictates of his faith in his daily life and work, and to observe, record and ultimately report the doings of those around him. He found his situation strangely restful – when he allowed his secret imperative to take a back seat in his mind. How extremely unlike the relentlessly bustling, rude, discourteous, insensitive, thoughtless, profoundly irreligious England he regularly inhabited, the ship seemed to him to be a haven of civilization, ordered, calm, dominated by the unchanging rituals and requirements of his faith. But of course it was also a place of ill-caged hatred and possibly deadly danger. Like that of Sayed Mohammed, like that of Ahmed himself, the calm face hid something deeper, darker.

Ahmed pushed open the door into his cabin, already reaching for the taps over his little bedside basin, already thinking *I am performing wudu . . .*, his lips unconsciously moving to form the word, '*Bismillah . . .*' But his attention was brutally wrenched away from his preparation for prayer, almost as if he had been attacked by a gang of crusader enemies. His cabin had been searched. Very thoroughly searched. Nothing seemed to have been taken, for everything seemed still to be there – from his copy of the *Muslim Weekly* to his copy of the Holy Qu'ran. But nothing was quite as he had left it – and long years of habit and experience had trained him to leave things exactly. Nothing missing, maybe – but what might have been left behind? he wondered.

The back of his neck prickled uncomfortably. His heart gave a lurch – the kind of sensation in his chest that he thought he would never feel again now that he was no longer an undercover operative gathering intelligence among the radicalized students in the FAST University of Peshawar. Before he started on the long and tortuous journey that had led him to Heritage Mariner, London Centre and Al Azhar. His eyes narrowed and his mind moved on to a different plane entirely. But he did not hesitate or deviate. The man he was pretending to be would never have noticed the disarrangement of his possessions.

The man he was pretending to be, therefore, would complete his preparatory prayer. He would go through the *wudu* rituals swiftly and fluently, pausing only when the voice of the muezzin called. Would complete his preparations exactly as he had done every day during the weeks he had been aboard.

Then he would leave without a second look or backward glance and go swiftly to the little library, where Chief Engineer Saleh Meshud and he would go through the *Dhuhr* side by side as brothers should. Saleh, who had welcomed him aboard those weeks ago with an open-heartedness rooted both in good nature and in genuine relief that he at last had the help he needed. Saleh, whom the infidel warders called Archie, because he chose to shave his head, and seemed to the ignorant and unbelieving to be bald. Shoulder to shoulder as brothers, standing, bowing and kneeling through the four cycles as required, their *taqiyah* skullcaps establishing their faith and purpose where their white overall uniforms never could. Needing the mullah's directions, however – and Saleh's little compass that pointed to the *Qiblah*, because the March sky outside the mean window behind them was laden with leaden clouds.

Brothers as ship mates – even aboard this forsaken tub. Brother engineers, though the younger had trained in Peshawar and the older at Heriot-Watt near Edinburgh. Brother Pakistanis – though one had come here via two generations in Glasgow and the other through one generation in Lewisham. Brothers in Islam. Brothers in *Umma*, the worldwide federation designed to bind every Muslim man to every other. Overcoming, with men of good heart, even the rift between Sunni and Shi'ia. For without the *Umma*, how may the faithful man achieve the five pillars – or the twelve exhortations – be he Sunni or Shi'ia? To whom will he profess his faith? Beside whom will he perform *Salah* prayers? With whom will he fast at *Ramadaan*? To whom will he donate his *zalat* charity?

Zalat not merely of giving but also of doing. It was the *zalat* of doing that took so many young Muslims to the poorer parts of the world where their actions could do the most good. That – and the combination of circumstances arising from links with villages only a few generations in the past where grandparents, uncles and cousins still lived, the universal brotherhood of Islam and the requirement of pilgrimage to Mecca for everyone seeking salvation. And with whom will he travel that holy journey, the *Hajj*?

Beside whom, Sunni or Shi'ia, will he begin his *jihad* – if all the other ways still will not guarantee his place with the prophets in paradise?

Side by side with Saleh Meshud, therefore, Ahmed went through the rituals of prayer. His hands and lips, shoulders and back and body moved in the required gestures. He raised his hands. He lowered his arms. He bowed. He knelt. He rose and began again, affirming the pureness, the oneness, the greatness of God and reciting the first chapter of the Holy Qu'ran.

But it was all utterly in vain, for in his heart and mind he was not thinking the required thoughts that should ascend like a sacrifice to Heaven. The whole of the *Dhuhr* seemed to epitomize the duality of his life aboard. Of the prison ship itself, in fact. For while he conformed outwardly and fitted in like a good Muslim should, inwardly he was not a Muslim at all. Inwardly he was a spy. He was thinking, first, that it was most likely Governor Weeks or Chief Warder Burke who had searched his room. He thought of them rather than of anyone else aboard because if any of the other groups had begun to suspect him, it would not have been a subtle search – it would have been a knife between the ribs. Or a bludgeon on the back of his head. Or a blowtorch and some tricky questions.

The only fact that gave him second thoughts about the governor and his henchmen was that they had taken so long to get around to it. But they would have done this at some time or another, he thought, because he was an unknown quantity, outside their control. And what they could not control they would not trust, for they seemed to Ahmed petty and pathetic men.

For in spite of the fine words that had been said to Captain Mariner all those months ago, there were almost no Muslims among the guards. And those that there were seemed isolated. Lumped in with the other workers – like Saleh, like Ahmed himself – with the prisoners.

Beneath the ordered surface, the ship was broken into two main camps separated by fearful ignorance. Weeks, Burke and their men were ignorant and therefore suspicious of the mullahs, the cooks, the cleaners, the engineers and all the prisoners. And the Muslims aboard, sensing their fearful antipathy, were guarded – occasionally armed – against them. But of course they were also armed against each other. Prisoners against free men. Sunni against Shi'ia.

Ahmed had worked very hard at keeping a foot in both main camps, for he was here to get the lie of the land as well as watching Sayed Mohammed for Jim Bourne and Captain Mariner. But he had seen almost at once that it would be impossible to swim with both the dolphins and the sharks for any length of time.

The calculating spy inside the praying man continued to reason secretly that if it was Governor Weeks who had caused his room to be searched, then there would certainly be some kind of listening or watching device left somewhere. So they could keep an eye on him as effectively as they spied upon the prisoners. Perhaps he should search for such devices, therefore, although in such a way that he could find them without seeming to do so. If he found them, then he would know who had placed them there. For although such whispers of gossip as he had heard suggested that the prisoners might be in possession of makeshift weapons and other illegal stuff, none of them was capable of placing a camera or a microphone anywhere. Or, as far as he could see, had any reason to do so.

And if Weeks and Burke did not realize he knew he was being observed, he could very well turn the situation against them. A camera was a spy. And a spy is only as good as his information. It was one of the first rules of spycraft, as it had been taught to him, that if you ever found a spy you turned him and used him to your advantage. You never unmasked him, arrested him or locked him up, or worse – until he was utterly gutted, blown and useless as a pawn in the double game.

As Ahmed knelt beside the powerful figure of Saleh Meshud and touched his forehead to the floor, he thought back over the last day or so. If Governor Weeks and Chief Warder Burke had taken action, then it may have been that he had done something to trigger that action. But there was nothing that sprang to mind at all – for he was an extremely careful man and a surprisingly experienced spy, given his relative youth. But of course he had filled his life with spycraft instead of friends, family, wife, children . . .

The only break in routine during the last few days had been the visit of Professor Stark. Now that the ship was fully staffed and all the cells were full, she had come aboard to oversee the next step of the research – which Ahmed seemed to be one of the few people aboard to understand. She had interviewed half a dozen prisoners, including Sayed Mohammed. And she had passed out forms for everyone newly arrived to fill in.

Ahmed had filled his in on behalf of the man he was pretending to be – but that man shared his name, qualifications, profession and previous employer. That man was Ahmed Tewfik, late of Heritage Mariner, engineer. Rupert Bligh had not had the time – nor seen the necessity – to manufacture any complicated aliases. All he had done was to talk to his contacts in Counter-Terrorist Command and the ubiquitous Criminal Records Bureau to cover anything unexpected that might turn up when Tewfik's background was security checked for the sensitive job of fixing the pipes and wires aboard the prison ship *Discovery*. For, of course, a simple civil engineer was all this Ahmed Tewfik appeared to be.

When the rituals of prayer were completed, it was usual for Ahmed and Saleh to take early lunch. They left the library side by side, therefore, and walked quietly down towards the dining areas. In past days they had filled these walks – and indeed, much of the mealtime – with discussions about what work needed to be completed in the afternoon. Today Saleh began a similar conversation as they walked, but Ahmed hardly heard a word the big engineer was saying.

For he had just realized that there was, in fact, something missing from his room. The piece of paper he had been using – perhaps a little irreligiously – as a bookmark in his Holy Qu'ran. If he closed his eyes he could see the holy volume now – lying almost exactly where he had left it beside his bed. But the gilded top of the pages was a ribbon of unbroken gold – no scrap of blue writing paper protruded. He was certain. It was gone.

How foolish he had been not to realize sooner. How stupid he had been to bring the thing aboard – even though it was only an unconsidered trifle placed between the pages of the holy book. The one chink in his armour of anonymity; the one proof that he might not be precisely who he claimed to be. Mary Mariner's letter of thanks for the prayer-watch Christmas present.

TWENTY-SIX
BUURHAKABA

Mary's thank-you letter fell out of Pat Toomey's passport as he took it out in the passport control area of Peshawar International Airport. Unlike Ahmed, who had attended university here, Pat had not kept Mary's letter out of any sentiment. He was naturally less tidy, however, and had shoved the slip of bright blue writing paper in the inside pocket of his jacket after glancing through it back in January. It had remained there, forgotten, for a good two months. Until it insinuated itself between the passport pages now. He regretted the untidiness. The forgetfulness. He regretted the jacket, frankly, for it was unseasonably hot for March and the temperature outside was the better part of forty degrees Celsius.

Humming a few bars of the *Dies irae* from Verdi's Requiem, he placed the passport on the desk in front of the uniformed officer and stooped to retrieve the letter. When he straightened, his visa had been stamped. But the officer refused to let him have the passport for a disturbing couple of moments until at last he let it go and waved Pat through.

Those moments of hesitation – every traveller's nightmare – had simply been designed, Pat realized, to make doubly sure his face was recorded on the security camera which might have missed him as he stooped to retrieve the letter. Anyone else might have been unnerved by the experience, even so. But not Pat.

'It isn't only what you know. It's who you know . . .' he thought to himself as he pocketed his passport once more and walked through to baggage claim, still humming the *Dies Irae*. And Pat knew almost everyone there was to know, both here and in Islamabad.

Patrick Aloysius Toomey may have started out working undercover in Ireland, trying to track and turn members of every terrorist organization from the most dyed-in-the-wool Provisional IRA man to the most rabid UVF volunteer. But he had rapidly become aware of the international nature of the terrorist threat he was fighting. He had been scouted at Trinity by a SIS recruiter working with the Garda Intelligence branch and had undergone standard training in London, Norfolk and the Brecon Beacons.

He had started out in operations with an old stager called Leary who had been involved in tracing IRA funding and arms back to Libya and beyond in the old days. It had been Leary who got Pat up to speed on the way the PLO trained the Provos in their camps in the desert. How the guns and explosives being used against the Taliban in Afghanistan could all too easily follow the ancient drug routes down out of the

golden triangle through Pakistan, the Middle East and Turkey
to the streets of London and Belfast.

Other operatives looked west; concentrated on the US
fundraising, the strong-arming, bank robbing and the porn.
Pat looked east, even after Leary was vaporized by a car bomb
in the Shankill Road in the closing days before peace broke
out. For when the CIA started arming the Taliban to fight the
Russians even more effectively, suddenly a complete new level
of weaponry began to flow down from the Waziri hills, finding
its way eventually to secret little havens all along the Waterford
coastline. Thence up to Derry and the Bogside – or the
Waterside. And Pat went on to the commercial market and
found his way to London Centre.

So the man who started out working in the Crumlin Road
soon had contacts in Karachi. From Belfast to Kabul was not
such a big step. Or from Portadown to Peshawar, for that
matter.

Tariq Mahsud was waiting on the far side of the barrier as
Pat wheeled his bag out into the brightness. When they first
met, Tariq had been a major in the Special Forces Karrar
Counter-Terrorism Battalion. Whether he was still a Black
Stork or whether he had moved on – up, or out like Pat – was
something they no longer discussed. But the friendship still
stood; the favours were still owed – and would be honoured
when settlement was demanded. And in an environment where
almost every other man visible was wearing some kind of
uniform, Tariq's starched cotton short-sleeved shirt stood out
almost as much as Pat's rumpled and sweat-stained jacket.
Proclaiming them to be associates. Brothers of a sort.

Fortunately, Tariq's Honda Accord was air conditioned, and
Pat spent much of the twenty-five-minute drive into Peshawar
city cooling down and catching his breath. 'We going to the
office, Tariq?' he managed at last.

'The office has moved. Too easy a target, even these days,'
answered Tariq. 'I thought I'd show you Hayatabad. They've
been making good progress there. And even out in Shalman
Park there are enough hot spots to allow my laptop on to our
intranet – and on to the Internet come to that.'

'We're not going to sit outside are we?' asked Pat, who was
still recovering.

'No,' chuckled Tariq. 'You're booked into the Pearl Continental Hotel for a couple of nights. We're going to a safe house nearby. Heritage Mariner is footing the bill I hope, otherwise you may have to sell your house, your wife and your children . . .'

'As ever, these days. It's more than Security or Intelligence ever did . . .'

'I have a temporary office nearby, as I say. It's not next door but it's still just off Route Five.'

'Why not use the hotel?'

'Security. Sending the army into Waziristan didn't sort everything out, even if it seems to have chased many of the most powerful leaders away. They spread like the swine flu. Everywhere from Syria to Somalia. We still have the old problems here, though. Because they still have the old hatreds, the old contacts, the old funding. Access to the same old munitions. Truck bombs. Car bombs. Motorcycle bombs. Vest bombs. Belt bombs. Suicide bombers seeking *jannah* through *shahada*. Paradise through martyrdom. One guy a couple of years ago nearly killed the President with a bomb shoved up his backside. His *wudu* before his *shahada* must have been particularly thorough.'

'And his backside must have been pretty capacious.'

'You might think so. I sometimes think that they'll pack explosives into anything that'll move and blow themselves and everyone else away.'

'We had a boat bomb at Chatham what, seven months or so ago . . .'

'I know. The trial's just about to start from what I hear.'

'At the London Central Criminal Court. The Old Bailey, yet. The people I work for were involved. They'll be giving evidence.'

'And the boy facing the charges, Sayed Mohammed, is the one you're checking up on now.'

'That's about the size of it. Just like old times.'

'It's a long way to come, though,' observed Tariq, turning off Route 5 into the great, as yet unnamed blocks of Hayatabad. 'We have secure communications and video conferencing now. You can even book your rooms at the Pearl online from anywhere in the world.'

'I know. But I'm a groundwork man. You know that. And I

really feel it's important, you know? I've been working on this off and on for months and this is the point I've reached in the inquiry. I'm not out here just trying to build up my carbon footprint, Tariq. In fact I've a nasty feeling my carbon footprint has just taken its first step. Its first step of many.'

Tariq brought the Accord to a halt outside an apparently vacant property. A property awaiting the interest of an extremely well-off purchaser, by the look of things. 'Fair enough,' he said. 'Come into my parlour.'

At least it was cool inside the house. And the one room that Tariq and Pat were going to work in had been well prepared for them. Tariq set up his laptop and linked it to a system that looked as though it would enhance its capabilities by at least one order of magnitude. Pat found a fridge in the corner and pulled out a couple of bottles of ice-cold fizzy water. As he unscrewed the top of his he started talking.

'Sayed Abu Minyar Mohammed al Hajj flies out of Heathrow with a couple of his cousins, Raashid and Saami Tantawi, December twenty-eighth 2010. All legal and above board. Working with the Islamic Humanitarian Association, which is a registered and recognized charity with us. With which organization they have travelled abroad before, both individually and as a group. Which, among other reasons, is why we are keeping a careful eye on them. We have the flight number and all that stuff. We have photos of them going out through passport control, which I'll tell you how to access in due course. On a memory stick here – if your airport security haven't wiped the memory. But even if they have, you can access the original files. Oh, the joys of Windows Seven with its online memory dumps. Anyway, they fly PIA to Peshawar with a stopover in Bahrain. They arrive here in the evening of December twenty-ninth.'

'And I have pictures of them coming off that flight through passport control. There are cameras in baggage collection too but they were not caught on those last time.'

'OK. The Tantawi boys return in March 2011. St Patrick's Day as chance would have it. That's the seventeenth. PIA again. Exactly the same flight – but in reverse. And we have pictures from passport control and from baggage handling. Cases all checked. Clean. Nothing incriminating in them at all.' Pat sounded faintly disappointed.

'We have records of their whereabouts and doings in the interim, Pat,' Tariq sympathized. '*Zalat* of charitable work in Waziristan. Under the eyes of the army of course. I have a report here from a lieutenant in the Intelligence Corps. But the Islamic Humanitarian Association is a recognized charity here too. It is even loosely federated with the Red Crescent. If they were plotting anything of a terrorist nature they would have to have been almost unbelievably cunning – for, as I say, there were eyes on them at all times.'

'But it's not the Tantawi boys we're interested in, is it? Not at this stage, anyway. It's Sayed Mohammed. And as far as I've been able to establish through all those weary months of trawling through the Internet and whatnot, Sayed Mohammed stepped off the PIA flight, picked up his cases, posed for your security pictures and then vanished off the face of the earth.'

'We have no record of him up in Waziristan,' agreed Tariq. 'There seems to have been no reported sighting of him . . .'

'Of his papers? Everyone here has papers . . .'

Tariq, scrolling through his records, shook his head regretfully.

'But surely that should have started alarm bells ringing? Boy arrives. Boy steps off plane. Boy vanishes.'

'Even in the UK I believe thousands of people vanish every year. It is the same here. Girls disappear. Boys vanish . . .'

'But not *this* boy! Tariq. Not this boy. I mean, someone over here knew enough to send a standard alert to Counter-Terrorism in London. *Registered suspect gone AWOL.* That sort of thing. But didn't anyone here follow it up?'

'No. But I agree, it's not good enough. He seems to have slipped through the net somehow. But then again, consider this. If he had actually vanished, surely his cousins would have raised the alarm. They did not. Therefore they knew where he was . . .'

'Or at least they had expected him to drop off the radar all along,' insisted Pat. 'And that might just explain why no one here did anything more than warn London and then sit on their hands, I suppose. I can see that.

'But to drop off the radar here means he must have had an alternative identity. False papers. And that's why I'm here, Tariq. I can't get someone tracing false papers over the Internet.

Especially if we're not even sure whose name the papers might be in.'

Tariq sat back until his chair creaked, looking at the screen of his enhanced laptop. His water stood untouched as he thought. At last he said, 'No ideas that could help us get started, Pat? No aliases that your boy may have used before?'

'The best one I could come up with is Sam Newton . . .'

And so, for the next few hours they trawled through every record they could find of all movements by UK visitors to Pakistan with a name that might be anything like Sam Newton – or any variation upon it. And indeed, the ghostly Mr Newton had come and gone through Pakistan from one end to the other. But in 2009. Sam Newton was in Peshawar in late October 2009, for instance, at the time of the horrendous bombings there. Staying at the Hotel Grand on Tehkal Road. Eating at KFC and Pizza Hut before the backlash against the Americans. Then at Chersee Tikka House. Then only in the hotel restaurant.

Tariq placed the information in the same file as that containing information about Sayed Mohammed's first visit in July 2006 with the Islamic Humanitarian Association. A visit cut short by the accident that had killed or injured several of his party, including Aamil Tantawi and Dr M.F. Abu-Sharkh, who had given such a moving interview to a local news network from his hospital bed.

'But it's Christmas 2010 to summer 2011,' cried Pat in frustration. 'That's when we need to track him down!' As he spoke, he gripped the back of Tariq's chair and stared distractedly into the wide screen of the laptop with its Arabic script, highlights and flags. He knew enough Arabic to recognize the names in the file Tariq was updating. The names in the beautiful, fluid script belonged to Aamil Tantawi and M.F. Abu-Sharkh. But not the flags, which were a new addition to the program. 'What are those flagged up for?' he asked, distracted.

Tariq clicked on the flag beside Aamil Tantawi's name. A picture and a paragraph popped up. A security photo from Peshawar International Airport, showing a young man with his hand out waiting for his passport to be returned. 'It's the most recent picture on record – dated July 2006 and taken at Arrivals. Underneath is the standard record of all the stamps and visas immigration saw in the passport – the number was scanned straight in and recorded there, see? No visas – either a first visit or a new passport. Ticket information patched in automatically – booking reference, flight number, seat location, departure from where – Heathrow in this case – destination where – Peshawar of course. Stopover at Muharraq International Airport, Bahrain Island recorded. Arrival time. Departure. It's all there. There are click-throughs to other associated files. I could check even further, but it's not really worth it: the rest of the entry is the report of the boy's death in the drone strike that wounded Dr Abu-Sharkh.' He hit the red box in the top right corner and the pop-up closed.

Then he clicked on the flag beside Abu-Sharkh as well. Again, a pop-up picture and a paragraph. In this picture, dated 30 December 2010, Dr Abu-Sharkh appeared to be a surprisingly young man with a full head of dark hair and a considerable beard. He wore thick-rimmed tinted glasses that must have had the immigration officer wondering whether or not to demand that they be removed. 'That's odd,' said Tariq. 'This was taken at Departures. And there isn't a matching image from Arrivals. Let's see what else we've got . . .' He clicked on a little click-through and the next earliest security picture appeared. Showing an older, slighter man with grey temples and a tightly trimmed grey beard. 'Oh dear,' said Tariq. 'Oh dear, oh dear, oh dear.'

But Pat was already dragging his chair over, his heart thundering in his chest. An instant later he was sitting shoulder by shoulder with Tariq. 'First things first,' he said breathlessly. 'Where was the good doctor going in December 2010?'

'According to this pop-up, he was off on quite a journey,' answered Tariq, coming back to the full-bearded young man. 'As representative of the Islamic Humanitarian Association, he was en route to Islamabad. With onward flights to Baghdad and Damascus already booked, by the look of things. Then back to Berbera en route, apparently, for Buurhakaba. Which would be logical I believe, for, according to these records, it is where the good doctor was born. But it is also by all accounts where a good number of wanted men who escaped our armies in Waziristan and the Americans in Afghanistan have fled to. Buurhakaba.'

'Buurhakaba! Hell's teeth, Tariq! I thought I knew Pakistan

inside out and back to front. But that's a new one on me. I've never even heard of the place!'

'Possibly because it's not in Pakistan at all,' said Tariq thoughtfully. 'You're certainly going to be putting carbon footprints all over the map if you propose to follow this route.'

'Oh, I'm going to follow him all right. But where on earth am I going? If this place Buurhakaba isn't here in Pakistan, where is it?'

'It's in the middle of Somalia.'

TWENTY-SEVEN
TRIAL

Robin Mariner looked round Court Number One of the Central Criminal Courts in London, often called the Old Bailey. She was seated in the visitors' gallery because she had no official business here. But so small was the court room itself and so massive the demand for seats, she had little choice in the matter. If she wanted to be here when Richard and Mary were called to give their evidence, then she had to be here for the whole proceeding. The whole proceeding up to that point, at any rate – for it looked as though the trial would stretch on into the Olympic summer and beyond.

With a strange sensation almost of unreality, Robin looked across at the dock. The last time she had been in here, Richard had been sitting in that dock, suited in black worsted and facing a charge of murder. The charge had stood briefly under legislation of a previous administration, repealed now, by which certain officers in any organization could be held criminally liable for corporate murder if anyone was held to have died as a result of that organization's failures in health and safety.

Richard had found himself facing the charge in a test case whose media profile had been almost as high as Sayed Mohammed's. As the one available committee member of a charity that sent youngsters out on training expeditions aboard

tall ships, he had been held liable for murder when the captain
and first officer of the square-rigger *Goodman Richard* had
apparently been lost.

But the experience had hardly put him off his charitable
work. He had stood as Master of the London City Guild of
Merchant Venturers and in that capacity had raised thousands
and thousands of pounds. Even now, as past Master, he was
deeply involved with the Venturers', the Guild's and the City's
preparations for the London Olympics. A chance, as he had
explained to her – and to anyone else who would listen – to
do something really big for charity. For the City. And, indeed,
for the country.

Both his Jetcat *Lionheart* and the square-rigged training
vessel *Goodman Richard* would be involved in the water
parade that was planned as a fundamental part of the opening
festivities in just over three months' time. And Richard was
considering adding *Poseidon* to the list, for – even if the government DA Notice limited the number of people who knew it
– *Neptune* had saved a good deal of the real estate currently
being polished up for the summer's orgy of sport. Large
sections of the Olympic facilities were built by the side of the
Thames, and the main areas in Stratford were also accessible
by water. Down the Thames and up Bow Creek, which opened
on the north bank opposite the O_2 Arena. Then on into the
River Lea that flowed through the Creek to the Thames, though
there was no chance of getting really big shops up that far.

The Lea Valley was one of the widest and lowest areas of
the north bank – some of it actually lying below sea level and
almost all of it, as far back as Stratford itself, below the high
water mark of the Thames which was contained by barrages,
barriers and locks. Indeed, the thirty or so miles of navigable
waterways running up into Essex were further controlled at
first by barriers and later by locks. And, in spite of the fact
that the main channel was a good ten feet deep, and almost
as wide as the Thames at Kew, it was no place for ocean-
going vessels. Richard proposed to stop his Merchant
Venturers' water parade outside the O_2 itself and join in the
fireworks display there.

Distracted by thoughts of the bloody man, Robin looked
back at the dock, which remained stubbornly empty, for the
accused continued to refuse to recognize the court. Indeed,

Sayed Mohammed repeatedly refused to recognize any English court or jurisdiction. And therefore, taking its precedent from the European Court in the case of at least one Bosnian leader accused of crimes against Islamic humanity, the trial was proceeding without him.

'The prosecution's case is simple, my Lord,' Quentin Carver-Carpenter, QC, leading council for the CPS, was saying, his beautifully modulated voice raised as he attempted to over-come the grapeshot rattling of the hail against the windows as though this particular early April shower had escaped from the last Ice Age or was warning that the next one was danger-ously close at hand. 'We will prove to the ladies and gentlemen of the jury beyond a reasonable doubt – indeed I may say beyond any shadow of a doubt at all – the following facts.'

He held up his long, pale, artistically aristocratic fingers as he counted off the points, switching his considerable atten-tion fully on the jury as he did so. 'That Sayed Abu Minyar Mohammed al Hajj had habitually associated with known and dangerous terrorists. That he was related to one man killed by American counter-terrorist forces near the Pakistani/Afghan border on the clearest possible proof of terrorist involvement, a man called Aamil Tantawi. That he was at Chatham in company with another such man – to wit, the bomber who actually detonated the deadly device. A man called Saami Tantawi. We will prove this through DNA evidence as well as through testimony. Some of which testimony is actually from the grieving head of the dead man's family. Their father, Hassan Tantawi. Mr Tantawi will speak on behalf of a family who adopted and protected Sayed Mohammed when his own parents tragically died, whose sons this man radicalized and led astray in return.

'We shall present evidence from unimpeachable sources – some of whom have travelled across the world to give their testimony – that Sayed Mohammed has visited terrorist training camps in Pakistan, Afghanistan and elsewhere. We will hear from his teachers, men and women of unimpeachable reputa-tion, who have seen their efforts to guide his studies and his charitable work into the paths of responsibility and rectitude all come to nothing. You will be left in little doubt that he has been – and still may be – in regular contact with some of the most desperate and dangerous terrorist leaders still at large.

'But, should all this be too much the currency of cheap and incredible spy fiction for you, ladies and gentlemen of the jury, we will finally prove to you the following. That, having organized the atrocity at Chatham – and allowed someone else to die in the execution of it – the prisoner, who dares not stand before you today, stole a gun from an officer of Counter-Terrorism Command. An officer rendered temporarily helpless by the effects of the outrage itself. And that he used that gun to assault a police officer in the execution of his duty, attempting to murder him, with malice aforethought as the old saying goes. That it was the purest chance that he wounded the officer's gallant canine companion instead. And that he was in the act of taking a second – surely fatal – shot at this brave officer when his colleagues brought matters to a conclusion with a taser device, thus certainly saving the constable's life.'

There was a lot more in the same vein but Robin's attention wavered once again. She was only called back to focus on the proceedings when the beautifully theatrical voice mentioned '. . . evidence from an experienced sea-captain who was quick-thinking enough to commandeer the only lifeboat left seaworthy – and who used this lifeboat to retrieve the accused from the river within mere moments of the explosion. From the captain's daughter, who actually performed artificial respiration on the accused and may well have saved his life. From the first officer to arrive on the scene. And from those of his colleagues who were most intimately involved. And even – and I believe this is among the first times this has happened in a British court of justice – we will hear evidence from the Under Secretary of State for Criminal Justice and Offender Management, who was unfortunate enough to be caught up in the outrage herself . . .'

'Pretty dry stuff, then?' asked Richard that evening, looking up from his *Financial Times*. They were camping out in the company flat above Heritage House and had just finished a ready meal Robin had grabbed from Marks & Spencer on the way back from court. The remains of a cold herb-roasted chicken and salad lay between them, with very little of a rich chocolate pudding and three-quarters of a bottle of South African shiraz.

'Are we allowed to discuss it,' she demanded a little tartly, 'you being a witness and all?' She poured more of the wine into her glass.

'I think it's only juries that aren't supposed to discuss proceedings,' he answered easily. 'We can ask Mary in a couple of days' time when she comes home for the early Easter break. It's just as well we didn't drag her away from her studies, by the look of things.'

'Still, she's got pretty important exams next term. She won't want to waste time hanging around . . .'

'Robin! It's *Mary*! She'll be hanging around the Old Bailey! She'll think she's in heaven. I could do with her thoughts right now, though.' He folded the pink paper and put it on the table. 'I know it's only a couple of days since Pat Toomey finally arrived in Somalia, but the *Times* says there's very little doubt that the combined leadership of the Taliban and Al Qa'ida are in hiding there. Almost all of the leaders who escaped the Pakistani army's Path to Salvation assault in Waziristan. And if Sayed Mohammed went there to talk to them then it has to be germane to the case.'

'Talk it over with Tom Clark,' she suggested shortly. 'He got you started on this . . .' She didn't say *waste of time*, but her tone implied it.

'I talked it over with him yesterday, didn't I tell you? No? Sorry! Things have been so hectic lately that I don't know whether I'm coming or going. He said to let it ride unless Pat found something more solid. As far as he knows the CIA are taking care of that aspect.'

'The CIA?'

'Apparently their man at Grosvenor Square has agreed to give evidence. That chap we were discussing at the last full board.'

She shook her head in disbelief. 'The CIA,' she said again. 'Maybe you should talk it over with someone at MI5.'

'Jonathan Evans the director perhaps. Or Sir John Sawyer at MI6.' He chuckled.

But before the conversation could proceed any further Richard's phone rang. He answered it and listened for a few moments of unaccustomed quiet before hanging up. 'That was the new Master of the Merchant Venturers,' he said. 'He's got a problem with the Olympic preparations. Mind if I pop across to Guildhall?'

Robin eyed the bottle of shiraz and the pink paper on the table. Beside the article he had been talking about were tonight's TV selections. She saw the names George Clooney and Brad Pitt. 'Pop away,' she said more brightly. 'I think I'll find some pleasant company . . .'

The trial stopped for Easter, during which time Mary and William arrived home – both laden with enough exam preparation work to more than fill the month of their vacation. But while William remained at Ashenden walled in with piles of books, Mary went back up to London with her parents when proceedings started again on Wednesday 11th April. As Richard had observed, she found the practical experience of the law at work better than any amount of reading. And after she and her father finally gave their evidence to Carver-Carpenter and explained the facts all over again to the counsel for the defence – a disturbingly spooky experience in the absence of the accused – Robin relinquished her seat in the gallery and Mary moved in for the duration.

In fact Quentin Carver-Carpenter had constructed his prosecution in exactly the opposite way to the narrative of his opening remarks. Motivated perhaps by juries' reluctance to credit the sheer scale of previous cases. To believe that young men raised and educated in England would travel abroad to be trained as terrorists and bombers. That they would coldly construct explosive devices out of sugary drinks and hair products. That they would plan to smuggle these aboard large numbers of aeroplanes hoping to detonate them all at once. A hesitation to believe this that stood even in the face of taped evidence, photographs and suicide videos. An unwillingness to believe through year after year and retrial upon retrial.

Perhaps wisely, therefore, Carver-Carpenter concentrated first upon establishing that Sayed Mohammed had been involved in the Chatham bombing. And once he had convinced the jury that the absent accused was a terrorist bomber who had attempted to shoot one policeman with a handgun stolen from another, he moved on to the wider reaches of the case he had described.

Thus it was Mary who heard CIA man Harvey Swann's confident Bostonian tones describe the structure of both the

Taliban and Al Qa'ida after the Pakistani army's Path to Salvation invasion of 2009, when the hills and valleys of Waziristan had been closed to them. How they had moved to failing states such as Somalia where they could regroup, financed always by that tiny tithe of oil wealth that their billionaire families allowed to trickle away in *zalat*, as well as by the running sore of drugs production that even the US army had been unable to stanch. How they were supplied with arms and material from wherever the pirates at the coast could steal or smuggle it. And how the knowledge, expertise, arms and explosives were all too often targeted at the unbelievers against whom the men pursued *jihad*. Targeted and effected through radicalized young men such as the Tantawi brothers and their sinister cousin Sayed Mohammed.

She watched with tears running down her cheeks as the dead boys' father, Hassan Tantawi, explained that he had taken into his house and family the young man who had destroyed them all.

She watched, with bated breath, as the internationally famous mathematician Professor Diana Stark briefly explained how he had studied in her department at Imperial; how his records showed he was perhaps the most gifted student the university had ever had.

And she observed, almost unaware that she had ceased to breathe, as Dr M.F. Abu-Sharkh explained how he had first met Sayed Mohammed, how he had taken him abroad to perform *zalat* in Pakistan. How he now understood that the boy had fallen in with bad company and begun to spread his poisonous ideas. Ideas that eventually developed into terrible, shocking action. How he had seen and understood none of this at the time. Or even suspected it in the wildest of his dreams. How, even as a student studying the mathematics of weather patterns at Imperial, Sayed Mohammed – calling himself Sam Newton – had seemed most keen to fit in with an English society that he apparently held in the highest regard. Hiding the evil within him from his teachers as effectively as he had hidden it from his family. Until he revealed his true, but secret, nature and came near to destroying them all as he had destroyed the Historic Dockyard at Chatham.

But it seemed to the frozen, breathless, ultimately terrified Mary that even as he delivered this easily plausible version of events to the jury, Dr Abu-Sharkh's cold and threatening gaze was fixed simply, solely and unwaveringly on her.

HOPE

TWENTY-EIGHT

STORM

It seemed to Richard that he was swept into an increasingly violent storm of activity as the Olympics approached. Like the redoubtable Captain McWhirr in his favourite short novel, Joseph Conrad's *Typhoon*, he hung on for dear life and tried to keep control as the power of the thing closed over him and desperately hoped he would get through it all in one piece. He hadn't felt so disturbingly powerless since seventy-five cubic kilometres of water had hit him at the mouth of the Yangtze a year or two back. With much of the city of Nanking, it seemed, as flotsam on the foaming crest. But, as Robin had observed when they were using *Neptune* to free the half-deflated boom from the explosive *Richard Montgomery*, they had managed to come through that all right.

What Richard found utterly frustrating, however, was the fact that he was supposed to be in charge. But, as Robin pointed out when he worried that the going was getting a bit too tough, this was all his own fault. He had volunteered. He had said of course he could do it. Because of course, he believed he could. In the past, he had always managed to pull the chestnuts out of the fire – no matter how hot it got. And he believed the future would be the same.

So he fought to keep on top of everything at Heritage Mariner. At the same time he was using more and more spare time on the Merchant Venturers, their fundraising, their profile enhancement, their support of the City institutions and the rest. And, at the centre of their plans, their place in the great water parade that would be part of the centrepiece for the Olympic opening ceremony on the evening of the rapidly approaching Friday 27th July. At least he persuaded them to agree that *Poseidon* and *Neptune* should join their water parade. Even though no one seemed to believe that there would only be an Olympic Games because the plucky vessels had averted a disaster that might well have flooded not only the Lea Valley but a good deal more of London besides.

While convincing his sceptical Merchant Venturer colleagues, he was also fighting off powerful requests from the Home Secretary and her increasingly demanding Under Secretary of State for Criminal Justice and Offender Management that he add to their stock of prison ships. Especially as the *Discovery* experiment was going so well. A claim that ran precisely counter to the occasional reports he was receiving from an increasingly nervous Ahmed Tewfik.

Sayed Mohammed's trial dragged on interminably in the background. In the face of the accused's intransigent refusal to join in the business of the court, he was returned to his cell aboard *Discovery* – to Ahmed's increasing worry – and proceedings continued without him. Immediately after hearing Dr Abu-Sharkh's testimony in late April, Mary had reluctantly returned to her studies and her exams. But she was back again and seated in the Old Bailey in time for the closing arguments at the beginning of July. William was finished by then too, but he was tempted away by Ashenden, his sporting friends and the Greatorex girls. He planned to be back in town for the Games, however; though the south coast sailing sections at Weymouth and Portland tempted him sorely.

When, way back in the past, as the Easter holidays ended and exams began to loom, Mary had discussed with William the fact that something about Abu-Sharkh frightened her, he had simply laughed at her at first. When he saw she was serious, he advised her to keep her worries to herself. Experience had shown that Father would fuss over her until she was smothering in cotton wool. And Mother was a million times worse. So she returned to the Old Bailey with one or two misgivings, noting every detail of procedure for the next level of her law studies. And if she sometimes had the disturbing feeling that she was being watched, she remembered the bracing conversation she had had with her cheerfully overconfident brother and dismissed such childish and fanciful worries from her mind. Even though, with her father consumed and her mother down at Ashenden, she was increasingly alone in the Heritage Mariner London flat.

*   *   *

In among everything else, Richard found time to pass on Pat's reports alongside Ahmed's concerns to Tom Clark as they came in, but they never reached Carver-Carpenter or found their way on to the news. The one brief contact that Tom and Richard shared suggested that the Director of Public Prosecutions was so concerned about the way the crucial show trial was going that he had refused to admit anything that wasn't already part of the case. No matter how important it looked – or how much it might help his cause. He was worried that any major new input would result in the whole lot being thrown out and a retrial being demanded. And the costs which *that* would entail were unacceptable. More, indeed, than his job was worth at the moment.

Even the redoubtable Harry Blake didn't want to hear Ahmed's fears about her favourite project. She had more than enough to worry about as the world and his wife descended for the *Sportfest* of the Olympics. Not counting the political, financial, social and sporting celebrities. The better part of ten million tourists. Bringing with them a raft of problems, infections, contraband; attracting all the worst elements in the country, in the Continent – and seemingly in the western world. Like a plague of leeches come to suck out of them whatever could be sucked. Providing disturbingly effective cover for those who came with deeper, darker motives still.

The weather fell into the pattern that had become familiar from almost every summer since the millennium. The blazing heat of May and June fooled no one at the Met Office into predicting a barbecue summer for the millions planning on a staycation to watch the Games. Late September promised well and there was likely to be an Indian summer in late October. But for July and August the canny computers at the Met Office and the BBC predicted nothing but a series of deepening depressions bringing unseasonable cold, rain, and storms.

The kind of extreme weather events that damaged wide areas of Sussex and Kent in the summer of 2000. Wales and the South West in Summer 2001. That nearly destroyed Boscastle in the south of England in the summer of 2004. That nearly ruined Carlisle in 2005, Sheffield and South Yorkshire in the summer of 2007, Gloucestershire and Wales in the summer of

2008, Durham and areas near it in the summer of 2009; Carlisle, Cockermouth and much of Ireland in the winter of the same year. If July and August 2010 had been marginally better, 2011 had still produced sufficient flooding and damage in the West Country to outperform Sayed Mohammed's efforts in Chatham by at least one order of magnitude. But London seemed to have escaped the worst of it.

Until now.

Muammar Faisal Abu-Sharkh, Doctor of Philosophy, Professor of Mathematics, eased his left leg. The blasted and withered limb had hurt incessantly from the moment the American Predator drone had launched its missiles at him and his little training school all those years ago on the Afghan border. He raised the twisted hook of his left hand and thoughtlessly scratched the scar-smooth flesh of his left cheek. He was aware of none of his burning discomfort. Even his relentless hatred of the crusaders who had done this to him was subsumed by the mathematician within him.

On the central of the three screens in front of him was the graphic of a weather system. A real weather system that was currently – his eyes flicked down to the clock – as of 21:02 hours on Thursday 26th July 2012 – out over the North Atlantic. All that evening the doctor had been watching it head in past Cape Farewell at the southern tip of Greenland and along the Denmark Strait towards Iceland. There was nothing particularly unusual about it. Nothing apparently to explain the kernel of excitement the sight of it had brought to his scar-bound chest. The pressure at the centre of the low stood at 996 millibars. But it looked to be falling. And what was interesting was that south of it, along the Atlantic coast of Ireland, a surge of icy water from the melting Arctic Ocean sucked south by a fluke in the Gulf Stream had super-chilled the air immediately above it. Generating a ridge of unusually high pressure, which stood currently at 1030 millibars. The computer screen showed the pressure gradient between the systems bunching together like contours on a map. On a land map such a configuration might suggest a steep cliff falling into an abyssal valley. On Abu-Sharkh's weather map it suggested storm-force winds.

Still scratching his burning cheek with his all but useless

left claw, his focus absolute, he pressed a series of buttons with agile right-hand fingers and the map leapt into fast predictive motion. The low pressure system span past Iceland, deepening swiftly as it went. The high pressure followed it, intensifying as cold air was sucked out of the Arctic by the low-pressure system. Another leap of those agile fingers, and the ghost of another system overlay the predicted path of the one he was watching. Tiny green figures in the bottom left-hand corner span through the hours of two late days in January, but the date remained the same: 1953.

The prediction and the record ran in parallel. Hurricane-force winds tore across Scotland. A huge hump of water, generated by their fearsome force, swept down the east coast of England. Pairs of figures predicted that, if the computer program was right, a flood was on its way that might match the terrible flood of 31 January 1953.

Smiling grimly, Abu-Sharkh moved his focus to the South East and watched the double image spread into the Thames Estuary, a blue wash spreading over sand-coloured coasts and grey conurbations lined with neat white streets. He reached forward and tapped in 1947. A slightly deeper tone spread along the river. But it spread farther and faster, for there were floods coming downriver to meet the surge coming up.

'I wonder,' whispered Abu-Sharkh, unconsciously speaking English. He glanced up at the second of his three screens. A news service was reporting on final preparations for tomorrow's Olympic opening ceremonies. Helicopter shots were filmed from high up the Lea Valley, looking back towards the Thames. The bright, rain-washed pictures showed the Olympic Village, the stadium, the Aquatics Centre, the O_2 beyond the Thames in the background. Then it lifted and the camera zoomed in to the roof of the Excel Centre on the north bank by the Royal Victoria Dock.

A touch or two on the computer keyboard raised a map of the areas of London that were shown on the TV screen, clustered around the twisting blue snakes of the Thames, Bow Creek, the Lea. Abu-Sharkh tapped in 1953. A blue surge swept up the Thames and spread. He tapped in 1947. The blue spread further. The O_2 and the Excel vanished under it. So did the Aquatics Centre, the stadium and the village itself. Stratford. West Ham on one side; Hackney on the other.

He took his mouse and moved his cursor over the main Olympic venues. As he did so, figures appeared above them, showing their capacities: 32,000; 17,500; 80,000; 17,300; 20,000. He was a professor of mathematics. He added up the figures in his head. At 6 p.m. tomorrow when the opening celebrations were fully under way, there would be 166,800 people packed into those venues alone. Not to mention the fact that among them would be the entire British Cabinet, the American Secretary of State and her large contingent, half the government ministers and more than half of the crowned heads of Europe. Almost the entire political command structure of the infidel army of brutal crusaders who had turned his suffering body into such a perfect representation of his broken and suffering homeland.

He dragged the map back downriver towards the estuary, opening out the zoom so that the graphic showed the Thames Barrier and the Albert Dock above it, with the City Airport in between. Lost in thought, he dragged it further still, past Barking, Dagenham and Rainham, all with their marshes doomed on the north bank. Past Erith and Greenhythe at risk on the south. Past Grays on its little promontory, which might survive, and Tilbury with its doomed docks. Gravesend opposite would be smashed by the surge as well as flooded, if all went well.

Then, with a twist of his whole right side, Abu-Sharkh opened the map almost to its fullest extent, so that the Barrier with the low-lying areas it was designed to protect lay at one side of the screen and the mouth of the Medway with Southend a few miles to the north lay at the other. And the Lower Hope lay in the middle. With Gravesend at the bottom of the reach and Thames Haven at the top. And Cliffe in the middle, with Cliffe Fort sitting squarely on the waterside.

He put the computer mouse down and reached for his cell-phone. He speed-dialled a number and pressed the instrument to his ear. As soon as the voice answered, he said in English, 'Go.'

Then he broke the connection and sat back, his heart beating almost uncontrollably. He touched the computer keyboard. The picture of the Lower Hope vanished, returned to the unadorned schematic of the low-pressure system in the Denmark Strait. In the few moments he had been focused on his plans for London, the pressure had fallen to 978 while the ridge of high pressure near Galway had risen to 1032. Even better than his model had predicted. If this carried on, the surge would arrive at nine tomorrow evening, at the climax of the opening celebrations. That was neat. That was almost mathematical.

He reached for the phone again. Speed-dialled another number. 'Yes?' came the answer.

'Call the cab and get the girl,' he said.

When the flat's phone started to ring, Mary put down the surprisingly tasty Olympic veggieburger that she had grabbed from a nearby burger bar, fired the remote at the TV, cutting Johnny Depp off in mid-flow, and picked the handset up on the sixth ring. 'Yes, Dad?'

'It's Dad, darling . . .' Father had obviously been preparing a speech, she thought. But only Mother and he used this number. And she guessed it must be him because she had just hung up after a heart-to-heart with her. Lucky she liked cold veggieburgers. She'd have to nuke the fries, though.

'Yes, Dad?' she prompted again.

'I'm still at Guildhall,' he said. 'I don't know when I'll get back. Can you grab something to eat OK?'

'Been down. Done that. Sharing it with gorgeous Johnny Depp when you called.'

'Sharing it with *who*? Oh . . .'

'It's OK, Dad. Don't fuss. I'm a big girl and there's a security system like Fort Knox downstairs. And the twenty-four-hour Crewfinders office full of really butch secretaries upstairs. I have your cell number on speed dial and you have my iPhone number. What's the worst that could happen?'

'OK, darling. I'll stop fussing. All right, James, I'm just coming. That's right. First *Lionheart* then *Poseidon*. *Goodman Richard* last. Order of speed. Fastest first. Not that there's much difference between the first two. And not that they'll be going faster than Slow Ahead in any case . . .' The line went dead.

Mary hung up, picked up her veggieburger. Hit the remote. Johnny Depp snapped the brim of his trilby hat, reached for his Thompson sub-machine gun, said, 'Well . . .'

And the doorbell buzzed.

'I'm afraid I'm going to have to nuke you too,' Mary told the long-suffering veggieburger as she crossed to the security screen. 'Hello?' she said, squinting at the back of someone's head on the security system's TV screen.

Diana Stark turned her face into the light. 'Is that Mary Mariner?' she said a little breathlessly. 'Would you mind awfully if I popped up for a quick word, my dear? It's terribly important!'

Mary hit the ENTER switch. She didn't think twice.

TWENTY-NINE
NESSUN DORMA

The wall of icy, sluggish high-pressure air stretching from wave-top to troposphere between the Western Approaches and the Denmark Strait ruthlessly trapped the lighter, warmer, more turbulent air to the east of it. That air became caught between the rock of its eastern edge and the hard place of the cold front reaching down across East Anglia, into Holland and the Low Countries. It agitated the already restless imprisoned atmosphere by hurling winds at hurricane speed along the edge of it, into the intensifying gyre of the depression.

Over the land mass of the West of England, from Cornwall and Devon, over Wales to the Borders, the Scottish Lowlands, the Highlands and the Isles, the increasingly tempestuous warmer air was forced to rise and cool at rarely precedented rates. A rampart of torrential storms formed ahead of it and swept in over Bournemouth, Reading, Oxford, Luton and Stevenage. There were waterspouts on Southampton Water and a series of tornadoes recorded between Bishop's Stortford and Stansted. More than a month's worth of rain fell along the squall line during the first three hours of Friday 27th July.

The Emirates flight from Mogadishu via Paris was the last allowed into Heathrow on the evening of Thursday 26th. Pat Toomey was one of the first passengers off it. Leaner, tougher, much more deeply tanned than he had been when he left. Harder and fitter than at any time in his life since he finished his training in the Brecon Beacons. And he was possessed of a burning desire to reach Heritage Mariner.

Pat had changed so much in the months he had been following in the cooling footsteps of Sayed Mohammed – occasionally alias Sam Newton but most recently Abu-Sharkh – that the officer at immigration had to take a second look at his passport photo. Then a third. Which endeared neither of them to the queue of exhausted but impatient travellers bursting to get into the city for the Olympic celebrations.

Because he was travelling light, Pat went through customs and baggage claim first. Because the airport was being forced to close by a cataclysmic thunderstorm, there were fewer people than usual queuing for taxis. Because the new Pat Toomey didn't bother with a drop of rain – even a drop that seemed big enough to fill Dun Laoghaire bay – he got a taxi surprisingly swiftly. Because of all of this and his simple relief at being home safe and sound in one piece, he found he was filled with fizz and energy. And that was just as well, he thought, for he had some pretty important news that he needed to share with Richard Mariner – or with Jim Bourne if Richard was busy.

Since he could rely on Heritage Mariner to reimburse him, Pat told the cabbie to take him straight to the office, showing him a wad of £10 notes that he had managed to exchange for a combination of Somali shillings and euros at the bureau de change at Orly. The cabbie wouldn't have the faintest idea where London Centre was, so Pat simply said Heritage House, corner of Leadenhall and Bishopsgate.

In spite of the rain, which caused occasional whiteouts on the motorways and disturbingly sudden side-streams washing out of uphill crossroads in town, the cab made good time. The only downside was that the cabbie talked relentlessly about the Olympics on the tacit assumption that only someone recently returned from Mars would be out of touch. Somalia in that regard seemed to Pat closer to Pluto.

The cab pulled up at the address Pat requested just in time for the frowning Irishman to see two figures hurrying out of the private entrance to the Heritage Mariner flat and across the pavement into a minicab. He thought he recognized Mary, but it was hard to tell because it was still sheeting down with rain and her collar was turned up. He assumed the woman with her was her mother. Idly, almost unconsciously, he noted the number of the minicab painted on its side. The women climbed aboard, the door slammed and the minicab pulled away. His own driver turned around. 'That'll be seventy-five, mate. Seventy-five on the nose.'

Pat leaned forward, reaching for his wallet. 'For seventy-five you can take me a wee bit further on,' he decided.

Everyone at London Centre was up and active. '*Nessun dorma* tonight, Pat,' said Jim as he welcomed his operative home and guided him, dripping, across his office. 'Or tomorrow, until the water parade's gone by and everyone is home safe.' He took Pat's sopping bag and put it in the corner, where it silently started creating its own puddle. Then he shook his hand enthusiastically. 'Jesus Christ, look at you! You look like one of these athletes in for the Olympics.'

'Don't be silly. I'm far too old,' laughed Pat, suddenly very glad indeed to be home.

'Old you may be, my man. Fit you have become. How'd you do it?'

'Living in a war zone for nearly three months with nothing much to eat or drink,' answered Pat, accepting a very large Jameson's whiskey and putting a little water in it. 'You either end up quick or dead. But where's Richard? I've got some pretty crucial news.'

'You'll be lucky to get hold of him. It's the big day tomorrow. Still. Can you try it on me and let me make a decision?'

'I guess.' Pat took a sip of the whiskey and continued. 'Look. I brought you up to speed with what was going on. You remember?'

'You and your tame Black Stork, Tariq Mahsud.' Jim nodded. 'You were off via Baghdad and Damascus to Buurhakaba in Somalia. You were following someone travelling on Dr Abu-Sharkh's papers. Forged papers, I'd guess. It was the Pakistani counter-terrorism people's contention that what was left of Al Qa'ida's high command was hiding somewhere near there. Which seems logical for all sorts of reasons . . .'

'Quite,' interrupted the new, more forceful Pat. 'There were money men and arms experts in Damascus and Baghdad, but no one who seemed about to pull off anything on a global scale. Somalia was different, as you say. You can get anything in – or out, come to that – via the pirates on the coast. Even with half the maritime nations in the world patrolling up and down trying to keep their vessels safe . . .'

'With limited success. Look at that couple from Tunbridge Wells a couple of years back. I mean I ask you, *Tunbridge Wells!*'

'The country is pretty lawless in the interior. A failed state, really. Even with the US Marines on patrol with yet more of their Predator and Reaper drones. If you move fast and keep your head down you can get away with pretty much anything.'

'OK, I follow you. So if I was Al Qa'ida and I'd just been booted out of Afghanistan and Waziristan but I still wanted to pursue my personal *jihad* against the war on terror . . .'

'Then that would be your destination of choice, as they say. Precisely.'

'And Abu-Sharkh popped out there to see them? Or the guy using the Abu-Sharkh papers.'

'Sayed Mohammed. He was there from February to May 2011. I can give you precise dates. At the end of May he flew back to Islamabad and went on to Peshawar. Then Abu-Sharkh disappeared and Sayed Mohammed returned to England. Counter-terrorism in London had been warned that there was something fishy by the Pakistani authorities when Sayed just vanished off the face of the earth in January. But the border protection people weren't expecting him back when he came out of nowhere nearly six months later, and he slipped away from them. What Sergeant Stone would call a SNAFU, I believe.'

'Indeed. He slipped through their fingers and disappeared again,' mused Jim. 'Just in time to help his radicalized Saami Tantawi pack the stolen gin palace *Jupiter* with explosives and blow the crap out of Chatham.'

'Yes and no,' countered Pat. 'He brought nothing back with him. Except perhaps contacts, expertise and a plan. Someone else had the explosives. Someone else, who helped them pack the boat with those explosives, then simply walked away. That's the problem. They set it up, walked away and they're still out there. And maybe they have more. Explosives, if not boats.'

'Abu-Sharkh? He knows Buurhakaba. I thought he was born there.'

'He was. And he maintains dual citizenship even now. Which is of course why it was so useful to use his papers. But he's never been back since he got out. No. Not Abu-Sharkh. But someone else visited the place just after Sayed Mohammed had returned to Islamabad via Mogadishu. I couldn't believe it so I checked and double checked. Then I came straight back to tell you face to face because it wasn't something I wanted to trust even to company code.' He looked around the room. 'We are secure in here?'

'Yup,' said Jim, frowning.

'OK. It was Diana Stark. Diana Stark was there for the last two weeks in August. Slipped in. Slipped out. God knows where she was supposed to have been but she was actually in Buurhakaba. And talking to the Taliban. Not to mention Al Qa'ida.'

'Shit! There's no end to the damage she could cause if she's gone over.'

'No end to the damage she might already have caused, you mean. Wasn't it on her advice that the Home Secretary put all the most dangerous terrorist suspects in one place at one time? And in a ship, come to that, now I think of it! God, what a great escape that would be. Even Steve McQueen on a motorcycle couldn't hold a candle to that one!'

'Shit and double shit! I'll get straight on to Richard at once.'

Richard sat silently in Jim's office, looking through the exhausted ghost of his reflection at the bright nuggets of rain sheeting down into the graveyard far below. His mind was racing. He must tell Harry Blake that the chief advisor on one of her most precious policies was possibly a terrorist sympathizer – possibly a terrorist. But he could only do that if he could furnish her with unassailable proof. For, despite the high regard in which he held the Home Secretary, he was well aware that she was above all a politician. And, especially after the furore over MPs' expenses and the string of fiascos since, she was likely to be hypersensitive to public opinion. And public opinion could be swayed so easily by appearances. If she appeared to have made a massive error of judgement in trusting Diana Stark then she was dead. If, however, she appeared to be taking swift and decisive action in the face of incontrovertible proof, she was on her way up the next step to Number Ten. Examples of each circumstance seemed almost without number – even during the last few years. Though the line of political graves stretched far, far further than the list of new Prime Ministers. 'And you couldn't bring any evidence back with you?' he asked at last. 'Hard evidence?'

'What did you expect?' asked Pat. 'A signed affidavit from Osama bin Laden? A clip of the meeting on YouTube? A Taliban tweet on Twitter?'

'You know that's not the way it works, Richard,' emphasized Jim gently. 'And if anyone in government knows that too, then it has to be the Home Secretary.'

Richard sighed. They were right. But so was he. And this kind of knowledge could be bitterly dangerous. He recalled vividly a section from Shakespeare's *Antony and Cleopatra* where the three most powerful men in the Roman world, Antony, Octavius Caesar and Lepidus, fall into a drunken sleep after a party of reconciliation with their greatest enemy Sextus Pompeius. Sextus's lieutenant suggests it would be a good idea to kill them. And Sextus sacks him on the spot. If he had *done* it he would have been a made man – lieutenant to the ruler of the world. But because he just *said* it, he was utterly destroyed.

Politics never changes, he thought. And he pulled out his cellphone.

A little envelope icon flashed on the screen and warned him he had a text message, but he ignored it. He had more important business. 'Please connect me with the Home Secretary. It's Richard Mariner,' he said. 'Yes, I know who she's having dinner with. This is crucial. She may want to convene COBRA.'

She didn't.

'Richard. Do you know who I'm dining with?'

'Of course. Look Harry, I wouldn't have disturbed you if I didn't think—'

'If it's something *that* important, then we can't discuss it on the phone, can we?'

'It's to do with *Discovery* and the advice you've had . . .'

'Well, talk it over with Diana Stark!'

'*That's the problem*, Harry . . .'

There was a short silence. Then, 'I tell you what, Richard.

You get your concerns organized into some kind of form and
bring them to the House. If I'm not back, Gloria Strickland
will be there. I'll warn security. You alert her. She has my
direct panic number. My Guy Fawkes number. Do I make
myself clear?'

'OK,' said Richard. 'Let's see what we can take to Gloria
Strickland. Diana Stark is Al Qa'ida. Has been for a while.
Abu-Sharkh into the bargain, I'd say. They've been controlling Sayed Mohammed. Three brilliant mathematicians. Who
don't seem to have posed any threat worth following up on
because – face it – how scary is maths? Maths and weather
forecasting?'

'But,' interrupted Pat, 'there's something going on. Because
both Sayed and Diana have been playing footsie with Al
Qa'ida in Somalia. And Sayed blew up Chatham.'

'Which begs the question,' supplied Jim, 'are they clever
enough to be using Chatham as a lift-off to something larger?
The result of the Chatham outrage is *Discovery*. And the men
specifically selected to be placed aboard her. All of which
Diana Stark suggested and oversaw. So it's logical to assume
that *Discovery* is part of any plan that's going on, if our suspicions hold water. The eyes of the world are on London at the
moment. If *Discovery* upped anchor and sailed away tomorrow,
for instance, the government would fall.'

'There has to be more to it than that!' Richard shook his
head. 'These people aren't in the business of regime change.
They kill people. They blow things up. They've had a hard
time lately. Pushed into corners, networks smashed all to
pieces. Supplies drying up. Recruitment shot to hell. What
they need is a spectacular even bigger than 9/11. Big time.'

'So,' said Pat. 'What if they were hoping to do a bigger,
better job than they did at Chatham? What if *Discovery* is
full of explosives? What if they're hoping to sail her up to . . .
I don't know . . . the Thames Barrier, say, and blow her up
there . . .'

'I've been aboard her,' said Richard. 'I think the governor
isn't up to much, but I can't see that they've had a realistic
chance to smuggle sufficient explosives aboard to do any real
damage to the Barrier.' He looked at Jim. 'Has Ahmed given
any hint of that much munitions going aboard?'

'Nothing. He's worried, though. There are things going on aboard that he can't get a handle on. Things he doesn't like. But nothing on that scale.'

'But even so,' said Pat. 'Even if they'd got a really massive bomb aboard, what are they going to do with it? Blow up Southend? The Isle of Grain? I mean, if there was a really big explosion in the Thames Estuary, what would be the outcome? A wave a couple of metres high washing upriver. And even that would take a really big explosion. If they had any plans at all along those lines then they'd need, what? . . .'

'A bloody great explosion. A spring tide and a storm surge,' said Richard. 'They'd need something that was already coming up the river on the same scale as the 1947 flood, or the 1953. The sorts of floods the Barrier was designed to stop. Then, on top of that, when the whole system was already at full stretch, they'd need to add their extra wave. Something enough to wash over the top of the defences and flood the river systems behind them. Maybe flood the City itself.'

'Do you think they could do anything like that?' asked Pat, frowning with concern.

'Not likely,' answered Jim dismissively. 'What would they need? A flood. A surge. A bloody great explosion. And a sodding great crowd of people all packed along the river just behind the Barrier.'

'No,' said Richard. 'No, Jim. Hang on there just a minute . . .'

THIRTY
DISCOVERY

It was well after midnight before Richard, Pat and Jim organized their thoughts well enough to present them to Gloria Strickland. Richard sent the other two off to bed and caught a taxi to Westminster across a city buzzing with excitement and anticipation.

The wee small hours suited the Under Secretary, thought Richard idly as he watched her going through his notes on

the far side of the desk in her surprisingly modest parliamentary office. Or it might just be the fact that, like her boss
Harry Blake, she had been out to a formal dinner earlier and
was dressed up to the nines. Or, according to the dictates of
the latest fashion, the threes rather than the nines. He could
see almost as much of her now as he had seen in the after-
math of the Chatham incident. *And*, whispered Robin's ghostly
voice, as though she were a little devil sitting on his shoulder
instead of safely asleep in Ashenden, *she's not working too
hard at keeping herself covered up, is she?*

'This isn't what you would call hard evidence, is it?' she
observed at last.

'This is intelligence, Gloria. Not law. Think MI5 not DPP.'

'I understand that, Richard. But even Jonathan Evans would
have problems accepting a bundle of ifs and maybes like this.
The Director of Public Prosecutions would simply boot it out
of court. What have you actually got? Diana Stark may have
visited Somalia. May have contacted terrorist leaders there.
May be involved in a terrorist plot of some kind at some
level.

'But what on earth are they going to do? They're all mathematicians. Her area may be relevant. So we need to look at
the policies she's had her fingers in. Yes. That includes
Discovery. But the other two are glorified weather forecasters.'
She looked out of the window. The rain had eased and the
clouds were beginning to break; there was the promise of a
moon. 'How can that be seen as a terrorist threat? Especially
when one of them is safely under lock and key.'

'I don't know,' answered Richard, who was beginning to
flag. 'I suppose you need to check that everything aboard
Discovery is still OK. And perhaps you should check with the
Met Office into the bargain.'

'I'll tell you what I'll do,' decided Gloria. 'I'll check with
Governor Weeks myself.' She glanced at her watch. 'It's a
bit late now. The communications blackout aboard stops us
contacting them the same as it stops anyone else. We do it
like the helicopters and whatnot that have to land on her –
line of sight communication. I'd have to wake up a whole
bunch of people between here and Southend to get a signal
through – to wake up the governor himself. I'll do it in the
morning.' She gave a half smile and added with gentle irony,

'Like everyone else, I expect I'll have lots of time on my hands then.' In the face of his stony silence, she pouted. 'All right,' she flirted a little. 'As it's you, I tell you what I'll do. If there's anything out of whack when I talk to Governor Weeks in the morning, I'll go down there with some security men and take a look myself. OK? Will that *satisfy* you?'

Richard was as unmoved by the double meaning as he was by the lowered lashes, the way she was playing with her hair and the power cleavage very clearly on display. 'That'll do,' he said ungraciously. 'Met Office?' he persisted.

Gloria swung the laptop on her desk round so he could see the screen. She clicked on an icon. 'Everyone has been ordered to keep an eye on today's weather,' she said. 'I think the Mayor has it hot-wired into his dreams. So many of the ceremonies are due to take place outside during the next few days. Including your Merchant Venturers' water parade from here at Westminster Pier to Greenwich, starting in what –' she glanced at her watch '– sixteen hours' time.'

The weather map came up and she adjusted the screen again. 'Weather warnings are organized in the RAG system. Red for severe, amber for take care— But what am I saying? Explaining weather prediction to a barnacle-chested sailor . . .'

The bright green map of the British Isles was suddenly covered in colour and surrounded by tiny writing. She clicked immediately on London and the South East and a more detailed map sprang up. There were areas of red in an arc from the west to the north, over the Cotswolds, the Chilterns and the Downs. The red was beginning to move into the waterways that flowed out of them. Snakes of amber wound down into the Thames Valley from all directions. 'Flood alerts on all sorts of waterways. The river systems have been pretty much at full stretch all summer,' said Gloria. 'If you can call it a summer.'

Richard's gaze raked down the coast, from the bright red in the Wash to the amber in the Thames Estuary. 'Looks like there's a surge coming too,' he said. 'Click back on the full map, would you?'

The entire British Isles returned. Scotland was a uniform red. 'Gales, severe gales and storms. Winds at damaging speeds,' Gloria said.

The east coast of Scotland and England from Wick to the Wash was red. 'Possibility of a tidal surge. Coastal flooding possible in some low-lying areas.' She read out the tiny words for them. 'Thank God for the Thames Barrier!'

Gloria's pager sounded. 'Right,' she said decisively, drawing herself up and sitting back. 'That's my call to arms. No rest for the wicked.' She closed the laptop and looked Richard squarely in the face. 'You've warned the Home Secretary about your concerns,' she said formally. 'You've alerted me. I will take action if I think I need to. You need to leave it to me now and get on with staying on top of your other priorities. It won't do the Honourable Guild of Merchant Venturers – or indeed the City Guilds of London – any good at all if your boats start bumping into each other in the middle of the Thames with a couple of hundred million people watching on TV. Not to mention the millions that will be in the city itself and the hundred thousand or so in the Olympic venues everywhere from Greenwich to Stratford, waiting for the formal opening ceremony.'

The Palace of Westminster security staff seemed happy enough to arrange for a cab, but Richard had hardly settled into the back seat and said, 'Heritage House, please, corner of Leadenhall and Bishopsgate . . .' when his phone started ringing.

'Mariner?' he answered, not recognizing the incoming number.

'*Poseidon* here,' came the reply. In the nanosecond before George Trevor, captain of the DSRV *Neptune*'s mother ship, uttered his next words, Richard's exhausted mind imagined that he was speaking to the real Poseidon. The Greek god. Lord of the great waters, earthquakes and natural disasters. It felt oddly apt to be speaking to him, especially as it was his emblem, the horse, that Ulysses left outside Troy. A big wooden horse secretly packed with soldiers. It seemed likely to Richard that Diana Stark was doing something similar with *Discovery*. A Trojan horse if ever he had seen one.

'I have Captain Han Solo for you,' continued Captain Trevor, who had clearly caught up with Robin's little *Star Wars* joke. 'Sounds important to me.'

'Han*cock*!' came the familiar voice of the tug captain faintly in the background.

'What? There aboard with you?'

'No, he's in the Medway. On the radio. Can I patch him through?'

'Yes of course. Hello, Captain Hancock? What's so important? What can I do for you?' asked Richard. It took him a moment to realize that the patch via *Poseidon* had failed and he was speaking to dead air. He switched off the phone. 'Change of plan,' he said to the cabbie.

Poseidon was currently in the Upper Pool, just downriver of Tower Bridge. As the cab retraced its route towards the Thames, following the Embankment to Monument and over London Bridge to Tooley Street, Richard contacted Captain Trevor again. 'I'm just on my way out to you. Can some of your people meet me at the steps on Shad Thames?' he asked.

'Certainly.'

'Any idea what Captain Hancock wanted?'

'As far as I can see, he wants to borrow *Neptune* . . .'

Richard stood on *Poseidon*'s command bridge looking upriver towards the Victorian Gothic glory of Tower Bridge. The central span would have to be raised at least twice tomorrow just for his convenience alone, he thought. Once in the morning when they were assembling the ships upstream, off Westminster. And once again when they all processed down to Greenwich. *Poseidon* and *Lionheart* might just squeeze under but *Goodman Richard*'s four tall masts were far too high. And *Goodman Richard* was by no means the tallest ship in the parade. So little time, he thought; so much to do.

'Weather's moderating,' observed Captain Trevor. 'Though my weather predictor says there's a chance of a bit of a surge at high water sometime around ten tonight.'

The radio buzzed. Richard picked up the headset. 'Yes, Captain Hancock?' he said.

'It's this blasted boom, Captain Mariner. It's broken loose again. I mean it's nowhere near the exclusion zone or the danger area this time, thank God, but it's burst and beginning to sink. I don't mind waiting here like an eternal doorman tugging it open and tugging it closed. It's easy money, to tell you the truth. But when the blasted contraption's as leaky as a sieve . . . Look. You couldn't send me down that little miracle worker of yours, could you? Inject some compressed air into the thing and wake the bugger up again . . .'

'No can do, Captain. I'm sorry. *Poseidon* is part of the parade here. Her place is booked and it would muck up the whole show if we started fiddling about with it now. I suppose I could get *Neptune* down to you slung under a chopper, but we'd have to control it from here and I frankly don't think we have the range. If I was at Greenwich I might be able to give it a go for you. But there's no chance from here, and we're bound upriver in a couple of hours' time. You'll just have to do your best I'm afraid. Still. The tide there must be on the turn . . .'

'Yeah. Low water was at oh two fifty. A couple of hours since . . .'

'There you are then. Use the extra depth. It's what we did last time, used a making tide . . .'

After he hung up from the disappointed and irate Captain Hancock, Richard suddenly realized that he had been slack – to put it mildly – in his husbandly duties. Without further thought he pulled out his cell and called home. 'Hello, darling?' he said as the receiver was picked up. 'Hello?'

'Richard! God! What time is it? What's the matter? Are you all right?'

'I'm fine, darling. Rushed off my feet, but—'

'It's Mary! What's the matter with Mary?'

'Nothing, darling. I talked to her a while ago. She was tucking down with a veggieburger and a good film on the box. I just wanted to tell you everything's fine and I love you . . .'

Silence. For a moment he thought she had been cut off – like Captain Hancock when the patch had failed. But no: 'Do you know what *time* it is?'

'Well . . .' He looked up at the ship's chronometer. 'It's just coming up to five . . .'

'Four fifty. *In the morning, Richard!*' She took a long, shuddering breath. 'Have you been to bed yet?'

'What? No. I haven't as a matter of fact.'

'Where are you? The flat? London Centre?'

'Aboard *Poseidon*, actually . . .'

'Don't explain. I don't have the patience. Look, darling, get your head down. There'll be a bunk aboard you can use. A slop chest for basics like pyjamas if you want to bother with them. You know your schedule for tomorrow is pretty tight. As is mine. And yours starts at nine – aboard *Poseidon* as it happens, unless you need to change. Stay there and get some rest. OK? Hang up now and call me at nine.'

'OK, darling,' he said. 'Speak to you in four hours.' Just as he broke the connection, he heard her snarl sleepily, '*Bloody man!*' And he smiled as he blew a little kiss at the phone.

Four hours later the phone's alarm went off, but Richard was already awake. He pressed the speed dial for Ashenden and listened to the click of connection and the purring of Robin's bedside phone. But then everything he could hear was drowned by the clattering of a helicopter swooping by very low indeed. Still with the instrument to his ear, he crossed to the porthole in the cabin wall and watched the chopper as it swooped away downstream. He wasn't certain, but he could almost have sworn that it was the Westland that had carried Harry Blake, Diana Stark and himself down to *Discovery* all those weeks and months ago.

Gloria Strickland looked down at Tower Bridge as the top turrets seemed to swing by just above her head. There was a lean, futuristic, slightly dangerous-looking ship down there. Probably something to do with Richard Mariner, she thought. It looked sleek enough and cutting-edge in that slightly menacing, disturbingly attractive way that Richard seemed to have perfected.

Richard Mariner had been on Gloria's mind ever since she had pulled herself out of her lonely bed ninety minutes ago. And indeed, he had taken a leading role in the half-remembered dreams that had filled the four hours of sleep she had enjoyed last night. Richard, and the promise she had made to him at some ridiculous time this morning. She had arrived back in her parliamentary office at a little after eight, and at eight thirty she had got hold of the House of Commons switchboard. 'Get me the *Discovery*, please,' she had ordered. 'I want to speak to Governor Weeks himself. Call me when you have a line.'

The switchboard had never let her down before. So when at eight forty-five they had reported back that it was currently impossible to contact the prison ship, she had been utterly stunned. Then, abruptly, incandescently enraged. At Richard for having made her promise by being so unattainably gorgeous. At herself for having made such a silly bargain in the first place, like a stupid schoolgirl flirting with the captain of rugby. At herself again for deciding to honour the insanely inconvenient promise now – on today of all days. But mostly at Governor Weeks for failing to answer her call – for refusing to get her off the painfully sharp hook of her own foolish making. So she snatched up the phone again. 'I need a chopper to take me to Southend,' she snarled, 'At once, please.'

The Westland delivered her in little more than fifteen minutes, through a gusty restless morning better suited to early April than late July. It followed the river closely enough for her to catch one or two landmarks familiar from earlier trips. The Dome, the Olympic Village, the Barrier, City Airport. Newham, Dagenham, the great marshes of Rainham and Purfleet where, she suddenly remembered, Count Dracula himself had wanted to buy a house. Then Gravesend, surrounded by foam and the Lower Hope running due north above it, with the three strange forts guarding the waterway against historical riverine invasions. Star-shaped Tilbury Fort, with the Coalhouse Fort on the Essex bank above it. And semi-derelict Cliffe Fort opposite. Then suddenly they were over Thames Haven and beginning their descent over Canvey Island towards Southend.

The chopper touched down briefly in Southend, outside the land-based sector of the *Discovery* prison system. There was just time for her to confirm that communications with *Discovery* itself were still down – even though the line of sight was clear enough for her to see the long aerial above the grey-painted bridge out on the slow brown water. There were three new warders waiting to go out, so she took them aboard, thinking of her promise to Richard that she would go herself – and that she would take security with her.

Ten minutes later the helicopter was settling on the landing area on the rear deck of the ship, still without having made any contact at all with *Discovery*. The pilot cut the motors. The door at the rear of the bridge house opened and Chief Warder Burke marched out, every bit the martinet as ever. With relief welling up at this return to normal service, Gloria swung out of the door and stepped on to the deck, stooping forward and protecting her hair with her hand. The warders stepped down behind her. Burke stopped rigidly in front of them. 'Welcome aboard, ma'am,' he said. 'If you would follow me to the governor's office . . .'

He swung round and was marching back towards the bridge before Gloria had a chance to register much more than the pallor of his face. How wide his eyes had seemed to be. And, now that he had turned away, that he seemed to have put on weight since her last visit.

Then the five of them were at the door and Burke was leading them through. After the blustery brightness outside, the corridor was surprisingly dark. But Burke marched purposefully forward and the others automatically followed him – until several things happened in a sequence so rapid that, in spite of seeing it all in dreamlike slow motion at the time, Gloria seemed almost instantly to lose track of the detail. Half a dozen men stepped out of a side corridor and surrounded them. The Under Secretary of State found a gun pointing at her face, the face of the man holding the gun concealed by a black and white *keffiyeh* scarf that reached up across his head in the style made famous by the late Yasser Arafat. Burke was tearing at the buttons of his uniform jacket, babbling, 'Take it off. Take it off . . .'

Out of the corner of her eye – for she found she could not look away from the gun or the masked face behind it – she saw a belt of white brick-like objects being removed from around Burke's waist. As soon as it was off, the chief warden seemed to sag like a deflating balloon.

Gloria Strickland tried desperately to think of something to say. But nothing would come.

The gun did not waver, but a hand came up and loosened the mask, pulling it aside. She recognized the face. And realized that, ever since the trap had been sprung, she had known with a sickening certainty whose face it would be.

'Thank you for bringing yet more hostages,' said Sayed Mohammed quietly. 'More martyrs to the cause. And a nice new helicopter to help us through any emergencies we have not calculated for.'

They put Gloria Strickland in a cabin with the only man of Arabic appearance aboard who didn't seem to be on their side. 'It's hopeless,' he whimpered brokenly. 'We're all going to die!'

As he spoke, he wrote on the margin of a page torn from the *Muslim Weekly* in writing just big enough for her to see: BUGS. He looked around the little cabin they were locked in. He tore off the word and popped it in his mouth.

'Looks like it, Ahmed,' she answered, reading his name off his overalls and trying to make her voice sound as defeated as his. Her mind raced like a rat in a maze with no exits.

'They just took over the ship. It must have been so carefully planned. The guards didn't stand a chance. They had knives. They made Burke open the arms cupboard. Then they had guns. They have *explosives*! Someone smuggled some aboard!' He wrote PROF STARK. Tore it off and ate it.

'A *lot* of explosives? *How?*' She couldn't help herself.

'Not much. I didn't see . . . I don't know . . .' He wrote: BIG I.E.D. IN BOWS. He looked at her questioningly. She nodded. She knew it stood for Improvised Explosive Device. The rat in the maze started trying to work out what things on a ship they could turn into a bomb. A lot, she thought. A hell of a lot.

But Ahmed was still writing: SOME C4? TRIGGER? He tore it off, slowly and silently, slipping it into his mouth and chewing earnestly.

'Have you any idea what's going on?' she asked. At the moment, under the circumstances she was not inclined to trust anyone aboard. Especially people she was casually shoved into bugged cabins with.

'Not really. I can't imagine,' he babbled brokenly. He wrote: HELP? RICHARD MARINER?

She began to consider trusting him a little. She frowned. Shook her head: No. Oh, how I wished I had listened to Richard, she thought.

'They can't have brought anything aboard big enough to do much damage, surely?' she said, almost as though she was speaking to herself. 'I mean, what could they actually do?'

'I don't know,' he whimpered brokenly. 'I just want to get off. Go home. I don't want to die.' He started snivelling. He wrote: DETONATE THE RICHARD MONTGOMERY. He started to cry as he looked at her. He was a very convincing actor indeed.

And suddenly Gloria Strickland felt like crying too.

For real.

THIRTY-ONE
CALL

R ichard strode back to the centre of the cabin as the helicopter clattered away downriver. The call had clicked through but he hadn't heard the connection because of the racket. 'Richard?' said Robin again.

'We need to agree itineraries for the day,' he said, suddenly fizzing with energy and excitement. 'Mine is pretty rigid. I have to move my ships up through Tower Bridge in very precise sequence between now and twelve. They're not going to open the span all morning – not with London so busy. And ten million tourists milling about. So there's a really tight schedule on that. We'll be leaving the tall ships at Custom House Pier to join us later and the smaller ships will go on upriver to the meeting point. Leaving those that won't fit under the bridges waiting to pick us up as the parade comes back downriver.

'Then, from midday to four, the main part of the parade is forming up all along the river between the Palace of Westminster and St Thomas' Hospital, sprucing up and getting ready for action. Four to five I have a chance to get back to the flat and change. It'll be tight but I think I'll have time.

'From five security really gets tight. The royal yacht is out of mothballs for the occasion and she'll take pride of place, of course. Once everyone is aboard her then we're ready for the off at six. As far as I know the royal party will be joined by the Mayor, the PM, the Secretary of State and several other VIPs. Six till seven thirty we progress down to Greenwich, taller and taller ships fall in alongside us as we go. Big spectacle. *Huge*. Fire-control vessels spraying hoses, police vessels flashing blue lights, horns and sirens hooting, every flag and pennant a-flutter. You know the kind of thing.

'The royal yacht docks at Coldharbour Jetty on the north bank opposite the O_2 and the royal party with their VIP guests go off up the A102 towards Stratford in a fleet of Rolls-Royces and so forth. With the rest of us following on. Main ceremony at the Olympic stadium and all ancillary buildings from eight to ten. Mega-screens, searchlights, huge parades. Fireworks. The lot.'

'Your suit?' demanded the ever-practical Robin.

'In the flat. With the rest of my kit. I've just got time to shower, shave and change. Formal lounge suit – the new one from Gieves. Three-piece. Very tailored. No uniforms or Merchant Venturer clobber. We'll need to fit in at the stadium ceremony too. And at the grand reception afterwards. No time for changes on the way I'm afraid.'

'OK,' said Robin's voice at the far end of the phone line. 'So I'll be waiting at the flat all changed and ready to go. My hair's booked in at that place on Bond Street at one on the dot. I'll be at the flat by three and ready to get out of your way by four. I'll see to Mary. I'm bringing William up. I promised we'd use the Bentley – he's hardly sat in it and Mary seems to have lived in it during the last few weeks.'

'They're sure they don't want to come with us? On *Poseidon* and then up to the stadium? The reception's out of the question, of course.'

'They'd rather die. At the last time of checking, they were planning on watching it all on the huge screen at Monument outside the Bank of England, then bringing some friends back to the flat for a party.'

'Fine.' He did not say *be careful with the Bentley*. After all, it was she who had done all the test drives with Andrew Assay when they had been preparing his surprise. 'I'll have a word with Mary when I see her. I don't want—'

'I'll have talked to both of them before you even get there. And no one – *no one* – will be allowed into our bedroom. I'm really going to need some beauty sleep when this day is over and done with!'

While Richard was sucked into the frenzy of his responsibilities during that morning, he had little opportunity to study the weather forecast. And his main focus when he did so was to do with atmospheric pressure, cloud cover and precipitation. He didn't want it to rain on his parade.

*   *   *

Dr Muhammar Faisal Abu-Sharkh had a different focus on much
the same matter, however. With Professor Diana Stark at his
shoulder, he was seated in the upper room of the ruined Cliffe
Fort. They had done just enough work on the place to make it
weatherproof and habitable. A little generator chugged away in
the room below – where Mary Mariner, their insurance policy,
lay in a drugged sleep bound with black duck tape. The little
generator supplied sufficient power to augment the portable
solar panels they had set up on the roof looking away into the
huge open sky above the Lower Hope. Enough power to keep
their laptops alive – and wi-fi'd to the Internet. Enough power
to keep their radio working and, via the tall aerial they had set
up beside the solar panels, in line-of-sight contact with
Discovery. The panels and the aerial were the only signs of
occupancy. Abu-Sharkh had decided that utter secrecy was their
best defence, so they hadn't even arranged any guards. He was
trusting to luck and the will of Allah. And with good reason.
Even the materials with which they had furnished the little room
had been purloined from Imperial and from the offices of the
bankrupt cement works on the far side of the fort wall. Which
remained surprisingly well stocked while the executors worked
out what to do with the disposable assets.

Like any good researcher, Abu-Sharkh was aware of the
danger of overreaching himself. Of pushing a theory beyond
its defensible limits, carried away by an idea that was simply
a bridge too far. But the circumstances unfolding on the screen
in front of him were making him adapt his original plan on
an almost minute-by-minute basis.

Diana's original mathematical model had prophesied how
effectively a shipful of like-minded men could be taken over,
even in the face of stronger resistance than the warders had
actually presented. Then, with a little of Thom's catastrophe
theory added to the basic chaos model, it had predicted that
the turning point of such an action was the addition of someone
like Sayed Mohammed to the already potent mix. A mix in
a situation, of course, already neatly foreseen as a result of
the previous terrorist spectacular at Chatham. The whole thing
had run so smoothly it had seemed more like a self-fulfilling
prophecy than a mathematical model.

The only problem had been in keeping a sufficiently low
profile to avoid detection during the time Sayed had been held

invisibly and silently by the authorities waiting for them to venture out of hiding, like tigers coming after a hunter's tethered goat. Especially as Diana, like any passionate convert, had been impatient – impetuous. But in the earlier days, when he had used his scars and his powerful beliefs to turn her to his ways, he had taught her the fundamental rule of obedience. And so they had managed it in the end with surprising ease and efficiency.

Abu-Sharkh's original doctoral thesis, applying post-Gleick chaos theory to the flood patterns of the Indus, had given him hope that he could apply his researches effectively to the Thames. And, by a simple reversal of some elements, do an untold amount of damage through flooding as well as through pyrotechnics if he could use the prison ship to make the wreck explode. But the extra element of the Olympics had made him put his plan on temporary hold. And now it seemed that the weather itself was offering the chance to add exponentially to the damage. And so, as the morning of Friday 27th July gathered towards midday, the doctor sat glued to his computer screens.

The picture of the surge sweeping down the east coast of England was augmented by readings from the SMOS satellite launched from Russia in November 2009 – aptly enough while eastern Scotland was fighting with disastrous floods around the coastal city of Aberdeen. Abu-Sharkh kept running his satellite-enhanced predictive programme, watching the storm-generated, wind-driven hump of water spread out of the Wash and swing round the bulge of East Anglia, overfilling Breydon Water at Great Yarmouth and the Waveney at Lowestoft, turning the Broads into an inland sea. Overwhelming Aldeburgh and washing away Orford Ness.

In the bottom left-hand corner of the screen a timer was running. A corrective to his earlier programme, which was at once a temptation and a warning. Orford Ness would be awash at 7 p.m. So his earlier calculations were out by around half an hour. But that error presented a further temptation.

As the predictor showed the hill of water overwhelming Felixstowe and Harwich, he pressed another series of buttons. And the relentless rising of a strong spring tide was added to the movement of the storm surge. The programs showed that the two surges would arrive more or less together off the mouth of the

River Medway at nine thirty tonight. A combination that would test the flood defences on the river to their utmost. And if the cataclysmic destruction of the bomb-filled wreck could be timed to coincide with that, then Abu-Sharkh would have created the flood that London had been fearing since 1953. At the very moment that the Olympic fireworks went off and the eyes of the world were fixed on the city.

Entranced, he factored into his predictive machine the third element that might be expected to result from the underwater explosion and watched as a wall of water filled the estuary. In colourful graphic, it destroyed Canvey Island and Stanford Le Hope, filling the Lower Hope itself but flooding the Essex shore, thrown westwards over the Coalhouse Fort by the physics of the cataclysm. Destroying Tilbury and Gravesend, but leaving Cliffe Fort relatively untouched. Then on up the narrowing waterway, over the helpless Barrier, through the Albert and Victoria Docks, drowning City Airport and the O_2 opposite and flooding the Lea Valley as far as Stratford and beyond. Taking the Olympic Village and everyone in it away. Just like the flood of 1947 – which Londoners had only just cleared up by the time they hosted the 1948 Olympics.

Abu-Sharkh glanced across at Professor Stark's computer. It showed the Met Office maps. Their warnings were a little behind his own – and significantly lower. They had clearly underestimated the power and potential of the storm surge. He wondered whether they had factored in the spring tide due this evening. He noted they had registered high tide at Southend just a couple of hours ago. Of course they had no idea whatever of his plans to add to the incoming swell at the top of the next high tide. It was perfect. The predictions would lull the weather forecasters and authorities they advised into a false sense of security. Like the time when they had famously said, 'Hurricane? There will be no hurricane . . .'

Suddenly full of excitement, he reached for the radio.

'Yes?' came the answer to his call.

'Sayed?'

'Yes.'

'We wait for the next high tide. Due nine thirty tonight. Let me talk to Saleh Mehsud.'

'Be quick, it is almost time for *Dhuhr*.'

As he waited for the engineer to answer, Abu-Sharkh thought

how strange it was to be ordering such actions at such a distance. Or how apt. After all, the American Predator drone that had all but destroyed him on the Afghan border had been flown by a boy probably no older than Sayed, sitting six thousand miles away in a control room at the USAF base at Creech, Nevada.

'Mehsud here,' came the voice in his ear.

'You are sure? Certain?' The detonator aboard *Discovery* was the only element of the entire plan Abu-Sharkh did not control. Not only his chance of success, but his chances of survival afterwards rested on this. When he planned to return home to Buurhakaba in secret – to take his rightful place among the men he had first begun to work with, in the wild valleys running between Afghanistan and Waziristan, in the great pre-Predator days. That was the reason he was compromising security with this call.

'The professor's C4 will trigger a device we have improvised in the bows of the boat. It consists of a combination of fuel oil, cooking oil, and all the extra gas canisters we have been ordering for the galley. We only just have enough fuel left in the bunkers to get us across the estuary. But we've just finished siphoning a good deal of avgas out of the Secretary of State's helicopter. Added to which we have the full range of pressurized fire-fighting equipment Health and Safety insist we have aboard – much of which is incredibly dangerous in the wrong hands. And even a sizeable collection of small personal pressurized canisters we have taken from our search of the ship – everything from shave foam and aftershave to deodorant. Packed under pressure as it is, it will be more than enough to blow the forecastle open and trigger the one thousand seven hundred tons of high explosives aboard *Richard Montgomery*. I guarantee. Then this ship and all aboard her will become the shrapnel in the grenade – the nails in the car bomb. The devastation in the surrounding areas will be almost incalculable.'

Abu-Sharkh broke contact then. *Almost incalculable*, he thought – and that was *before* the wave washed on upriver.

A gentle but insistent tinkling broke into his thoughts. It was Diana Stark's alarm, warning them that it was time to prepare for noon prayer.

*   *   *

At noon Robin was snarled in traffic. Tower Bridge Road was nearing gridlock because the central span was being raised yet again and the beautiful smoke-grey Bentley was right in the middle of it. 'Call this number,' Robin ordered William. 'It's the hairdresser in Bond Street. Tell them I may be late.'

Two minutes later the obedient William terminated the call. 'They said if you're late you lose your booking,' he informed her. 'The next time they can fit you in after that is the third week in August.'

'Right. It looks as though the span is coming down at last. I'll bet your father is somewhere at the back of this mess. Call Heritage House and tell them I want a cab waiting at main reception in twenty-five minutes' time. Will you get a bloody *move on*!' This last was addressed to the car in front, whose driver seemed to be sightseeing rather than driving with any sense of purpose.

Twenty minutes later, Robin was parking the Bentley in the Heritage Mariner car park. She bundled William out and loaded him with the stuff from the capacious boot. 'Take this up to the flat,' she ordered. 'Get Mary to help you put it neatly in my room. She'll know what needs hanging up and what doesn't. Now, if that sodding taxi isn't waiting, heads will roll!'

William just managed to fit into the lift. Five minutes later he eased himself through the flat's door, leaving the key in the lock. 'Mary?' he called. But there was no reply. He huffed the bundle of clothing across to the room his parents used and let it cascade on to the double bed. 'Mary?' he called again. When there was no reply he made a faint gesture towards laying the clothes out tidily then strolled into the sitting room. There was a half-eaten veggieburger and some cold chips on the little table by the security videophone. He took a bite. 'Hey,' he said. 'That's not bad. I think I'll get a hot one of those.' Miraculously, on the way out he remembered to pull the key out of the lock.

William bought the biggest burger he could find and a mega serving of fries, taking a walk as he ate it all. Town was heaving with an amazing number of people. He checked out the big screen down at the Monument which he and his sister were planning to watch tonight, along with a select band of friends who even now were on their way into the City. He bought a can of Coke and drank it as he watched the massive screen. Then he bought a packet of his favourite chocolate-covered chocolate chip cookies and took them back to the flat to eat.

He was on the last one when the phone rang.

'Yup?'

'Who is that? Mary?'

'It's William, Dad.'

'William. Thank God. Look, this is really important. I want you to get the suit bag and the shoes from the wardrobe in the bedroom and bring them down to Westminster Pier at once. Get the people at reception to order you a taxi. Have you enough money for the fare?'

'Sure, but I—'

'Good. Look, I wouldn't ask this if it wasn't important. Can you do it?'

'Sure.'

'I'll be waiting at the pier in half an hour.'

As things turned out, it took William the better part of an hour to deliver Richard's suit and shoes to Westminster Pier, and when at last he clambered out of the taxi there was no sign of his father at all. But *Poseidon*'s cutter was waiting. As was a crewman with a note. William cheerfully paid off the cabbie, climbed amenably aboard and took his father's formal clothes out to the ship himself.

It was after four when William finally found his father in one of *Poseidon*'s officers' cabins. But Richard was in the middle of a call, and even the terminally laid-back William saw at once that things were not proceeding well. 'No,' his father was explaining into the phone with the extra-patient, ultra-understanding tones he only ever used on Mother. 'I won't be able to get back to the flat. William, thank God, is here with my clothes. I'll have to get changed aboard. Why don't you get reception to call you a cab and get down here as quickly as you can?'

'It'll take three-quarters of an hour,' called William helpfully. 'That's how long it took me, anyway . . .'

'I'm sure your hair did cost nearly three hundred pounds, darling,' said Richard, waving his chilled-out offspring in. 'And I certainly know how much your outfit cost. But we were always going to have to take a cab, darling. It's not normally more than a fifteen-minute ride.'

There was a short silence – a silence at Richard's end of the call at any rate. He gestured fiercely and William put the suit bag on the bunk, with the shoes on top of it. Then his father continued, 'No, I haven't seen her, darling. I expect William has. Just a minute. I'll ask him. William, have you seen Mary? No? No, he hasn't, dear. Yes, of course she'll have left a message if she's gone anywhere. Nothing in the flat? Not on the message board? No I can't look at my texts, dear, I'm talking to you on my phone. What, dear? Yes. OK. Five minutes.'

Richard broke the connection. He tossed the instrument to William. 'Will, take a look at that, will you? See if there are any text messages from Mary. I have to get changed and back on the bridge in pretty short order.'

Richard shrugged off his jacket. He moved the shoes, treading off the ones he was wearing, opened the zipper on the suit bag and pulled his new suit trousers free.

'Here it is,' said William. '*Going out with Professor Stark.* That's it.'

He looked up. His father was standing rigid. William had never seen an expression like that on anyone's face, let alone Richard's.

'What time did the message come?' Richard grated.

William checked. 'Just after ten last night. Are you OK, Dad?'

Richard was in motion. Pulling his shoes and jacket back on. 'Call your mother,' he ordered. 'Tell her Mary's gone missing. No! Tell her we're coming back. Now. Tell her we're on our way.'

Ten minutes later *Poseidon*'s cutter was back at Westminster Pier. But in the interim, a disturbing change had come over the place. There were three police cars sitting where William's cab had pulled up. And a wall of policemen in hi-vis jackets and black stab vests were standing where there had been a gaggle of gaping tourists half an hour ago. Richard glanced at his watch: 4.45. The really high security was not due to appear for at least half an hour yet and yet here were wall-to-wall CO19 Special Operations officers. He went cold all over. Pushed straight up to the nearest officer. 'I have to get through,' he said. 'It's important . . .' He was about to add . . . *life or death.*

But the policeman was shaking his head. 'Not possible I'm afraid, sir. Total security. No one on and no one off.' He saw the look in Richard's eyes and shifted his position a little. His Glock handgun caught the light and the Heckler and Koch MP5 across his chest swung out a little. 'It's an emergency, I'm afraid, sir. Anyone trying to push through gets restrained. We have permission to use lethal force if the circumstances dictate. They're even briefed to shoot down unauthorized over-flights. Choppers and such.'

But then a kind of recognition registered on his face. 'Wait a minute. I know you. You're the bloke who was involved when Pat Zalewski and his dog Brandy got their medals. Pat's a mate of mine from way back. I remember seeing your picture . . .' He looked around, almost guiltily. Some sympathy slid into his tone. 'You may not have heard, sir. But there's a huge flap on. Gloria Strickland MP, the Under Secretary of State for Criminal Justice and Offender Management, has vanished. She went down to inspect the prison ship *Discovery* before ten o'clock this morning and she's completely disappeared. They think it may be terrorists, sir. Especially after that incident that you and Pat were mixed up in at Chatham last year. So they've closed everything down all across the capital and along the river until the Olympic ceremony's safely over and the VIPs are home safe and sound. Or until they find out just what on earth is going on.'

THIRTY-TWO
PARADE

Robin Mariner almost exploded into Jim Bourne's office half an hour later, dragging a sheepish Sergeant Stone in her wake. She would have turned all the heads in London Centre – male and female – even had she not been spitting fire. She was, after all, coiffed and frocked, booted and spurred for a reception at Buckingham Palace. It was obvious to every woman there that her hair alone had cost an astronomical sum, and to every man that it had been money well spent. Her little black number was literally that – one of Graeme Black's more severely tailored and exclusive creations. And, aptly enough, her shoes were by Prada. Because she was in the devil of a temper.

'That bloody man,' she said to Jim as she loured at him over his desk, 'has got himself trapped aboard one of his boats by this Gloria bloody Strickland security situation. They won't let him off. They say if he tries to use the chopper they'll shoot him down, though personally I think he should take the risk and try it!'

'What's the matter, Robin?' asked Jim, a little overcome, looking to Sergeant Stone and Pat Toomey for brotherly support in the face of this Chanel-scented Valkyrie.

'The bloody man has lost my daughter!' she snarled. 'Mary went off at ten o'clock last night with this wretched woman Diana Stark and she's vanished off the face of the earth.'

Jim sat down, frowning. 'I'll report it right away—' he began as he reached for the phone.

'Don't bother. Richard's already on to Tom Clark, his police inspector friend. But apparently they're setting up Gold, Silver and Bronze commands in both Essex and Kent over Gloria's disappearance. Tom's alerted the missing persons section at the Met about Mary as she seems to have vanished here in town, but they're at full stretch, what with one thing and another. Jesus *Christ*, what a day for the wretched girl to get herself kidnapped!'

This spate of words was enough to deflate Robin, so that she sagged on to the chair opposite Jim. It was also sufficient to drown out Pat's diffident question, 'But wasn't she with you last night?'

There was a tiny silence before Robin slewed round to look at the tanned Irishman. '*What?* What did you say?'

'Last night. Tennish. Maybe ten fifteen. When I got in from Heathrow. I thought I saw Mary getting into a minicab. Wasn't that you with her?'

'No, it damn well was not me with her. It was Professor Stark by all accounts. Wait a minute, though. You *saw* that?'

'I did. But I didn't think . . .'

'Well, think *now*, dammit. Jesus. You men . . . You said a minicab. Not a black cab?'

Pat hesitated, frowning. Calling on the kind of tradecraft

he had been taught in his spying days: never forget a detail. 'No. It was a minicab. I know because it had its logo on the side – you know the way they do, with a contact number?'

'A contact number!' shouted Robin, her face alight with relief. 'Brilliant! What was it?'

But Pat shook his head apologetically. 'No idea.'

'Oh, for crying out—'

Jim interrupted Robin's howl of frustration. 'The logo then. What was the logo, Pat?'

Pat closed his eyes, looking at the rainswept picture in his memory. Letting the side of the cab form naturally – not forcing it. Waiting for the picture to come. Waiting for the pattern to clear. Waiting to see and understand the logo. 'ECZ DALL,' he said at last. 'Some kind of name I'd guess. Dall certainly.'

'Could ECZ be initials?' suggested Robin more temperately. 'E.C.Z., like for Edward Christopher Zachary? Google it, Jim. ECZ Dall Minicabs.'

Jim obediently called up the search engine of his computer and typed *ECZ Dall Minicabs* into the box. A tenth of a second later the screen was full of blue writing. 'Nothing relevant comes up. Some cabs in Dallas, Texas. Dallas Fort Worth area. Lots of stuff in what looks like Greek and Arabic. Cyrillic maybe. Konstantinos Nikolopoulos, whoever he is. Lives in Dallas. Nothing of any use to us.' He sat back, frowning.

'ECZ. What could that be?' persisted Robin, like a terrier with a bone. 'Think, Pat, *please*! In the meantime, Jim, put *Dall* in and see what comes up, would you?'

Both men obeyed. Jim spoke first. 'First thing it asks is: Do we mean DELL minicabs? Then we get a slew of stuff about computers. Dell, of course. Then we're on to Dallas again. Scrolling down. More of the same. Hey, this is interesting. Cab company in SW8. No . . .'

Robin sat up suddenly. 'Wait a minute! Pat,' she spat. 'Think. Could it have been a code like SW8? Could it have been DA11?'

Pat frowned, mentally re-examining the picture in his memory. 'Not DALL but DA11. Yes. I guess it could indeed . . .'

'And maybe EC2 instead of ECZ?' added Stone, getting into the swing of things suddenly.

'EC2 DA11. That would make sense,' said Jim. 'I'll Google that now . . .' There was a moment of silence, then, 'Bingo! EC2 DA11 minicabs. Specialists in East London and Kent. Reduced fares and special offers between London and Dartford. Head offices Crooked Lane, Gravesend, Kent. It's actually postal district DA12, but it looks like the place to me.'

'Call them,' ordered Robin. 'Ask them about last night.'

But the man who took Jim's call regretfully declined to give the information requested.

'Of course he did,' said Robin. 'Information about kidnapping is probably covered by the Official Secrets Act. Or some other piece of imbecilic legislation. Right! Give me the phone. And get ready to go to sunny Gravesend. We'll see if we can set up a little parade of our own.'

William had never seen his father like this and was utterly awed. Like a theatrical director, Richard had set up all the elements of the water parade for which he was responsible. He had briefed everyone, drilled them and rehearsed them to perfection. And now that things were under way there was nothing for him to do but wait in the wings and hope that all went well. Except that he wasn't waiting in the wings. He was on the bridge and in command. But in command of an entirely different situation.

As the parade began to move in its prearranged sequence behind the royal yacht down the Thames beneath the bridges and under a clearing evening sky, Richard was the calm heart of a tornado of activity.

It wasn't enough that the parade was clicking together like clockwork outside the bridge windows. That ships – taller and taller ships – were peeling away from piers and jetties all along the riverside and falling into place, flags flying, hoses squirting, sirens hooting. On the bridge itself, Captain Trevor and his crew were working like a well-oiled machine in a sort of balletic frenzy. At the centre of which stood Richard, like a rock.

He had accepted a call from Robin a while ago and, after a brief but powerful conversation with her, had called up his friend Chief Inspector Tom Clark. As he waited for connection, he had called across, 'Will, is your phone charged up?

I'm not sure my battery will last much longer and the ship's system isn't compatible . . .'

'Yeah,' answered William, too chilled to check. 'Charged to the max.'

Richard knew his son too well to stop there. 'Credit?'

'Oh. Shoot. Maxed out. Forgot. No credit left . . .'

Richard lobbed his wallet across the busy bridge at his son. 'Get the debit card. Put a hundred pounds on to your account. I may need it soon. You can keep what's left. Hello, is that you, Tom? Tom, listen. Sorry to disturb you again but this might be important. Robin's traced the cab that picked up Mary and Diana Stark last night. It's from Gravesend, so it's logical to suppose that's where they were headed. What is there down there that might fit into this situation? Nothing springs to mind. Tell me about it. But listen, wherever they are, at least part of the point must be that they can communicate with *Discovery*, surely. Have you got GCHQ or whoever monitoring radio traffic down there? Don't ask me how I know. Just suggest that they look out for narrow band, focused transmissions passing between the areas of Gravesend and Southend. Get back to me on this number if anything comes up. Oh, and by the way, I think Robin's on her way to that cab office. From the sound of things you might want to get a squad car over there. To give the cab operator some kind of protection if nothing else.'

'Right,' said Robin. 'I'll take Pat in the Bentley with me. Jim, you take your laptop and keep searching for anything else that comes up under this wretched cab company. Or the area round Gravesend, especially along the river there. Sergeant Stone. Can you come with us?'

'You couldn't stop me, ma'am. That girl's kind of a good luck charm for all of us . . .'

'She'll need some good luck to survive when I get my hands on her. Have you got a car?'

'Got a Range Rover in the garage downstairs. Old but sprightly. I keep her maintained to top spec myself.'

'Perfect. Got everything? Then let's go—'

'Just a moment, Robin,' said Jim a little sheepishly. 'I think, under the circumstances . . .' He crossed to the wall and slid a picture back, revealing the front of a safe. He spun the lock and opened the door, pulling out a case made out of black composite. 'Insurance,' he said, looking around the other three men, frowning earnestly. 'Not very legal, but . . .'

'If it's a Glock 9mm with a red-dot sight, then I'm your girl,' said Robin grimly. 'I can hit a gnat at a hundred metres with a red-dot Glock. Let's go.'

Richard was familiarizing himself with William's state-of-the-art phone when his own more modest cell went off. There was a number not a picture. Not Robin then. Not Mary miraculously reappearing. 'Hi, Tom.'

'You took your clever pills this morning, didn't you?' came Tom's familiar voice.

'They find anything?' asked Richard, suddenly tense and breathless.

'What you'd expect from a quick scan of radio signals. Taxi cabs. Emergency services. Air traffic . . .'

'And?' Richard was controlling his impatience with difficulty. He rolled his eyes at William, who gave a shrug and a grin of support.

Tom chuckled grimly. 'And a high frequency narrow-band radio signal they weren't expecting. What they've been able to get clear is just coming through to me. I'll be passing it on up through Jan at Silver to Chief Constable Peake at Gold, but I thought I'd bring you up to speed as you're so closely involved, so to speak . . .'

'Because I am where *you* put me, Tom! And so is my daughter.'

'Perhaps. *Mea culpa.* Are you listening? Here's the first bit:' Tom's voice took on a more formal tone as he read off his computer screen the words that the radio watchers had found: '. . . *we've just finished siphoning a good deal of avgas out of the Secretary of State's helicopter.*'

'My God, Tom. Where did that come from?'

'*Discovery.*'

'And any idea where it was being received?'

'Wait. There's more coming through.' Tom's voice went dead as he read the next section. '*Packed under pressure as it is, it will be more than enough to blow the forecastle open and trigger the one thousand seven hundred tons of high explosives aboard* Richard Montgomery. *I guarantee.*'

'My God, Tom. My God. Where was this being broadcast to?'

'No real idea. The radio boffins can triangulate the source. But not the reception area.'

'Wait a minute, though. Wait a minute, Tom. I think we can. They have to be using the line-of-sight for this – the same as Governor Weeks and the legitimate powers aboard did. All communications are cloaked except for narrow-band line-of-sight radio signals to allow choppers and so forth to come aboard. But it was *only* line-of-sight. And if we take a rough line from *Discovery* towards Gravesend, where Robin's headed after that minicab company . . .'

Richard's voice tailed off. He too closed his eyes. 'What you doing, Dad?' enquired William, fascinated.

'Trying to get a mental picture from the last time I was on *Discovery*'s bridge,' Richard answered. William looked around *Poseidon*'s bridge where Captain Trevor and his crew were going about their business in that perfectly rehearsed, thoroughly professional manner as though Richard, his son and the horrific conversation were not there at all.

Like Pat Toomey in a similar situation, Richard cleared his mind. Focused on the image that remained in his memory from the last time he had looked through *Discovery*'s clearview. What he had seen from this same bridge as they lowered *Neptune* into the river after the dangerously drifting boom. The wide grey estuary, the low humps of the Kent coast opposite. The mouth of the Medway. The shallows above the mudbank where *Richard Montgomery* lay. Sheerness in the background. The Isle of Sheppey. The Isle of Grain. The tall whip-thin blade of an aerial rising unexpectedly in the farthest distance behind the grey hump of Grain. The way it had caught his attention again from the chopper above the Lower Hope.

'Tom? Tom. Are you still there? I think they're in the old fort at Cliffe.'

'Cliffe Fort,' said Pat as he broke contact with Richard a few minutes later. 'It's on the Kent bank of the Lower Hope Reach. He's told the Chief Inspector but everything's locked down tight because the Secretary of State is at risk. They're pretty sure she's on that prison ship – but the whole thing's rigged to blow up, apparently, so they're going softly-softly.

Negotiators first, by the sound of it. They aren't going to send in the SAS any time soon.'

'That's all right by me,' grated Robin. 'I'm bringing in the Paras. Well, Sergeant Stone at least. And negotiation is the last thing on my mind! Cliffe Fort, you say? Kent bank of the Lower Hope?'

'Cliffe Fort,' Pat confirmed.

'Punch it in the SatNav and tell Jim to see what he can find on the Internet, would you?'

Richard stood at Captain Trevor's shoulder looking down into *Poseidon*'s electronic chart display. William stood at his father's shoulder, trying with difficulty to keep up with what was going on. Outside on the river, the parade was coming to a halt. Away on the left, the royal yacht was heading for Coldharbour Dock. If William had bothered to look up he would have seen the O_2 in all its glory on his right. He didn't. He was looking down and concentrating with all his might.

The computer display showed details of the Thames Estuary. Even to William's untutored eye it was obvious which lines marked the banks, but there were other lines and figures: two bright dots and some sort of calculator running in the bottom right-hand corner. 'What is all this?' he asked.

'North bank. Southend,' explained Richard, pointing towards the top of the screen. 'That's the line of the watermark at the moment. If you watch carefully you'll see it moving. Those spinning figures calculate the way the tide will rise for another hour or so until nine thirty.'

'Is it real?' asked William. 'Or is it some sort of program?'

'Bit of both,' Captain Trevor supplied. 'The tide and the depth variations are in a standard program. The bright lights here and the calculator have been factored in by your father to calculate how long it will take this green light here – *Discovery* – to get to this red light here – *Richard Montgomery*.'

'OK,' said William, turning to the screen next door. 'Then what's this reading that seems to be coming up this other estuary? I mean, it's the same basic picture but the figures and the colours are all different . . .'

'That's the Met Office feed,' answered Captain Trevor, his voice suddenly a shade uncertain as his mind strove to match the two subtly – crucially – different computer images.

'That's a storm surge,' said Richard slowly. 'There's a storm surge coming in on top of the tide. That's what they're waiting for! I'll bet that's what they're—'

Richard's cell began to buzz. He picked it up. '*Discovery*'s on the move,' said Tom Clark.

THIRTY-THREE
HOPE

Robin came down the A2 a good deal faster than the speed limit allowed. But the road was empty and she cared not at all about the number of speed-camera flashes she saw in her rear-view mirror. She just hoped that the local police were too preoccupied to come chasing girl racers tonight.

'I think that's five so far,' said Pat helpfully as she negotiated Blackheath at sixty miles per hour and swung into the sharp right out towards Kidbrooke and the dual carriageway.

'We'll hit the dual carriageway soon,' she grated. 'Then I'll really show you what this baby can do!'

'The seat belts are pre-tensioned, aren't they?' he asked a little nervously.

'Don't be a scaredy-cat,' she said. 'And if you are fixated on the rear-view, then make sure Sergeant Stone is keeping up. That Land Rover is awesome in its own way but it's hardly built for speed . . .'

'Jim,' said Pat into Robin's cell. 'We're just coming through Kidbrooke and down on to the dual carriageway. Where are you?'

But he never heard the answer, because Robin put her right foot down hard and the snarling of the motor filled the cabin for an instant as she shifted up to sixth gear. A neat little spoiler appeared in the rear-view and distracted Pat even further.

Poseidon too was approaching her fastest safe speed as she rounded Greenwich and powered southward into Bugsby's

Reach. Richard had completed a terse conversation with Tom
Clark, which had covered all the obvious alternatives.
Alternatives Tom had already discussed at Silver and Gold
level – and which his superiors had chewed over with as many
of the Cabinet as were sharing the PM's limousine.

Although the police and security services were on full alert,
there was no chance of getting a rapid response team aboard
Discovery. The SAS would be happy to try, but the result of
any error would be the loss of the boat and all aboard her –
even if she didn't trigger the bomb-laden wreck she was
heading for. The loss of an SAS team, an entire top-flight
prison staff – not to mention the Under Secretary of State
directly responsible for them – was too high a price to pay
unless there were absolutely no options left. Both the Home
Secretary and the Prime Minister agreed. The same logic ruled
out the RAF and the Fleet Air Arm's offers to blow *Discovery*
out of the water before it got anywhere near *Richard
Montgomery*. And organizing any of the ships in the bustling
estuary into a floating barrier was a non-starter given the time
frame, even for the coastguards.

But Richard believed he had an alternative, and his plan
was swinging into action now under William's wide and
admiring eyes. There was absolutely no time to lose. Apart
from anything else, it seemed that *Poseidon* had to be out
through the Barrier before the incoming surge forced it to
close.

As the slim-hipped, needle-sharp corvette pushed down the
reach, so the crew at Richard's orders bustled about on the
foredeck and the poop. There was a helideck behind the bridge
and here the ship's powerful little Westland was kept tethered.
By the time *Poseidon* was swinging eastward into Woolwich
Reach with the Barrier rearing dead ahead, a blaze of white
and silver under the searchlights, the Westland was off and
hovering just above the foredeck. As the helicopter matched
its speed to the ship's, it lowered a rope. The team that had
been busy on the foredeck attached the rope to the top of the
remote vehicle *Neptune*. The instant the rope was secure, the
Westland's crew was winching *Neptune* up into the air,
swinging her like an odd-shaped orange conker away over the
huge raised sails of the Barrier and off east, downriver into
the gathering evening.

'Better ease her speed a little as we shoot the Barrier,' Richard observed.

George Trevor said something about grandmothers sucking eggs, but William noticed that the forward impulse did indeed ease as the long, sleek vessel went through the Barrier like a lean grey cat through a flap. As she slid into the wider river beyond, Captain Trevor's hand tightened on the helmsman's shoulder and the ship picked up speed once more, pounding between the out-thrust piers of the Woolwich Ferry with a dirty gold bone in her teeth.

William crossed to the right-hand side of the bridge and strained to look back along the widening wake as the Barrier began to close behind them. As the ship swung north into Gallion's Reach, William ran to the left like a schoolchild at a fair, and watched in utter fascination until the tight-closed barrier was hidden behind the Custom House buildings and warehouses at the mouth to the King George V Docks.

'Hey, Will,' called his father. 'Want to see something neat?'

Side by side father and son pounded down to the control room in *Poseidon*'s bulbous bow. Will sat in the seat sometimes occupied by Robin while Richard flicked the switches that brought the machines around them to life. 'We have fully trained operators on board of course,' he said. 'But this is the kind of assignment that requires leading from the front. Like Lord Cardigan leading the Charge of the Light Brigade . . .'

His busy fingers called up the maps familiar to William from the bridge. One showing the green dot of *Discovery* moving slowly across the estuary towards the red dot of the bomb ship. The other showing the incoming tide massively augmented by the spreading stain of the storm surge. 'Like Colonel Custer leading his cavalry at Little Bighorn . . .'

In the centre, on the largest screen of all, there suddenly appeared an aerial picture of the river, speeding past below as *Neptune*'s cameras came on line. William didn't know it, but they were showing the Lower Hope. In one corner of the reach was a promontory that ended in what looked like a ruined castle pushed hard against a derelict cement works. The setting sun gleamed on what appeared to William to be solar panels and a tall whip aerial. 'Like King Harold leading his housecarles in hot pursuit when Duke William the Bastard of Normandy seemed to be in full retreat at the Battle of Hastings,' said Richard.

'Hey,' said William, the reluctant history student, suddenly catching on to the drift of his father's words. 'Didn't King Harold *lose* the Battle of Hastings?'

Gloria Strickland felt foolish and frightened both at once. The moment the young man she was incarcerated with felt the engines beginning to turn, he had ripped the mattresses off the bunks beside them and wrapped her bodily in one of them. Then, as she sat there like a dumpling, he had bundled the bedclothes around her, turned on the taps in the little bedside basin and started showering her with water. She felt like a Russian baboushkha, shapeless and hooded. She knew she looked increasingly wet and incredibly stupid. But she knew too he was trying to protect her from what was bound to be a cataclysmic explosion. And, she thought queasily, as she had learned from past bitter experience, a girl can never be wearing too many clothes if there's going to be a big explosion.

William found that some of the writing on the river chart that showed the tides and the slowly converging red and green lights, gave the names of the sections *Poseidon* was racing through. Under normal circumstances, he suspected, the speed limits enforced by the river police and other relevant authorities would have made each stretch of the ancient river pass at a sedate pace. But now, with Captain Trevor at the helm breaking every law Richard told him to, things were very different.

No sooner had William registered that they were in Barking Reach than they were powering along Halfway Reach beyond it. No sooner had they swung through Erith Reach than they were in the middle of the Long Reach. It was while they were in the Long Reach that the faraway *Neptune* was lowered into the water hard by the *Richard Montgomery* and Richard started testing her systems. To see, quite apart from anything else, if she would answer to his instructions with so much solid Kentish mud lying between them.

Richard had not been sitting silently or idly as reach succeeded reach. Captain Trevor had reversed the radio signal that he had so patently failed to patch through to Richard's phone uncounted hours ago. Captain Hancock of the good ship *Atlas* had replied almost at once, and his natural truculence had melted away in the face of Richard's terse description of the current situation. Not least because if the bomb-laden wreck went up, then Hancock and his command would be swamped under the resulting tsunami. If they hadn't been blown to smithereens first.

At Richard's request, he roused his opposite number on the tug *Ajax* and the pair of them began pulling the leaky boom out of the mouth of the Medway, racing to position it between the *Discovery* and the *Richard Montgomery* before the two collided.

'Where are we, Will?' asked Richard abruptly.

'Coming out of Clements Reach into Northfleet Hope,' answered William. 'And it's just coming up to nine o'clock.'

Richard sat back and eased his shoulders. His face looked strange in the multicoloured light from the video screens.

'How's it going, Dad?'

'I can't control *Neptune* anywhere near well enough yet. She's just sitting there at the moment. We'll have to get closer before I try again. There's . . . what? Gravesend Reach, then the Lower Hope, then we're out into the estuary and nose-to-nose with *Discovery*.'

'That's about it, I guess,' said William. He added, 'We don't want to do that though, do we? Go nose-to-nose with *Discovery*?'

There was a tiny silence before Richard said, 'I wonder what your mother's up to.' As though that was an answer to William's nervous question.

'That was the A227 up to Gravesend. We're the next major exit,' said Pat. 'There's a roundabout. Junction one of the M2 will be second exit on your right, but we'll be going first exit left up the A289 to North Rochester, Higham and Cliffe. Six kilometres' time. Five minutes, not much more, even though there's a couple more roundabouts before it.'

'We'd have been there ages ago if it wasn't for these sodding roundabouts,' snarled Robin, gunning the motor and shooting away from the Singlewell roundabout, testing the nought-to-sixty stats again.

The phone purred. Pat answered it. 'Cliffe Fort. Gottit,' said Jim's voice. 'Palmerston Forts website. Photos, map, the lot. We'll work out a plan of assault as we go. Sergeant Stone wants to know, what's our ETA?'

'Five minutes to the M2 turning. Five minutes up the dual carriageway to the north of Rochester, then fifteen, maybe twenty minutes out to Cliffe on the minor roads. Twenty-five to thirty minutes all in all. OK?' said Pat.

'OK with us,' answered Jim. 'But it's getting really hard to keep up with you. That is one *fast* car. And I tell you, in this light it's as near invisible as makes no difference!'

The signal to prepare for evening prayer rang through *Discovery*. The mullah was under restraint with the warders, so Sayed Mohammed gave the direction to Mecca, for he was captain of the vessel now, just as Saleh Meshud was the chief engineer. But of course Sayed was a mere mathematician rather than a sea captain. He aimed the ship at the point to which his computers directed him. He asked Sayed to supply him with the power to get there. He knew when to ask that the bomb be detonated – and Dr Abu-Sharkh was there at the far end of the radio link to help with that. But he had no real understanding of the instruments below the clearview other than the basic propulsion and guidance.

Sayed and Saleh stood side by side on the restored bridge – still softly furnished as Governor Weeks's office – and went through the three repetitions of the *Maghareb* rituals shoulder to shoulder for the last time. *Discovery* was making slow progress across the estuary, for her anchor winches had not functioned as well as they had hoped and she was dragging a good deal of chain behind her. And, as she had been refitted inside rather than outside, her bottom was foul with weed. But Sayed's calculations were almost identical to his master's and there was still time to reach their final destination.

As always, the prayers filled Sayed with happiness and holiness. He completed his final prayer and crossed to the clearview to stare out across the shadowy river. It was all but empty. Only a couple of tugs in the distance were fussing about in the mouth of the Medway. They were probably doing something with the boom there, he thought. And that, too, had been part of the original calculation. After the Chatham bombing the fearful authorities had put barriers and booms across all the rivers opening out of the Thames, except for the docks by the Thames Barrier itself. Booms and barriers that would stop the wave from dissipating. Would funnel it, in effect, make it focus more fiercely, hurling all its terrible force at the Barrier. Through the Barrier. Beyond the Barrier at the Olympic park like the floods of 1947 and 1953.

Watching the mouth of the Medway again Sayed thought back to the day that his cousin Saami and he had steered the cruiser *Jupiter* into the river at the start of this. He had come full circle now. He felt literally uplifted. He was nearing the end of a long, hard road.

There was almost nothing left to look forward to now. Except *Jannah:* Paradise.

'That's it,' called Richard triumphantly. 'I have full control of *Neptune* now. Tell Captain Trevor to stop her now, Will. Where are we, son?'

'Somewhere in the Lower Hope,' supplied Will, even as the racing motors went into reverse and the shuddering hull slowed to a stop. 'Just behind the Isle of Grain,' said Richard thoughtfully. His speculation ended there. He concentrated all his attention on what he could see through *Neptune*'s systems.

The big picture on the centre screen showed the green soup that gulped down the golden beams of the DSRV's powerful headlights long before they revealed anything important. But Richard soon had the sonar up and the gently pulsing readout began to define shapes in front of the intrepid little vehicle, and distances between them. A box at the top right plotted *Neptune*'s position against a readout from Google Earth, and as Richard became more confident of its location, he went to larger and larger zoom. 'William,' he called as he worked. 'I want you to sit here by me and keep a careful eye on the two estuary maps you saw up on the bridge. I want you to give me distances between the five highlighted vessels, OK? *Discovery* is the green one. *Richard Montgomery* is the red one. *Neptune* is the bright blue dot and those two yellow blobs are the tugs *Atlas* and *Ajax*. They're blobs because the thing making them seem to spread out a bit towards each other is the boom they're pulling into position. Got all that?'

'It's like an old computer game, Dad. No sweat.'

'Good. But there's more. I need you to give me a countdown minute by minute. And warn me if the big red storm
surge seems to be speeding up or slowing down. At the moment
everything's going to come together at nine thirty. And how
long is it till then?'

'Thirteen minutes and counting,' said William, sounding as
though he was beginning to enjoy this game. It was, he thought,
certainly more fun than the party he and Mary had planned.

'What time is it?' demanded Robin.

'Just gone a quarter past,' answered Pat.

'Fifteen minutes should do it, though,' added Sergeant Stone.
'If you'll agree to the battle plan.'

The four of them were standing between the Bentley and
the Land Rover at the junction of the B2000 and a long,
straight, almost Roman road which led out across the flooded
marshes to the fort. The road was the better part of four kilometres long and the fort was only visible in the distance
because it was high enough to be framed against the last glow
of the sunset. Or what of the sunset was left to show between
the ragged storm clouds in the west.

Nearer at hand, there were wide grey marshes and flat grey
lakes already darkening through smoke to thundercloud as
they reflected the sky overhead. In the utter, before-the-storm
stillness, a low fog was beginning to form, writhing and
bubbling uneasily – as though vampires, werewolves and
zombies were getting ready to rise out there.

'Well,' temporized Robin. 'I agree we'll all *fit* in the Land
Rover, but it's noisy and it's slow and it's really easy to see.
I thought surprise was a crucial element.'

'It is,' agreed Sergeant Stone. 'But I don't see the alternative.'

Robin popped the Bentley's boot open. 'Sergeant, if you
get in there and kick hard enough, I think you'll find that the
panel immediately behind the seats will give way quite easily.
Then, if you and Jim don't mind squeezing in a little, Pat and
I can set the seats right forward and give you legroom. It
won't be for long, I promise you.'

'It won't,' said Pat. 'This thing goes like the clappers and
she drives like a demon.'

'If we're quick I won't even need to use the lights,' persisted

Robin. 'And you said yourself the car is almost invisible in the shadows . . .'

Five minutes later they were ready.

'*Right*,' said Robin.

'Hang on *tight!*' advised Pat. But his voice was lost in the snarl of the motor.

Robin let the clutch up and the Bentley was off. The road ahead was utterly straight, and had been well maintained by the defunct cement company in the past. She left the lights off. There was no chrome about the car – every bezel, sill, bumper and grille was smoky. The windows were tinted. Her paint was grey velvet. She vanished into the mist like one of Count Dracula's children of the night.

Two seconds into the wild ride, Robin had the Quickshift up into second and they were doing well over thirty. Two seconds later, they were coming up towards seventy. Four seconds later the Quickshift was in fifth and the Bentley was doing one hundred miles per hour. Four seconds after that the Quickshift was in top and the engine was purring slightly less loudly than Pat was humming.

Moving forward at more than two hundred miles per hour along a strange road in the misty dark, seemed to his shrieking subconscious to call most urgently for the *Agnus Dei* from Mozart's final D minor Requiem Mass. After all, it was what Mozart had been working on when Salieri had him murdered.

You don't get much closer to God than that.

A little more than ninety seconds after Robin let the clutch up, she was braking – thankfully in almost complete silence. The four kilometres between the B2000 and the fort had simply vanished in the meantime. The Bentley coasted silently to a halt at the top of a narrow promontory. Like the water-shed ridge on a mountain range, the road was the highest point of the little isthmus. Immediately before the front tyres was a forty-foot drop into the river. On the right, the cement works fell steeply away into shadow and silence. On the left was the topmost roof of Cliffe Fort. Two sets of solar panels lay open on it and a tall whip aerial reached up into the lowering sky like some kind of lightning conductor.

Robin opened her door silently and stepped out. She found she was moving on tiptoe and holding her breath. In equal silence, Pat was climbing out of the passenger seat. If he was still humming Mozart he was doing it in his head. Side by side they crept back to the boot and Robin eased it open. Two pale faces and four wide eyes stared up at her. She gestured with a curt jerk of her expensive hairdo and they began to struggle out. As they did so, she went off on her first reconnaissance. The Prada shoes were not at all practical. But the Graeme Black outfit made her almost as hard to see as the car.

Jim took out his gun and Sergeant Stone produced a nasty-looking commando knife. Pat closed his massive fists into bony clubs the size of big York hams and Robin considered going back for the tyre iron. But she decided to rely on the big strong men instead, and apply a little brain while they were exercising their brawn. Then the four of them were tiptoeing across the roof, looking for a quick and quiet way down.

That was what they were doing when they heard a man's voice shouting, 'Now! Now! Now!'

And the order was followed almost immediately by the massive *BOOM!* of the explosion.

Richard and William watched as *Atlas* and *Ajax* tugged the half-inflated boom out of the mouth of the Medway and dragged it into position in front of *Discovery*. Richard positioned *Neptune* using a combination of sonar readout and satellite tracking, as William counted the minutes down and kept an eye on the incoming storm surge.

'Ten minutes dead, Dad,' warned William as *Neptune* settled into position. On the screen in front of Richard it was possible to see the sonar picture of the sunken wreck swinging out of view as *Neptune* turned to face the oncoming 'V' of *Discovery's* bomb-packed bows. But in between them hung the sagging curtain of the boom, its upper balloons leaking quite badly now, its ghostly chains hanging limply.

'Still coming,' said the voice of Captain Hancock, patched through from the bridge – successfully this time. 'He doesn't seem to suspect anything.'

'OK,' said Richard. 'Hold it there. I'm coming out closer to you.'

'Nine minutes, Dad. And that surge looks to be getting ahead of itself.'

'OK. Thanks, Will,' said Richard. 'He looks like he'll be over the boom in about four minutes, Captain Hancock. Hold steady there. Watch out for a surge coming in when the tide is at full flood.'

'That's about five minutes too.' Captain Hancock sounded nervous.

As well he might, thought Richard. 'Precisely,' he said.

Richard flicked the screen to show what *Neptune*'s rear sensors could discern. The wreck of *Richard Montgomery* was terrifyingly close. But then, of course, it needed to be. He flicked back to the forward sensors and gasped. *Discovery*'s bows seemed to have leapt forward in the moment he had looked away. They were sweeping in above the sagging boom now.

'Two minutes, Dad. Surge about to arrive . . .' said William in his most laid-back tone.

Hell's teeth, thought Richard. He seemed to have missed out on over a minute's countdown. He sent *Neptune* surging forward, arms unfolding, equipment ready.

Everything heaved sideways. The water seemed to writhe and twist, threatening to hurl the little remote away like a bubble in a hurricane. But Will's words had just given Richard time to prepare. The intrepid little vessel stayed on station. *Discovery*'s bows ground over it, heading relentlessly towards *Richard Montgomery*. Richard let off a string of swear words in his mind that he would never have dreamed of uttering in front of his beloved son. The amateurs aboard *Discovery* had calculated for the surge almost as well as he had himself.

'Now!' he shouted. 'Now, Hancock! Now!'

The boom was scraping along the prison ship's foul old keel as the forecastle head plunged onwards and down towards the wreck. Any moment now Sayed Mohammed would detonate *Discovery* and the whole bloody lot would go up. But on his shout, the boom began to tighten and rise as the tugs pulled apart as hard as they could. Desperately, Richard pressed the buttons in front of him and prayed.

And, just at the crucial instant as he had planned, hundreds of cubic metres of compressed air hissed into the sagging balloons of the boom, even as the tension between them was tightened by the tugs. The buoyancy released by the injected gas was augmented even further as Richard drove *Neptune* herself full-thrust towards the surface, crashing the game little vessel like an iron fist on to the point of *Discovery*'s bow.

The calculated downward plunge of *Discovery*'s laden fore-castle hesitated. Reversed. Like a racehorse leaping the highest fence at the Grand National, *Discovery* reared over the top of *Richard Montgomery*. The whole of the vessel seemed to stagger as though it had received a powerful uppercut. Which, Richard thought grimly, she had.

And then the entire bow section blew open.

Discovery leapt up, lurched back then plunged forward once again. The shock wave from her exploding bow burst the boom, obliterated *Neptune* and tore into the riverbed. *Richard Montgomery*'s masts and funnels tumbled – to be brushed bodily away by the inrush of the storm surge sweeping in through the estuary towards the river itself.

The rearing, plunging prison ship was carried onwards by her own massive momentum until her shattered bow plunged into the soft flank of the Yantlet Flats less than a hundred metres out from the flooded shore. The whole ship juddered to a stop and slowly rolled over on to its left side, settling at an angle slightly more than forty-five degrees from the vertical.

Sayed Mohammed and Saleh Meshud picked themselves up, surprised and deeply disappointed to be still alive. Sayed looked through the oddly angled clearview at the dark, forbid-ding shore. The first of the night's rain lashed across the foredeck. He hauled himself to the console and gave the last order of his all too brief captaincy. 'Abandon ship.'

As Saleh and he hesitated on the down-slope of the deck, preparing to jump into the surging water so close below, the sky in the western distance was suddenly, magically bright-ened. The fireworks celebrating the Olympic opening ceremony lit up the sky above Stratford, above Greenwich, above the whole of London.

Richard and Will ran up on to the command bridge. Captain Trevor was standing rigidly, looking east across the hump of the Isle of Grain. 'Seems like you pulled it off,' he said. 'I thought we were done for when I heard the explosion. But apparently not. Looks like we live to fight another day.'

'Don't relax too soon,' warned Will, without thinking.

'There's a storm surge coming round the corner that can only go from bad to worse.'

Even as he said it, a wall of white breakers abruptly exploded into visibility in the shadows ahead that had been Thames Haven and spread across Mucking Flats as though some unimaginable sluice gate had been thrown wide. The entire upper section of the Lower Hope was suddenly something between a cataract and a maelstrom, as the storm surge came foaming upriver at the speed of a galloping horse.

'Oh my God,' said Captain Trevor. 'Give me full ahead. NOW!'

At the instant he said this, the sky was lit up with fireworks. The white foam at the peak of the onrushing water was suddenly rainbow-coloured.

'Wow,' said William. 'That's so *cool*.'

It was Richard who realized what they needed most urgently under the circumstances, apart from enough power to stop them being swept back into the middle of Gravesend High Street. 'Lights!' he ordered. 'All lights, full beam.'

Robin's little commando unit used the shouting and the explosion to cover their rush downstairs. The stairway was an external one and they ran down in single file from the roof to a kind of balcony outside a gaping doorway. There was no door. Had the man and woman inside the room not been focused so absolutely on the display on the laptop computers in front of them, they would certainly have noticed what was going on behind them. Robin, Pat, Jim and the sergeant stepped in through the doorway, eyes everywhere. No sign of Mary. No sign of guards either. And the most dangerous-looking weapon seemed to be the walking stick beside the man's canvas chair.

Such was Diana Stark's and Muammar Abu-Sharkh's over-confidence and concentration on what the laptops were showing, that they had no idea what was happening until Robin, flanked by her modest army, said, 'Excuse me . . .'

Stark and Abu-Sharkh both swung round, riven with shock and horror. Diana Stark sprang to her feet, but her companion was slower to do so. The red dot on Jim's Glock moved purposefully between them. Not knowing what else to do, the pair hesitantly started to raise their hands above their heads.

'Where,' demanded Robin, 'is my daughter?'

Diana Stark pointed to a hole in the floor. Robin strode across to it and looked down into the darkness. A set of stone steps led down into deeper and deeper shadow. Shadow that chugged quietly and smelt of petrol fumes. Of course, she thought bitterly, the one thing no one had remembered to bring was a torch. But the Olympics sprang to her aid. Not with a torch, but with a firework display. There was enough light from the celebratory pyrotechnics to guide her way down the steps. And at the bottom she could just make out the outline of someone lying on a makeshift bed.

Robin ran down the steps and across to Mary. She pulled the somnolent figure up into a sitting position. Mary stirred sluggishly, but was too tightly bound to do much. It was obvious at once that Robin would never be able to cut away the duck tape, so she held her still-drugged daughter against her breast and bellowed, '*A little help here!*'

Pat Toomey was halfway down the steps with Sergeant Stone just above him when the storm surge hit. Water exploded up through the gaping stairwells leading down to ground level and in through the open windows. Robin was inundated almost instantly. Vicious currents and counter-currents of icy water tried to trip her up, suck her under and wash her away. The generator failed as soon as the water hit it, spilling petrol as though a major artery had been severed. But Robin's concentration on Mary was absolute. Her will to get her daughter to Pat Toomey on the stairs was overwhelming. She handed the mummy-like bundle up. Felt him take her weight and lift her away.

Then she staggered helplessly as the power of the stinking water gripped her afresh. Her shoes went first and then her balance. Any minute now, she thought, she was going upriver with this lot. And what would be found floating face down when the surge and her last long swim were over, heaven only knew.

But Pat's hand seemed to come down itself almost from heaven and he caught her. As her head broke the surface she had the impression of Mary being lifted up by Sergeant Stone, framed against the unearthly gleaming of the reflected firework display. And then someone switched on a set of lights slightly brighter than the sun.

Ten minutes later they were all standing beside the Bentley on the only safe and dry section of the whole promontory. The terrorists were securely under Jim Bourne's gun. Sergeant Stone was cutting the last of the duck tape from Mary's sagging form with his commando knife. And Pat was commiserating with Robin.

'Jeezus,' he was saying. 'I have never seen such an expensive fashion statement go up the creek so quickly. Five minutes ago you put the Queen in the shade. Now you're giving drowned rats a bad name.'

Jim suddenly added, 'And I think we can safely assume that's your husband bringing your sadness and shame into the light, because that's *Poseidon* sitting out there blazing like a bloody bonfire!'

And for some reason she would never be able to fathom, this suddenly seemed to Robin one of the funniest things she had ever heard.

EPILOGUE

'Hey,' said William. 'Look at this!' He held up his phone. The screen was big enough for everyone around the breakfast table to see. 'Its on one of the Internet newsfeeds,' he said, and read aloud: 'HEROIC MARINERS SAVE LONDON FROM DISASTER. How's that for a headline?'

Richard looked up from his *Financial Times*. The printed headlines on the page he was reading were more like:

> *Gravesend counts the cost of floods.*
> *Barrier survives worse than expected storm surge.*

And:

> *Olympics Opening Ceremony – money well-spent?*

He looked across at Robin, who gave a tiny shrug. Much like the gesture with which she had bid farewell to the sopping black rag that had once been haute couture of the highest order. But she was still sick at heart about her hair.

They shared a moment of silent understanding. They had never courted headlines. In fact they preferred it when their good works went unnoticed by the Third Estate.

'More toast and marmalade?' she asked, almost dismissively. 'Anyone for more tea?'

'I'll have a cup, Mum,' said Mary, who was beginning to perk up after her ordeal. After the hospital had given her an enthusiastic all-clear and the opiate drugs she had been fed were right out of her system. And especially now that Professor Stark and Dr Abu-Sharkh were safely under lock and key.

'What does it say, Will?' asked Richard easily, reaching for the toast.

'I'll read it to you,' said William enthusiastically, scrolling the story up on his telephone screen.

> 'Heroic mariners Captain Wilfred Hancock and Captain Nigel Pugh saved England from a security disaster at the very moment the Olympics were opened when they foiled a concerted attempt by some of the most dangerous terrorists in captivity to escape from the prison ship *Discovery*. Using the security boom from the mouth of the River Medway, of which they had been in charge since the atrocity at Chatham, they drove the ship on to the mud bank of the Yantlet Flats and stopped one of the most daring escape attempts from any English prison in recent years. Gloria Strickland MP, Under Secretary of State for Criminal Justice and Offender Management, who was briefly held captive aboard the vessel, has suggested that the two captains should be given an award for gallantry . . .

'Hey, Dad, this isn't right. It doesn't mention any of us at all. This *sucks*. Dad, why are you laughing? Dad? Mum? Jesus. *Parents* . . .'

Notes and Acknowledgements

Readers will easily see influences as diverse as Peter Ackroyd, James Bond, John Le Carré and Charles Dickens – as well as Joseph Conrad. But *The Prison Ship* actually began with the BBC programme *Coast*. In an edition on the Thames Estuary, the presenter mentioned the wreck of the *Richard Montgomery* with its cargo of Second World War explosives – still possibly lethal today. Every element of the story is, like the wreck, grounded in as much solid fact as possible. Such was my desire to write about the Thames itself that I studied the river – its history and so forth – in great detail. Or those parts of it relevant to my story: from the Pool of London to the Lower Hope, where the River Thames becomes the Thames Estuary. And where, incidentally, Cliffe Fort is exactly as I have described it. Though I admit I have tinkered a little with the Isle of Grain and made no mention of the power station that dominates the confluence between Medway and Thames.

Research on the Internet revealed details of the ship's position and condition up to 1999 – the last Coastguard survey I have been able to find.

Friends were very willing to add expertise and experience as I fleshed out my ideas. I must thank Peter Halsor, who lent me his charts and sailing companions to the east coast and the estuary. Phil Booth, who supported me with a detailed breakdown of all levels of emergency response – the Gold, Silver, Bronze system. And John Mazzey, who briefed me on the fire service's likely responses to an explosion aboard *Richard Montgomery*; it was he who suggested that it 'would be raining nuts and bolts in Tunbridge Wells' if the ship ever went up. A particularly disturbing image as we were in the Pantiles when he said it. Finally I must thank Sam Dalton and everyone else at Chatham with whom I spent a very fruitful day in July 2008 planning the near-total destruction of the Historic Dockyard where they work.

The other main elements of the simple plot begin with the prison ship of the title. The then Home Secretary John Reid last gave such vessels serious consideration in 2007, less than a year before I began serious work on the first draft. And, with the prison population as it is, who knows how soon some other Home Secretary will return to those same thoughts?

Both chaos and catastrophe theories are real. I consulted James Gleick's *Chaos* for the basic elements of chaos, but I had studied René Thom's catastrophe theories in some depth for an earlier planned story that never saw publication. Put at its most (over-) simple, the combined theory goes something like this: There are elements in the most random events that will form patterns and there are mathematical models that will predict these patterns – weather forecasting is the most obvious, and Lorenz's famous 'butterfly effect' is based on an early weather model. Thom then suggests that there are points in the formation of these patterns where changes will occur – which can also be predicted and perhaps controlled. The point at which a threatened dog will stop backing into a corner and attack instead. The point at which a slowly bending branch will snap. This work is really being used to predict and try to control threats such as international terrorism, in much the way the very fictional Professor Diana Stark suggests. If I may quote the much-maligned Wikipedia on the subject: 'Mathematical modelling is currently being used to manage security policy. Specifically, scholars and practitioners of security studies are tackling the new challenge of managing terrorism.'

Next, the nature of the terrorist threat within this story itself. I have literally taken it from the headlines. As I worked on the main body of the story, the newspapers were full of the conviction of the young men from Newham, High Wycombe and Blackburn accused of trying to smuggle liquid bombs aboard aircraft. Of their links to worldwide terrorist organizations and of the continued threat of terrorist 'masterminds' in Pakistan, Afghanistan, Somalia and elsewhere. These required only a little change to move them out of dangerous reality into fiction.

Finally, all the information about flooding is also real. As with all of my 'green' research since *High Wind in Java*, I use *The Ecologist* and *The Week*. Both magazines, like *National*

Geographic, are indispensable to my work, and I am happy to acknowledge the debt here. Although it seems inconceivable that the Thames Barrier would ever be breached – even given Richard Doyle's research for his fine book *Flood*, and the parallel efforts put into the more recent film and television production of the same name. It is however a fact that South East England and the London Basin are both sinking while sea levels are rising and extreme weather events both inland and in the North Sea seem to be intensifying. (Though my description of the storm and the subsequent movement of water down the east coast is taken from the great flood of 1953.) Added to which, the location of main facilities for the 2012 Olympics in the Lea Valley has been twice inundated in the floods of 1947 and 1953. There is even a fascinating if chilling Environment Agency map available on the Internet which overlays all of the Olympic facilities with the high-water marks of those terrible events.

Peter Tonkin
Tunbridge Wells, November 2009